EARTHRISE

Ace Books by William C. Dietz

GALACTIC BOUNTY

FREEHOLD

PRISON PLANET

IMPERIAL BOUNTY

ALIEN BOUNTY

McCADE'S BOUNTY

DRIFTER

DRIFTER'S RUN

DRIFTER'S WAR

LEGION OF THE DAMNED

BODYGUARD

THE FINAL BATTLE

WHERE THE SHIPS DIE

STEELHEART

BY BLOOD ALONE

BY FORCE OF ARMS

DEATHDAY

EARTHRISE

EARTHRISE

William C. Dietz

ACE BOOKS, NEW YORK

EARTHRISE

An Ace Book
Published by The Berkley Publishing Group,
a division of Penguin Putnam Inc.,
375 Hudson Street, New York, New York 10014.

Visit our website at
www.penguinputnam.com

Copyright © 2002 by William C. Dietz.
Jacket art by Edwin Herder.
Jacket design by Pyrographx.

First edition: September 2002

Library of Congress Cataloging-in-Publication Data

Dietz, William C.
    EarthRise / William C. Dietz.—1st ed.
        p. cm.
    ISBN 0-441-00971-9
    I. Title.

PS3554.I388 E17 2002
813'.54—dc21
                                    2002018684

PRINTED IN THE UNITED STATES OF AMERICA

10   9   8   7   6   5   4   3   2   1

For Marjorie, with all my love.

EARTHRISE

1

DEATH DAY MINUS 80

WEDNESDAY, MAY 13, 2020

Man is born free: and everywhere he is in chains.
—JEAN-JACQUES ROUSSEAU
The Social Contract, 1762

HELL HILL

The sun had risen, the early-morning air was crisp, and Manning could see his breath. From his vantage point, standing atop the vast stack of cargo modules known as "Big Pink," he could also see a generous swath of the strange almost surreal landscape in which he and thousands of slaves had been forced to live during the last few months. Months that felt like years.

What he and everyone else referred to as "Hell Hill" was located on a finger of land once known as Governors' Point, located just south of the once thriving city of Bellingham, Washington. A place that had once been home to a well-respected state college, a small but charming central business district, and a population willing to trade the hectic pace of a city like Seattle for the pleasures of kayaking on Puget Sound, snowboarding on Mount Baker, and hiking in the Cascades.

But that was prior to February 28, 2020, the day that the Saurons destroyed the cities of New York, Paris, Moscow,

Madrid, Cairo, Beijing, Sydney, Lima, Rio de Janeiro, Johannesburg, Tehran, and New Delhi.

The worst damage was inflicted by powerful energy cannons mounted on Sauron spaceships. Dreadnoughts that measured almost a mile in length, were more than two thousand feet wide, and carried upward of twenty thousand aliens plus the slaves required to support them.

Though unable to descend through the atmosphere, the largest battleships had no difficulty firing their weapons from space itself. Earth's atmosphere shrieked in protest each time a bolt of energy tore through the air. Those located within a half mile of the impact experienced a chest-thumping concussion, and if they were fortunate enough to survive, could watch skyscrapers topple, bridges collapse, and entire neighborhoods erupt into flame. The fires spread to suburbs, grasslands, forests, and jungles. Soon the entire planet was wrapped in a blanket of thick gray smoke.

But that was little more than the beginning. Confused by the nature of the attack, and uncertain as to who the instigators had been, the humans turned on each other. The cities of Bombay and Islamabad were consumed by mushroom-shaped clouds, while three neighboring countries launched subnuclear missiles at Israel.

All of this occurred not over a period of months, not over a period of weeks, but in a matter of *three days*. Nor was the attack over when the orbital shelling finally ended. That's when the Saurons employed space-to-surface missiles against hardened military installations, when the systematic carpet bombing started, and when swarms of manta-shaped alien attack ships sought to clear the skies, roads, and freeways of human life.

With the exception of assets which their superiors had identified as potentially useful, the Sauron pilots destroyed anything that moved, including airplanes, trucks, cars, and the long ragged columns of refugees that snaked out of the cities searching for shelter.

More than 3 billion people died, enough to eliminate any immediate resistance, but not so many as to drive the human race to the edge of extinction.

No, the Saurons were careful to stop short of complete annihilation, not because they had a system of ethics, but because they *needed* the survivors. Needed slaves to construct the enormous citadel-like fortresses within which a new generation of Saurons would hatch, each killing its progenitor during the birth process, and each taking its place within the complex racial hierarchy upon which the alien culture had been built. A social structure in which each caste had a distinct function: The Zin governed, the Kan fought, and the Fon performed menial work, or *would* have performed menial work had it not been for the diminutive Ra 'Na, a slave race upon which the aliens were heavily dependent.

A relationship which over hundreds of years had become so entrenched that something approaching a symbiotic relationship had evolved. A reality that helped explain why many of the whip-wielding Fon overseers carried Ra 'Na technicians on their chitin-covered backs even as they forced thousands of humans to ascend Hell Hill.

The reason for this became apparent as one of the Fon flexed his deceptively slender legs, propelled himself high into the air, and landed some thirty feet away from the point where Jack Manning stood. The Ra 'Na, a relatively small being with reddish fur, a short muzzle, and brown beady eyes absorbed the shock with slightly bent legs, and murmured into a handheld radio. The process of herding the secondary slave race to the top of the hill had to be coordinated, and he, like many of his peers, took pride in a job well done. His mount's whip made a loud cracking sound as the neatly braided leather cut into a human back, and the victim fell face first into the heavily churned mud.

Manning winced. He knew, as did those around him, that the whipping, like the ceremony thousands of humans were about to participate in, was part of an elaborate effort to keep the slave population under control. A task made increasingly difficult, as word of the birthing leaked to the previously ignorant Fon, and to segments of the human population as well.

Even as the Zin called Hak-Bin strove to complete the great fortress at the top of Hell Hill—the resistance movement continued to gain strength. Especially now that the humans realized that the entire Sauron race would be momentarily vulnerable once the nearly simultaneous birthing process started.

All of which explained why the aliens had gone to such great lengths to find a hospitable planet, build their defensive citadels, and install the automated weapons systems designed to keep enemies at bay. Had they remained in space, had they undergone the change there, the entire race would have been vulnerable to the Ra 'Na.

Manning's thoughts were interrupted as Vilo Kell's voice came over the security chief's military-style headset. "Snake Three to Snake One . . . Over."

Manning did a 360 and used the elevated vantage point to scan the surrounding rooftops, shacks, clotheslines, and stacks of firewood. Below, down in the heavily rutted streets, the Fon continued to jump from place to place. Their harakna hide whips popped like firecrackers. "This is One . . . go. Over."

"We're ready—or as ready as we're likely to get. Over."

"Roger, that. Stand by . . . The Big Dog is on his way. Over."

Manning turned to the man who stood beside him. He had even features, quick intelligent eyes, and medium brown skin. "Time to go, Mr. President."

Alexander Ajani Franklin, the onetime governor of Washington State, the politician the Saurons had chosen to head their puppet government, the individual many humans referred to as "Frankenstein," and the man who Manning and hundreds of resistance fighters were counting on to lead them out of slavery, managed a wry smile. "Yes, it would be rude to keep Hak-Bin waiting."

"Rude *and* dangerous," Manning responded gravely. "I don't know what the bastard has to say—but it must be important. Important enough to take thousands of slaves off the job and sacrifice six hours' worth of production."

Franklin lowered himself through the hatch and looked up into his security chief's face. "I don't care what Hak-Bin says . . . it's what he might *do* that bothers me."

Manning's eyebrows rose slightly. "Such as?"

Franklin shrugged. "Such as a show designed to get our attention, scare the crap out of us, and reassert Sauron control all at the same time."

"That's an interesting idea," Manning said slowly. "Did you pick up on a rumor of some sort?"

"Nope," the president answered as he ducked out of sight. "But that's what *I* would do if *I* were a Sauron. Let's hope Hak-Bin is different."

Manning hoped . . . but knew it was a waste of time.

■ ■ ■

Dr. Seeko Sool, University of Nebraska, class of 2011, was in the process of suturing a cut when she heard her nurse say, "You can't go in there!" followed by a loud commotion and a clang as something hit the metal floor.

Little more than a makeshift curtain served to separate the surgery from the rest of the cargo-module-sized clinic. The walls were painted green and badly in need of washing. The Kan warrior jerked the flimsy divider aside, shuffled into the space within, and regarded Sool with a baleful gaze.

Her patient, a man dressed in gray rags, seemed to shrink, as if trying to disappear.

Like all his kind, the Sauron had a sharklike snout, three backward-pointing skull plates, and large light-gathering eyes. His highly specialized chitin shifted to match the paint on the wall behind him. Sool blinked as her eyes attempted to focus on the miragelike image. The voice, as reproduced by the translator clipped to the Kan's combat harness, was harsh and grating. "Slaves have been ordered to assemble on the top of the hill. You are a slave. You will depart *now*."

Sool used the needle holder to gesture toward her patient's foot. The wound was only partially closed. "We can't leave yet . . . not until I finish suturing this cut."

The patient, a skinny almost skeletal figure who had managed to survive almost three months of brutal slavery by doing exactly what he was told, jumped off the table, snatched a boot off the floor, and hopped toward the door. A thin strand of 4-0 nylon snaked after him. The Kan produced something like a predatory grin. " 'Now' means *now*."

Sool sighed, put the instrument on a Mayo stand, and removed her disposable gloves. Then, with her nurse in tow, she left the clinic. The crowd flowed upward as if determined to defy gravity.

■ ■ ■

Hell Hill's original profile, as viewed from the opposite side of the ironically named Pleasant Bay, had been that of a gently rounded hill covered by mature evergreens.

Now, after months of work by thousands of slaves, the long-abandoned stone quarry at the base of the hill had been reopened, most of the trees had been cut down, terraces had been cut into the steep side slopes, and empty cargo modules had been stacked for use by the slaves. A sort of instant city that the humans had modified and expanded as they proceeded to create a sub-rosa economy.

Higher up, the hill wore a necklace of freshly built crosses. The lumber, all of which had been looted from a yard in nearby Vancouver, Canada, had a slightly greenish hue. Each piece wore a small white tag intended to reassure its new owner that it had been pressure treated and would last for the next twenty years, a fact the Fon named Mal-Dak was unaware of and unlikely to take much comfort from.

Like most of his lowly caste, Mal-Dak had been forced to queue up for any number of things over the years—but the opportunity to be crucified had not been one of them. Not until now, as the line shuffled slowly forward and the unfortunate Sauron had a moment to reflect.

The focus of his thoughts was the fact that insofar as he knew, based on the roughly two standard years' worth of memory currently available to his mind, he had never joined or even commingled with the organization called the Fon Brotherhood and was therefore innocent of the charges lodged against him.

Had Mal-Dak been acquainted with the now notorious Bal-Lok? Who, along with some twelve members of the nascent organization, had been foolish enough to attack a Kan checkpoint? The answer was "yes," but knowing someone and belonging to their organization were two different things. Something he had explained over and over but to no avail.

Assuming the Kan who arrested him had been truthful, and there was no reason to suspect otherwise, Hak-Bin had ordered his subordinates to identify and crucify "twenty guilty parties." No less and no more. How could everyone ignore the obvious unfairness of that?

Mal-Dak's thoughts were interrupted as a Kan shouted an order, a cross was raised into the upright position, and a Fon hung upside down with his arms stretched to either side. The Sauron made a pitiful bleating sound which ended abruptly when a Kan kicked him in the jaw. Though conscious, and in pain, the Fon no longer had the capacity to speak.

That's when Mal-Dak felt graspers lock onto both of his arms, heard a Kan say, "Now it's your turn," and was wrestled onto a newly constructed cross.

"No!" Mal-Dak shouted. "It isn't fair! I'm innocent!"

"That's what they all say," a warrior said unfeelingly. "Now mind the way you act—humans are watching. Here's an opportunity to show them that even the lowliest and most insignificant members of the Sauron race can die without complaint."

Mal-Dak was about to object when an order was given, his cross was raised, and the world turned upside down.

Then, his weight hanging from the plastic ties that secured his wrists and ankles, Mal-Dak was left for the crows. There were hundreds of the fat black birds—and they circled the morning's feast.

■ ■ ■

The few surviving members of the Fon Brotherhood had learned a thing or two during their organization's short but tumultuous life.

The first learning ran contrary to everything they had been taught since birth: Fon were as intelligent as the Kan and Zin . . . a fact many had proven by teaching themselves to read.

The second learning was that humans, especially *white* humans, who claimed to be part of something called the "brotherhood of the skin," were completely untrustworthy.

The third learning was that even though the white humans had tricked Bal-Lok and sacrificed their brethren to the Kan as part of a complicated slave scheme, the Fon had proven their valor. Though dead, every one of their bodies had been found facing the enemy with a weapon at pincer.

Now, having learned those things, the Fon Brotherhood was in the mood to teach a lesson of their own: the meaning of respect.

Jonathan Kreider, a.k.a. Jonathan Ivory, a name he had chosen as a way to celebrate the lack of pigmentation in his skin, didn't know he was being hunted until the trap had already closed.

Flushed out of hiding by the Kan, the racialists had been absorbed into the steadily growing crowd and pulled toward the top of the hill.

There were fewer of them now, after the disastrous assault on the Presidential Complex, and the loss of brave Hammer Skins like Parker, Boner, and Marta Manning, a hard-core racialist who, had it not been for the efforts of her brother Jack, would almost certainly have killed Alexander Franklin.

But six remained, which by either coincidence or divine intent was the exact number mentioned in Ezekiel 9:1-2: ". . . Then he called out in my hearing . . . 'Let those who have charge over the city draw near, each with a deadly weapon in his hand.' And . . . six men came . . ."

A skin nicknamed Tripod was the first skin to die as a Fon dropped off a roof and buried a six-inch blade between the unsuspecting human's shoulder blades. Four of his companions died within seconds of each other. The last of them took a pipe to the side of his head, staggered through a complete circle, and collapsed.

Ivory, who caught the motion from the corner of his eye, started to turn. He never made it. *His* Fon, the one to whom the ancestors had given a mental likeness of the racialist's features, struck the back of the human's head with a length of two-by-two. It was a glancing blow, but sufficient to drop Ivory in his tracks. There was the jolt of the blow, followed by an explosion of pain, and the long fall into darkness.

The Fon, satisfied with his grasperwork, jumped to a

nearby roof. A debt had been incurred . . . and a debt had been paid.

The racialists, their bodies left to rot, were but a small down payment on the long bloody day to follow.

■ ■ ■

Consistent with the fact that they had what amounted to a genderless society, the Saurons had a marked tendency to regard their slaves in much the same manner as earlier generations of humans viewed horses. The aliens placed a definite premium on size, strength, and, to a lesser extent, on color, favoring blacks over browns and browns over whites, in what observers like ex–FBI Agent Jill Ji-Hoon knew to be conscious racism.

So, given the fact that *she* had white skin, stood six-foot-two, and had the broad shoulders of a competitive swimmer, the onetime law enforcement officer was often chosen for tasks which the alien overseers considered to be physically demanding but appropriately menial. That's why she was not especially surprised when a Kan leaned over the parapet above, ordered her team to meet him on the plaza below, and promptly disappeared.

The team, what the Saurons considered to be a matched set in terms of physical ability, consisted of Ji-Hoon and three reasonably well built men. Two had come on to her and failed. Only the third, a man named Escoloni, remained true to his wife. Something Ji-Hoon admired. Their eyes made contact as they maneuvered the five-hundred-pound block of limestone into place on top of a long, gently curving wall. It was the last oversize brick of that particular run and fell into the assigned gap with a gentle thud.

The six-foot-long steel pry bar clattered as Escoloni allowed it to fall on the stone pavers. "So," the man everyone called Loni, said sarcastically, "what now? High tea?"

Ji-Hoon grinned and used a faded red bandanna to wipe

the sweat off the back of her neck. "Don't I wish . . . No, some kind of shit detail most likely."

Loni looked doubtful and gestured to the dry set wall that circled the citadel's third level. "Shit detail? What do you think *this* is?"

"There's worse," the man named Hosker said somberly, "unless you think the stone mules actually enjoy what they do."

An entire lexicon of slang words and terms had evolved on and around Hell Hill. The term "mule team" referred to those slaves assigned to haul the quarter-ton blocks of limestone up the hill. A backbreaking job that could have been performed in a tenth of the time through the use of machinery. But the Sauron Book of Cycles dictated otherwise, that was the rumor anyway, and Ji-Hoon believed it. She had seen the stonemaster poring over what appeared to be a large volume of weatherproofed manuscripts and heard the overseers refer to it.

The way Ji-Hoon understood the matter, the Book of Cycles, plus the memories that the stonemaster had inherited from his ancestors, laid out not only the plans for the temple itself, but the methods used to build it. Processes and procedures long outdated but still adhered to. A practice reminiscent of some human religions. All of which meant that Hosker was correct. There *were* worse things than setting stone.

The slaves made their way down to the plaza below, were automatically berated for being too slow, and ordered to follow a path that switchbacked down to the beach. A large manta-shaped shuttle wallowed in the swells offshore, looking for all the world like some sort of prehistoric sea animal, its atmosphere-scarred skin slick with spray. It was difficult to walk, what with thousands trying to make their way upward, and the team was forced to halt.

The Fon opened a passageway with his whip, and much

to her surprise, Ji-Hoon noticed that many of the individuals thus punished directed dirty looks to *her*, as if she and her teammates were responsible for the alien's actions. It didn't make sense, but what did? The crowd parted, the work detail passed through, and wondered what awaited below.

■ ■ ■

The Ra 'Na were a clever race, and like most shuttles of its tonnage, this particular craft had been designed to serve a multiplicity of purposes. The main compartment could be used to transport cargo or converted for passenger use. And, given the fact that there were various kinds of passengers, three different seating configurations had been devised. There were slings for the Saurons, large, oversize seats for the humans, and smaller, better-upholstered chairs for the Ra 'Na, who, having been being forced to build them, saw no reason to compromise their own personal comfort.

That being the case, Dro Tog, along with his many peers, could hardly complain about the size, fit, or comfort of their respective seats. As for the overall ambience, well, that was another matter. The cargo compartment, which had most recently been used to transport canisters of a liquid presently being brewed deep within the bowels of factory asteroid Λ-12, still stank of sulfur, and made Tog nauseous. Or was it the overly large lunch consumed just prior to departure? Or the nature of the outing itself? An exercise the entire College of Dromas had been *ordered* to take part in.

"Please join Lord Hak-Bin in a lavish entertainment." That's what the so-called invitation read, although the prelate harbored the suspicion that the "lavish entertainment" wouldn't be, not by *his* standards, which were the only ones that mattered. Conscious of the fact that his thoughts were less than politically correct, and fearful lest someone pluck them from the ethers, Tog eyed his peers.

They were an eclectic group, some attired as he was, in

finery intended to highlight their importance, while others, the dour Dro Rul foremost among them, modeled robes so plain they resembled little more than sacks cinched at the waist and secured with lengths of utility cord. A self-righteous crowd who loved to pontificate about concepts like freedom and considered themselves to be morally superior.

Still, regardless of political affiliation, none of the prelates were especially cheerful, although some, Rul being an excellent example, were more dour than all the rest. Why? Because he took everything too seriously, because rather than accommodate the Saurons, as common sense dictated that he should, Rul was determined to *fight* them, a surefire recipe for disaster. Especially since he and the rest of his reckless ilk had already agreed to align themselves with the human resistance movement. If the poorly coordinated rag-tag bunch could be characterized as a "movement."

Yes, Tog thought to himself, no wonder my stomach feels upset! Fools surround and beset me from every side. Tog's musings were interrupted when a heavily armed Kan entered the room and stomped a big flat foot. The signal, which was the nonverbal equivalent of "Hey, stupid, pay attention!" reduced the compartment to shocked silence.

Though slaves, the Ra 'Na were *privileged* slaves, and the Dromas were most privileged of all. *Too* privileged, according to Dro Rul . . . who sensed something different in the air. Something ominous. When the Kan spoke the prelate paid close attention. Rather than the polite but slightly condescending manner in which the Saurons normally spoke to individuals of his rank, a more coarse form of address was being used. Was the Kan's tone intentional? Or was this particular individual simply out of sorts? The answer would soon be apparent. "So," the warrior began, his voice hard and flat, "we have arrived. Inferior beings will rise, move to the forward hatch, and make their way ashore."

Though the shuttle was not equipped with view ports, a

large vid screen occupied most of the forward bulkhead. A single glance was sufficient to confirm that a significant stretch of water lay between the ship and the much-abused beach. No one moved.

There was silence for a moment followed by the sound of a rather hesitant voice. It belonged to Dro Por, one of Tog's sycophants, a prelate best known for his ability to recite honas rather than interpret them. "Excuse me, lord, but given the fact that the ship remains offshore, and I see no sign of the smaller craft required to ferry us to land, how should we proceed?"

It quickly became apparent that the Kan had not only been waiting for some such comment—*he had been counting on it*. In spite of the hard inelastic nature of his mouth parts, the alien managed what amounted to an evil smile. The warrior smiled evilly. Por appeared to wilt under the weight of the Sauron's stare. "In addition to the technological expertise of which you and your kind are so endlessly proud, it's the great Hak-Bin's understanding that the Ra 'Na people love to frolic in the water, a pleasure long denied your inferior race during the journey through space. That being the case, you will no doubt enjoy the opportunity to *swim* ashore."

There was no doubt about the fact that the Ra 'Na like to swim, more than that were *designed* to swim, as attested to by the webbing located between their fingers, not to mention the fact that their spacecraft were designed to lift off from and land on water. Something the land-loving Saurons continued to resent but lacked the technical expertise to change. No, Rul, along with every other Ra 'Na in the compartment, knew that the order had nothing to do with their preferences and everything to do with Sauron domination.

By forcing the Dromas to swim, an activity most were no longer adept at, the master race was not only asserting its power but sending a message as well: The church hierarchy serves at *our* pleasure, the church hierarchy has privileges, and the church hierarchy could lose those privileges. Stay in line, and keep the Ra 'Na people in line, or suffer the consequences.

All of those thoughts, those realities, were running through Rul's mind as he stood, released the fastener on his unadorned robe, and allowed it to fall. Now, with the exception of a loincloth, and his soft brown fur, the prelate was naked. His voice rang loud and clear. "We accept the invitation . . . The last one ashore hosts the rest to dinner!"

Some individuals, such as Tog, looked aghast. But the majority of his peers understood what Rul was up to and moved to support him. They stood, dropped their robes, and formed a furry line. The Kan watched in amazement as the Ra 'Na pushed, shoved, and crowded their way into the lock. Appalling though it seemed, the slaves were actually enjoying themselves! The lesson went untaught. Would he be punished? Yes, quite possibly . . . And that in spite of the fact that he had done little more than follow orders.

Tog, one of the last to emerge from the ship's lock, was more than a little self-conscious about his large potbelly, and eyed the open water ahead. Unlike some of his peers, who were known to fritter away hours on self-indulgent exercise programs, it was *his* habit to put work first, remaining at his desk while other less responsible Dros frolicked in the gym. Individuals like Dro Rul, whose sleek, water-slicked head was already halfway to shore, closely followed by a coterie of less skilled but enthusiastic lackeys.

Tog eyed the glassy-looking water at his feet. Would he make it? Or ignominiously drown while thrashing about? With the rest of Ra 'Na in the water, and only one chubby specimen left to go, the Kan gave Tog a push.

The prelate made a satisfying splash, remembered how to swim, and kicked for shore. The water was cold, the rest of the Dromas would reach shore long before he did, and demand a feast. If life could get worse, Tog couldn't see how.

That's when a wave slapped him across the face, salt water flooded his open mouth, and a leg muscle began to cramp.

■ ■ ■

Most of the gaunt humans who trudged up the winding road had little if any knowledge regarding the true purpose of the structure they were being forced to build, the activities of the resistance movement, or the relationship between the Ra 'Na and their masters. All they knew was how hungry their stomachs felt, how sore their feet were, and the highly corrosive manner in which the unending fear ate away at what remained of their humanity. For them the climb up the hill was one more act in a largely meaningless series of acts which they lacked the means to put into perspective.

Consistent with standard practice, as well as a personal commitment to keep Franklin alive, Manning requested that the chief executive officer use his Sauron-authorized helicopter or one of the big black SUVs to reach the top of the hill.

But, typical of what often seemed like the president's contrary nature, Franklin refused. A decision that verged on suicidal since to travel on foot would make the chief executive officer vulnerable to racialist snipers, freelance assassins, and a mob of people who hated collaborators, and might very well turn on the CEO. And not only him, but those assigned to protect him as well.

And, making a nearly impossible situation worse, was the fact that the security team had been ordered to leave any weapon that couldn't be concealed beneath their clothing behind, a presidential imperative that would make the bodyguards seem less threatening, but limited them to handguns, sawed-off pump guns, and a pair of submachine guns.

That being the case Manning, Kell, Amocar, Wimba, Mol, Orvin, and Asad had every reason to be concerned as they left the relative security of the presidential compound and eased their way into the crowd.

In an effort to make up for the lack of heavy weapons, the security chief had no fewer than four .9mm handguns hidden under his long duster-style raincoat, two in shoulder holsters, and two stuck down into his waistband. His right hand hovered near one of the weapons as the people closed in from all sides.

The trick was to create a protective bubble around the Big Dog, a layer of protective flesh that would absorb the incoming rounds and provide those who survived with time to throw the president down.

Once the chief executive was on the ground, there was very little the surviving members of the team could do except throw the ballistic blanket over him and return fire.

Then, depending on what mood the Kan were in, *maybe* they would help, although there was increasing evidence to suggest that Hak-Bin didn't trust his human pet anymore, and might fail to intervene.

The bubble held as the sour-smelling bodies closed in around the presidential party. Eyes stared from dark sockets, long, uncut hair hung down over bony shoulders, and foul breath fogged the air.

Franklin's face was fairly recognizable both because of his former position as governor of Washington State and because the Saurons had gone to considerable lengths to make it known via the heat-activated "talkies" they rained down from above. That being the case, people stared, muttered threats, and applied pressure on the bubble.

Manning was just about to pull his weapon and attempt to force them back, when Franklin did something so right, so natural, that the effect was almost magical.

There weren't very many children on Hell Hill, or elderly people for that matter, most being considered too weak for heavy construction work. But thanks to a moment of laxity, or just plain luck, some parents had managed to bring a child with them, and in spite of the fact that many had been killed by the recent cholera epidemic, a few survived.

One such, a scrawny little girl with a mop of blond hair had been forced to run in order to stay abreast of her mother, who—like many slaves—preferred to carry most of her meager belongings from place to place rather than risk leaving them behind. Bending at the waist, the politician scooped the child up, smiled reassuringly at the little girl's mother, and walked at her side.

Seeing the move, and the way that the youngster had started to play with Franklin's red ear tag, the crowd fell back.

It was one of those wonderful-horrible moments when Franklin demonstrated the full extent to which he could manipulate people and by doing so caused Manning to both respect *and* fear him. After all, what if *he* had been manipulated as well?

A whip cracked, the crowd surged forward, and carried the security chief along with it.

■ ■ ■

Drawn from every part of Hell Hill, and literally whipped into motion, the humans snaked their way upward in trickles, rivulets, and streams, surging at times, until friction slowed them down. Like drops of water in a slow-motion flood, Dr. Sool and her nurse were pulled along.

Crazy though it was, the doctor felt much the same way that a younger version of herself had felt during recess back in grade school. Freed from the demands of the classroom, or in this case the clinic, she experienced a certain lightness of being, a guilt-free joy, that flowed from what amounted to an enforced break in the seemingly endless rounds of work. That's why the medic experienced a sense of disappointment when she heard something squeal, and the crowd jerked to a halt.

Then, like ice exposed to heat, the people standing in front of Sool seemed to melt away. That's when the view opened, and she saw the Kan. The alien shimmered as his highly specialized chitin sought to blend with the background. Judging from the manner in which the warrior lay there, using both graspers to clutch his right leg, it appeared as if the Sauron had crashed on landing. A rather unusual occurrence. The squealing sounds became more urgent.

What the doctor did next came naturally, to her at least, although she would come to question her actions later on. Sool crossed the intervening space, knelt at the Kan's side, and noticed that the Sauron was bleeding. The blood was a watery green color, as if possessed of less hemoglobin, but still recognizable for what it was. The human tried to sound authoritative. "Remove your pincers so I can examine your leg."

The alien's eyes were like river-smoothed black stones. "*No.* Slaves, especially *white* slaves, must never touch one such as myself."

Sool could have told him that according to definitions used by some members of her race she was *black*, regardless of what her skin looked like, but knew it would be a waste of time. "A section of chitin fractured when you landed. You are bleeding. I'm willing to help."

"No," the Sauron replied stubbornly. "My brethren will come to my assistance."

Sool looked around. A crowd was starting to form. Some of the humans looked angry. A man shouted, "Kill the bastard!" and others murmured their agreement.

The doctor looked back to her patient. "None of your brethren are available at the moment. You can accept my help or bleed to death. The choice is yours."

The Kan attempted to sit, started to say something, and

fainted. Sool motioned to her nurse. "Dixie, check the pouch on the left side of his harness. It might contain a first-aid kit." The nurse did as instructed, discovered that it *was* a first-aid kit, and removed the contents.

Now that Sool had unrestricted access to the wound she could see that her original diagnosis was correct. The warrior's chitin had shattered—but not from the impact alone. No, based on a very superficial assessment it appeared as if the thin hairline cracks, or sutures, that normally divided one section of brown chitin from the next had been forced open from within. Not only that, but what should have been hard unyielding exoskeleton felt soft and nearly pliable. All of which was consistent with what Boyer Blue and his people had described as early manifestations of "the change." They estimated only a tiny percentage of the Saurons would die and give birth early but here it seemed was one of them.

Unknown to the Kan and those around him, a nymph had started to take shape within the warrior's abdomen and had already started to grow. Within a week, two at the most, signs of the transformation would become so obvious that the warrior would be whisked away and quietly put to death. The only thing the ruling class *could* do if they wanted to keep the upcoming birth-death day secret from the lower castes who they feared might panic.

"Here," Dixie said, handing Sool a wad of what looked like green steel wool. "Stuff that in the wound. It's a coagulant of some sort."

Sool eyed her assistant, who responded with a shrug. "Hey, I saw one of their medics take care of a cut. That's what *he* did."

Sool pushed the coagulant-soaked wad into the wound, noticed that the color started to change, and saw the bleeding stop.

"Spray this stuff on top," Dixie instructed, handing Sool

a small metal cylinder. "The goo will harden, apply pressure to the coagulant pack, and seal the hole."

The doctor grinned, followed the nurse's instructions, and noticed the sealant was brown. Did the first-aid kits supplied to the Zin come with *black* sealant? And were the Fon kits equipped with *white* sealant? Yes, she suspected that they did. A rather sad commentary reminiscent of segregation in the American South.

That's when a rock hit the Kan's head, another struck Dixie's back, and more clattered all around.

With a vehemence that surprised even her, the doctor shouted "No!" tugged the alien's t-gun free from the belt clip, and pointed it toward the crowd. That's when she felt for a trigger and realized there was none. The medic was still examining the weapon, still trying to understand how it worked, when two of the rock throwers were hurled from their feet.

The high-velocity darts, which had been fired from the top of a nearby observation tower, expanded on impact and blew chunks of meat out through their spines. The rest of the crowd scattered as a party of whip-wielding Fon arrived on the scene. The rescue party paused, watched silently as Sool laid the t-gun down at its owner's side, then shuffled forward.

Having been alerted by the observers high atop the minaret-like tower, the Fon came equipped with the Sauron equivalent of a stretcher. It consisted of two alloy poles connected by a network of adjustable straps. It took two of the functionaries less than three minutes to lay the device next to the injured Kan, lift him into place, and detail four humans to carry the warrior away.

That was when an overseer with a blood-encrusted whip approached Sool, ordered the medic to turn her head, and did something to her right ear. The doctor felt a tug, knew it had something to do with her ear tag, and heard a click.

Task completed, the Sauron shuffled away.

It was only after the functionary was gone that Dixie, her face a study in conflict, delivered the news. "I don't know how to tell you this . . . but he turned you into a red . . . No more double shifts for you!"

Sool took that in. For months she had been working nights for the Saurons, digging ditches for the most part, prior to grabbing a few hours' sleep, and opening the clinic. Now, thanks to the work exemption that went with the red ear tag, the medic could focus all her attention on patients. Would they assume she was a collaborator? Yes, most likely, but there wasn't a damned thing the doctor could do about it. The crowd surged forward and swept both women away.

■ ■ ■

At the top of the hill, near the plaza where a black canopy had been erected, those who had been crucified waited to die. The worst of the pain had passed by then . . . leaving Mal-Dak's extremities almost entirely numb. Though not much given to introspection, the process of being executed caused the Fon to look back on his life and wish that he could remember more of it.

All of which begged an important question: Why had the Zin been gifted with the capacity to recall everything that transpired while the Kan and Fon could look back no farther than two local years? Was that unfair? Or simply proof of what the ruling caste had long claimed: Beings having lighter chitin were inferior. No answer came to him.

Perhaps the Sauron's newfound interest in the whys and wherefores of life stemmed from the blood that rushed to his head or the sudden upside-down perspective which the cross provided. Whatever the reason, the Fon found himself making eye contact with an equally inverted human who hung not ten paces away. The slave was younger rather than older, had fur growing on his face, and piercing blue eyes.

"So," the man said stoically, "it looks like the old saying is correct . . . What goes around comes around."

The words were translated by the device still strapped to the Sauron's chest. Suddenly, and much to his surprise, Mal-Dak felt a strange kinship with the human. "What offense did you commit?"

The human grinned. "I told a Kan to take his t-gun and shove it up his ass."

"He must have been very angry."

"Yeah," the man said with evident satisfaction, "he was. How 'bout you?"

"The Zin needed to punish someone," Mal-Dak said simply. "I was chosen."

"That's a tough break," the human allowed sympathetically. "Or would be if it weren't for the fact that you deserve it."

Mal-Dak thought about all the slaves he had whipped, many for no reason at all, and realized that the same thing was happening to him. "Yes, I guess I do."

"Big of you to admit it," the man said dryly. "So, do Saurons believe in life after death?"

"Of course," Mal-Dak replied with certainty. "My ancestors speak to me when I sleep. They watch over me now."

The human seemed to consider the matter. "What about humans? Would that apply to us as well?"

Mal-Dak had never considered the issue before, but the answer popped into his head. "Of course. Just as Saurons need slaves in *this* life, we need slaves in the afterlife as well."

The man laughed. "You are one crazy bastard . . . You know that?"

Mal-Dak, who wasn't sure how to respond, chose to remain silent. Horns sounded, drums began to beat, and the sun speared the Sauron's eyes.

■ ■ ■

In spite of the great meeting about to be held, and the fact that construction work had temporarily been halted, there were some functions that not only had to continue, but were actually made easier by the momentarily empty streets. The never-ending process of body disposal was one such process.

The meat wagon, as it was generally known, consisted of a stripped-down pickup truck. It had been black once, but sections of paint had peeled, leaving patches of rust. A Fon named Hol-Nok sat high in the cab, a human called Cappy sat in the now empty engine compartment, and a team of eight slaves pulled the vehicle along.

The bodies, which were stacked in the back, were mourned by a flock of somber-looking crows. They rose like a black cloud whenever the truck bounced over an obstacle, and then, reluctant to part with such a fine feast, settled again.

Each day was pretty much like the one before, something that Cappy, who abhorred change, was glad of. He would get up, don his clothes, eat some gruel, wake the slaves, allow *them* to eat some gruel, put them in harness, collect Hol-Nok, and proceed to the top of Hell Hill. Usually before the artificial sun—or was it a moon?—had set and the real one rose.

It was important to accomplish that prior to loading any bodies since the pickup chassis was heavy, and there was no way the team would be able to pull the meat wagon up the hill while fully loaded.

Had he been asked, Cappy would have sworn that he hated his job, that the horror of it kept him awake at night, but that wasn't entirely true. No, the truth was that he was grateful for his job, one that required little more than a loud voice and a heavy foot on the brake. The fact that he identified himself as African American, and the slaves pulling the pickup were white, amounted to a bonus. Finally, after hundreds of years, the bastards were getting theirs. Black aliens, who would have thought?

Once the slaves halted the meat wagon at the top of the hill, and removed the latest crop of corpses from the crosses, it was time to wind their way down. It was a gentle journey during which the wagon stopped at all the usual pickup points, and the load continued to grow larger. Not a pleasant task, but better than letting them rot, which could lead to disease.

And it was that, the possibility of an epidemic, which accounted for the fact that Cappy and his subordinates had been excused from the day's festivities and ordered to work. Now, his chores having been accomplished in half the usual time, the human shouted words of encouragement to his team, waved to the guards on the gate, and guided the grisly conveyance out beyond the protective wall. From there it was a relatively short pull to the ravine where the bodies were routinely dumped and burned.

Cappy, his body swaying to the motion of the truck's side-to-side rhythm, took pleasure in the fact that the shift would end early, slapped the slaves with the reins, and urged them forward.

The Fon, who rode in the cab above and had yet to utter a single word during more than a month of meat wagon duty, continued to doze.

Meanwhile, in the pile behind him, a body started to stir. Jonathan Ivory sensed motion, gagged on the horrible stench, and felt a crushing weight. Not only that but his head hurt, *really* hurt, worse than anything he had experienced before.

The racialist rediscovered his arms, ordered them to push the weight off his chest, and discovered that they were far too weak. What *was* the oppressive weight anyway?

Ivory tried to open his eyes, discovered that they were glued shut, and struggled even harder. Suddenly, after persistent effort, they flew open. There wasn't much light down toward the middle of the stack, only what leaked in around the loosely packed bodies, but enough to see by. That's when Ivory found himself staring up into Tripod's blue-tinged countenance and knew what the weight was. Not only was the skinhead's corpse resting on his . . . there were more bodies all around.

Ivory tried to scream, realized that screaming requires oxygen, and settled for a sob instead. That was the moment that the subtle but persistent motion ceased, the racialist heard voices, and forced himself to think. Should he yell? In hopes of attracting attention? Or lie as he was? And continue to play dead?

The latter seemed safest, for the moment at least, and Ivory forced himself to lie perfectly still. He watched through slitted eyes as bodies above and to either side were lifted away. Then it was his turn, and pain lanced through the racialist's head as slaves grabbed hold of his extremities and lifted him free of the truck.

Cappy watched impassively as four members of the now unharnessed team counted to three, swung the body back and forth, and let it fly.

The corpse hit the top of the pile with an audible thump, made some sort of noise, and went limp.

Cappy heard the sound, and might have gone to investigate, except for the fact that bodies make a lot of noises. Farts mostly—which he had no desire to chase.

Ivory, eyes closed, regretted the groan. Would anyone investigate? No, it didn't sound as if anyone had noticed. All he had to do was wait for the slaves to depart and come back to life.

Something light landed on the racialist's chest, strutted up toward his face, and took a bite out of his cheek. A crow! It hurt like hell, and Ivory allowed himself to move subtly. The crow cawed, and the weight disappeared.

Metal clanged on metal, mostly unintelligible words were exchanged, and there was a moment of silence. Then, with no warning whatsoever, someone doused the racialist with what felt like cold water. Except that it *wasn't* cold water, it was gasoline, which the characteristic stench made clear.

Cappy had already struck the old-fashioned kitchen-style match, and it was already falling toward the pile of fuel-soaked corpses, when one of the bodies screamed "No!" came to its feet, and tried to run. The problem was that bodies, even dead ones, make a poor running surface. Not to mention the fact that they were sitting on many layers of gray ash, which gave under Ivory's weight.

That being the case the racialist was still on the pile, still high-stepping toward safety, when the fumes were ignited. Ivory heard the whoosh of suddenly consumed oxygen, felt warmth wash across his body, and knew he was on fire.

Cappy, his eyebrows raised in amazement, watched the fiery apparition dive off the pile, hit the ground, and roll. Just like they teach children to do in grade school.

The flames were out, and the pain had just begun, when Ivory regained his feet and started to run. The ravine led toward the east, so that's where he went. No one attempted to follow.

Gravel crunched as the Kan, who rarely left the comfort of the meat wagon's cab, shuffled up from behind. Cappy turned and was there to hear the only words the Sauron had uttered during their time on the job. "A dead human comes back to life, catches fire, and runs away. Now *that's* funny."

■ ■ ■

The team, with a Fon in the lead, had made its way down off the hill, through a cordon of heavily armed Kan, and into a sort of no-man's-land where all the humans had been intentionally evacuated. To join the assembly at the top of the hill? Or for some other reason? There was no way to be sure.

Like most humans, Jill Ji-Hoon knew very little about the race that had enslaved her, especially their culture, which meant that the steady beat of unseen drums, plus the occasional groan of a horn came as something of a surprise.

Music, no matter how simple, implied emotion, to Ji-Hoon's mind at least, and emotion suggested empathy, of which she had seen no evidence whatsoever. Why?

Be it right or wrong the ex–FBI agent had a theory . . . Perhaps the Saurons could feel empathy for each other, but, because they had been trained to perceive slaves in the same way a carpenter regards her tools, couldn't empathize with what they saw as a screwdriver or a pair of pliers. Did that make it okay? Hell no, but if true, it helped her understand.

Now, as the team made its way down toward a recently completed wharf, Ji-Hoon suspected that whatever chore she and her teammates had been chosen to do, it had nothing to do with blocks of stone.

Her suspicions were almost immediately confirmed when they rounded a stack of newly arrived pastel-colored cargo modules and a group of formally attired Zin appeared. They were clustered around a richly decorated sedan chair—the very thing that Ji-Hoon and her companions had no doubt been summoned to carry. One of the ruling caste hurried forward to berate the Fon for being late—just as Ji-Hoon and her team had been berated not a half hour before.

Then, dominance having been reestablished, the slaves were ordered into position. Their Fon, frantic lest some detail go awry, circled the conveyance and peppered them with threats. The Zin, all of whom wore pleated skirts and leather harnesses, watched impassively.

The ex-agent was directed to take the front right corner of the sedan chair, a position she liked, since it would allow her to see the terrain ahead. A seemingly trivial detail that would make the journey slightly more bearable and lessen the chance of injury as well. A rather important strategy in an environment where those deemed unfit for work were routinely executed.

Then, on an order from their increasingly officious Fon, the humans lifted the sedan chair up into the air. Judging from the object's weight, and consistent with the ex–FBI agent's expectations, the passenger was already aboard. It was impossible to verify, of course, but judging from most of the Saurons Ji-Hoon had seen, the typical alien weighed a hundred, maybe a hundred and twenty pounds, which meant that the sedan chair was heavier than the individual it carried.

So, assuming the conveyance weighed in at a hundred and fifty pounds or so, the total load was just under three hundred pounds. Heavy, but lighter than a typical stone block, a fact for which Ji-Hoon was grateful. It was a long way to the top of the hill, which the slave felt certain, was their ultimate destination.

Hosker, who had long since designated himself as the team's leader, called, "Your right, your right, left right," just as they taught him in boot camp, and it worked. The slaves moved forward, and the Zin, none of whom were used to walking, shuffled along behind. It was uncomfortable, and they were unhappy. Somewhere, as if aware of their pain, a horn groaned in sympathy. Meanwhile, the sun, which cared nothing for the beings who consumed its energy, inched higher in the sky.

■ ■ ■

Dro Tog, who had been rescued by two of his peers and towed ashore like so much flotsam, stumbled up out of the shallows, shook himself in a manner that sent hundreds of water droplets flying in all directions, and sought to recapture at least some of his dignity. A task made somewhat easier by sycophants like Dro Por, who hurried to offer their sympathies.

Then, having been chivvied into a column of twos, the clergy were ordered to march up the road. Dro Rul, who led the procession, looked ahead. Hundreds of Ra 'Na lined the sides of the road, where they could witness the manner in which he and the rest of the prelates had been humbled. A lesson the wily Hak-Bin hoped the technicals would share with their peers.

The prelate frowned, shot looks at his lieutenants, and started to sing. The hona, which had been written on their home world of Balwur, affirmed that no matter how hard the winds might blow, and no matter how high the waves might climb, all storms must eventually end, leaving tranquillity in their wake. First joined by those most loyal to him, and then by the rest, Rul walked with his head up, his chest out, and an expression of defiance on his face as the chant went out.

The crowd saw the loincloth-clad Dromas, the way that their ears were laid back, and knew something was amiss. Then, hearing the hona from which they had taken hope for so long, they were quick to join in.

Rul, who heard their voices, felt his heart swell with pride. Though poorly led at times, and susceptible to weakness, the Ra 'Na people were essentially unbroken.

The knowledge of that, the certainty of it, carried him forward.

■ ■ ■

In spite of the fact that the Zin privately referred to it as "the citadel," as if it was a single structure, the alien fortress actually consisted of three interlocking towers, a sort of three-leaf-clover configuration with each cylindrical structure being linked to all the rest via enclosed passageways and tunnels.

Now, as the tide of humanity carried Franklin and his security team to the top of the hill, the president was impressed by the vast size of it. Good or bad, right or wrong, here was an accomplishment on a par with the wonders of the ancient world. Especially when one considered the scant seventy-plus twenty-four-hour days in which the complex had been built.

Sheer windowless walls rose more than two hundred feet to crenellated towers, each topped with clusters of vents, ducts, and alien antennas.

And it was there, beneath long wind-whipped pennants, that specially trained Fon blew into their snout bags, forcing air through gigantic ground-resting horns to produce the deep foghornlike groans that announced the Great One's arrival.

Around the cluster of towers, and laid out with admirable precision, were concentric rings of crosses. Some were empty, the meat wagon having taken the dead away earlier that morning, but most remained occupied.

A horrible sight, which should have shocked the human, and would have, had it not been for the fact that Franklin, like most of the people around him, had grown used to such displays. One thing *was* surprising, however—and that was the unprecedented number of Saurons who had been crucified alongside the slaves. The politician noticed that all of them were Fon and thought he knew why.

The sudden emergence of the Fon Brotherhood, not to mention the attack on the Kan checkpoint only days before, had shaken Hak-Bin to his very core. So much so that the Sauron leader was willing to sacrifice some functionaries in the name of social discipline. An example not lost on the Kan or Zin either, for that matter. What with the clock ticking, and his entire race about to be reborn, the means would justify the end.

A situation the human could easily understand since most

of *his* race, those not actually murdered during the attacks, would be slaughtered the moment the fortress was complete. That was the plan at any rate—but one he and the rest of the resistance movement planned to counter. *If* they lived long enough to do so. Whips cracked as the crowd slowed, was forced to disperse, and ordered to face uphill.

A tightly arched black awning had been established at the foot of the north tower, and, judging from the Zin assembled there, was the point from which Hak-Bin would address the multitude. Rows of crosses served as decorations, speakers had been mounted on poles, and rows of sling chairs stood ready to accommodate Zin dignitaries. A Kan waded through the crowd, pointed toward Franklin, and motioned upward. Never one to miss an opportunity, it seemed that Hak-Bin wanted his "ruka" or pet, up where the rest of the slaves could see and hate him.

Franklin lifted the girl off his shoulders and placed her on the ground. She ran to her mother, who nodded and smiled. At least one convert had been made.

Then, protected by Manning and his security team, the president wound his way up to where a group of Fon functionaries stood. A murmur ran through the crowd behind him, and someone hissed. Franklin, who half expected an attack of some sort, made it to the flat area and turned to face the crowd. He could feel the full weight of their animosity. The sun chose that particular moment to duck behind a cloud. A shadow fell on the hilltop, and Franklin shivered.

■ ■ ■

Wave after wave of slaves arrived, were ordered to wait, and had little choice but to obey. There were no sanitary facilities, no arrangements for water, and those who sat, or tried to, were whipped onto their feet.

Sool, with Dixie at her side, was deposited directly in

front of the awning where whatever was about to occur would most likely happen. A privilege she could have done without. There was one advantage, however, since the vantage point provided Sool with an unobstructed view of Jack Manning, who, completely unaware of her presence, scanned the crowd. The fact that the medic found the security officer interesting, even sexy, never ceased to amaze her. Logically, based on all things that made sense, there should be no attraction whatsoever.

First, because *his* profession, which required Manning to shoot people from time to time, was completely at odds with *her* profession.

Then there was the matter of his inner life, a mindscape which she assumed to be less intellectual than hers, although she knew him to be well educated. Manning had a master's degree in geology no less . . . which might show a scientific bent.

Why the attraction then? If it shouldn't exist? Memories mostly, like the first time she had seen him, lurching in out of a rainstorm with an injured girl cradled in his arms. Or later, after the racialists abducted her, the manner in which he not only came to her rescue, but held her filth-encrusted hand.

So which was he? Sool wondered. A violence-prone maniac? Or a man capable of great tenderness? And what difference did it make? Since the doctor knew the security chief had been in love with Franklin's wife and crushed by her violent death.

Manning, his eyes hidden by the dark glasses that he and the rest of his team wore, looked in her direction. Something, Sool wasn't sure what, jumped the gap.

Damn, the medic thought to herself, I'm an idiot.

Manning smiled, and the sun came out.

■ ■ ■

Mal-Dak, still hanging upside down from his cross, had never thought about crucifixion before and never contemplated how terrible it could be. Rather than simply dying, as by other forms of execution, victims lingered for days until they succumbed to exposure. A long, horrible process that stretched forever.

The fact that the cursed black birds had already been stymied by the thickness of his chitin, and would soon attack his eyes, made the process even worse.

Now, only hours into his own personal hell, the Fon was thirsty. Not just a little thirsty, but *very* thirsty, to a degree he had never experienced before. A fact that seemed especially ironic since he, like his brothers, had suffered through endless days of rain. Rain that fell as a mist, rain that blew in sideways off the water, and rain that fell in torrents from an eternally gray sky. The very thought of it made his throat feel parched. And it was *that* thirst, *that* need, which was foremost in the Sauron's mind when Hak-Bin's procession drew into his upside-down world. Not that Mal-Dak *knew* the procession had anything to do with Hak-Bin, but surmised it from the noise, color, and movement.

Of one thing there was no doubt, however, and that was the fact that his misery, combined with the unjust manner in which he had been treated, combined to make him the very thing for which he was being punished: a rebel. A rebel who, more by luck than anything else, was about to generate an incident that would inspire *real* rebels, most of whom were standing around trying to look busy.

The moment occurred just as Ji-Hoon and her team, sweating heavily after the long hard climb, bore the sedan chair past Mal-Dak's cross. That's when the Fon, having struggled to muster the necessary saliva, moistened his mouth, and shouted a phrase which previously had no meaning to him. "Long live the Fon Brotherhood!"

That's the way the English-language version came out

anyway—although the original was somewhat different. The translation was picked up by the Ra 'Na PA system and relayed to the mostly human crowd. The words were meaningless to most who continued to stare at the ground.

But even if the vast majority of the humans remained unmoved—the challenge had an electrifying effect on at least one individual. The great Hak-Bin sat up straight, rapped the side of the sedan chair, and said, "Stop!"

Ji-Hoon heard the command, as did the rest of the team, and they came to a halt. Hak-Bin slid backward out of the sedan chair, found the ground with his feet, and scanned the area. The citadel loomed above, crosses cut the sky into odd geometric shapes, and humans carpeted one side of the hill. The vast unwashed stink assailed the olfactory sensors located on the inside of each wrist, and the Zin pulled elastic bands down to cover them.

All of it was the way Hak-Bin had visualized it, had arranged it, except for the offensive slogan. The voice belonged to a Fon, he knew that, partly because of the words themselves and partly because of the manner in which they had been said. Like most inferior beings, this one spoke the dialect typical of his caste. Hak-Bin eyed the surrounding thicket of crosses. "Which one?"

A Kan pointed at Mal-Dak, and the Sauron turned to look. The first thing he noticed was that this particular creature was nothing special to look at. A rather pathetic specimen he couldn't remember seeing before, though truth be told, the Zin had a hard time telling functionaries apart. He gestured with a pincer. "T-gun."

Reluctantly, because no warrior worth his chi parts with his weapon willingly, the nearest Kan surrendered his sidearm.

Hak-Bin accepted the weapon, made his way over to where Mal-Dak hung, and allowed the t-gun to dangle at his side. "You and your entire line are about to die."

Unlike a growing number of his caste, some of whom stood not twenty paces away, Mal-Dak knew nothing about the coming change. All he wanted to do was strike back, and words were the only weapon he had. He said the first thing that came to his mind. "All of us are going to die . . . and *you* sooner than some."

The words, which not only seemed to imply a knowledge of the great change, but the rather worrisome symptoms that plagued Hak-Bin of late, were far more effective than the Fon could have possibly imagined. The Zin felt sudden uncontrolled rage.

Mal-Dak saw the t-gun come up, knew what it meant, and was glad. Others might hang for days, might have their eyes pecked out, but he would escape. He would . . .

Hak-Bin squeezed the weapon's handle, the weapon barked, and the dart punched a hole through the Fon's thorax, hit the wood beyond, and blew the two-by-four in half. Like a tree falling in the forest, the cross toppled, and landed with a thump.

Much to Franklin's amusement the humans produced a scattering of applause, and the Sauron leader, who knew what the sound meant, felt a resurgence of anger. Had the entire universe gone insane? Would everyone, Sauron and human alike, be allowed to defy his authority?

Enraged by the manner in which his own object lesson had been turned against him, Hak-Bin raised the t-gun, shot the blue-eyed man in the head, and proceeded down the line of crosses, killing humans until his weapon ran out of projectiles.

Hak-Bin's anger had run its course by then, and the rational part of his mind was back in control. It questioned the true cause of his runaway emotions while simultaneously looking for some way to cover up.

Much to its owner's horror Hak-Bin tossed the t-gun aside, allowed it to plop into a mud puddle, and shuffled toward the canopy-covered dais. His retinue, which included Ji-Hoon and the rest of her team, followed. Dro Rul, along with the rest of his peers, had arrived by then, and stood off to one side as the Sauron took his place before the enormous crowd.

It was no coincidence that a flight of seven Sauron fighters chose that particular moment to roar over the slaves. People ducked and eyed the sky in fear.

Hak-Bin took note of the fact that the humans appeared to be cowed—and made the decision to dispense with his opening remarks. He took his place behind the dais and eyed his audience. "You continue to live for one purpose, and one purpose only, and that is to work. Not just any work, such as you did prior to our arrival, but meaningful work. Look at the temple behind me, take pride in what you have accomplished, and continue to live."

Hak-Bin paused at that point, allowing time for the words to sink in. "Or, and the choice is yours, you can die. For death is the fate assigned to all miscreants regardless of who they may be. This reality applies to humans, Ra 'Na, and Saurons as well. If you doubt me, turn your eyes to the sky."

Slowly, as if not quite sure they had heard correctly, the slaves looked up. Manning was no exception. The sky appeared to be clear—so the security chief was confused at first. Then he saw the black dot and heard the low-pitched hum. The lifter, just one of the many types of aircraft that the Saurons had stolen from the Ra 'Na and adapted for their own use, came in from the north.

It looked like a single blob at first, but that started to change. The single image morphed into an H-shaped aircraft with something that dangled below. A cargo module? No, it was too small for that. Whatever the thing was it twisted back and forth at the end of its tether and seemed invested with a life of its own.

"As I said," Hak-Bin intoned, his slightly stilted words booming out from the pole-mounted speakers, "*no one* is exempt from Sauron justice. Not even the stonemaster himself."

There was a muted gasp as the H-shaped shadow fell over the crowd, and whatever it was that kept the alien aircraft aloft roared, blasting the hill with jets of hot air. Grit flew, clothes flapped, and hair whipped from side to side. The object was clear to see by then—and it was the Saurons rather than the slaves who stared up in horror.

The stonemaster, who, only hours before, had been the second or third most powerful being on Earth, now dangled beneath the lifter at the end of a long black cable. It swayed alarmingly as the lifter lost forward motion and hovered above the citadel. "Remember what you are about to witness," Hak-Bin said gravely. "Remember as you watch over the slaves, remember as you haul stone, and remember when you dream."

Then, by means of a prearranged signal, an order was given. The lifter's copilot touched a switch, a coupling snapped open, and the stonemaster, still struggling to accept his fate, fell free of the cable. Strangely, or perhaps not so strangely, he never screamed. True to his calling, true to the knowledge inherited from his predecessors, and true to his own nature, the master architect spent the last few seconds of his life admiring what he had built, wondering why he had never thought to view it from that particular perspective before, and hoping his assistants would have the strength to deal with the political pressure from above, would refuse to compromise the citadel's structural integrity in the name of speed, and would hew to the instructions laid down in the Book of Cycles.

And that was when the Sauron's legs shattered against a partially completed dome, when shards of exoskeleton punctured his abdominal cavity, and light exploded before his

eyes. The sight of the Sauron's death affected different beings in different ways.

Sool winced and closed her eyes.

Franklin thought about how desperate Hak-Bin must be.

Dro Tog felt frightened.

Manning smiled coldly.

Ji-Hoon frowned.

And the man named Brian Banes finally snapped. A fact
which wasn't all that surprising in and of itself, especially
given the fact that the Saurons had murdered most of the
other patients in the mental hospital, sparing Banes because
he was big and strong. *Very* big and *very* strong.

Propelled by emotions rather than concrete thoughts,
Banes pushed his way through the crowd, sucker punched
one of the Kan warriors, and broke through the security
cordon. The ex–mental patient pulled the long heavily ser-
rated kitchen knife out of its homemade sheath, held it up
over his head, and charged up the hill. The roar of primal
outrage turned many heads.

Strangely enough it was Hak-Bin who first noticed the
would-be assassin. His first thought was to escape, to jump
out of danger, but he refused to let instinct rule. No, appearances were important, especially then, with so much at
stake.

That being the case, the Sauron resolved to stand his
ground, to place himself in the hands of fate, and wait for
one of his seemingly dim-witted warriors to kill the oncoming slave.

The truth was that in spite of the Zin's doubts regarding
their capabilities, no less than three of the shimmery aliens
had turned uphill and raised their weapons only to discover
that if they fired and even one of their darts flew wide, there
was a high likelihood that it would hit Hak-Bin or one of
the Zin dignitaries seated to either side of him. A definite
no-no. They were still contemplating, still trying to decide,

when Jill Ji-Hoon took action. Though some would question the ex–FBI agent's judgment later on—it was training rather than political correctness that put her body in motion.

Ji-Hoon, who, along with the other members of the team had been standing just downhill from Hak-Bin, waiting for the event to end, stepped out to block the madman's way. He saw her, roared some sort of challenge, and ran even faster. His legs pumped, his breath came in short gasps, and only one thing stood in his way. A tall woman with a look of determination on her face.

Though not responsible for Hak-Bin's safety, Manning and his team were responsible for Franklin, and the sight of the knife was more than sufficient cause. Coats were whipped aside, heavy weapons appeared, and they stood ready to fire. That was when Ji-Hoon decided to intervene, and the security chief raised his hand. Fingers came off triggers as everyone waited to see what would happen. Ji-Hoon waited for the would-be assassin to get a little closer, shifted all her weight to her left foot, and kicked with her right. The lower part of her leg slammed into Bane's midriff.

He seemed to hesitate, stutter-stepped in an effort to achieve more traction, and swiped at Ji-Hoon with the knife.

The ex–FBI agent jerked her head back, let the blade pass, and kicked her assailant in the right knee.

Banes felt something give, knew he was falling, and managed to recover.

Now, dragging one foot behind him, knife still in his hand, the ex–mental patient drove himself upward. Darts, fired from the top of the nearest observation tower half a mile away, blew divots out of the ground behind him, and those close enough to see what was taking place dove for the ground.

Ji-Hoon, who stood ready to hit her adversary again, was close enough to feel the warm spray as one of Hak-Bin's ceremonial guards finally blew the madman's head off.

Blood spouted, the corpse toppled, and Banes was free.

Hak-Bin, who still stood frozen in place, allowed himself to relax. Though dramatic, the assassination attempt made a poor conclusion to an otherwise powerful presentation. But that couldn't be helped, so the Zin looked out over the crowd, marveled at how quiet the scene was, and felt the first signs of the much-dreaded symptoms.

He would need privacy in which to wait them out, in which to scream unheard, in which to wish he were dead. That being the case, Hak-Bin kept his closing comments short and to the point. "You know what I require of you . . . You know the price of failure . . . You know what to do. Work hard, build well, and you will survive."

The last sentence was a lie, for his kind as well as theirs, but such were the words all of them needed to hear. They required hope . . . and the gift was his to give.

The multitude watched in silence as the great Hak-Bin summoned the sedan chair, slid into place, and was carried away. That's when a crow cawed, the slaves were released, and work resumed.

2

DEATH DAY MINUS 79

THURSDAY, MAY 14, 2020

Tyranny, like hell, is not easily conquered, yet we have this consolation with us, that the harder the conflict, the more glorious the triumph. What we obtain too cheap, we esteem too lightly: it is dearness only that gives everything its value.

—THOMAS PAINE
The American Crisis, no. 1, December 23, 1776

PUGET SOUND

It was nighttime, or would have been, except for the ghostly glow provided by the asteroid-mounted reflecting mirror the Ra 'Na had constructed on behalf of the Saurons and referred to as "the bounce."

Authorized by the now deceased stonemaster, and focused on Hell Hill so the humans could work around the clock, the intensity of the light started to fade a few miles to the south, where a group known as the Crips had established a temporary camp.

It was a pathetic affair, consisting of little more than a secluded cove, a jumble of weather-whitened logs, and a cluster of carefully camouflaged huts, none of which provided more than twelve square feet of usable living space. Veritable hovels by the standards of the indigents forced to dwell in them—but objects of delight to the wayward alien who floated belly up not fifty feet from the rock-strewn beach.

His name was Pas Pol, *Fra* Pol, the prefix Fra indicating his status as a member of the Ra 'Na clergy albeit the lowest rung thereof.

Not that Pol, who was or had been part of Dro Tog's diocese, had ever spent much time worrying about the needs of the religious bureaucracy. A fact that not only prevented his ascension to the next highest level of the hierarchy but kept him in perpetual trouble. A situation made worse when the wayward cleric surreptitiously witnessed a meeting in which Hak-Bin addressed his fellow Zin regarding the heretofore secret birth-death day.

Bishop Tog sat on the information at first, fearful that it might stimulate a revolt and thereby threaten the rather comfortable status quo. But the attempt to bottle the information up failed. Dro Rul learned of the secret, and the Ra 'Na resistance movement was born. An effort to which Fra Pol had dedicated both heart and soul.

There were dangers attendant to such movements, however—and the initiate had been forced to flee. Yes, the manner of his departure from the dreadnought *Hok Nor Ah* had been something less than dignified, but Pol not only managed to survive the experience, but wound up in a veritable Ra 'Na paradise thanks to the fact that the waters of Puget Sound were home to a natural buffet of bivalves, any number of which had already found their way into the initiate's well-rounded tummy. And into *other* tummies too, since the Crips not only lived off the abundant seafood themselves, but used the watery harvest to buy the medications that many of them required.

Not that such matters claimed much of the Ra 'Na's attention since his mind was mostly occupied with the sensory feedback attendant upon the act of swimming. An activity mostly denied his race during their long captivity and one for which their lithe, fur-covered bodies had expressly been designed. The sensation had something in common with weightlessness but managed to be better somehow. Pol loved the resistance offered by the water, not to mention its cool embrace and the way the unseen currents tugged at him. Surely Balwur, the Ra 'Na people's fabled home world, had been like this, only better if such a thing could be imagined.

The realities of the larger context couldn't be ignored, however, and much as the more sybaritic part of the cleric's personality would have liked nothing more than to extend his responsibility-free lifestyle for as long as possible, there wouldn't *be* a future if the Saurons had their way. Each time the sun disappeared in the west the great slaughter drew one day closer. A fact which meant that everyone who could do something *should* do something, and sooner rather than later.

Pol's thoughts were delightfully interrupted when a clanging noise was heard, and the camp began to stir. What the humans referred to as dinnertime had finally arrived. It was the best moment of the day except for breakfast, lunch, and the snacks that came in between.

Suddenly energized, the Ra 'Na rolled over and dove. The water was deliciously cold. Barnacle-encrusted rocks gave way to gravel that sloped up to a sandy beach. Pol stood the moment the water was shallow enough, waddled across the seaweed-strewn tide line, and shook himself like a water-soaked dog.

A depression surrounded by artfully stacked driftwood served to screen the fire pit from the water, but the top of the cook's head could still be seen. His name was Cecil. He was black like the Zin and a fine cook, or as Pol thought of him, a "flavorist." An important distinction since the humans had a not altogether healthy tendency to fry, broil, bake, and otherwise cook food that should have been dunked in flavor pots and served raw. Hence the term "flavorist," since the skill lay in the preparation of the condiments rather than the application of heat. In any case, Cecil, who liked his brood to arrive on time, shouted, "Come and get it!" which Pol hurried to do. Other members of the small, tight-knit community responded with an equal sense of urgency.

There was the ex–navy petty officer named Darby, her face scarred by a shipboard fire; Wily, who though paralyzed below the waist, insisted on dragging himself across the sand; Chu, one sleeve flapping in the breeze; Nakambe, whose left leg was two inches shorter than the right; Nok, who had lost one leg to cancer, but still made good time on a prosthesis; Slo-mo, who had the body of a full-grown man but the mind of a ten-year-old, and a black Lab named Whitey, who liked to play in the water almost as much as Pol did.

All of them, with Whitey dashing from one person to the next, converged on Cecil's carefully arranged fire pit. Baked salmon, which had been wrapped in seaweed and buried under hot coals, steamed on a freshly scrubbed plank. Clam chowder, thick with chunks of meat and canned potato, burbled in a well-blackened pot.

And, thanks to the nice collection of wine, which Darby had stumbled across in an isolated waterfront home, there were three bottles of St. Michelle Riesling, which stood like soldiers on a driftwood plank. Though lavish by the standards of Hell Hill, the Crips had grown used to such meals, and were quick to tuck in.

Cecil, hands on hips, smiled approvingly as slices of fish were transferred to plastic plates, bowls were filled to the brim with chowder, and Pol, his food having been prepared sushi style, started to vacuum oysters out of their shells. A somewhat noisy process that was accompanied by grunts of satisfaction.

No one took offense, however, since all the Crips were hearty eaters and not much given to the finer points of etiquette. That being the case, the first fifteen or twenty minutes of the meal passed with only a modicum of conversation. Then, once the worst of the hunger pangs had been assuaged, and those who wanted seconds had obtained them, the conversations began.

The nature of these interactions was usually the same. Chu would complain about the way in which she had been treated that day, Nakambe would tell her to shut up, Wily would attempt to make peace, and Darby, who not only steered the group's boat, but functioned as de facto group mother, would remain silent, partially eaten food resting on her lap, eyes focused on something the others weren't able to see.

Pol, having inhaled more than a dozen shellfish, and being in need of a rest prior to the second course, came to his feet, loosened the cinch of his loincloth, and took a mug of freshly brewed coffee over to Darby.

The sailor heard the crunch, crunch, crunch of the alien's footsteps and looked up. She liked Pol and smiled. That's what it was supposed to be anyway, except that the scar tissue refused to cooperate, and the expression resembled a grimace instead. She accepted the cup. "Thank you, Fra Pol, that was thoughtful . . . Have a seat."

The Ra 'Na accepted the invitation, took his place on the log beside her, and, much to his own surprise, started to act like the cleric he had trained to be. "You seem troubled, Darby. . . . Is there something I can do to help?"

Darby, who would have answered differently had Chu or Nakambe asked the same question, shrugged. "Not unless you can get rid of the Saurons, give me a new face, and bake some apple pie to go with this coffee."

Though presented in a lighthearted manner Pol knew the pain was real. Especially where her face was concerned. "I don't know what apple pie is, but I'm fairly sure our medical personnel could repair the damage done to your face."

Hope flared in Darby's eyes, held for a moment, then faded away. "The Saurons would never allow something like that."

"No," the initiate agreed, "they wouldn't. Which is just one of the reasons why we need to rise up and defeat them."

The human shook her head. "Fighting the Saurons is a waste of time. I took part in an attack that destroyed five Sauron spaceships. It didn't even slow the bastards down."

"Understood," the Ra 'Na replied, "but there's something you *don't* know. Something important."

Darby looked quizzical. "Such as what?"

Pol smiled and rows of tiny white teeth appeared. "Such as the fact that all of the Saurons will die while giving birth to the next generation—which means the slave races have a chance. *If* we work together, *if* we have courage, *if* we strike at the correct moment."

Darby had questions, lots of them, but the first was the one Pol was waiting to hear. "So what can I do to help?"

"*We*," the alien replied, "what *we* can do to help. The answer is out there . . . and our job is to find it."

IN THE FOOTHILLS OF THE CASCADE MOUNTAINS

Half-crazed by the pain from his burns, and fully expecting to be shot in the back, the newly risen racialist had blundered through the thick underbrush for more than a mile before coming to the conclusion that he was at least momentarily safe.

Then, desperate to find shelter and something for his burns, Ivory wandered for hours. In spite of the fact that most humans had been murdered, and the rest forced into slavery, a scattering remained free. That being the case, the racialist discovered that most homes had already been broken into and robbed of anything useful.

Ivory always went about it the same way. He would approach the prospective house, circle it, and pause to listen. Then, assuming everything looked good, he would sidle up to the often shattered door, push it open, and wait for some sort of reaction. A bird flew out once, nearly causing him to shit his pants, but that was unusual. A brooding silence was more common, broken only by the crunch of glass beneath the soles of his boots and the creak of interior doors.

There was stuff, tons of it, all scattered hither and yon where the looters had left it. Clothes, *lots* of clothes, intermixed with useless radios, CD players, clocks, irons, hair dryers, lamps, books, records, and on and on.

What he didn't find but desperately wanted were medical supplies, guns, knives, axes, sleeping bags, cookware, toilet paper, matches, backpacks, or any of the other things that the foragers could use, trade, or hoard.

There were a few victories, however, albeit minor ones, like an overlooked Teflon-coated frying pan, a fifty-foot length of clothesline, and a roll of paper towels. All the newfound treasures went into a canvas bag that the racialist carried Santa style over one shoulder.

Most valuable, however, especially where the burns on his torso were concerned, were some unopened packages of V-neck white undershirts. They were large enough to allow free movement, and the clean cotton felt wonderful against his skin.

Ivory spent the first night wrapped in a cocoon made from floor-length, fully lined, floral curtains, listening to the sounds the house made and the howl of a distant dog. There were a lot of dogs, all feral by then, and very dangerous. They couldn't open doors, though—which was one reason why the human chose to sleep indoors.

The room, which had previously been occupied by a teenage girl, smelled of spilled perfume. It seemed like a strangely inappropriate odor, hearkening as it did to a much happier time and what now seemed like unimaginable luxuries.

Finally, after what seemed like hours, Ivory fell asleep.

Ivory awoke with a start, managed to remember where he was, and wished his mouth tasted better. Strange though it seemed, the racialist had grown a little bit soft during his stay on Hell Hill. A fact which became all too apparent when he struggled to extricate himself from the curtain and realized how sore his muscles were. The burns were better, however, a miracle considering the possibility of infection and the fact that he had no antibiotics.

And it was later that morning, while tromping through a previously looted Ramada Inn, that Ivory discovered an unbroken mirror. That's when he saw the heavy growth of beard, the grimy skin, and the crusted-over burns. None were infected, not so far as he could tell, which was something to give thanks for. The great Yahweh had work for him to do, that was for sure, because nothing else could explain such extremely good fortune.

There wasn't any hot water, not with the power being out, but there was plenty of cold. The racialist used gallons of the stuff, not to mention three bars of individually wrapped soap and four previously white towels before he felt clean. The goatee came off, as did a month's worth of hair, leaving a gaunt, tight-skinned face.

Then, rather than don the filthy clothes that lay puddled on the floor, Ivory wrapped himself in an undersized terry-cloth robe and stalked the halls until he found a room strewn with male clothing. The racialist appropriated some clean boxers, tried on a pair of nicely pressed jeans, and was pleased to discover they were only one size too large. A brown belt with a cheap Western buckle took care of the size discrepancy, a blue T-shirt went up top, and a nondescript sweatshirt added warmth.

Then, having recovered his boots, not to mention his canvas booty bag, Ivory made the best discovery of all: an undisturbed storage room complete with a fully loaded maid's cart, which not only yielded six rolls of toilet paper, and some more clean towels, but a plastic bucket filled with foil-wrapped chocolate hearts!

The racialist filled his pockets with the tasty tidbits, crammed three into his mouth, and experienced something better than sex. Had anyone chosen to follow Ivory that morning, the trail of gold foil would have provided them with the means. Of course, no one did. On that particular day, in that particular place, Ivory was blessed.

ABOARD THE SAURON DREADNOUGHT *HOK NOR AH, (PRIDE OF THE PEOPLE)*

P'ere Has was eating a bowl of gruel when the Kan came to take him away. Not because other more flavorsome fare wasn't available, but because he felt the discipline involved would strengthen his soul and help keep temptation at bay.

Never mind the fact that Dro Tog, his immediate superior, placed himself under no such strictures. Has believed it was the responsibility of each person to define the precise nature of their relationship with the Great One and to conduct themselves in accordance with that belief. Success or failure was their affair.

So, having given *his* particular God a somewhat stern and unyielding demeanor, Has felt it necessary to find ways through which to demonstrate the extent of his devotion. That's why the priest had just scooped the last spoonful of tasteless porridge into his mouth, and was just about to scour the inside of his unadorned bowl with a crust of pan bread, when the hatch flew open.

The Kan, all members of the special security unit assigned to eliminate members of the Ra 'Na resistance movement, wasted no time on niceties. A pair of warriors grabbed the diminutive cleric, jerked him out into the corridor, and searched his body for weapons.

In the meantime, with no rules, regulations, or laws to stop them, other members of the security team ransacked the small sparsely furnished compartment. They found a combination computer–vid player, a collection of what purported to be religious cubes, and a carefully maintained robe used for religious services. The warriors also discovered an extra pair of sandals, a stash of closely scribbled notes, and a preslavery comb inherited from his now-deceased mother.

The lead Kan, who harbored fantasies regarding a stash of weapons, seditious writings, and a computer file containing a complete roster of the Ra 'Na resistance movement, gave a grunt of disappointment. The compartment concealed nothing more dangerous than the comb, no obviously seditious materials, and, if the roster was there, it was disguised in the form of code. Perhaps the scraps of parchment—or the computer's memory cache—would yield something. A possibility the specialists would no doubt look into. "All right then," the Kan said, shuffling out into the corridor, "take him away. The painmaster is not known for his patience."

Like all his kind Has was fluent in the language of his masters and the very mention of the painmaster was sufficient to loosen his bowels. One of the warriors swore, another laughed, and the noncom offered the Sauron equivalent of a frown. "Perhaps the slave isn't the only one in need of the master's attentions."

The noncom lacked the authority necessary to exact such a punishment, but there were other possibilities—and the warriors were well aware of them. The Kan hurried to obey. Has felt the Saurons lift his feet clear of the deck as he struggled to understand why he had been singled out for such treatment, and was hustled away.

The trip through the ship's crowded corridors was like

some sort of nightmare—the kind the cleric experienced in the wake of Tog's unreasonable demands. Except the painmaster was sure to administer something a good deal more unpleasant than a mere tongue-lashing. The certainty of that loosened the cleric's bowels once again.

There was a rational Has, however, a sort of overbeing who managed to remain detached in spite of the mewlings generated by its lesser self. It was that part of the Ra 'Na's personality that took note of the way in which passersby reacted to his presence. Not the Saurons, who were universally uninterested in his predicament, but fellow Ra 'Na, who could be expected to care.

Except that they *didn't* care, or didn't appear to, since to demonstrate any sign of sympathy could be interpreted as a sign of support for whatever crime the unfortunate cleric had obviously been found guilty of.

So, even as the Kan hauled Has away, the Ra 'Na remembered other times, occasions on which it was *he* who had averted his eyes, *he* who allowed the already condemned to be carried away without so much as a comforting look. In fact, Has was so lost in his own contemplations that it seemed as if little more than seconds had passed before the Kan whisked him through the checkpoint beyond which members of the slave races were not normally allowed to pass and didn't *want* to pass.

Then, after a quick series of left and right turns, Has was half-carried, half-dragged through an unmarked hatch and into the painmaster's dark domain. The decor, if that was the correct word, was consistent with instructions set forth in the Book of Cycles, which, ironically enough, dedicated most of its considerable pages to the subject of death.

Though served by a contingent of specially trained Kan, the painmaster was Zin, and therefore black. Thanks to knowledge inherited from his predecessors, the painmaster understood how important psychology could be when it came to wringing information out of recalcitrant slaves. He stood with crossed arms and was lit from below. The effect, which made his already intimidating countenance all the more terrifying, was often sufficient to elicit confessions in and of itself. A positive thing for the most part, unless the goal was to learn the truth, when fear could actually get in the way. Those who were susceptible to intimidation, or simply hoped to avoid torture, had an unfortunate tendency to confess to anything and everything regardless of whether they were actually guilty. A subtlety that his superiors, beings like Hak-Bin, often missed. But that was the way of it, and just one of the reasons why the ancient ones had seen fit to formally invest his particular line.

None of which was apparent to Has as the toes of his sandals skipped over the surface of the metal deck and fear seized his body. Confronted with the Sauron's carefully lit visage, the sight of rods heating in the forge, and the stink of previously singed fur, the Ra 'Na would have loosed his bowels yet again except for the fact that there was nothing left to give. All he could do was make a strange yammering sound as the Kan carried him over to a vacant spot on one of the bulkheads, strapped him into place, and backed away. A Kan moved to cut the subject's clothes away and soon left him naked.

It was then that Has realized that he wasn't alone. Bodies other than his decorated the walls. The compartment was dim, lit by little more than the forge and a scattering of deck-mounted lights, but the newly arrived prisoner could make out half a dozen Ra 'Na, two humans, and a ghostly white Fon—all suspended by straps similar to his. None of them seemed to be aware of the newcomer's presence, or if they were, chose to conceal that fact. Some knew from harsh experience that to demonstrate awareness was to invite more pain—something none sought to do.

Now, his entire weight suspended by the bloodstained

straps, Has watched in horrified fascination as the pain-master withdrew one of the glowing rods from his forge and shuffled across the deck. Having interrogated countless slaves, and knowing their areas of weakness, the Zin entered his regular routine. The first step was to provide the subject with a sample of that which could be. A quick flick of the wrist was sufficient to the task. Has flinched as the glowing tip of the red-hot implement touched the tip of his left ear. The resulting scream emptied his lungs.

The painmaster, who expected nothing less, started the slow methodical questioning. The answers, all of which were recorded, would be evaluated by others. "What is your name?"

"Has . . . P'ere Has."

"And your identification number?"

"RS47602."

"Good," the painmaster allowed deliberately. "You have been truthful so far. There are more difficult questions, how-ever, *much* more difficult, as those around you can attest. Now, consider carefully . . . How long have you been a member of the Ra 'Na resistance movement?"

Has stared at the rod's slowly yellowing eye as the in-strument wove intricate patterns in front of his face. He could feel the perspiration working its way out through his pores, trickling down along individual hair follicles, and wetting the outer surface of his fur. It was a trick question, he knew that, and clung to the truth. "I am *not* a member of the resistance."

Has actually heard his flesh sizzle as the rod touched his ear. The scream was louder than the one before.

The painmaster clacked a pincer in what seemed like an-noyance. "Come now . . . surely you are wrong. The Kan brought you here, correct?"

Has wanted to touch his badly burned ear, to *see* what it looked like, but knew he couldn't. Where was this line of questioning headed? There was no way to tell. "Yes, the Kan brought me, but I don't see . . ."

"Of course you don't see," the Zin interrupted, "inferior beings rarely do. The Kan are Saurons, true? And Saurons are infallible, are they not? All of which attests to the fact that you are guilty."

The *truth*, Has instructed himself, you must stick to the truth. The cleric braced himself against the pain about to come. "No, your eminence, I am *not* guilty. Not of crimes against the master race."

The painmaster started to bring the rod down onto the heretofore untouched ear but stopped short. The last answer intrigued him. "Ah, so you *are* guilty of something, what is it?"

"I am guilty of sloth," Has answered truthfully, "and of pride, envy, and occasional doubt."

The painmaster ran the still-cooling rod down the inside surface of the Ra 'Na's left arm, paused at the nearly bare axillary, and pulled the instrument away.

Though less intense than the injuries that preceded it, the burn made a river of pain, and Has jerked in the opposite direction.

"Don't toy with me, slave," the Zin warned ominously. "You won't *enjoy* the results."

"Yes, your eminence," Has gasped, "I *am* innocent, ask Dro Tog."

The painmaster examined the rod's tip, decided in favor of a touch-up, and shuffled toward the forge. "Who is Dro Tog? And why should I believe what *he* tells me?"

"Dro Tog is a prelate," Has answered earnestly, "and one of the most important leaders the Ra 'Na have."

The last part was not exactly true, given the fact than many of Tog's peers viewed him with something akin to contempt, but Has saw no reason to mention that. He was a subordinate after all—a relationship that mandated respect.

Having equipped himself with a fresh rod, the Zin returned from the forge. "So, which group does this paragon of virtue favor?" the Sauron inquired patiently. "The resistance? Or those who remain loyal?"

"Those who remain loyal," Has answered honestly. " 'Order is superior to chaos, the Saurons provide order, so why change?' That's what Dro Tog likes to say."

"How very perceptive of him," the painmaster replied. "This rod is extremely hot . . . Where would you least like to receive it?"

Has was tempted to lie, to name a part of his anatomy where the pain might be less intense, but managed to resist temptation. The truth—that was his only hope. "My genitals, eminence. I would least like to have the rod touch me there."

It was this simple statement more than anything else that convinced the painmaster of the slave's veracity and thereby brought the session to an end. Still, it was always best to leave subjects with something to remember, so the Zin brought the rod upward. Has heard his genitals start to sizzle, screamed the Great One's secret name, and fell into darkness.

ABOARD THE SAURON FACTORY SHIP *LA MA GOR*, *(SOURCE OF PLENTY)*

The *La Ma Gor*'s interior, once the very definition of well-defined order, had been literally transformed into a nightmarish maze of vats, tanks, and pipes, all dedicated to the manufacture of pink glop.

That's what the humans called it anyway, although their Ra 'Na counterparts, slaves like Toth, had another name for the substance. Loosely translated, the word meant "shit." However, regardless of what the viscous material was called, it refused to be constrained by the plumbing designed to contain it and continued to weep, ooze, and dribble from the countless joints that the archaic plans called for. Plans, which if rumor could be believed, came straight from the Book of Cycles.

What wasn't known, however, and was the subject of much speculation by Toth and his pals, was the glop's purpose. It wasn't food, they were sure of that, since not even Saurons could stomach something that looked like the glop did, nor was the substance medicinal, since no one had seen a member of the so-called master race rub, slather, or dab the stuff on.

All of which explained why Toth, having little else with which to occupy his rather active mind, had decided to solve the apparent mystery. An impulse completely in line with his history as a petty thief, slacker, and all-around miscreant.

The answer, if one was to be found, almost certainly resided in Kol-Hee's office, a space definitely off-limits to the likes of Toth. A fact which made the task of digging it out that much more interesting. But the Fon was no fool and literally wielded the power of life and death over his subjects, which suggested that a good deal of caution was in order.

That being the case, Toth made no attempt to tackle his objective directly, but chose a more roundabout method. A strategy that involved actually doing some work—an aberration that should have resulted in some healthy skepticism.

But, like the vast majority of his peers, Kol-Hee knew next to nothing about the slaves who worked for him, finding it far more convenient to assign them a single overall personality. One which characterized them as sub-Sauron, and in this case sub-Fon, which meant lazy, incompetent, and stupid. All of which was absurd, since the very fleet from which the Saurons took their power had been constructed by ancestors of those very same slaves. But Kol-Hee was blind to that, hadn't bothered to study Toth's rather extensive rap sheet, and was therefore vulnerable.

So, determined to solve the mystery of the glop, and discover why an entire ship had been converted to the production thereof, Toth went about his work. His title, like that of more than two dozen others, was "wiper." And, unlike the honorifics that some Ra 'Na had granted themselves, the name actually described what Toth did.

His job was to work his way through the maze of pipes that carried the glop from one containment to the next, find the places where joints leaked, and wipe them clean. A rather time-consuming chore that could have been eliminated via design changes and preventive maintenance. Something that any number of wipers had suggested.

But the Saurons, who normally listened to such input, especially where technical matters were concerned, had turned a deaf ear. Some saw this as one more example of their overweening arrogance, but Toth had a different theory. *He* believed only a finite amount of the glop was required and, once available, production would cease. A possibility that would account for the Saurons' otherwise inexplicable lack of interest in refining the process.

Most of Toth's fellow wipers had developed routines—patterns that carried them along and helped make the job easier. Toth had resisted that temptation as it would serve to limit his movements and thereby hinder his self-assigned mission. An apparent quirk that annoyed his turf-conscious contemporaries. "Go along and get along," that was their motto, and one which had served the slaves well. That's why the human named Gretchen growled at the Ra 'Na as he worked his way through her territory on a roundabout course calculated to terminate within Kol-Hee's office.

The Fon, who was a creature of habit, had exited his cage-like command post at roughly the same time during the last three shifts, and, assuming that the Sauron did so again, Toth planned to take full advantage of Kol-Hee's absence.

Meanwhile, as the wipers wiped and worried about their various prerogatives, Kol-Hee monitored a rack of jury-rigged readouts, compared the readings to the list he had been given, and noticed that all of them were higher than they should be. *Much* higher. As they had been for the last three shifts.

It seemed as if the Zin who was in charge of the factory, an overzealous type named Gon-Dra, was determined not only to meet the daily quota, but *exceed* it. Regardless of the potential consequences. Would the idiot finally listen to reason? No, probably not, but Kol-Hee felt it was his duty to try.

That being the case, the Fon backed out of the sling chair, shuffled out onto the catwalk, and headed for the bank of lift tubes.

No sooner had lift tube's door whispered closed than Toth dropped his glop-soaked rag, climbed up onto the catwalk, and hurried toward the office. Gretchen hollered, "Hey, fur ball, what are you doing? Trying to get us killed?"

But the Ra 'Na ignored the question, knowing as he did that while his peers were rule-following wimps, they weren't likely to tell on him, and that's all that mattered.

Toth entered the cage, ignored the mysterious readouts, and went for the computer terminal. A pincer-friendly joystick and clicker had been installed for use by Saurons—but when the wiper touched a small out-of-the-way button, a tiny keyboard extruded itself from the machine's casing. Like most of his kind, the Ra 'Na had a natural affinity for machinery, and more than that, knew that back doors had been established for every computer system aboard every ship his people had designed. Which was to say the entire fleet! Knowledge he had used to get himself into trouble on more than one occasion.

So, having brought up a menu that Kol-Hee didn't even know existed, it wasn't long before Toth found what he was looking for. A heavily encrypted file which the not-too-tech-savvy Zin believed to be completely inaccessible but which the petty criminal hacked into within a matter of minutes. And that's where he was, reading about something called birth-death day, and a substance called the birth catalyst, when a Klaxon went off, vat number 12 exploded, and four of his fellow wipers were killed by flying shrapnel.

The force of the blast hurled Toth into a bulkhead, bounced his head off the metal hull, and left him unconscious.

Ironically enough it was the big rawboned woman named Gretchen who scooped the Ra 'Na into her arms, ran the length of the catwalk, and made it through the opening before hatch 17 slammed shut. No fewer than three surveillance cameras captured the human's escape.

That's when vats 10 and 11 blew, the rest of the slaves in that part of the ship were killed, and Kol-Hee won his ongoing dispute with Gon-Dra. The *pressures were* too high . . . and someone would have to pay.

HELL HILL

Ironically enough mornings were typically cold on Hell Hill, even spring mornings, and Manning held his hands out toward the wood-burning stove. The first step in preparing his frigid fingers to work on the week's duty roster. A much-dreaded chore.

That being the case, Manning felt a distinct sense of relief when Kell entered the duty room and flashed a characteristic grin. "Got a minute?"

"Absolutely . . . especially if it's something that would prevent me from working on the duty roster."

"Your wish is my command," the ex-Ranger said solemnly. "Remember the woman who saved Hak-Bin's pointy butt?"

"Yeah," Manning replied. "Who could forget?"

"Well, you sent for her, and she's waiting outside."

"Name?"

"Jill Ji-Hoon. Ex–FBI agent."

"Really? Sounds promising. Lord knows we're under strength. Send her in. And Vilo . . ."

"Yeah?"

"Tell Amocar to write up the duty roster. Maybe he can get that right."

Kell grinned. "Roger that."

Based on a recommendation from Hak-Bin, and over Manning's objections, Franklin had appointed the somewhat mysterious candidate to the number two slot. Manning had been forced to keep him. That in spite of the fact that Amocar had a tendency to fade when bullets started to fly, liked to linger outside closed doors, and couldn't follow procedure much less teach it. A problem the security chief would solve one day.

Kell turned, pulled the olive drab USMC blanket to one side, and motioned the woman in. "The boss will see you now . . . step on in."

Ji-Hoon nodded, passed through the door, and found herself in a sparsely furnished steel cargo container. Some of the cubes were smooth on the inside, even shiny, but not this one. Judging from all the scrapes, scratches, and dents something heavy had broken loose in transit and played merry hell with the interior prior to being unloaded.

Beyond the heavily blackened stove, and the tall rangy man who stood in front of it, the compartment contained some mismatched chairs, a beat-up black leather couch, a scattering of boots, jackets, and one pair of plaid boxers, a hand-lettered sign that said "SAFE YOUR WEAPONS." A none-too-clean deck and a rack of assault weapons completed the decor. Not a very imposing room.

The man turned to offer his hand. "Agent Ji-Hoon . . . welcome to the Hilton. I'm Jack Manning."

Ji-Hoon had long been a believer in first impressions, and there was something about this man that she liked. The hand was big and warm. "Thanks, I think."

Ji-Hoon was tall, *so* tall that Manning could look straight into her eyes, and he liked what he saw there. A wary sort of centeredness, as if the ex-agent knew exactly who she was, including both the good *and* the bad. Small feathers had been added to the red ear tag, thereby transforming it into something similar to jewelry. The security chief pointed with his chin. "The tag . . . a present from Hak-Bin?"

Ji-Hoon nodded. "I was surprised to say the least."

"He's unpredictable that way," Manning responded, "a fact that makes him all the more dangerous. Take a load off . . . You know why I sent for you?"

Ji-Hoon took a chair. "No one said . . . but I have a theory. You're looking for foot soldiers."

Manning hooked a chair with a boot, dragged it into position, and sat facing the back. "In a word, yes, although I need something a cut above foot soldiers. I need people who believe in what they're doing, who think before they shoot, and who can play both offense *and* defense."

The agent raised an eyebrow. "Let's start with the first item you mentioned. What exactly would you expect me to believe in? The need to protect collaborators?"

Manning nodded. "Fair question. I could sign up fifty self-styled gunslingers by noon tomorrow. People who understandably want to escape their present job assignment, hope to obtain more food, or simply like to shoot things.

"Believers believe that in spite of the shitty situation we find ourselves in, and the role Franklin has been forced to play, he's the best leader available."

Ji-Hoon started to say something, but Manning held his hand up. "Hear me out . . . Yes, I know he was a bit slow coming around to the role of patriot, and yes, he made some mistakes. But that's in the past. Maybe you've heard rumors about how various resistance groups are coming together . . . Well trust me, that's *because* of Franklin, not in spite of him. He's the best hope we have to destroy the Saurons, set our people free, and reclaim Earth."

Ji-Hoon searched Manning's face for any indication of insincerity, cynicism, or guile. She found none. "That last part—about destroying the Saurons. Are you serious? Or just trying to suck me in?"

"I'm serious," Manning replied. "*Very* serious. The opportunity will come less than eighty days from now."

"How?"

"Join and I'll tell you."

"And if I don't?"

Manning shrugged. "I'm only authorized to have fifteen people. You walk, and I keep looking."

The opportunity felt right and beat the hell out of wandering aimlessly around Hell Hill watching everyone else work. "All right then—count me in."

"Good," the security chief replied enthusiastically, "we're lucky to have you. Just one thing though . . ."

"What's that?"

"Next time someone tries to kill Hak-Bin . . . get the hell out of the way."

HELL HILL

It was a crisp spring morning, the kind that offers a promise of the summer to come, and puts winter firmly in the past. Most of the denizens of Hell Hill society were well into the first shift's routines by the time the small group of Kan and humans came together near the bottom of "blood run," the very foot of the path over which so many blocks had been carried.

The limestone slab weighed upwards of five hundred pounds, and except for the fact that one edge had been rounded over, making it appropriate for use as a capstone, this particular chunk of rock was no different from thousands of others already carried to the summit of Hell Hill. No, what made the tableau different was not the nature of the burden itself, but the group assigned to carry it.

Dressed as they were in crisp, white, ankle-length robes, and absent the filth that typified most mule teams, this group looked like angels somehow fallen to Earth. Sister Andromeda, the Star Com's founder, stood in what she hoped would be interpreted as a position of dignified outrage.

Early on, during the first stage of the Sauron invasion, she had mistakenly believed that the aliens were a gift from God, and their depredations were a necessary evil, a cleansing meant to clear the way so the human race could take the next step on the ladder of spiritual evolution. A belief which explained why Andromeda had been willing to help the Saurons, and why they, desirous of a biddable workforce, had allowed, no *encouraged* her group to grow so long as the cult continued to be what Hak-Bin referred to as "a positive influence."

But now, as she, along with five of her most senior acolytes waited for the order to proceed, the cult leader understood the nature of her error. Rather than the paragons of wisdom she had supposed them to be, the Saurons were by way of a test. Before humans could ascend to a higher level of consciousness a sifting process must necessarily take place. A process during which the wheat would be sorted from the chaff. Then, once the Saurons left, she and her followers would found a new society based on precepts provided by her. In the meantime she had been forced to provide the Fon

Brotherhood with a limited amount of support.

Did Hak-Bin know that? Or believe that he knew? If so, that might explain why the Kan had been ordered to provide Andromeda and her followers with an object lesson. There was no way to tell . . . Although if the Sauron was certain, *really* certain, it seemed logical to believe that she'd be hanging upside down from one of the crosses up on the hill. All she and her followers could do was acquiesce, haul the limestone block to the top of Hell Hill, and hope for the best.

Like some of the other Kan who had spent a significant amount of time on and around Hell Hill, Lik-Maa had developed a sort of grudging respect for the humans and their overall resiliency.

Not *this* group, however, who, like the upper echelons of the Ra 'Na hierarchy, had discovered means by which to avoid the really hard work by supporting rather than opposing the system imposed by his race. Understandable? Yes, but far from admirable.

So, feeling as he did, Lik-Maa was determined to make sure that the human who called herself Sister Andromeda and her acolytes came away from the experience with a very real appreciation of what their less fortunate peers experienced on a daily basis. The Kan clacked his pincers. His voice boomed through the translator strapped to his chest armor. "Pay attention. Rather than the four people normally assigned to move a block of stone up the hill—you have been allowed *six*. A decision that takes into account the fact that you lead sedentary lives while the rest of your kind perform hard physical work every day."

Andromeda took note of the criticism, was surprised to learn that individuals like Lik-Maa even considered such matters, and made room for the new data in her overall view of what Saurons were like. The Kan seemed to shimmer as his chitin tried to imitate the water off to the west. "Now," the Sauron continued, "bend over, grasp the wooden cross-pieces, and lift."

The humans obeyed. The block wobbled as the weaker members of the team struggled to support it. The stone tipped dangerously, but came right as a couple of fairly well built men managed to get their shoulders under it, then steadied as the entire group shared the weight.

Andromeda, one of two women in the center position, was surprised by how light the burden was until she realized that the men, all of whom were taller than she was, bore most of the load. Something she was secretly glad of.

"So," Lik-Maa said sarcastically, "the hard part is over. Now all you have to do is reach the top of the hill."

Andromeda had been through many hardships during her life. She had been two years old when her father abandoned his family, twenty-seven when her husband did much the same thing, and thirty-one when her only child was killed in an automobile accident.

Nevertheless, the next hour and a half were the most difficult of her life. The block of limestone not only grew heavier with each passing minute, but became more and more central to her existence. Though little more than an abstraction at first, the block took on additional weight as the men started to tire—and the cultist fought to keep her footing. More than that she could smell the raw earth that still clung to the bottom of the object she carried, she could feel the cold texture of it, and she could taste a layering of sea salt. Or was it her own sweat?

Then, as if passing through some sort of permeable barrier, the limestone block was suddenly within her, redefining who she was, restating Andromeda's purpose. Not long after that, about a third of the way up the hill, Sister Andromeda started to think of the burden as a living being, and of herself as little more than two of its many legs.

The acolyte named Mandy fell at roughly the halfway

point, was whipped back into position, and started to cry. Not a wailing sound, there was too little oxygen for that, but sobs that sounded like gulps. Tears tracked down across her grime-covered cheeks, and Andromeda wanted to offer the other woman some sympathy, but couldn't muster the energy. The rock was in charge and refused to share her with anyone else.

What happened next was well under way before Andromeda knew it was taking place. A man, one of the hundreds who occasionally sought solace within one of the Star Com's steel "temples," saw the white robes, knew who these particular humans were, and shouted to a friend. Together they pushed their way in, brought fresh muscle to the task, and the rock surged forward.

It wasn't long before onlookers started to pace the rock, *more* volunteers joined the group, and still more, until Lik-Maa watched in astonishment as the lesson was transformed into a processional, and the limestone rock seemed to float over the crowd. Even more amazing, to the Kan at least, was the fact that white humans, brown humans, and even elite black humans took part. The caste mixing, though distasteful, was also inspiring, though he couldn't say why.

And so it was that Saurons, humans, and Ra 'Na alike turned to look as the momentarily ebullient slaves swept onto the top of Hell Hill, dropped the block into its assigned slot, and cheered like victorious football fans.

That was the moment when Lik-Maa realized that the humans were crazy—and felt the first tendrils of fear enter his belly.

SOUTH OF HELL HILL NEAR SAMISH BAY

The room was small and grimy, in keeping with the carefully blacked-out building to which it belonged. Some ancient file cabinets occupied a grungy corner, where they continued to guard files that belonged to Ed's Plumbing, and a man sat on the edge of the metal-framed military-style bed where Ed himself had occasionally snatched a nap. His face was too strong to be classically handsome, his hair was peppered with gray, and his eyes were unremittingly serious.

Deac Smith was tired, extremely tired, which made sense given not only the extent of his responsibilities, but the energy with which he tried to fulfill them. Just back from a long and somewhat painful midnight horseback ride, the resistance fighter was about to turn in when he heard a knock on the door. Smith made a face. "Who is it?"

"It's me," a gruff-sounding male voice responded. "Who were you expecting? The tooth fairy? Come to tuck you in?"

There was only one man who dared speak to Smith like that, the same man who had served at his side in the Rangers and spent the same amount of time in the saddle that he had. None other than George Farley, U.S. Army staff sergeant, retired, and Smith's second-in-command. The resistance leader grinned in spite of himself. "The tooth fairy couldn't possibly be that ugly . . . So come in then get the hell out. I need some shut-eye."

The door squeaked as it opened. Farley, also known as Popcorn to his friends, stuck his head in. He had chocolate-colored skin, quick, intelligent eyes, and needed a shave. Hair, which had been almost entirely black just months before, was shot with gray. "You have visitors."

Smith pulled a combat boot off, noticed the hole in his wool sock, and sighed. "I don't want any visitors—especially at this time of night. Tell them to come back in the morning."

"One of them is a young petty officer named Darby," Farley said dispassionately. "The same Darby who took part in the attack on five Sauron spaceships and destroyed every damned one of them."

"*Darby?*" Smith demanded incredulously. "Darby? I figured she was dead. Why didn't you say so? That woman deserves the frigging Medal of Honor!"

Farley smiled and stood to one side as the single-booted ex-Ranger limped out through the door. A battery-powered lantern hung from a hook in the ceiling. Darby stood in the cone of light thrown down onto the dirty linoleum floor. She saw Smith appear and the way his face lit up. He hobbled across the room to give the ex–petty officer a very unsoldierlike hug. "You're alive! That's the best news I've had all week. Where the hell have you been?"

Darby, who was both surprised and pleased by the warmth of the greeting, smiled to the extent that the scar tissue would allow her to do so. "I went fishing . . . and here's what I caught."

Darby stepped to one side and turned to discover that Pol had climbed up onto a human-sized stool, turned his back to the room, and was busy sorting through the parts that littered Ed's plywood workbench. She sighed. "Pol . . . this is the man I brought you here to meet."

Pol snapped one last component into place, heard a "click" as a connection was made, and touched a tiny button. The image of a fierce-looking Kan blossomed in front of the Harley poster tacked over the grease-stained bench. The Sauron started to speak. The dialogue sounded like a long series of clicks and squeaks.

Smith stepped in to get a closer look. "Who the hell is that?"

"Sector Commander Muu-Dak," Pol said calmly. "Briefing his troops."

"About what?" Farley asked, equally fascinated.

"Boring stuff," Pol said offhandedly. "You know, troop movements, logistics, that sort of thing."

The ex-Rangers looked at each other in amazement. What the ratty-looking Ra 'Na had been able to do in a matter of a few minutes was more than their best tech heads had been able to accomplish during the last month.

Darby, who had a pretty good idea what the two men were thinking, gestured in Pol's direction. "Deac Smith, George Farley, meet Fra Pol. He would like to join the resistance movement."

Smith, one boot still held in his hand, limped to the workbench. "It's a pleasure to meet you, Fra Pol. We have more equipment like that . . . stuff we captured. A lot of it needs work. Would you be willing to look at it?"

"Certainly," Pol said, watching his hand disappear inside Smith's sizable paw. "I will assist in any way that I can."

"Then welcome to the resistance, son," Farley said. "The pay sucks, you'll probably get killed, but it beats a hitch in the United States Navy."

Darby gave the ex-Ranger a one-fingered salute, and the humans laughed.

The joke was lost on Pol, who, for reasons he wasn't quite sure of, and contrary to all common sense, felt like this was home.

SOUTHEAST OF HELL HILL

The main problem with Jonathan Ivory's plan, beyond the fact that it was crazy, had to do with the amount of patience required. However, assuming he wanted to hitch a ride on a Sauron road train, which he did, and assuming he wanted to trim weeks off the journey to Racehome, the racialist had very little choice. All he could do was camp out on the concrete overpass, wait for enough time to pass, and hope he wasn't fast asleep at the critical moment.

Ivory had dreams about that, nightmares so vivid that on one occasion he awoke to find himself standing at the guard-rail, screaming as the phantom convoy pulled away.

Not that wakefulness was much better. More than once he thought he heard the growl of engines, and gathered his meager belongings, only to discover that his mind was playing tricks on him. The freeway was empty, there was no line of vehicles approaching from the north, and the wait continued.

Worst of all, however, was the time when the growl of engines brought the racialist out of the woods to the west, and the Sauron road train was *real*, but headed in the wrong direction. Did that mean that another convoy, one headed toward the south, would be along soon? Or did it mean just the opposite? There was no way to know.

Strangely, when the moment finally came, it was the vibration rather than the noise that awoke Ivory from a fitful sleep and sent him scurrying toward the walls that ran along both sides of the overpass. The entire structure started to shake, as if in the grip of a low-intensity earthquake, and left little doubt that something heavy was on the way.

The racialist peeked over the edge, saw the tractorlike vehicle at the head of the Sauron convoy, checked to see if roof guards had been posted, was relieved to see that none were visible. That being the case, he ducked down again.

There would be Kan within the armor-clad vehicles, plenty of them, all heavily armed. All it would require was one curious warrior, a single fifty-foot jump, and Ivory would be history.

The bridge vibrated even more as the Sauron road train approached and the human scrambled to gather what few belongings he had.

Then, as the tractorlike lead vehicle passed under the concrete span, Ivory climbed to the top of the rail, where he stood like a windblown scarecrow and watched as dull, bird-splattered metal passed beneath his feet. Some sort of hieroglyph appeared, an ID number that would allow Sauron aircraft to identify the convoy from the air, then it disappeared as well. Ivory wanted to land on the last of the cars, theorizing that it was less likely to have any Kan lurking within, and wondered if the impact would be heard. "No" meant he would survive for a little bit longer, "yes" was equivalent to a death sentence.

"No, yes, no, yes." Who could tell? The last car in the train drew near, Ivory took a long deep breath, put his faith in Yahweh, and jumped. There was a solid thump as his boots hit, less than two seconds in which to fall flat, and "feel" the bridge deck pass not more than a foot overhead. Then, lying prostrate on his stomach, the racialist began to count. "One, and two, and three, and four, and five, and six . . ."

When the total hit 120, or the equivalent of two minutes, Ivory stopped. There had been no sounds of alarm, no change in the car's back and forth sway, no reason for alarm.

Relieved, and suddenly very tired, the racialist rolled over onto his back. The sun inched higher in the sky, warmed the metal roof, and made him drowsy. Ivory threw a forearm across his eyes, wondered if there was something more he should do, and fell asleep.

ABOARD THE SAURON DREADNOUGHT *HOK NOR AH*

Unlike most of the Ra 'Na-sized passageways aboard the *Hok Nor Ah*, corridor [*] had been constructed to allow various kinds of utility vehicles to transport equipment from one end of the ship to the other. That meant there was sufficient headroom to allow low-level jumps. Something that made the passageway a favorite with the Saurons. A fact which Dro Tog was coming to regret.

His escort, which consisted of two bored Kan, stood at the intersection and peered back over their shoulders. They shimmered like spirits only half-seen. The prelate, whose short, stumpy legs were already pumping at what he considered to be an excessive rate of speed, sensed their impatience and did his best to waddle even faster.

That was sufficient to make his heart quicken, but what

really caused his pulse to pound was the nature of the summons itself. The great Hak-Bin had sent for him! A signal honor—but one which the cleric would rather have done without.

Or was it an honor? What if he had done something wrong? And the Saurons were about to crucify him? No, the condemned were treated in a much different manner. So what in the six blue devils was going on? All he could do was wait and see.

Tog caught up with the Kan who jumped and landed fifty standard units up corridor. The prelate had little choice but to hoist his robe, scurry forward, and hope that the torture would soon end.

And, as if the Great One had decided to answer Tog's prayers, it wasn't long before the Kan turned down one of the many side passageways that intersected the ship's axis and were forced to resume their usual shipboard slip-slide shuffle. That allowed the prelate to settle his robes and resume something akin to a dignified pace.

Now, as passersby stared, Tog felt a moment of pride. And why not? He not only occupied one of the highest ranks his race was permitted to have, but had been summoned by no less a personage than Hak-Bin himself. And whatever the matter was it must be important. Otherwise why the summons? How many of those passing to the right and left could say the same? None, not a single one.

And so it was that Tog, oblivious to the subtle looks of disgust directed at him from every side, followed the Kan under an arch and was ushered into what looked like an airlock. Fear stabbed the cleric's belly. Were they going to blow him out into space? No, while his knowledge of the ship was far from perfect, the prelate knew he was nowhere near the outside surface of the hull. Where then? And why?

Conscious of the fact that the Kan were watching him, Tog drew himself up, stepped through the hatch, and did his best to remain as expressionless as possible while the chamber was sealed. Nothing happened at first—which made him nervous. Then the inner hatch cycled open, Tog moved toward it, and something strange started to take place. The prelate felt lighter, *much* lighter, and was just starting to absorb the implications of that when his sandals left the deck. He had entered one of the ship's null-gee zones—areas where certain kinds of work and medical therapies could take place free of gravity. Like all of the fleet's Ra 'Na slaves, Tog had been raised in space, and once freed from the weight of his obese body became suddenly graceful.

Tog flipped upside down, used his feet to push off the overhead, and dove through the hatch. His trajectory was perfect. His hands touched the deck beyond with just the right amount of force, he performed a somersault, and emerged in perfect position. Head "up," to the extent that there was such a thing in zero gee, and feet "down."

There was a clacking noise, and Tog turned in the direction of the sound. What he saw surprised him. Hak-Bin, his body swathed in multiple layers of what looked like flimsy black gauze, floated not twenty units away. Globe-shaped lights, both equipped with air jets, floated above and to either side. Another globe, this one positioned to provide the Sauron with a back light, hung above and behind. The rest of the chamber was dark and therefore mysterious. Beyond what Tog could see, there was what he could smell, and the Ra 'Na's supersensitive nostrils detected a not altogether pleasant odor. An amalgamation of smells, as if one scent had been used to hide another, and none too successfully.

The clacking stopped. "Nicely done," Hak-Bin said in a patronizing manner. "I have long admired the grace with which your kind can move in zero gee. Even my most athletic warriors are clumsy by comparison."

Here was the great Hak-Bin, addressing him personally,

and saying something nice! How could this be? Fear rose to block Tog's airway. It was difficult to speak. "Thank you, eminence, but you are too kind. Even the least of your warriors is much more graceful than I."

Hak-Bin, who was used to such lies, and expected nothing less, waved a pincer. "Thank you for agreeing to come."

Had the Kan warriors extended some sort of invitation? No, Tog couldn't remember any . . . But maybe they were supposed to and forgot. "Thank you for the invitation, eminence. It was my pleasure."

Hak-Bin nodded as if the answer was completely believable. "I'm sorry we won't be able to spend much time on the ceremonial aspect of your investiture—but these are pressing times. Construction has slowed, the temples have fallen behind schedule, and every unit counts."

Tog was mystified and mustered the courage to probe. "Investiture? Would your eminence be so kind as to explain?"

"Sorry about that," Hak-Bin replied with wave of a pincer, "I assumed my staff had briefed you . . . It seems rumors have started to fly, nonsense for the most part, but fire sufficient darts and one will hit something eventually. According to one such story the entire Sauron race will die and give birth at the same time. Have you heard anything of that nature?"

The fact was that Tog *had* heard of something like that, from the scalawag Fra Pol no less, and refused to believe it. Until now that is . . . and his audience with Hak-Bin. Tog was a lot of things, many of which were less than admirable, but he wasn't stupid. Suddenly, armed as he was with the information that Pol had overheard, plus the evidence in front of his eyes, the cleric knew the undeniable truth: The Saurons were not only going to die, just as Pol claimed they would, but Hak-Bin had already started to change. That's why the Zin was living in zero gee, that's why his body was swathed in fabric, and that's why he smelled. The thoughts raced through his mind at incredible speed, and the prelate would have sworn that his face was expressionless, but he must have been wrong. Hak-Bin clacked a pincer. "Ah, so you *have* heard the rumors?"

Tog considered his options. A "yes," would indicate that he had heard things which should have been reported. A "no," would come across as a challenge. The cleric decided to gamble. "Yes, eminence. I heard the rumors and did everything in my power to quash them."

"Yes," Hak-Bin said easily, "you did. Which has everything to do with your presence in my chamber. Even after hours of what the painmaster describes as a most rigorous regimen of torture, your subordinate, one P'ere Has, continued to speak of your devotion. A most remarkable session indeed. Perhaps you would care to thank him."

There was a sudden gust of colder air, the sound of sequenced air jets, and a small stretcher floated out of the darkness. Retros fired, and it coasted to a stop. Has, his features slack, lay as if dead. One ear had been burned almost beyond recognition, the other was badly singed, and who knew what lay beneath the crudely applied bandages.

The prelate shivered. To suffer yet remain loyal to a superior . . . Not only was Has stupid—he was crazy as well . . . Something for which Tog was extremely grateful. But what to say? That it was kind of the Saurons to let the cleric live? That they never should have tortured him in the first place? That they were scum? No, none of those alternatives would go over very well, and that being the case, Tog attempted something neutral. "Yes, well I am most grateful for the manner in which Has sustained the truth."

Hak-Bin stomped a foot in approval, remembered where he was, and clacked a pincer instead. "Yes, it's important to show loyalty to those who are loyal in return. Especially when one occupies an extremely important position."

The words brought Tog's ears up and forward. "Position? What position?"

Hak-Bin savored the slave's eagerness and raw lust for power. The whole thing was so easy—almost *too* easy. "Why the position of Grand Vizier, what else?"

Tog had no idea what the title meant, but knew no one else had it, not even Dro Rul. "Why thank you, eminence. May I inquire as to the exact nature of my responsibilities?"

"Of course," Hak-Bin replied affably. "As I indicated earlier there is at least some truth in the rumors that are floating around. My brethren and I *will* die on or around what the humans call July 31. Some seventy-three days from now."

Tog, who wasn't exactly sure of how to react, bowed his head. "Eminence, I am truly sorry to hear that."

Hak-Bin waved a pincer. "Thank you, but there is no need for regret. Each of us will live on in the memories of successors. Just one of the many ways in which our race is superior to yours. Once born, our descendants will require the services of loyal servants such as yourself. Not the entire Ra 'Na race, mind you, since there are those who might try to take unfair advantage of our momentary weakness, but a strong nucleus from which the subclass can soon be bred.

"In fact, plans have already been laid to ensure that three out of four of the surviving Ra 'Na will be female, so that individuals such as yourself will have ample opportunity to pass their genetic materials along to the future."

Tog felt his emotions lurch from horror to lust. Thousands upon thousands would be put to death . . . but what could *he* do? Nothing . . . nothing at all. To align himself with the resistance would be madness. The survivors would require experienced leadership, a sort of benign dictator capable of managing their affairs, literally planting the seeds required to grow the race. Tog felt himself start to harden and pushed the sensation away. The time for fantasies would come later—*after* he escaped from the chamber. "And in the meantime, eminence?"

"And in the meantime you will do all in your power to ensure that the citadels are completed, that members of the Ra 'Na resistance movement are identified and eliminated, and the fleet is fully provisioned and ready for departure when the next generation of Saurons has need of it."

"So, the journey will continue?"

Hak-Bin looked as surprised as a member of his race was capable of looking. "Of course . . . Our people shall be bound together until we find the planet called Paradise."

"And then?" Tog asked, astounded by his own audacity.

"And then we will all live in harmony," Hak-Bin lied smoothly, "equals in the eyes of the great creator."

Tog recognized the line for it was, an excellent way to give the surviving Ra 'Na something to pin their hopes on, and stored the nugget away. "Thank you, lord, I will do my very best."

Hak-Bin fought a sudden cramp and sought to bring the conversation to a close. "I'm sure you will. Members of my staff will contact you. You may leave now."

Tog looked at P'ere Has and felt a sudden surge of unexpected tenderness. "May I take P'ere Has with me?"

"Of course," the Zin said dismissively. "You are the Grand Vizier . . . the entire Ra 'Na race is yours to command."

And so it was that Has survived, the Saurons forged a new weapon, and another day came off the clock.

ABOARD THE SAURON DREADNOUGHT *HOK NOR AH*

The compartment was darkened—lit only by the glow of a red light. It began to flash on and off. Shu awoke as she often did to the persistent buzz of the alarm and the knowledge that something horrible had occurred. The injured Ra 'Na came in all shapes and sizes with medical emergencies as varied as they were. Lacerations, burns, fractures, infections, and more. She saw them all.

Of course that was what she had been trained to do, and was happy to do, except that as the Saurons pushed the slaves harder there were more casualties.

Shu rolled out of bed, slipped her feet into a pair of sandals, and joined other medical personnel who were rushing to their stations.

Shu entered the emergency receiving station, nodded to a bleary-eyed assistant, and waited while the attendants wheeled the patient into the compartment. He was conscious and clearly agitated. Attendants transferred the male to the examining table, strapped him down, and left.

Shu removed a stylus from a tray, placed the tip on a black dot that had been inked into the fur-free inner surface of her patient's left arm, and looked up at the wall screen. Though spared the indignity of ear tags such as the humans were forced to wear, the Ra 'Na were subjected to something that Shu considered to be even worse: an implant that contained information regarding who they were, the kind of training they had, and a complete record of disciplinary problems if any.

Still, the medical information stored in the wrist chip was valuable, and the medic soon knew everything there was to know about the wiper named Toth. He had suffered a broken leg three years before, was allergic to a commonly used antibiotic, and had been labeled as a borderline sociopath. In fact, as Shu skimmed Toth's voluminous disciplinary record, she was reminded of a friend, a certain somewhat disreputable cleric named Pas Pol. Some claimed he'd been killed—while others insisted that the initiate was alive and well.

Either way Shu's patient was a handful and clearly wanted to tell her something. Toth reached out to grab the medic's arm. "Listen to me . . . I got a look at their files, and the

Saurons know that by now. When they come for me you must tell them I never spoke anything other than gibberish."

Shu assumed her patient was delusional and nodded agreeably. "Just lie back and relax. You'll be up and around in no time. Please release my arm so I can go to work."

"No!" Toth said emphatically, his grip tightening even more. "Everything that I'm telling you is true. Later, when it's safe, find those with the courage to fight back. Tell them that the entire Sauron race will die in approximately seventy-three days—and that a new generation will be born. The few days in between represent the only chance our people have to achieve their freedom. They must seize the opportunity or all is lost."

Shu was about to reply, about to say something soothing, when a lab tech stepped into the compartment. "Sorry to interrupt, but a pair of Kan are headed this way. They want a patient named Toth."

"You see?" Toth demanded fiercely, "it's just as I told you . . . Now listen carefully—The material manufactured aboard the *La Ma Gor* is some sort of birth catalyst, a substance the Saurons require in order to quicken their young. Destroy it and you destroy them. Do you understand?"

Shu wanted to say "yes," that she did, but the Kan chose that particular moment to enter the compartment, and the wiper appeared to convulse. Toth arched his back, made choking sounds, and thrashed from side to side. The effect was quite convincing, but the senior Sauron, a noncom named Dru-Laa, appeared unmoved. "Is this the slave named Toth?"

"Yes," Shu replied quickly, "but it won't be possible to speak with him."

"We don't want to speak with him," Dru-Laa said emotionlessly, and shot Toth in the head. The dart blew the top half of Toth's skull off, and sprayed blood, bone, and brain tissue across a bank of metal cabinets.

The t-gun swiveled in Shu's direction. "What did he say to you?" the warrior demanded, his voice devoid of intonation.

"Nothing," Shu replied, as she backed away, "you saw him. He was completely incoherent."

There was a long hard silence as death stared at her through huge saucer-shaped eyes. Then, based on who knew what criteria, Dru-Laa holstered his weapon and gestured to his companion. Together they left the compartment.

Shu, overcome by grief, collapsed in tears.

■ ■ ■

It was evening, the real sun had just started to set, and it was too early for the orbital reflector to cast its ghostly glow over the land. Dozens of cook fires sent smoke spiraling up from makeshift chimneys to be caught by the wind and sent off toward the east. Snatches of conversation could be heard, along with the sound of an improvised string instrument and the distant clang of tools.

Even as Manning's feet carried him through the streets and toward the clinic, he wondered if he should go there. Yes, the cut was real enough, sustained while working on the defenses that protected the Presidential Complex. But did the injury require stitches? Or was the laceration little more than an excuse to see Dr. Sool? And if it was an excuse, why would he need one? Because of Jina's death? Even though his relationship with the president's wife had never extended beyond a single kiss? Did any of his maunderings make sense? No, the security chief concluded, they didn't.

But his feet continued on their journey, and soon, as if drawn there by some invisible force, Manning found himself standing outside Dr. Sool's clinic. There was a line, albeit a relatively short one, and the security chief was debating whether he should join it when Sool, coffee cup in hand, wandered out through the door. The doctor wore light blue scrubs, scrounged by some admirer, and bisected with dots of dried blood.

Sool's face lit up when she saw him, and she made her way over. "Jack! This is an unexpected pleasure . . . Is the president okay?"

Manning grinned sheepishly. "Yeah, he's grumpy, but otherwise fine. I cut my arm . . . but I'm not sure if it needs stitches."

"Come on in," Sool said, gesturing to the makeshift clinic. "I'll take a look."

"I'll get in line," Manning replied. "Those folks were waiting when I arrived."

"Don't be silly," Sool said, loud enough so her patients could hear, "even I get to take a break once in a while. Dixie has to see them first anyway. We don't charge for our services, but we try to keep some records. It makes the job easier if you know their histories."

Manning followed the doctor inside, said hello to Dixie, and stepped into the so-called examining room, which was actually no more than an area that could be curtained off from the rest of the cargo container. "Sit on the stool and let's see what you did to yourself," Sool said as she plucked a pair of disposable gloves out of a box and pulled them on.

Manning knew that as with so many of the supplies used by the clinic, the gloves had been brought there by Jina Franklin. Where would such things come from now he wondered? The security chief made a note to speak to his team.

The doctor's hands were gentle as they removed the dressing to reveal a two-inch cut. "It turns out that you *do* need stitches," Sool said sternly, "so stay right there while I set things up."

Given the fact that the clinic lacked an autoclave, as well as the power required to run one, instruments were boiled.

That included needles as well. Having dipped a pair of tongs into antibacterial solution, Sool used them to reach into a pan of slowly boiling water and grab a pair of needle holders. The instrument looked like a large hemostat except that it had a blunt nose and short jaws. With the needle holders in hand, the doctor pushed a selection of curved cutting needles around the bottom of the pot until she found one that met her needs.

Then, with the needle firmly clamped in instrument's jaws, it was a simple matter to feed some suture material through the needle's eye and secure it by pulling the nylon back through the slot at the end of the holder's slightly parted tip. Though far from sterile, the procedure was the best she could do.

Knowing how few supplies Sool had to work with, and mindful of the horrendous injuries she dealt with on a daily basis, Manning refused a topical anesthetic and focused on her rather than the pain. As the doctor fought to push the much-dulled needle through the security chief's leathery epidermis he saw the very tip of a tiny pink tongue emerge from the corner of her mouth. The sight was endearing somehow, and Manning found himself transported back in time to a vision of a little girl seated with legs crossed, as she worked on a puzzle. "So?" Sool inquired gently. "Do I get an answer or not?"

Manning realized he had missed something, and apologized. "Sorry, I was distracted."

"By the pain?"

"No, by you."

Sool looked up into his eyes, liked what she saw there, and felt her heart jump. It was silly, not to mention unforgivably juvenile, but real nonetheless. A fact which made her next words all the more perverse. "What about Jina?"

It was a stupid thing to say, motivated by jealousy more

than anything else, and Sool regretted the words the moment that she said them.

Manning flinched, as if reacting to the needle, and pain clouded his eyes. Sool felt him pull back and cursed her own stupidity. He had been there, trying to reach out, only to have her slap him down.

The security chief smiled gamely. "It was that obvious? Look, I was out of line, it won't happen again."

A voice inside Sool screamed, "Please, I want it to happen again!" But it was too late. There was an uncomfortable silence as Sool placed a dressing over the stitches, Manning thanked her, and pulled the curtain aside. Seconds later he was gone.

There were no interior walls, which meant that Dixie, working only a few feet away, had been a witness to the entire conversation. The clinic was momentarily empty, and she stood, hands on hips. "You know, for such a smart doctor, you are one stupid lady."

Sool nodded sadly. "Yup, that pretty much sums it up. I'll find time to cry about it later tonight . . . In the meantime, patients are waiting. Okay, who's next?"

SOUTHEAST OF HELL HILL

The horse nickered, and shook its head back and forth, as it continued to pick its way down the trail. The Ra 'Na, who had been strapped into a car seat intended for human juveniles, was himself facing backward. Though not especially cold, the night was pitch-black, and without benefit of the light-intensification goggles that the human wore Pol could see very little beyond Hell Hill's distant glow, the occasional glint of a star, and for one brief moment, the steady blink, blink, blink of running lights as a shuttle descended toward the water off to the west.

Could the Saurons "see" them? Using the infrared detection equipment the Ra 'Na had designed for them? Yes, without a doubt. The combined body heat generated by a human, a Ra 'Na, and a horse would show up as a ghostly green blob meandering across the countryside below. Visible, but not worth pursuing given the number of deer, elk, and large farm animals now free to roam the countryside. Or so the humans claimed, although Pol, who knew the Saurons a good deal better than they did, knew that a sufficiently large blob of heat was almost certain to attract a fighter if not a barrage from space.

Still, uncomfortable though the horseback trip was, it certainly beat trying to keep up with the long-legged humans on some sort of cross-country hike. So, having nothing in particular to do, Pol fell asleep and remained that way till the sound of voices and a sudden wash of white light served to wake him up.

The Ra 'Na initiate blinked as he straightened up to look around. The room was huge. It had a high ceiling, electric lights, and featured gray concrete walls. Most were lined with shelving, a lot of it, all loaded with carefully arranged equipment. Not *human* equipment, as Pol might have expected, but Ra 'Na, which was to say Sauron equipment, salvaged from who knew where. Judging from the smell, and the sounds that came from nearby, horses were quartered there as well.

A black-skinned human appeared, smiled, and introduced himself. He had short-cropped black hair, even features, and wore rimless glasses. The human had long slender fingers and they made quick work of the fasteners that held Pol in place. "Hello there, welcome to the skunk works. My name is Jared Kenyata . . . I hear we have a lot in common."

"We do?" Pol asked, allowing himself to be lifted down onto the cement floor. "Such as what?"

"Well," Kenyata said, grinning widely, "we both have trouble dealing with authority figures, we enjoy electronics, and we hate the fucking Saurons."

Pol's translator rendered the last part of the human's sentence as "intercoursing Saurons" which called for an immediate correction. "It's a pleasure to meet you Jared . . . but it's important to understand that the Saurons don't have intercourse."

Kenyata's grin grew even wider. "Yeah, the poor bastards don't know what they're missing, do they?"

Pol decided to ignore the fact that it was impossible for a Sauron to be a "bastard" in the technical sense . . . and went with what he now knew to be the human (male) version of humor. "Nope, them fuckers ain't got a clue."

The human laughed and gestured to the room. "So? What do you think?"

The horse had been led away. Pol saw that there were some additional humans, three in all, one of whom was seated at long workbench. "Where are we?"

"This is the basement of a church," Kenyata replied. "It looks like the building caught fire at some point, and collapsed, but the heavy-duty concrete floor held everything up. The wreckage provides the place with camouflage and helps to block radiated heat."

Pol eyed the steel crossbeams and the concrete floor above. "No offense, friend Jared, but the layers of concrete and wreckage won't be sufficient to protect us."

The human nodded agreeably. "You're absolutely correct. Listen, can you hear that humming sound?"

Pol's ears rotated to either side, and he agreed that he could.

"We have a generator," Kenyata explained, "which not only powers the lights, and the wall outlets, but a water pump as well. We use a portion of the well water for drinking . . . but the vast majority passes through half a mile of tubing woven into the wreckage. The constant drip, drip, drip of water helps keep the site nice and cool."

"Very clever," Pol said, happy to learn that his new friends were appropriately cautious. "So, where do the skunks come in? Do you ride them like horses? And what do they look like?"

Kenyata remembered the comment made earlier and laughed. "No, there aren't any skunks. Not real ones. The term 'skunk works' refers to a place where people work on some sort of project . . . often outside of the way that things are normally done."

"Ah," Pol replied, "now I understand. This is where we will work to how do you say it? Throw a monkey into the works?"

"A *monkey wrench*," Kenyata replied, "but yes, with your help we hope to do a much better job of tapping into Sauron communications, and then, if all goes well, we'll use their system against them."

Pol eyed the heavily loaded shelves. "Good. I like the way humans think. What's the fur dryer for?"

Kenyata followed the pointed finger to a small device with a flexible hose attachment. "That's a fur dryer? You could have fooled me . . . Is any of this stuff any good?"

Pol nodded. "Have no fear, friend Jared . . . we can make lots of monkeys. But first we must eat. Do you have any seafood?"

The human frowned. "Nothing fresh . . . Is canned tuna okay?"

"Tuna? What is 'tuna'?"

"It's a fish."

Pol nodded. "First we eat . . . then we work the dogs."

"*Like* dogs."

"Whatever . . ." Pol replied, his nose sampling the air. "Take me to the tuna."

SOUTHEAST WASHINGTON STATE

The road train was traveling at a steady thirty-five miles per hour. Not especially fast but consistent with the tractor's gearing, which had been set up with off-road conditions in mind.

There was no need for that, however, not with such a well-developed system of roads already in place, which explained why the Sauron convoy was eastbound on a secondary highway.

Ivory had been clinging to the roof of the trailer for hours by then, cursing the fact that he didn't have enough water, but reluctant to abandon his ride. He was half-conscious much of the time, not truly awake, but not really asleep either.

Perhaps, had Ivory had been less fatigued, and therefore more alert, he would have noticed the fact that the train had started to slow and prepared himself for what occurred next. But he wasn't and didn't.

The convoy jerked to a halt, doors banged open, and ramps touched the ground. Though not especially vigilant up to that point, orders were orders, and the Kan were supposed to check the entire train twice each day. The main purpose of the inspection was to look for maintenance problems, but security was an issue as well. Some of the feral slaves possessed projectile weapons, and liked nothing better than to take potshots at the road train from high in the hills.

One such individual had even managed to bag a Kan who had been riding atop one of the trailers. Subsequent analysis indicated that the warrior had been killed by a single .50-caliber bullet fired from twelve hundred yards away. That's why none of the warriors were willing to ride topside anymore, not unless an officer was present, which thankfully there wasn't.

The inspection was a routine and therefore boring chore—one which the Saurons had performed many times before without any results. That being the case, Rol-Baa could hardly believe his eyes when he made the necessary leap, felt his feet thump down on the trailer's metal roof, and saw the human lying prostrate two cars away.

The slave was still in the process of trying to sit up when Rol-Baa landed with one foot on the human's chest. The impact cracked two of Ivory's ribs and knocked the wind out of him. The racialist was still fighting for breath when the Kan aimed the t-gun at his head and uttered a series of incomprehensible noises.

There were no humans aboard the train, or hadn't been, so there was no reason for the warrior to wear a translator. He *did* need to communicate with the noncom in charge of the convoy, however, and proceeded to do so, using what Ivory thought of as "click speech" since that's the way the unmediated language sounded to him.

Rol-Baa listened to the reply via the radio attached to his combat harness, sent an acknowledgment, and jerked Ivory to his feet. Once the human was in motion a quick series of pokes, jabs, and shoves were sufficient to herd the unfortunate slave to the edge of the roof, where he was forced to sit, swing his legs over the side, and drop to the ground. There were no ladders attached to the road train for the simple reason that the Saurons didn't need them.

As the impact hit his ribs, the racialist screamed, clutched his side, and nearly fell.

Guided by another series of jabs, Ivory was forced to make his way to the very front of the tractor, where he was "encouraged" to mount the massive front bumper.

That was the moment when the human noticed the dimples that bullets had made in the vehicle's armor, a patch of dried blood, and four strategically placed Velcro-like straps.

The Kan were already in the process of securing him in place when Ivory realized that other slaves had been bound to the front of the vehicle before him, and, judging from the evidence, been killed by their own kind. By accident? Or as an act of mercy? There was no way to know.

Shortly thereafter the engines started, the road train jerked into motion, and Ivory started to pray. He beseeched the great Yahweh to save him, or, barring that, to put him out of his misery so that he could take his place in a heaven alongside all the other whites who had been judged as worthy.

But the minutes passed, the yellow line passed under the human's feet, and Ivory's prayers went unanswered. That's the way it *seemed* anyway, although sixty miles ahead, completely unaware of her husband's dire circumstances, Ella Howther, along with a force of some thirty skins, worked to put the finishing touches on a well-conceived ambush.

Unlike most of the women who had chosen to associate themselves with racialist doctrine during the years prior to the alien attacks, or, having nowhere else to go had aligned themselves with the White Rose Society since, Ella took a backseat to no man.

In spite of the fact that she was pregnant, or partly because of it, she worked to fill the vacuum left when her husband, along with a party of warriors, had departed for Hell Hill, where they had hoped to foment a revolution in which whites would rise up against both the muds *and* the Saurons.

Most of those who remained behind believed that Jonathan Ivory was dead, and had been for a long time, but Ella knew better. Her mother, the much-revered Marianne Howther, race wife to Old Man Howther, was given to dreams. *Important* dreams in which truths were often revealed. In one such dream she had seen Ivory struck down, only to rise out of the flames, and then, like Jesus himself, hang crucified for all to see. But dead? No, her mother had been certain of that, which meant that her baby would not only have a father, but a *race* father, to whom he could turn for knowledge and guidance.

In the meantime there was work to do, and with no one

else to take care of it, Ella would handle the chores herself. The site of the ambush had unknowingly been chosen by the Saurons themselves the moment one of their shuttles touched down on the surface of the small, undistinguished lake, released the sausage-shaped fuel bladder clutched beneath its belly, and lifted again. Such an abomination might be tolerated elsewhere, but not *here*, within the large, vaguely defined chunk of territory that the Howthers and their followers referred to as Racehome.

No, the racialists feared that the fueling station was an encroachment that, if tolerated, would soon lead to even more territorial violations and must therefore be dealt with in no uncertain terms.

There had been four guards, all of whom had been killed by a single sniper less than twenty-four hours earlier. Since that time two had been butchered and eaten while the rest of the meat had been salted and prepared for the journey home. The flesh was a good if a bit chewy—and welcome during a time when protein was hard to come by.

"Butchered" was a deceptive term, however, since the Saurons had been cleaned with almost surgical care, stuffed by a skilled taxidermist, and posed in and around the fuel station, where they gave the appearance of normalcy. A deception that wouldn't hold up for very long—but should be sufficient to lure the unsuspecting road train deep within the carefully established kill zone.

And so it was that Ella, along with her band of white warriors, settled in to wait for what might be days. A not-altogether-unpleasant prospect since it would provide the racialist with an opportunity to read, something for which there was very little time of late. So there she was, curled up with the American Institute of Theology (AIT) study guide, reviewing Seedline doctrine, when the Motorola Talkabout 250 walkie-talkie squawked in her pocket. Ella frowned, removed the device, and pushed the "send" button. "This is One . . . say again. Over."

The voice belonged to a promising skin named Hampton, who went by the name Too, after the many racialist tattoos that decorated his body. That being the case, it seemed natural to honor his request for the call sign Two.

"This is Two . . . The convoy is in sight. I see one tractor, six trailers, and no guards in sight. ETA ten minutes. Over."

Ella looked up at the evergreen-covered hill where she knew Too to be hiding. "Any sign of air cover? Over."

"Nope. Not so much as a crow. Over."

"Good. Stay where you are and keep a sharp lookout. I don't want any surprises. Over."

"Understood," Too replied, "and one more thing . . ."

"Yes?"

"The chits strapped some guy to the front of their tractor. Like a trophy . . . or a hostage. Over."

"Is he white? Over."

"Yes, ma'am."

"Then don't anybody shoot him. All right, take your places, and remember . . . Nobody fires until I do. Over."

There was a chorus of clicks as the rest of the team acknowledged Ella's order, released their safeties, and prepared to fire.

Meanwhile, less than a mile away, a Kan named Doo-Naa engaged in the Sauron equivalent of a frown, and clicked through the a series of radio frequencies. He had heard something, the warrior was certain of that, but what? Feral slaves were a loquacious lot, and even though there weren't all that many of them, it seemed their numbers were larger because of the fact that they babbled day and night. And, making a difficult situation worse, was the fact that the transmissions might be coming from nearly anywhere. Still, better safe than sorry, which was why Doo-Naa reported his observa-

tions to the NCO in charge, a relatively competent individual named Cis-Nor.

Cis-Nor took the warning seriously, ordered the driver to
reduce speed, and placed his entire squad on the highest
level of alert.

It was then, as the noncom scanned the screens racked
against the front bulkhead, that he noticed the first sentry.
The warrior stood on a slight rise—ready to respond should
there be an attack.

Cis-Nor allowed himself to relax a little as the train
turned off the main highway and growled into the small
state park. The fact that the fuel bladder was where it should
be, floating untouched at the center of the lake, made the
noncom feel even better.

The shore-based pump station was equipped with a
twenty-unit-long heavily armored hose. That forced the
driver to swing the tractor out toward the water, over a patch
of recently disturbed dirt, and into the same general area
where convoys always stopped. Ivory ran his tongue over
dry, cracked lips, saw the lake, and tugged at the straps.
"Water . . . I need water."

The word was little more than a croak, but the movement
caught Ella's eye, and she took a look through a small pair
of binoculars. That's when Ivory's face came into focus, when
she knew who he was, and when the road train ground to a
halt.

It was Jonathan! He was alive! Just as Mother said he
would be. She had never seen him without the goatee but
recognized her husband nonetheless. A sense of fierce pride
welled up to fill the racialist's breast as the tractor burped
compressed air, hatches whined up out of the way, and
ramps slid down to meet the sandy soil. You must concentrate, Ella instructed herself, and wait for the aliens to leave
the protection of the tractor and trailers.

The racialist aimed at the tractor's ramp, applied additional pressure to the submachine gun's trigger, and waited for one of the Kan to appear. Nothing happened.

Meanwhile, still confined within trailer three, and eager to go outside, Rol-Baa made use of his radio. "What's the delay?" the warrior wanted to know. "I'm tired of sitting in this metal box."

"Really?" the noncom inquired sarcastically. "Well, maybe you're tired of living. Take a look at those guards and tell me what's wrong with them."

Goaded by the other Sauron's tone, Rol-Baa took a second look. He could see two of the guards—neither one of whom had moved since the first time he had looked at them. Then, before the warrior could remark on how strange that was, Cis-Nor used one of the train's turret-mounted auto throwers to put a burst of darts into the ground less than one unit from a sentry's foot. There was no reaction. "It's a trap!" Cis-Nor roared. "Seal the hatches and get the train out of here!"

But it was too late. Though hopeful that the Saurons would come out where the skins could shoot them, Ella had a backup plan, and was quick to make use of it. The racialist thumbed a button, the explosives buried under the road train went off with a loud whomp! And trailer two was nearly torn in half. Rol-Baa was killed in the explosion, along with a another warrior assigned to the same car.

The driver, a quick-witted sort named Sus-Naa, hit the switch that would uncouple the tractor from the train and twisted the throttle. The vehicle lurched forward.

Outside Ella heard a sharp crack as a smaller charge was detonated, a seventy-foot pine tree swayed, and started to fall.

Ella held her breath as the tractor came up to speed, spewed gravel, and tried to escape even as warriors still trapped within the surviving trailers implored Cis-Nor to save them. Would the tree, falling as if in slow motion, hit the ground in time?

The racialist didn't think so at first, but then the tree seemed to fall more quickly, and smacked the ground directly in front of the tractor's blunt nose. Ivory felt the tip of a branch brush across his chest, wondered what caused the explosions, and felt very exposed.

Sus-Maa slammed the brakes on, managed to stop short of the tree trunk, and put the tractor into reverse. The Kan was backing away, looking for an escape route, when a skin named Boot fired the tripod-mounted launcher he and his companions had captured along with the fuel station. The foot-long missile slammed into the tractor's side, blew a hole in the vehicle's armor, and detonated inside the engine compartment. The subsequent explosion destroyed the main accumulator and put the vehicle out of commission.

That was when Cis-Nor radioed for air support, or tried to, only to discover that both his primary and backup frequencies had been jammed. Furious, the noncom took an assault weapon down from a rack, ordered Sus-Maa to do likewise, and came out shooting.

Ella squeezed her trigger, felt the submachine gun leap in her hands, and heard other weapons join in.

Most of the Kan died quickly, but Cis-Nor made it into the air, and was able to kill two white slaves before the enemy bullets found him. Some of the projectiles flattened themselves against his body armor, but others found his unprotected legs and another struck the side of his head. Killed instantly—the noncom crashed to the ground.

Ella knew that even if the effort to jam the Sauron transmission had been successful, and there was no way to be sure that it had, the activity itself was likely to draw the wrong kind of attention.

That being the case, the racialist knew there was no time to gloat. "This is One . . . Blow the fuel bladder and check the trailers for things we can use. I want the dead and wounded on stretchers. Nobody gets left. Quickly now, before all hell breaks loose. Over."

Each skin knew what he would be held responsible for and went to work. There was a dull thump as the fuel bladder blew, black liquid stained the previously crystal-clear lake, and trout started to die.

Boot, who had been assigned to deal with hostages and/or prisoners, was already in the process of cutting Ivory down when Ella arrived at the front of the tractor. "Look at what the bugs did to this poor bastard!" the skin said sympathetically. "He looks like hell warmed over."

Ivory heard the male voice and tried to focus. The face appeared as a white blob. The female voice was familiar somehow. "That 'poor bastard' happens to be my husband," Ella said coolly, "so please pay him the respect he deserves."

"Yes, ma'am," Boot said respectfully. "I'll take good care of him."

"See that you do," Ella said, and kissed her husband's sunburned cheek.

And it was then, as the skin hoisted Ivory up onto his shoulder, that the racialist got a good look at his race wife. She smiled—and Ivory knew he was home.

Meanwhile, up in orbit, a battery of ship-mounted weapons fired. A quick succession of six energy bolts, all targeted to the same patch of ground, ripped through the atmosphere. Ella heard what sounded like a runaway freight train, felt a ground-shaking thump, and saw an entire cluster of trees explode into a million splinters. They whirred as they slashed through the air, rattled across some of the trailers, and plowed furrows in the fuel-polluted lake.

One of them struck a skin between the shoulders, threw him down, and nailed him to the ground. Ella, with Boot at her side, started to run. Another freight train arrived, and another, until the entire world erupted in flame.

ABOARD THE SAURON DREADNOUGHT *HOK NOR AH*

A platform complete with a table and chairs had been erected in the otherwise empty compartment. Below the platform, positioned so it could be seen through the transparent tabletop and clear plastic floor, sat a large tank. And there, visible through the grillwork designed to keep him from climbing out, a Fon could be seen. The liquid in which he was immersed was active, like water put on to boil, except that the motion was generated by a chemical reaction rather than heat. The acid, diluted so the process would take longer, ate at the Sauron's chitin. Eventually, after most of his hard exoskeleton had been dissolved, the acid would bite into his internal organs. Then, while still experiencing the agony caused by that, and no longer able to hold his head up, the Fon would collapse in on himself and sink to the bottom of the tank. Knowing that, and hoping for some crumb of mercy, Kol-Hee stared up through the transparent floor in a futile attempt to make eye contact with Gon-Dra, the Zin who had been his supervisor, and was in all truth responsible for the disaster aboard the factory ship, *La Ma Gor*.

But, having successfully blamed Kol-Hee for the explosions, and the subsequent shortage of birth catalyst, Gon-Dra was not about to demonstrate what might be interpreted as signs of sympathy for the unfortunate Fon.

Still hopeful of attracting the attention of the beings seated above him, Kol-Hee used his nose to push against the gridwork that held him in place, but with no success. His snout was wrapped with tape, his pincers had been secured with plastic ties, and only his feet remained unbound. The Fon could lift one foot then the other—but that was the extent of his freedom. None of which seemed to be of interest to Hak-Bin, Gon-Dra, Dro Tog, and a Zin named Len-Dar, all of whom were gathered to discuss the shortage of birth catalyst.

Hak-Bin, who had seen fit to restore gravity to the chamber to accommodate the requirements of the acid bath rather than his guests, was swathed in folds of black fabric. The extent to which his body had become swollen, and the odor that emanated from it, were factors the others sought to ignore.

"So," the Sauron leader said gratingly, "I believe all of you understand the nature of the situation. Every drog of birth catalyst lost through Kol-Hee's incompetence must be replaced. The facility on the *La Ma Gor* will be repaired, a new factory will be constructed on the planet's surface, and the time schedule will be adhered to."

The Zin turned toward the single Ra 'Na. "It will be the Grand Vizier's responsibility to mobilize the resources necessary to make these things happen and keep the slaves at the highest possible level of productivity. Do I make myself clear, Vizier Tog?"

Tog struggled to control his hard-pressed digestive system as the acrid odor of dissolved chitin found its way into his nostrils and threatened to summon his lunch. "Yes, eminence, you do."

Meanwhile, just below their feet, Kol-Hee tried to scream as the acid found its way through thinner sections of chitin and burned his flesh. That was impossible at first, thanks to the tape that secured his snout, but when the stronger sections of his exoskeleton suddenly transformed themselves into white paste, and the acid rushed in, such was the Fon's agony that he broke the tape and emptied his quickly melting lungs. The resulting sound made Tog's fur stand on end, pushed his ears back along his skull, and caused his hands to shake.

Hak-Bin glanced down in time to see the functionary's now-unsupported head vanish beneath the surface of the acid bath even as the sound was cut in half. The Zin looked back up. "You heard Kol-Hee—need I say more?"

Those in attendance agreed that he didn't—and were quick to leave. There was work to do, a great deal of it, and every reason to hurry.

ABOARD THE SAURON DREADNOUGHT *HOK NOR AH*

Lock ^◇* had been designated for use by slaves and was heavily used. That being the case, the metal bulkheads along either side of the passageway were shiny up to the level of the average Ra Na's head but dark and grimy above that. And, because normal maintenance programs had been suspended in order to put the maximum number of slaves to work on citadel-related projects, many little things had started to slide. Lights had burned out, a layer of trash littered the deck, and Ra 'Na graffiti had started to appear on the once-immaculate walls. Some of it was openly rebellious—a sure sign of how thinly the Saurons were stretched.

A line of approximately thirty rather bored Ra 'Na technicals shuffled forward as a pair of equally bored Kan waved scanners over their wrist chips, verified that they had the necessary authorizations, and allowed the slaves to the enter the shuttle's lock.

Med tech Shu, her pulse pounding in her ears, tried to look as blasé as those around her, but discovered that was difficult to do. Especially since the chip implanted in her wrist rightfully belonged to a recently deceased com tech named Mas. Did the Kan know Mas was dead? Killed when the shuttle she had been riding in smacked into a large chunk of orbital debris? Just one of thousands if not millions of such obstacles the Saurons had allowed to accumulate around the planet below? No, there was no way that they could. No one had been present when Shu switched *her* chip with the one removed from the other female's body and closed the incision.

It was a brilliant plan, or that's what Shu thought at the time, but now she wasn't so sure. Once they saw her arm the Saurons were almost sure to notice the tiny incision on the inside surface of her wrist and the makeup that had been applied in an attempt to conceal it.

Or, failing that, how could the warriors miss the fact that the picture that would show up on their screens didn't match her face? They couldn't, which was why her entire body started to shake, and the med tech worried that she might faint.

Now, as Shu approached the checkpoint, she questioned her own logic. The whole thing was absurd . . . Rather than perform surgery on herself, and assume another identity, why not share her knowledge with someone in authority. Dro Tog perhaps . . . or Dro Rul. Surely they would know what to do.

But whom to trust? Many believed that Tog was a collaborator, especially since his controversial decision to accept the title "Grand Vizier," and Rul was something of a mystery. Some claimed he was hip deep in the resistance movement; others said not.

So, to whom could she turn? The answer was Fra Pol, assuming he was alive, and somewhere on the planet below. But first she had to get there, something that now seemed next to impossible as the male directly in front of her was cleared through the checkpoint and allowed to board the waiting shuttle.

Shu extended her hand, watched Kan wave his wand over the chip, and eyed the nearby screen. Though similar in age, and overall body mass, the two females were otherwise quite different. Mas was prettier for one thing, having the small, even features that males preferred, and fine golden fur. Shu on the other hand was a good deal more plain, having a nose that was a tiny bit too long, and mottled brown fur. It seemed to the Ra 'Na that no one, not even a Sauron, could mistake one for the other.

The med tech winced as the other female's image appeared, forced herself to remain motionless, and awaited the inevitable confrontation. It never came. Most Saurons, Kan included, saw their slaves as interchangeable work units and believed that the Ra 'Na looked alike. Small, furry, and weak. What more did one need to know? That being the case, the warriors glanced at the image, saw what they expected to see, and waved Shu through.

Thirty minutes later the shuttle bucked its way down through Earth's atmosphere, emerged from the cloud cover, and headed west. The broad glittering expanse of the Atlantic Ocean could be seen beyond the armored view port, and Shu felt an unfamiliar lightness of being. The sensation took her by surprise, and it took a moment to realize what it was. Freedom . . . the feeling was *freedom* . . . and the reality of it filled her heart with joy.

HELL HILL

Though originally quartered with other members of the security team, José Amocar had snored, farted, and barfed all the others out of the cargo cube, thereby creating what amounted to a private compartment for himself. Having colonized the entire space, his previously untidy habits had mysteriously disappeared.

The clothes that had once littered the floor had been hung on a pole suspended from the ceiling, tops together, all facing the same way, pants in a row, boots arranged below.

The food, which he had been known to leave out until maggots hatched within, was sealed within matching pieces of Tupperware and were stored in a scrupulously clean cooler.

The five-gallon bucket, once full to overflowing with the results of Amocar's infamous bowel movements, was now nearly empty and decorated with no less than three self-adhesive deodorizer disks, all acquired during trips with President Franklin.

So, while primitive by pre-Sauron standards, Amocar's apartment, plus its location four levels above the stench of the street, amounted to a penthouse within the context of Hell Hill's endless misery.

That's why the security agent actually enjoyed the moment when the windup alarm clock went off, when he swung his feet out onto the carefully placed throw rug, and retrieved the .9mm from its place under his pillow. He had thick black hair, a round moon-shaped face, and a barrel-shaped torso. Each day was an opportunity, and he paused to consider the one that lay ahead.

Not only was the knowledge that Amocar was better off than the vast majority of those around him well worth getting up for, there was the knowledge that the next twelve to sixteen hours would almost inevitably produce an opportunity for personal profit and the aggregation of personal wealth. Wealth as measured by what Amocar thought of as the three P's: possessions, pleasures, and privileges.

Amocar grinned. Not that the three categories were mutually exclusive. Take Agent Jill Ji-Hoon for example . . . Would fucking her in the ass constitute a pleasure or a privilege? And once fucked would she qualify as a possession? A long, tall piece of extremely personal ass? Yes, the security agent decided, she would. Something to be enjoyed, humiliated, and eventually discarded. And there were a number of ways to rid oneself of surplus women . . . some of which were quite pleasurable in and of themselves.

Amocar stood, produced what he was sure qualified as a world-class fart, and followed his erection toward the red plastic basin. Life, the kind *he* wanted to live, was as good as it could possibly get.

■ ■ ■

Jill Ji-Hoon had taken a quarter cube in a stack just down the road from the Presidential Complex. It was a crowded, noisy, but not altogether unpleasant co-op-style complex established by a pair of women, both of whom had been crushed by a runaway stone block a couple of months before.

A crude memorial consisting of small limestone blocks surmounted by a Star of David, a ceramic vase, and two pairs of well-worn work boots sat just outside the front door. A handful of wildflowers had been placed in the vase, and Ji-Hoon wondered where they had come from as she left what the residents jokingly referred to as the Hell Hill Hilton, and stepped out onto the street.

Improvements had been made, especially where flow was concerned, but there was no way to make the open sewer seem like something that it wasn't. Not given the brown color, sluggish current, and horrible smell.

However, like many of the hill's residents, Ji-Hoon had mastered the ability to step over the ditch, confront the stench, and still keep her breakfast down. The walk to work served as a reminder of just how fortunate she was. At a time of day when most slaves were already on the job, risking their lives to construct the Sauron citadel, she had risen only an hour earlier. Even better was the fact that with the exception of Amocar, the ex–FBI agent liked the people she worked with and rarely took shit from the Saurons.

Not only that, but she was armed, which meant that unlike the dozen or so people who hung themselves each night, Ji-Hoon could always shoot herself, a normally dubious privilege that she now took comfort from.

Yet, in spite of all the misery, signs of hope could be seen in the increasing number of babies, a window box in which colorful primroses had been planted, and the occasional patch of bright black-market paint.

Thus buoyed, the agent passed through the heavily guarded main gate, nodded to the agents posted there, and followed a path that cut left along the stack's rocket-scarred façade and passed into a canyon of shadow, for it was there, in a half cube well removed from the office occupied by Manning, that Amocar maintained his personal lair.

Ji-Hoon paused, checked the Timex Ironman watch that had been issued to her along with the rest of her gear, and saw that she was right on time. Always a good thing, especially when reporting to a new boss. Even if it was Amocar.

The ex-agent rounded the corner, followed the path, and found the crudely cut hatch. A white marker had been used to print the words "The office of El Segundo, Nock Before Entering," across the metal, and, judging from the manner in which "knock" had been misspelled, Ji-Hoon had a feeling that Amocar had lettered the sign himself. Ji-Hoon put on what she thought of as her game face, rapped on the door, and heard the low-pitched reply. "Come."

Hinges squealed as she pulled the hatch open and stepped inside. The first thing the ex-agent noticed about the interior was how tidy the space was—something that seemed to be in conflict with the stories she'd heard.

The second thing she noticed was that the beat-up metal desk, salvaged from Lord knew where, had been placed on top of a crudely constructed platform. A stratagem that put Amocar above those who sat in front of him, or would have, had Ji-Hoon been shorter.

The third thing the newly recruited female agent noticed was the fact that a heavily veined dildo had been placed on the single guest chair. That meant she could pick the object up, sit on top of it, or continue to stand. She chose the last option.

Amocar grinned. The expression, plus the rounded shape of the man's head, reminded Ji-Hoon of a flesh-colored jack-o'-lantern. He gestured toward the dildo. "Hey, no offense. Just a little present . . . Okay, a *big* present, but you're a big girl.

"In fact, rather than allow ourselves to get bogged down

in all that job assignment stuff, let's see if that hummer fits."

Ji-Hoon knew it was a no-win situation. If she was shocked, and allowed it to show, Amocar would take pleasure from that. If she wasn't, and complied with his request, that was a win as well. The ex–FBI agent kept her voice flat and level. "Does Manning know about this?"

The grin grew even wider. "Why no, sweet buns, I don't think he does. Not that it matters a whole lot, since Franklin himself appointed me to the team and ain't about to let me go. Not if he knows what's good for him . . . Besides, it would be my word against yours. So, unless you would like every shit-ass detail this organization has to offer, I suggest that you drop those pants, grab the edge of my desk, and get ready to play. Who knows? You might even like it."

One aspect of Ji-Hoon's mind took note of the fact that Amocar had a hold on Franklin, or believed that he did, and wondered if that was true. Another met force with force. Her grin was as big as his and mocking as well. "I'll tell you what . . . You want a piece of this, how 'bout you come and take it? Or you can go for that .9mm and we'll see who's fastest. Whaddya say, pin dick? Let's rock 'n roll."

Amocar pulled his hand away from the gun butt and forced a smile. "Okay, shit for brains, have it your way . . . You want all the shit details? They're yours. Franklin's heading uphill this morning to give some sort of rah-rah speech. Manning wants a bullet catcher running next to both sides of the car. You're elected."

Ji-Hoon nodded as she backed toward the door. "I'd keep that dildo if I were you—just in case something happens to the real thing."

Amocar struggled for a suitable rejoinder, and thought he had one, but the hatch had closed by then. The words caught in his throat and made it difficult to breathe. Somehow, in ways he didn't fully understand, Amocar had been bested. He didn't like that, not one little bit, and a price would have to be paid. Not just any price, but the *highest* price, the penalty called death.

3

DEATH DAY MINUS 65

THURSDAY, MAY 28, 2020

When those states which have become accustomed to live in freedom under their own laws are acquired, there are three ways of trying to keep them. The first is to destroy them, the second to go and live therein, and the third to allow them to continue to live under their own laws, taking a tribute from them and creating within them a new government of a few which will keep the state friendly to you. For since such a government is the creature of the prince it will know that it cannot exist without his friendship and authority . . .

—Niccolò Machiavelli
The Prince, 1513

SOUTHWEST OF HELL HILL

Shadow slipped on shadow as Manning followed Smith deeper into the woods. The sun had set long before, which was why both men wore night-vision goggles salvaged from the ruins of Fort Lewis.

The security chief had made use of such devices before, but only on training exercises, and didn't care for the unicorn-like lens that stuck straight out in front of his face, what amounted to tunnel vision, and the need to cope with a surreal landscape.

Thanks to the ambient light provided by the moon, the

orbital mirror, and the stars, Manning could theoretically see out to approximately seventy-five yards, but that was out in the open rather than deep in fifth- or sixth-generation evergreen forest. A forest that seemed determined to whack Manning with moisture-laden branches, toss him over half-rotted logs, and dump him into half-seen gullies.

None of which seemed to apply to Deac Smith, who slid through the trees with the surety of an elemental spirit, paused to listen every now and then, and waved the security chief forward. Manning swore under his breath, followed the greenish white blob through a swiftly flowing creek and up the opposite slope.

Both men paused there while the ex-Ranger checked the riverbank for footprints, found nothing remarkable, and continued on their way. Manning looked left and right, confirmed that other blobs were crossing the creek to the east and west of them, and knew they were members of Deacon's Demons. A paramilitary group that consisted of veterans, historical reenactors, and hard-core survivalists. The kind of people who still knew how to hunt, fish, and survive in the wild. More than that, the kind of people who didn't sort people out according to the color of their skin, the way they worshiped God, or who they slept with so long as they loved freedom and were willing to fight for it.

The trail, which was little more than a deer path, led them deeper into the trees, and Manning felt the forest close in around him. It wasn't the sort of place where the Kan were likely to lie in ambush since they preferred open areas where they could jump. But the forest was perfect for humans. Racialists, like the group his sister had been part of, bandits, more interested in loot than freedom, and religious groups, all on multiple missions from God.

Though not necessarily out to get Franklin specifically, any group strong enough to survive was heavily armed and often unpredictable. A factor that made an already difficult situation even worse.

The trees began to thin, the light level increased, and so did the clarity of the images that Manning could see. There was an open area ahead, what he knew to be stacks of logs off to the right, three ghostly loaders, rows of neatly stacked lumber, and a building that glowed as if lit from within. It had been a sawmill once, a relatively small one, but large enough for this new purpose.

Smith paused, spoke on a channel other than the one Manning had been told to monitor, and waved the security chief forward. "The area is secure," the ex-Ranger said confidently, "all except for the interior of the building, and that falls to you."

Manning nodded. "Thanks! Your people did one helluva job. Let's turn them inside out."

Smith knew what Manning meant. Having swept the surrounding area and secured the perimeter, it was time for the Demons to take up defensive positions within the clearing. Positions prepared over the last few days and strong enough to withstand an infantry-style assault launched from the edge of the forest *or* an orbital bombardment. Not for a sustained period of time—but long enough to evacuate the resistance leaders. A subject on which Manning had been somewhat vague.

Smith, who had seen what the Saurons could do to people, understood the concern. He didn't absolutely need to know how that part of the plan would work, so he didn't. "Yes, sir. My people are taking up their defensive positions now. We'll be ready in five minutes."

"Good," Manning said approvingly. "Don't forget that one of the people I'm supposed to protect is *you*—so get your butt inside as soon as you can."

Smith smiled. "Sir, yes, sir."

"And you know where you can shove the 'sir,' stuff," Manning said with a wave. "Right where the orbital mirror don't shine."

Smith grinned and watched the blob jog toward the sawmill. What method would Manning use to bring the president in? the resistance leader wondered. The noise generated by a helicopter would alert everyone for miles around, produce one hell of a heat signature, and point a big red arrow right at the sawmill. But Manning wasn't stupid . . . or was he? The ex-Ranger had a tendency to be somewhat cynical where civilians were concerned—even ones he liked.

Manning was about twenty yards from the building by then. He removed the goggles, clipped them to his harness, and flipped a switch. The wire-thin mike curved down in front of his mouth. "Snake One to Snake Two . . . Over."

There was the sort of delay that Manning had learned to expect from Amocar followed by the flat wary sound of his voice. "This is Two—go. Over."

"Status? Over."

"Everything is A-OK. Over."

"Good. Hold where you are . . . over."

"That's a roger," Amocar confirmed. "Out."

There was a click as Amocar went off-air, and Manning wished for the thousandth time that Kell, not Amocar, was his second-in-command. There wasn't much he could do about it, however—not so long as Franklin continued his sponsorship. Not because the chief executive thought Amocar was especially outstanding, but as a check on Manning, a man originally chosen by Hak-Bin himself, and forced into his present position. Yes, the relationship had evolved since then, but not to the point where Franklin was willing to reverse himself on the subject of Amocar and potentially lose face in the process.

The security chief crossed the invisible line of demarcation that served to separate security zone *two* from security zone *one*, and was immediately challenged. "Hold it, bucko . . . and keep those hands in sight. If you know the word then cough it up."

Like all of Manning's agents, the African-American female had been chosen because of her intelligence, attitude, and experience. Unlike most of the security types, Manning knew Garly Mol had a preference for cold steel, as evidenced by the knives stashed on various parts of her anatomy. Not that the ex–Border Patrol agent was averse to using firearms—as the ugly little Heckler & Koch 9 mm MP7 submachine gun made perfectly clear.

"Save it for the bad guys," Manning replied lightly. "The password is: 'rhino.' "

Mol grinned and jerked the barrel of her weapon up toward the sky. "Nice to see you, boss . . . How was the stroll through the woods?"

"It sucked. Smith and his people are crazy . . . but what else is new? How 'bout our guests? Have any arrived?"

"Only one so far," Mol replied, a smile stealing over her face.

"What's so funny?"

The ex-agent shook her head. "I wouldn't want to ruin the surprise. Go see for yourself."

Manning shrugged, admonished the agent to keep her eyes peeled, and walked toward the blacked-out building. It seemed to crouch there, anchored by the darkness. A generator purred somewhere nearby. A great deal of time and energy had been spent trying to disperse the engine's heat. Would it work? Only time would tell.

One of the shadows had more substance than all the rest, and the security chief was far from surprised when it took two steps forward and morphed into a rather formidable man. Jonathan Wimba was six and a half feet tall, weighed more than 250 pounds, and had belonged to ROTC while in college. It was later, while doing his time in the army,

that the sociologist mastered the care and feeding of the
M62 machine gun now leveled at Manning's midsection.

The weapon, a direct descendant of the classic M60, fired
caseless ammo at the relatively poky rate of 550 rounds per
minute. So slow that an artiste, a person like Wimba, could
fire single shots if he chose to. "Pick an animal," the security
agent growled, "and keep those hands where I can see them."

"Rhino," Manning replied, and was relieved when the
machine gun went vertical. "How's it hanging?"

Wimba grinned. "Long and limp . . . How 'bout you?"

"Short and shriveled. Maybe you army guys enjoy running through the boonies, but I'll take a sidewalk every
time."

Wimba laughed. A deep, rumbling sound reminiscent of
distant thunder. "I'm with you, boss . . . *especially* at night."

Manning nodded his agreement, felt for the door handle,
and pulled it open. "Keep 'em peeled, Jonathan—there's a
whole lot of strange shit out there."

"You can say that again," the big man said, as a feral dog
howled somewhere in the distance. "You can sure as *hell* say
that again."

But Manning was inside the building by then. Heavy
fabric had been draped over a makeshift frame to create an
effective light lock. Manning felt for the opening, slipped
through, and squinted into the electric lights.

The interior of the building was two and a half stories
high. It smelled of lubricants, sawdust, and freshly brewed
coffee. Down at the far end, above some enormous doors,
blank windows stared out over a maze of motionless machinery.

Manning noted that some of the wood stored outside had
been brought back in and hammered into a crude but serviceable conference table. And it was that, along with some
mismatched chairs, that would provide a focal point for the
upcoming meeting. *If* those who had been invited actually

showed up, *if* they could put their differences aside, and *if* the Saurons left the humans alone for a while. It seemed like a whole lot of "ifs," but not to Franklin, who was eternally optimistic. "People are basically good," he liked to say. "The United States is proof of that, so give them a chance."

The words sounded good, almost *too* good, coming as they did from a man who had flirted with being, if not actually functioned as, a collaborator prior to finding the patriot within. Still, even though Manning harbored no illusions about Franklin or his past, he continued to take hope from the man's words. Especially when he heard the chief executive talk about the United States of America. Even though the country lay in ruins, Franklin refused to give up on it. He truly believed that the Saurons were vulnerable, that alliances could be forged, and the nation brought back to life. And it was that, more than anything else, that made the man worth protecting.

The security chief's eyes had just come to terms with the light when Amy Vosser, Franklin's newly named executive assistant, bustled over. She had gray bowl-cut hair, a face held together by worry lines, and the manner of a marine corps gunnery sergeant.

"Mr. Manning—I'm glad you're here . . . It's 9:00 P.M. and the president's guests have yet to arrive."

The words were delivered in an accusatory tone, as if the security chief was at fault somehow, and caused him to raise an eyebrow. "I'm in charge of the president's security, Ms. Vosser . . . *not* the punctuality of his guests. Besides, one of them *has* arrived, or so I was told."

Vosser produced an audible sniff. "The guest, *if* he qualifies as such, is over there. Agent Asad was assigned to babysit him."

Manning, curious as to why this particular resistance leader had been found wanting by two people as diverse as Mol and Vosser, followed the woman's blunt finger. There was a series of staccato hissing sounds as the security chief rounded a massive piece of equipment and entered the far aisle. Asad was there all right, along with a scraggly adolescent who sported a chain-mail shirt made out of what looked like aluminum beer tabs, a battered belt comp, and raggedy spray-cloth pants. They ended a good three inches above a pair of well-worn REI hiking boots. A fairly common look by pre-Sauron standards. Not so typical, and clearly homemade, was the bandoleer of spray cans that the youth wore bandit style across his scrawny chest.

One such can hissed loudly as the teenager made one final pass over the highly stylized four-foot-by-six-foot sketch that decorated the wall, took two steps back, and paused to admire his work. It showed a Kan, one foot planted on a woman's chest, ready to shoot her in the head. In spite of the fact that the Sauron wore a sneer, something the chitinous creatures simply weren't capable of, the characterization worked. Though not especially realistic, it was supposed to evoke emotions, a goal which it certainly achieved.

More than that, the security chief knew that the artist, an individual who went by the name Cyan, was the leader of a group that referred to itself as The Free Taggers, a sort of free-form tribe comprised mainly of children. Children who took enormous risks to post their anti-Sauron graffiti where slaves could see it, and sometimes paid with their lives. Manning had seen their little bodies crucified heads down with spray cans jammed between their teeth. Asad, who wasn't all that much older than the graffiti artist beside him, nodded approvingly. "That's rev, man, truly rev. Hey, I want you to meet my boss, Jack Manning."

The street artist turned, nodded in a perfunctory manner, and said "So where's the prez? Let's get this shit in gear."

"It's a pleasure to meet you too," the security chief answered dryly. "Now, if Agent Asad would be so kind as to escort you over to the conference area, we'll see how many of your esteemed colleagues have arrived. Then, depending on the answer, maybe we can 'get this shit in gear.' "

The threesome arrived back in the conference area to discover that the rest of the resistance leaders had arrived and were being guided, instructed, and downright bullied into the chairs chosen by Ms. Vosser. Dro Rul, who had risked his life to visit the planet's surface, was assigned to a child's high chair located between Professor Boyer Blue and Deac Smith. The woman called Storm, clan leader for the Sasquatch Nation, and Doo-Nol, one of the few surviving members of the Fon Brotherhood, were placed on the same side of the table as Sister Andromeda, who, in the wake of the humiliating journey up Hell Hill, had decided to throw in with the resistance movement. Unless she didn't like what they said, in which case she would pull out and go her own way.

Franklin, who was watching from the windowed office located at the other end of the building smiled. Those who didn't know any better would assume that the effort to tweak the seating was just one more manifestation of Vosser's high-control personality. Others, who knew the players as *he* did, would note the way Rul had been placed between two utterly reliable humans, and the manner in which Sister Andromeda had been paired with the representative from the Fon Brotherhood. Organizations that had befriended each other in the past. Or would the word "used" be more accurate? Whatever the case, a relationship existed, and he would take what he could get. As for the heavily tattooed Storm, well, who knew? She and the clan she represented were something of an enigma, so one position seemed as good as the next.

As for the Free Tagger named Cyan, he had been seated at the foot of the plywood surface, where he had already produced a fistful of Magic Markers and was drawing a mural on the tabletop.

Now that the resistance leaders were in place Franklin was eager to start the meeting. Something he couldn't do without a green light from Manning. He turned to Amocar, who, along with a heavily armed agent named Lucky Lu and the newly inducted Jill Ji-Hoon, had been assigned to guard the president. "Call your boss . . . ask him what we're waiting for."

Amocar, who liked nothing better than to see friction between Franklin and his chief of security, already had his thumb on the "transmit" button when Manning spoke in his ear. "Snake One to Snake Two . . . Bring him down."

Though disappointed, there was little Amocar could do beyond acknowledge the order and lead Franklin down the stairs. Something he did with considerable drama.

Lu rolled his eyes, and Ji-Hoon smiled, as they followed Amocar and Franklin down to the main floor.

Deac Smith watched Franklin and his bodyguards emerge from the heavily shadowed aisle with something akin to relief. Franklin had obviously been brought in first, probably by horseback, and stashed on-site. Now, with the conference already under way, Smith would have been willing to bet his pension that the chief executive's helicopters were waiting somewhere nearby, and would be used to extract Franklin and his guests should that be necessary.

Of more immediate concern, to Smith's mind at any rate, was the fact that all of the guests were presumably armed. Something both Manning and he had argued against but Franklin had allowed. "After all," he said, "we're asking them to come onto our turf, without so much as a single bodyguard. If you take their personal weapons, I doubt they'll come. I know I wouldn't."

Security was the last thing on Franklin's mind at that particular moment, however. He missed his wife more than ever now as he followed Amocar out into the makeshift conference area, saw the participants turn to look, and realized that she wasn't there, seated in the back, her eyes filled with pride.

Suddenly it took every bit of courage the politician could muster to produce the professional smile, greet each individual by name, and take his place at the head of the table. He chose to stand rather than sit. A none-too-subtle trick that put him in control. Franklin chose his words with care. "Thank you for coming. There is a great deal to discuss—and not a lot of time in which to discuss it. By the time the sun rises in the morning the fate of our various peoples will be sealed. It's assumed that your presence here indicates at least some interest in a unified resistance movement—and that will be our first topic of discussion."

Franklin made eye contact with the only Sauron in the room and inclined his head. "With the single exception of Doo-Nol, who will die and give birth on or around July 31, the rest of us have a choice . . . That brief moment in time, those few days when the Sauron race is vulnerable, represents our only chance to survive, and for the Fon to gain their freedom.

"That's why the first thing on the agenda is the question of leadership. Not just political leadership—but military leadership as well. I hold the title of president thanks to the enemy rather than a vote of the American people. That being the case, I will step down if that's your will.

"Ideally, according to the traditions and laws of our country we would hold an election, one in which every individual would cast their vote, but that is one of many freedoms denied us. Because of that you will act in place of the Electoral College—and vote on behalf of the people you represent.

"In keeping with guidelines distributed prior to this meeting, each one of you will be given five minutes in which to state your group's position, and, should you wish to do so, to nominate yourself or some other member of this group as the coalition's leader.

"After each individual has been afforded an opportunity to speak there will be half an hour of general discussion followed by a forced vote. The person receiving the most votes will lead the coalition.

"Anyone who no longer wishes to participate can leave now. By doing so those who remain agree to bind themselves *and* the organizations they represent to the coalition, as well as the goals, strategies, and tactics that it may subsequently adopt. Once conditions return to something resembling normal, the coalition will dedicate itself to the restoration of the United States government. Are there any questions?"

There was no sound other than the rhythmic squeak, squeak, squeak of Cyan's marker as Franklin looked from one face to the next. "All right then," the politician said, soberly, directing his next comment to Vosser. "Let the record show that all present agreed to the process as described—and agreed to honor whatever decisions the majority of the group may arrive at.

"Let's begin by hearing from Clan Leader Storm. She represents a group that calls itself the Sasquatch Nation. Ms. Storm?"

Storm had a long, serious face. Her eyes, which were dark and shiny, smoldered with passion. Her voice had the singsong quality of someone reciting frequently uttered cant. "The Sasquatch Nation was meeting near Concrete, Washington, the day before the virus attacked Mother Earth. Some of the attendees fled, and were presumably killed, but the vast majority of the group, some four hundred in all, took their camping gear and retreated farther into the woods. It was difficult at first, but, thanks to the Great Mother's bounty, we managed to survive. Now, like antibodies in her global bloodstream, we stand ready to attack the alien virus and thereby destroy it.

"In fact, given the terrible damage done to the Great Mother we find it hard to understand why one of the alien viruses has been allowed to sit at this very table, and hereby request permission to kill it."

So saying, Storm produced a well-oiled .357 Magnum, turned to her left, and pressed the barrel against the side of Doo-Nol's elongated head. The hammer made a loud click as it went to full cock.

Manning, who had stationed himself between Franklin and the door, pulled his weapon and aimed it at the woman's head. Not in an effort to save the Sauron, but to protect Franklin, should Storm's weapon swing in the president's direction. Amocar, Ji-Hoon, and Asad were careful to keep their attention focused on the other participants, the doors, and each other. *If* someone fired, *if* bullets started to fly, it was important to avoid hitting Franklin or one of their teammates.

The president held up his hand. "Hold it right there, Ms. Storm. Like his white brothers, Doo-Nol is a member of a persecuted minority with goals that are compatible with ours. What better way to help the Great Mother than to turn virus against virus?"

If Doo-Nol thought the human's words were somewhat cynical, he showed no signs of it but continued to stare straight ahead.

The silence stretched long and thin as Storm considered the politician's words, eased the hammer down, and made the handgun disappear.

Boyer Blue, one of the few individuals in the room who had arrived unarmed, allowed himself to release a pent-up breath. Franklin, the man he had once dismissed as a collaborator, had done it again. In spite of a not-altogether-healthy love of power, and an all-too-pragmatic approach to obtaining and keeping it, the politician had an almost magical ability to span what appeared to be unbridgeable gaps.

Franklin nodded. "Thank you . . . I urge the rest of the delegates to keep their weapons holstered for the balance of our discussions. Now, given Ms. Storm's statements, it seems only fair that Doo-Nol be given an opportunity to speak."

Doo-Nol looked from left to right. The Sauron didn't know whom he disliked the most, the Zin, for the manner in which they treated members of his caste, the humans, for trying to capitalize on the brotherhood's suffering, or himself, for the way in which he had betrayed the master race. Or were the eternally arrogant black and brown Saurons members of the same race to which he and his brothers belonged? No, not judging from the way he and his kind were treated, all of which justified his otherwise inexcusable perfidy. Now, if only he could convince the resistance to practice what amounted to selective murder, the humiliation of dealing with lesser beings would be worth it.

In spite of the fact that most of the aliens didn't consider slave talk worth learning, the aliens actually had a natural facility where foreign languages were concerned, and Doo-Nol, like Hak-Bin himself, had gone to the trouble to learn the dominant tongue. That being the case, his words carried a good deal of the passion which the Ra 'Na-designed translators had a tendency to remove. "Earlier, when slave Franklin spoke of the few days during which my race will be vulnerable, he addressed not only *your* opportunity but *ours* as well."

The Sauron scanned the faces around him. "I know what most if not all of you are thinking . . . Why should we care about the Fon? Like slave Storm, you can't wait for all of us to die. Yet it was slave Blue who conspired with juveniles like slave Cyan to teach my caste to read, and it was slave Andromeda who arranged for her followers to assassinate the Zin named Xat-Hey, to protect our nascent movement.

"Nor has the relationship been one-way . . . Later, after

brother Bal-Lok formed his ill-advised alliance with the ones you call racialists, and failed in his attempt to kill slave Franklin, the surviving members of our brotherhood sought to temper the reprisals that followed. So now, as you plan your assault on my race, I ask that you spare the Fon. Allow our nymphs to live, help them board their ships, and they will leave your planet forever."

Dro Rul, silent till then, pulled himself up to stand on the high chair's padded seat. He might have looked absurd, like an otter on two legs, but somehow didn't. His ears lay back against his head, his teeth were bared, his body rigid with outrage. The prelate's anger was clear in spite of the translator's tendency to leach the emotion out of the words it processed. "Human Storm is correct . . . Your species *is* like a plague, a disease that lays waste to entire planets and kills without compunction. There can be *no* forgiveness for your crimes, there can be *no* mercy for your kind, and not a single nymph can be allowed to escape. Even now, here among us, you think and refer to us as 'slaves.' You and your brothers must die, not as a punishment, but to prevent the spread of a contagion."

There was a moment of silence as Storm nodded, Cyan drew, and Franklin waited to see what would happen. The Sauron's voice was hard and flat. "Call us what you will . . . but face the truth. Even if you bide your time, attack the citadel on Hell Hill, and kill each Sauron who takes shelter within, my race will *still* survive. What you fail to realize is that a *second* citadel was constructed elsewhere on your planet."

"*Yes*," the Fon continued, directing himself to a visibly shaken Dro Rul. "You didn't know that, did you? Just because you believe yourselves to be more intelligent than we are doesn't mean you actually are. So you invented spaceships? So what? Which race was enslaved? Yours? Or mine?

"So," Doo-Nol insisted, "*if* you want to know where the

other citadel is, you will comply with my demands . . . More than that you will ensure the survival of *my* kind . . . in return for the survival of *yours*."

Franklin felt his stomach sink. Here, like a bolt of lightning out of the blue, was a whole new threat. Even if the resistance attacked the citadel on Hell Hill, and even if the attack was successful, the Saurons would still survive. The meeting disintegrated into chaos.

ABOARD THE SAURON DREADNOUGHT *HOK NOR AH*

Too unhappy to jump, and in no particular hurry to reach his destination, Mon-Oro shuffled along one of the ship's bustling corridors and used the time to contemplate his fate. Most Zin, Mon-Oro included, had at least some ambition and tried to live their lives in a manner that would generate respect from their peers. Respect, which, when layered onto the accomplishments of those who preceded them, would eventually elevate the entire line to a primary position within the ruling caste. A gradual process that could take thousands of years. That was the manner in which Hak-Bin's line had risen to ascendancy—and that was the way that Mon-Oro and his ancestors hoped to accomplish the same thing.

Before any such elevation could take place, however, there were challenges to be met. Some were enjoyable, and some were not. And today, with the all important birth-death day looming ahead, Mon-Oro found himself burdened with the most unpleasant task of his extremely long life.

The Zin, the vast majority at any rate, wanted to send a message to Hak-Bin, and Mon-Oro had been selected for the task. A distasteful and somewhat dangerous errand that would require the not-altogether-willing messenger to tell the highest-ranking individual in Sauron society numerous things he didn't want to hear.

Mon-Oro turned a corner, passed one of his brethren, but

was so lost in his own contemplations that the other Zin's greeting failed to register on his consciousness.

Among the issues Mon-Oro had been instructed to raise was the extent to which the construction of the birthing chambers was running behind schedule, the so-called catalyst crises, and the basic question of fairness. After all, the rank-and-file Zin wondered, given the fact that more than a score of early changers had already been put to death rather than allow the slaves to learn about birth-death day, then why should Hak-Bin and his nymph be somehow exempt?

Perhaps, many of them thought, a new leader should be chosen, and *his* line elevated to very apex of Sauron society. It was a legitimate question, or so it seemed to Mon-Oro, although he had no desire to ask it. Especially since Hak-Bin was known to be cranky of late, and, if sufficiently incensed, could have his visitor shot.

Why me? Mon-Oro wondered pitifully, especially so near the end of a life successfully lived? The answer was obvious. Some of his peers worked to advance their lines via out-and-out aggression. Others, those who thought themselves clever, chose to wander the labyrinthine world of Zin politics, where they attempted to plot, scheme, and manipulate their way into power.

Still others, a relative handful, chose to pursue the strategy adopted by Mon-Oro's antecedents and now entrusted to him. They sought to be honest with their peers, to honor the promises they made, and to avoid the web of interlocking alliances, groupings, and cliques within which so many were trapped.

Mon-Oro knew it was this perception, this reputation for neutrality, that explained why all the various factions within Zin society were willing to entrust him with such an important task. *If* he succeeded, and *if* he survived, the respect for his line would go up a full notch. A considerable achievement indeed.

It was with that sobering thought that the Zin found himself standing outside the null-gee chamber in which Hak-Bin had chosen to closet himself while a Kan asked the same question again. "Greetings, lord, how may I assist you?"

"My name is Mon-Oro . . . I'm here to see Hak-Bin."

The Kan tilted his body forward in the Sauron equivalent of a bow, servos whined, and the lock opened. The entryway yawned like a widely opened mouth and consumed the emissary whole.

Meanwhile, waiting within, Hak-Bin hung weightless, suspended in space. Air jets hissed as the three globe lights sought to maintain positions relative to each other. The rest of the compartment fell into darkness.

The Zin had been warned of Mon-Oro's visit, and though not privy to the exact content of the messages the intermediary had been asked to carry, had a pretty good idea of what the topics would be. In fact, Hak-Bin knew full well that if the situation had been reversed, he would have been among the most vocal of critics.

But the situation *wasn't* reversed—which meant that he had to hang on. For himself, for his nymph, and for his line. A not-so-silent group of crotchety old has-beens who haunted his dreams.

The inner hatch opened, a gust of cold air stirred the black tentlike garment intended to hide Hak-Bin's extremely swollen body, and Mon-Oro entered the compartment. Though not as bad as some, the visitor's movements were still clumsy compared to those of even the least capable slave, and Mon-Oro spent the better part of three units getting himself positioned before Hak-Bin. The senior Zin took advantage of the interlude to consider the individual with whom he was about to negotiate.

Though reasonably well groomed, Mon-Oro's chitin had not been oiled in some time, which left it flat and dull.

Nothing to be especially ashamed of but consistent with a somewhat studious and externally focused personality. Though clearly apprehensive, Hak-Bin saw determination in the set of the other Zin's shoulders, and knew that to be one of his adversary's strengths.

As for weaknesses, well, those who follow the path of accommodation are very often in love with compromise, a mutually deluded mentality in which the parties to a particular dispute manage to convince themselves that something is better than nothing, and therefore agree to half-witted, often unenforceable, nonsense.

Yes, Hak-Bin thought to himself, a little bit of appeasement, followed by what looks like a compromise, should be sufficient to buy some time. Then, assuming that certain initiatives came off as planned, the whole matter would soon become moot. "So," the Sauron said, careful to choose a casual form of address, "our brethren chose *you* to convey their concerns. Not an easy task . . . You have my sympathy."

Grateful for the manner in which Hak-Bin had both seized the initiative *and* broached a rather difficult subject, Mon-Oro was quick to follow up. "Thank you, lord. I wish the circumstances were different."

Hak-Bin gave a single up-and-down nod of his elongated head. "We have that wish in common . . . but such is not the case. That being said, please allow me to address the first of what I am sure is a long list of issues that you were asked to pursue. *Yes*, as everyone has no doubt figured out by now, my nymph has plans to enter the world a bit early. Something I oppose as strongly as my brethren do—since there is a great deal of work to be finished.

"*Yes*, I could hand over the reins of power to a qualified candidate, someone like yourself for example, but hesitate to do so with birth-death day almost upon us . . . The manner in which the Sauron race traditionally invests absolute power in a single individual confers many benefits upon our people but entails some risk as well.

"For example, who, outside of myself, understands the complexity that we now face? Who stands ready to step in, assume *all* the responsibilities attendant to my office, and would be able to do so without making mistakes? The birthing draws near—and with it comes the possibility of extreme peril. The truth is that we find ourselves in something of a conundrum . . . We need the slaves to construct the citadels that will protect us—yet the slaves are the greatest threat to our safety.

"Sometimes, in my darker moments, I wonder if we should put every single one of the lesser beings to death early. But what if we fail? The humans are especially hard to kill—and at least some of them are likely to survive our efforts at sterilization.

"And what then? Even if the subsequent birthing were to be successful, our nymphs would emerge to find themselves stranded on an alien planet, and, lacking the knowledge required to operate the fleet, would be forced to remain here, waiting for some other spacegoing race to land. An interlude that might last for thousands—or even hundreds of thousands of years.

"No," Hak-Bin said, doing his best to sound reluctant, "should I discover the means to delay the moment of birth, and thereby extend my life, however briefly, I have the clear obligation to do so. Not for myself, or my line, but for the benefit of the Sauron race."

Mon-Oro was impressed. Hak-Bin had been warned, that was to be expected, but the quality of his response was higher than anticipated. Especially with regard to the rationale behind why he should be allowed to live—in spite of the fact that others had been put to death. Well aware of the fact that his host could turn on him like a hunt-crazed harakna, the emissary was careful to proceed with caution.

"Though impressed by the well-phrased manner in which your arguments were put forward, lord, I remain curious where the issue of life extension is concerned, and wonder if your eminence would be so kind as to elaborate? Is such a thing possible?"

Fearful lest the full extent of his activities make him appear to be excessively calculating—Hak-Bin offered a partial truth. "Yes, I believe that it is, although research continues. *If* I'm correct, and *if* the process proves successful, *all* our brethren will benefit."

Mon-Oro could do little more than float there and admire the manner in which Hak-Bin had at least momentarily turned the tables. Not only had the ranking Zin made a fairly believable case for why the rest of the Saurons should let him live for as long as possible, he had raised the possibility that some sort of procedure could be used to the benefit of *all* the early changers, thereby benefiting not only the changers themselves but individuals such as Mon-Oro, who, like so many others had come to greet the least little ailment with something akin to horror. Was this *it*? Was the headache the first in a string of symptoms that would herald the change? The mere possibility was a form of torture. "Thank you, eminence, I will carry the news to our brethren. And the citadels? And the birth catalyst? What should I say regarding those matters?"

Hak-Bin made note of Mon-Oro's nearly subservient tone, knew he had triumphed, and was careful to hide it. "Tell the brethren that I share their concerns, that I will soon undertake dramatic steps to hasten the construction of the citadels, and that a new catalyst factory will soon come on-line."

Mon-Oro felt a strong desire to ask what steps, but sensed that to do so would be an error. Had Hak-Bin wanted to divulge such information, he would have—and nothing

Mon-Oro could say was likely to make a difference. "Thank you, eminence, I will tell them."

"No, *thank you*," Hak-Bin said with all the false humility he could summon. "The task given you was both difficult and demanding. The race owes you a debt of gratitude."

Mon-Oro left after that, and the nymph, as if intentionally quiescent for the duration of the interview, started to stir. Hak-Bin used the inside surface of his pincers to massage his badly swollen abdomen. "Were you listening, little one? And did you learn? I hope you did. Your time will come soon, *very* soon, but the interim will require patience."

It was possible that subsequent movement, and the pain that accompanied it, were a matter of coincidence. Hak-Bin doubted that, however—and was thankful that no one could hear him scream.

SOUTHWEST OF HELL HILL, IN THE ABANDONED SAWMILL

Though still in session, the realization that the resistance would have to deal with two citadels had sucked most of the energy out of the proceedings.

"Mr. President . . ." The voice seemed to come from a long ways off. Franklin forced himself to focus.

Dro Rul, who—for reasons not entirely clear—had either climbed onto, or been placed on top of, the conference table, stood not two feet away. Another Ra 'Na, a female judging from the way she was dressed, stood at his side. Blue spoke, and Franklin realized that it was the historian who had summoned him back. "Mr. President, Dro Rul has something to tell you, something important."

Rul indicated the female at his side. "This is Med Tech Shu—she risked her life to visit the surface. George Farley brought her to me. I believe she has something important to share."

The story of how Shu had exited the Sauron shuttle, managed to escape into the woods, and subsequently been captured was a good deal more complicated than that, but the med tech knew it was neither the time nor the place to go into that.

Now, with the entire group hanging on every word, Shu told the resistance leaders about the orbital factory set aside to manufacture birth catalyst and the manner in which it had been destroyed.

Gradually, as the med tech told her story, Franklin felt the first stirrings of rekindled hope. Then, as the full ramifications of the newly revealed intelligence dawned on him, hope turned to outright excitement. "Let's see if I understand . . . Insofar as we know every single one of the Saurons will require a quantity of this catalyst in order to reproduce successfully. Damn! If we could destroy the entire supply of catalyst—there would be no need to attack the citadels!"

Doo-Nol, painfully conscious of the fact that the advantage had somehow been snatched away from him, struggled to understand. Birth catalyst? *What* birth catalyst? He'd never heard of such a thing . . . But the Zin loved their secrets—and this could be one of them. In fact, many of the functionaries had questioned the miles of plumbing that the recently deceased stonemaster had insisted on, and wondered what all the pipes were for. Now he knew. The slaves were staring at the Sauron by then, so Doo-Nol tried to appear nonchalant. "I swear I knew nothing of this substance . . . it's one more reason why my brethren and I oppose the Zin and their endless machinations."

Smith looked cynical, as did some of the others, but Franklin saw no point in trying to counter the alien. No one in their right mind would trust Doo-Nol in any case. The important thing was to focus on the way in which the existence of the birth catalyst should impact their strategy.

The president came to his feet. His eyes swept both sides of the table. Blue noted the energy there and marveled at the way things worked. Was this the way it had been during the early days of the American Revolution? Great men and not-so-great men lurching back and forth between hope and despair? Yes, the historian thought, it probably had, and the possibility made him feel better.

"So," Franklin began, his eyes flicking from face to face, "the situation continues to change. Time passes quickly, so let's move forward. Based on this new intelligence I suggest that we dedicate our efforts to identifying the location of whatever infrastructure the Saurons will attempt to build, and having done so, destroy those facilities. No catalyst— no nymphs. It's as simple as that."

Opposition came quickly and from a predictable source. Doo-Nol backed his way out of the sling chair, rose to his full height, and clacked his pincers. "This proposal goes too far! While my brethren and I can support violence directed to a more equitable sharing of power—we can never be party to what amounts to genocide. Unless each one of you agrees to withhold your support, the Fon Brotherhood will be forced to withdraw from the alliance."

Franklin looked at Blue, the historian looked at Dro Rul, the Ra 'Na looked at Smith, the ex-Ranger looked at Cyan, the Tagger looked at Andromeda, and she looked Franklin in the eye. "This is our chance, perhaps our *only* chance, and we *must* take advantage of it."

"Hear, hear," Storm put in. "The cult lady has it right."

The president nodded his agreement. "I'm sorry Doo-Nol . . . but we're going to move ahead. That being the case, it would be best if you were to wait somewhere else while we complete our deliberations. You will be released when the meeting is over."

"Wait a minute," Smith objected, leaning forward over the table. "What's to prevent Doo-Nol from ratting us out? The chits think their secret is safe. Let's keep it that way."

"Who can he tell?" Franklin asked reasonably, "without being crucified for doing so?"

"It's a problem," Smith conceded, "but who knows what kind of story he might concoct? Hell, given enough time, the bastard might schmooze his way out of it. We're at war," Smith said grimly, "and there's no room for mercy. Not where Saurons are concerned."

"Right on!" Storm put in. "Let's roast the sucker . . . Rumor has it that the chits cook up pretty good."

Well aware that he should have been less forthright, and afraid that the slaves would kill him, the Sauron backed away. That's when something hard touched the back of Doo-Nol's skull, and the Fon knew it was a weapon. He closed his eyes and waited to die.

Cyan looked up from his tabletop mural. "Shoot the geek if that's what you want to do . . . but we could tag him."

The rest of the group was surprised to hear from the Tagger, and heads swiveled in his direction. "Okay," Franklin said, "what do you have in mind?"

"A really cool paint job," Cyan said thoughtfully, "the kind that won't come off for at least a month."

"I don't get it," Storm said critically. "What difference will *that* make?"

Blue had worked with the Taggers before and thought that he understood. "Give the young man a chance. Say we agree . . . What would you paint on him?"

"First a base coat," the graffiti artist said thoughtfully, "then some slogans. 'All power to the Fon,' . . . stuff like that."

Doo-Nol's eyes popped open. "The Zin would kill me!"

"Precisely," Franklin agreed coolly. "Which is why you'll want to keep a very low profile until the paint wears off."

The chief executive officer turned to the Tagger. "Good suggestion, Cyan . . . Better use some heavy-duty paint, or he'll scrub it off."

Cyan nodded thoughtfully, selected some cans from his bandoleer, and pointed to a spot some ten feet from the table. "Put him over there . . . I'll work on him while the meeting continues."

Doo-Nol had little choice but to cooperate, and Franklin turned to Vosser. "Where were we?"

Vosser, apparently unmoved by anything that had occurred so far, delivered an editorial sniff. "Thanks to the excessive amount of time devoted to Mr. Doo-Nol and his issues, we are running some twenty minutes behind schedule. Both Ms. Storm and Mr. Doo-Nol had their opportunity to speak. I assume Ms. Andromeda would go next. No nominations have been tendered so far."

A can hissed as Cyan sprayed a white base coat onto the Sauron's already white chitin. "Okay," Franklin said, "let's move on . . . Sister Andromeda? It's your turn to speak."

SALMON NATIONAL FOREST, IDAHO

Jonathan Ivory awoke from a deep, nearly comalike, sleep and almost panicked when his eyelids refused to open. It was as if someone had glued them shut, and the racialist was pawing at them when he heard a stir, followed by a high-pitched girlish voice. "Mrs. Ivory! Mrs. Ivory! He's awake! Come see."

One eyelid popped open soon, followed by the other. It was still difficult to see as the gummy substance continued to impede his vision. Hands gripped his wrists, and a familiar voice said, "Janey will clean the gunk out of your eyes, and everything will be fine."

Ivory allowed the hands to restrain him, knew they belonged to Ella, and felt a sudden flood of emotion. There was relief, gratitude, and something else. They had been thrown together by circumstance and more or less forced into a union consistent with the needs of the white race but not based on much else. But now, in spite of the way the union had come about, the racialist realized that he had come to have feelings for her. Feelings that extended beyond the politics of race, beyond his sexual requirements, and into what he regarded as new territory.

"There," Ella said softly, "you can open your eyes."

Ivory took his race wife at her word, opened his eyes, and found himself looking up into her hard but handsome face. It softened slightly. "You look like hell."

"And you look like heaven," Ivory croaked. "Where am I?"

Ella took note of Ivory's response, as well as her response to his response, and decided that there was nothing incorrect about the pleasure she felt. "You're at Racehome . . . in our bedroom."

Ivory struggled to sit up. His entire body was sore. A plain-faced girl rushed to shove pillows behind his back. It was an honor to do so. There had been a contest to see which of the preteens would be allowed to serve Ivory, and she had been chosen.

The chamber was just as the racialist remembered it. The room had been hewed from solid rock. No one could be sure, but, judging from the rails that passed through the arched entryway and terminated somewhere beneath Ella's queen-size bed, there was reason to believe that the alcove had once served as a siding, a place where her great-great-grandfather could remove one ore car from the line and push another into place.

Now, thanks to an enormous armoire, plus some colorful hangings, the space had been transformed into a bedroom. That's when Ivory noticed that a change had been made to the mural that occupied the wall opposite the bed. The wreath normally associated with the German Knight's Cross had previously been used to frame a symbolically faceless warrior. The kind of man who could be anyone, anywhere, hidden within society. Now, staring sternly out into the room, Ivory gazed on his own likeness. The sight of it sent a chill down his spine. He turned to look at his wife.

Then, as Ivory's eyes met Ella's, he realized something else. Her face was a little fuller, her breasts seemed larger, and the once-flat stomach displayed a slight bulge. A weight gain? No, his wife was pregnant!

Ella, who had been waiting for that exact moment, monitoring her husband's face to see what sort of emotions might appear there, was pleased with results. There was no mistaking the look of pleasure followed by manly pride.

That was the moment when Ivory remembered the Sauron road train, the manner in which the chits had secured him to the front of the tractor, and the subsequent attack. He frowned. "You were there . . . in the middle of a firefight. What about the baby?"

Ella raised an eyebrow but was secretly pleased. "We're short of good leaders. So many of the men who come our way are either too strong or too weak. It's good to have you back."

"It's good to *be* back," Ivory replied. "There's a lot of catching up to do."

"Yes," Ella agreed. "There certainly is. Do you feel up to a walk?"

Ivory swung his feet over the side of the bed and groaned. "Everything hurts. Is there any aspirin around?"

Ella looked at the plain-faced girl, who immediately scurried away. She took her husband's arm. "Here, let me help. Once you have a shave, a shower, and some breakfast you'll be good as new."

Ivory doubted that, but enjoyed the process, especially when his wife stripped her clothes off, helped him into the shower, and used a bar of Ivory soap to lather his entire body.

Then, when he was almost impossibly hard, Ella threw her arms around Ivory's neck, kissed his throat as he lifted her up off the floor, and made little mewing sounds as she welcomed him into her warmth. Ivory, who was used to the

Ella of old, braced himself for what promised to be a nearly violent mating.

But this was a different woman, or that's the way it seemed, as Ella appeared to savor the moment and took her time. Finally, after both were drained both physically and emotionally, it was his turn to bathe her. He did so slowly, reverently, taking a moment to kiss the curve of her swollen stomach.

Then it was back to bed, to rest, and catch up. He told her about his travels, about life on Hell Hill, the attempt on Franklin's life, the way so many Hammer Skins had been killed, and his journey home.

Later, after an enormous breakfast, Ella took the recently returned racialist on a tour of the onetime gold mine, which her father, commonly referred to as "Old Man Howther," had inherited from *his* father, and now served as the very heart of the area which the white supremacists called Racehome.

In spite of the fact that Mrs. Howther, her daughter and a hard-core cadre had already moved into the mine prior to Ivory's departure for Hell Hill, a great many improvements had been made. Not only that, but the facility was home to more people, a lot more, many of whom wore what looked like white nightshirts.

Everyone seemed to know who Ivory was—and most addressed him as "sir." Ella sought to explain. "Incredible as it may seem, word of your exploits found its way out of the camp on Hell Hill—but people would respect you even if it hadn't. The fact that you went there and fought for the race puts you on a par with our greatest heroes."

The words were all Ivory had ever hoped to hear and more. That meant he should have been happy, *very* happy, but he discovered that he wasn't. Recognition was nice, but recognition without actual power didn't mean much, and the purposeful way in which the skins went about their daily activities suggested that someone else was calling the shots. Ella? Maybe, but for some reason he didn't think so.

Ivory's thoughts were interrupted by the tinkle of multiple bells. He looked in the direction of the sound and saw four men in white jerkins round a corner farther down the shaft. They bore a stretcher, and Ivory was still wondering why people were in such a hurry to get out of the way when Ella pulled him aside. Some of the bystanders, his wife included, brought their hands together as if in prayer.

Bells jingled, and the stretcher swayed as it passed them by. The racialist caught a glimpse of bright blue eyes, an explosion of age-wrinkled skin, and a puddle of wool blankets before the conveyance was gone. "Who, or what was that?"

For the first time since his return Ivory saw Ella frown. "You may recall that my father prophesied that during the time of troubles the great Yahweh would send three people to help us. A leader, an assassin, and a saint. You are the leader, the woman named Marta Manning was the assassin, and Reverend Dent is the saint."

Now Ivory understood. He thought the prophecies were nonsense, but the Howthers believed in them, and he had gone along. Especially given the fact that the first prediction worked in his favor. But now, with some guy named Dent horning in, things looked different. And who was Dent anyway? The name had a familiar ring . . .

Then he had it! Of course, the man on the stretcher was none other than the controversial minister, and sometime-radio-talk show host named *Raymond Dent*. A self-confessed Racial Conservative, who was known for his right-wing politics, and the frequent target of attacks by the Zionist Occupational Government or ZOG.

The Jews, the muds, and all the other servants of the devil claimed Dent was racist, something he never publicly owned up to but was nevertheless. The question was why? Because certain radio stations would drop his broadcasts? Thereby silencing one of the few voices who spoke the truth? Or because he made a good living telling racialists what they wanted to hear?

Not that it mattered because Ivory had already decided that he didn't approve of Dent and wanted to get rid of him. Something he couldn't tell Ella or anyone else for that matter. That being the case, the racialist was careful to keep his voice neutral. "Raymond Dent? The talk-show host?"

"That's right," Ella said proudly. "He was on the air in Missoula when the Saurons attacked. He told the people who believed in Yahweh, the people who understood the need for a great cleansing, to meet him at the radio station's transmission tower.

"The station went off the air shortly after that, he jumped in his car, and headed toward the tower. He was almost there when a chit fighter appeared out of nowhere, slagged the front of his Lincoln, and injured both of his legs. People, *his* people, pulled Dent out of the wreckage and carried him away. It was a miracle."

Not for the first time, Ivory wondered how his race wife could be so smart and so stupid, all at the same time. Dent had been lucky, that's all, and Yahweh had nothing to do with it. The racialist was careful to hide his true feelings while he probed for more information. "So, how did Reverend Dent wind up here?"

"My father appeared on Reverend Dent's show years ago. Later, once the broadcast was over, they talked for a long, long time. Daddy told him about Racehome, about his vision for the future, and the Reverend never forgot. That's why he told his followers to bring him here, where he could preach the word of Yahweh, and the race could be reborn."

And the miserable bastard could take advantage of the supplies the Howther family had stashed in their mine, Ivory thought cynically. "That's an amazing story," Ivory said truthfully, "so the folks in the white shirts carried him all the way from Missoula?"

"That's right," Ella confirmed, "and it wasn't easy. They had to break up into small groups, travel only at night, and maintain contact via radio. Approximately half the flock were killed en route, but the other half made it. Thanks to them, and their knowledge, we now have an underground farm. Plus a radio station! Later, when the time is right, the saint will resume his broadcasts. Come on, I'll show you."

As Ivory followed his wife down the main shaft, then off into side tunnels and their associated galleries, there was little he could do but be impressed.

It seemed as if Dent's followers were a cut above the motivated but often dysfunctional riffraff so often attracted to the racialist movement. People like the men who had accompanied Ivory on the trip from Denver. Death on muds, and filled with the lord's spirit, but poorly educated. Certainly not capable of putting together extensive underground farms fed by miles of black irrigation tubing and supplemented by a rich combination of human waste and bat guano.

Add grow lights, powered by a diesel generator dedicated to that purpose, plus some natural sunlight, brought down via carefully arranged mirrors, and the people of Racehome had fresh vegetables. Not sufficient to live off of, but a healthy, vitamin-rich supplement to the military MREs and canned goods that made up the bulk of their diets.

Not that underground life was easy. No, it took work, *hard* work to bring more than a thousand wheelbarrows of topsoil down from the surface, to mix it with fertilizer, and fill the wood-framed trays. It also required labor to plant, weed, and harvest, all activities that the white-shirted "Dent heads" seemed to somehow glory in.

Ella introduced Ivory to a man named Tracks, a former marijuana grower, who possessed considerable expertise where underground crops were concerned and seemed typical of the newcomers. He had long, lank hair, a narrow face, and beady brown eyes. They blinked every few seconds, in time with some neurological tic, and were linked to the manner in which he spoke. The words came in codelike bursts. "Glad to meet you. Heard plenty . . . Welcome back. Yeah, we're doing okay. In two years, maybe three, we'll be self-sufficient."

Ivory raised his eyebrows in surprise. "You're planning to live down here long-term? What about the holy war? Why not drive the Saurons off planet, harness the muds to your plows, and live on the surface?"

Tracks blinked in surprise. "You're kidding, right? How you gonna do it? With two or three hundred skins? I don't think so."

Ella pulled him away after that, to see the underground pen in which four pigs and a pathetic-looking Fon were waiting to be slaughtered, but Ivory's mind lagged behind. Still another danger had made itself known, not elements of the much-hated ZOG, but an enemy that lurked within.

NEAR THE MAYAN RUINS OF NAKABE, GUATEMALA

A bolt of lightning zigzagged across the sky, sent thunder rolling across the land, and announced the coming of the rain. It pinged the metal roof as if experimenting with a new instrument, found the surface to its liking, and beat it like a drum. There were holes, tiny for the most part, but each produced its own miniature waterfall. Some of the slaves turned their faces upward, and allowed the cool wetness to splatter against their faces, while others moved, seeking the dry spots, thereby sending ripples out through the crowd of roughly three hundred men and women. Some, so tired that their sleep verged on a state of unconsciousness, remained right where they were as the water fell from above.

Sleep was a boon, the only medicine they were likely to get, and therefore precious.

The weak, flickering light came from a scattering of battered kerosene lamps, all of which were protected by homemade umbrellas and regarded as community property.

The dry season, which ran from late December through mid-April, had ended, or so Jones believed, although she had no longer had the access to the cell phone, PDA, and belt comp through which the complexities of life had once been managed. Those had been taken away from her the day after the Saurons landed and took possession of the surrounding area.

In fact, with the exception of a stainless-steel Gator pocketknife, discovered where some tourist had lost it, a Bic lighter stolen from another slave, a cheap Timex, and some ragged clothes, Dr. Maria Sanchez-Jones had nothing beyond life itself. Something she planned to hang on to for as long as possible.

That's why she paid close attention when a Kan unlocked the doors and pulled them open. The air was warm and humid. Not that much better than the fetid stuff trapped within the shed. Not just any shed, but *her* shed, the one that she and other anthropologists had once used to clean, sort, and classify bits of material removed from the Mayan ruins. But there had been fans back then, *big* fans that had been flown in from Mexico City, and ran 24/7. Not anymore, though, not without power, and not for the comfort of slaves.

The Kan shimmered as his chitin sought to match the jungle behind him and waved a pincer at a group of approximately thirty humans. His voice was flat and hard. "You will exit the building."

Jones was automatically suspicious since the Kan were creatures of habit and nearly always did everything the same way day after boring day. When they didn't, when patterns were broken, it meant something unpleasant was about to happen. Now, as the slaves were ushered out of the shed a full two hours before their shift was scheduled to start, she knew it was bad. The only question was *how* bad.

Had she been seated toward the rear of the group, Jones might have done what she thought of as "a fade," kind of hanging back and melding with those who were slated to stay. Something often made easier by her relatively small stature. At five-two and 105 pounds it was relatively easy to hide.

But that wasn't going to work this time, not so close to the doors, which left the anthropologist with little choice but to obey. She got to her feet, followed the others outside, and felt the raindrops explode against her brown skin. Skin which, thanks to the regard that the aliens had for pigmentation, had sometimes served to shield her from the often horrible jobs reserved for *los blancos*. But not this one, whatever it was, since the people around her were a mix of Hispanics and *gringos*. No blacks, however, since they were housed in quarters reserved for overseers.

It was dark, without so much as a hint of light in the eastern sky, and only the glow of distant work lights to guide them. Thunder rumbled, the rain fell more heavily, and soon soaked her clothes. Jones felt her nipples harden, knew they would be visible through the thin fabric of her T-shirt, and crossed her arms in front of her chest.

Kevin Blackley, a *blanco* who had the misfortune to be on-site visiting the ruins when the Saurons landed, raised his eyebrows and ran his tongue over his lips. He was actually kind of good-looking in a smarmy sort of way—and buff, thanks to the hard physical labor. Previously prominent love handles had disappeared, his upper body was much more muscular, and he looked good with a two-day growth of beard. None of which was sufficient to counter the fact that he had an IQ only slightly above that of a Chihuahua.

Ever since Blackley had been assigned to her work team roughly a month before, and become aware of the fact that Jones had represented Mexico in the Miss Universe pageant five years earlier, he had dedicated himself to getting into her pants. Something that wasn't about to happen.

Jones ignored the suggestive look, fell in behind a Guatemalan housewife named Irene Irigoyen, and followed her toward the temple beyond. Her fellow slaves referred to the structure as the *iglesia de diablo,* or "church of the devil," and hated the structure with every atom of their beings. An emotion that Jones certainly shared, but was tempered to some extent by the dispassionate more academic aspect of her being, a persona that couldn't help but draw parallels between her experiences and those of the ancient Mayans. They too had struggled through the heat and humidity to cut limestone blocks from the same quarries to which the Saurons had been attracted.

They too had struggled to carry quarter-ton blocks of stone to the sites where their amazing temples had been constructed.

And they too had stumbled, bled, and died during the process.

The irony of that, the fact that Jones had been enslaved in order to build structures similar to those she sought to study never ceased to amuse her. But not now, not as the file of ragged-looking humans followed the alien warrior through the drenching downpour and toward the nearly completed temple. Now Jones focused her extremely sharp mind on the question of what was taking place and why.

The temple crouched on a slight rise. In spite of the lights, which the Ra 'Na had rigged so the humans could labor through the night, the structure was only half-visible through the veil of driving rain. It consisted of three towers connected by box-shaped galleries. There were doors, but no windows, skylights, or other apertures. In that regard the temple, if that was an accurate description, was reminiscent of the Egyptian pyramids. A fact the anthropologist found troubling.

The pyramids basically had two functions. The first was to impress the hell out of anyone who saw them, a goal clearly met, and the second was to protect the mummy or mummies within, something they failed to accomplish.

Egyptian temples on the other hand, like most such structures, were much more open. Yes, some were reserved for priests and or high-ranking members of society, but still featured large rooms or chambers where people could congregate.

How to explain the Sauron temple then? With its maze of small, seemingly identical rooms? The complete absence of a nave, or similar space, and miles of seemingly useless plumbing?

And, if the aliens were even half as religious as they claimed to be, and truly planned to leave once the temple was completed, where were the behaviors, rituals, and symbols normally attendant upon a religion?

Such thinking was ethnocentric, of course, the anthropologist knew that, but given all the energy the Saurons had expended in order to construct the temples, it seemed as if such an important social construct should have an impact on daily life.

Now, as the group neared the temple, Jones saw that the crudely made scaffolding that still cloaked the structure's façade, along with the adjacent work areas, were empty of humans, and guessed that the second shift had been dismissed early and sent to the food troughs. Not only that, but one of the rarely seen Zin was present, complete with an entourage of Fon, Kan, and two of the Ra 'Na technicals.

A globe-shaped light, held aloft by some unseen force, floated above. With the exception of the furry aliens, who seemed to glory in the rain, the rest of the XTs huddled beneath black mushroom-shaped umbrellas.

The humans were ordered to stop, which they did. Some stood heads down—waiting for whatever orders might come. Others, Jones included, scanned the area, on the lookout for something, anything, that might provide an advantage.

The black Sauron rated an umbrella of his own. He was the local stonemaster, a rather harsh taskmaster named Dun-Dar, who, unlike his recently deceased counterpart to the north, had a passion for detail. An extremely wet Fon struggled to keep the protective device centered over his superior's elongate head as the Zin paused to address the slaves. He waved a pincer at the towers behind him.

"Our temple nears completion. Like all such structures, it must be protected from the ravages of time, weather, and those who might attempt an unauthorized entry.

"A security system has been installed to counter such break-ins, and you have been selected to test it. I warn you that this activity should be carried out with the utmost caution lest you be injured or killed."

Even the most cowlike humans raised their heads, and the crowd seemed to sway as people looked for some way to escape. But a contingent of Kan had moved in to surround them, which left the slaves with nowhere to go.

"The security system was designed to keep intruders out," the Sauron continued. "That's as much information as I can provide without compromising the integrity of our test. You are now free to approach the temple in any way that you choose and attempt an entry. Any slave who manages to get inside will be freed. Any slave who fails to find a way in will be killed by the security system, or by the Kan. The test will last for one-twenty-fourth of a planetary rotation. Let the exercise begin."

The slaves looked at each other, mumbled various swear

words, and broke into groups of two or three. Friends mostly, people who looked out for one another, and mated pairs as well.

Jones, consistent with her extremely independent personality, was going to tackle the problem alone until Blackley sidled up, treated her to one of his shit-eating grins, and said, "So, Doc, what's the plan?"

The anthropologist started to tell the American to fuck off, but, for reasons she wasn't quite sure of, decided to let him stay. She even went so far as to produce smile number three, the one calculated to reduce most males to highly malleable mush, and allowed her arms to fall away from her clearly outlined breasts. "First we scope things out—*then* we make a plan."

"Works for me," Blackley said amiably, "but it won't be easy. The system the fur balls installed includes motion detectors and calibrated heat detectors."

Jones looked at her companion in surprise. "You seem to know quite a bit about security systems."

Blackley shrugged. "I own, no *owned*, an alarm company up in KC."

Jones didn't know where "KC" was and didn't care. "So give it to me in English. What does 'calibrated' mean? In this particular context?"

" 'Calibrated' means that our body heat will trigger the sensors, but theirs won't."

"Why?"

"Because we're warm-blooded and they aren't," Blackley explained. "Not to mention the fact that their chitin may shield some of the heat they generate internally."

In spite of the fact that Jones had given considerable thought to the question of Sauron physiology, including the impact it might have on their behaviors, language, and tools, the whole heat thing had escaped her, and that made the anthropologist cross with herself. If an idiot like Blackley could figure it out, then *she* should have done so as well. Jones pushed the reaction away in order to deal with the situation at hand. One that might get her killed if she continued to waste valuable time. "Come on," Jones said, "let's scope this out."

Blackley nodded and kept pace with the woman as she walked along the western wall. Rain trickled down over his cheeks, but he made no effort to wipe it away. A recently installed cluster of sensors tracked their movements. Six slaves jogged past. They had a large piece of timber and seemed hell-bent on some sort of plan. A Kan, clearly assigned to monitor their activities, hopped along behind. Blackley envied the other slaves their apparent certainty, wondered if he was aligned with the correct person, and knew it was too late to change.

"So," Jones said, her eyes scanning the battlements above, "if the motion detectors sense movement, and the heat reading is consistent with Sauron physiology, what happens then?"

"It's my guess that once the system registers an acceptable heat signature, the subject is allowed to enter."

There was a staccato bang, bang, bang as a semiauto t-gun fired off in the distance. There was an abbreviated scream followed by abrupt silence. The people who had the long length of timber or some other group? Both humans looked in the direction of the sound, but the temple blocked their view. Still, the sounds spoke for themselves. One or more people believed they knew how to break in, had put their theory into practice, and paid the price.

The commotion was a distraction, and Jones managed to push it aside. "What about guests? The motion detectors go off, three blobs of heat approach one of the entryways, and only one of them falls within acceptable parameters. What then?"

Blackley started to turn, started to look back at the Kan.

Jones grabbed his arm. "Keep your eyes over here . . . Now answer my question."

Blackley could see where the questions were headed and felt a lump form in the back of his throat. He thought he knew the answer, believed he was right, but there was no way to be sure. A system designed by humans would require each and every individual who entered the facility to provide some sort of positive ID, ranging from a simple PIN code to more exotic possibilities, like retinal prints, or a DNA match.

But the Saurons were different. It didn't take a degree in xenopsychology to see how arrogant they were—especially where issues of control were concerned. Would the master beings allow the Ra 'Na to design a system that would force them to symbolically submit? Or would they refuse? Blackley swallowed the lump.

"There's no way to be sure of course . . . but it's my guess that the system was programmed to assume that the Saurons are *always* in control, which means that a guest, a slave, or a chimp would be allowed to enter the temple so long as it was accompanied by a Zin, Kan, or Fon."

"Bingo!" Jones said. "That's my guess as well. Shall we bet our lives on it?"

"Okay," Blackley said reluctantly, "but how . . ."

"We position ourselves in front of an entrance," Jones interrupted, "call one of the Kan over, and kill him. Then, before his body can cool, we drag the bastard through the door."

"*Kill* a Kan?" Blackley demanded incredulously. "Right in front of the bugs? Have you lost your mind?"

"Maybe," Jones allowed, as she looked at her watch. "We have forty-six minutes left. Have you got a better idea? One we can execute in that amount of time?"

Blackley *didn't* have a better idea, and now, with so much time off the clock, wasn't likely to come up with one. Would the Saurons simply stand and watch while a member of their race was murdered? All in the interest of a security check? No, it didn't seem likely, but he could take one of the bastards with him, and there was something to be said for that. "Okay," Blackley said nervously, "I'm in."

"Good," Jones answered firmly. "I'll call him over. You immobilize his arms—and I'll kill him."

Blackley glanced at the nearest Kan and back again. "Let me get this straight . . . *You're* going to kill him?"

"That's right," Jones confirmed grimly, "assuming you shut the hell up so we can get on with it. Follow me."

With her somewhat reluctant accomplice in tow, Jones made her way across the causeway that crossed a still-dry moat. The entranceway, surmounted by alien glyphs not to mention two sensor-controlled weapons pods, lay just beyond. Opposing rows of overarching lights brought the area into sharp relief. How close could she get before the dart throwers fired? There was no way to be sure, so Jones stopped halfway across the bridge, turned, and waved to the nearest Kan. "Hey, bug face! Get your ass over here!"

The warrior seemed to consider the request for a moment, leaped into the air, and was already falling when Jones yelled at Blackley. "Grab the bastard's arms!"

The warrior, an individual named Wen-Opp, heard the words via the translator clipped to his combat harness, but hit the ground before he could react to them.

Water splashed away from the bug's podlike extremities as Blackley threw himself forward. The Sauron staggered under the impact, wasted a fraction of a second wondering if the slave was suicidal, and tried to free the assault weapon clutched across his thorax.

Blackley, his once-flabby arms strengthened by months of forced labor, started to squeeze. The bug hug turned out to be surprisingly effective. So much so that the human heard the Kan's chitin creak and wondered if he could make it break. That seemed like a good idea so he squeezed even harder.

Jones circled to the left, attempted to pull the knife free of her pocket, and discovered it was caught. She should have pulled it first, should have held the weapon blade out against her leg before yelling at the Kan, but that was water under the bridge. Now, as Blackley clasped the alien to this chest, and the Sauron struggled to free himself, the anthropologist managed to release the knife and open the blade.

Other warriors, alerted by the commotion, not to mention Wen-Opp's cries for help, were quick to respond. Two were in midjump, and more than halfway to the causeway, when the stonemaster spoke via their radios. "Stop! Not a single grasper shall touch the slaves. Can the temple defend itself? That's what we're here to test."

A noncom, the one to whom Wen-Opp had reported for the last twenty-five years, objected, but to no avail. Dun-Dar was determined to avoid the kind of mistakes made to the north. Better to lose a single Kan than an entire structure packed with vulnerable nymphs.

In spite of the fact that Jones didn't know much if anything about entomology, it didn't take a genius to realize that while the Saurons were equipped with what amounted to armor, there were seams where various plates came together, each one of which represented a point of vulnerability. The problem was to choose the right one, drive the blade into a constantly moving target, and cut something vital.

Wen-Opp felt a new source of strength as naturally produced chemicals entered his blood. He twisted his torso from side to side in an attempt to throw the human off. "Cut him!" Blackley yelled. "The bastard is getting stronger! I can't hold him for much longer."

Jones gritted her teeth, stepped in close, and managed to drive the stainless-steel blade into the spot where Wen-Opp's short leathery neck disappeared into his heavily ar-

mored thorax. Then, hoping to cut a major blood vessel,
nerve bundle, or other structure, she sawed back and forth.

The Kan squealed like a pig, squirted watery green blood,
and tried to free his arms. Blackley managed to hang on,
however, the knife cut through something important, and
the bug went limp. That was the moment Jones had been
waiting for, and she wasted no time. "That's it! We killed
the sonofabitch! Drag him to the door!"

Blackley obeyed, and with the woman's help, towed the
dead warrior across the causeway. Green goo smeared the
walkway.

Dun-Dar and his retinue had moved in close by then and
watched from the other side of the bridge. The Zin, his
umbrella protecting him from the worst of the rain, stood
like a judge at an old-fashioned hanging. Additional warriors, summoned by the commotion, shimmered as their
chitin sought to match the gray-green jungle beyond.

Jones walked backward, her hands under Wen-Opp's
armpits, while Blackley gripped the alien behind his knees.
"They're watching," the anthropologist said through gritted
teeth, "to see if our plan will work."

"And if it does?" Blackley grunted, lifting the carcass
higher to clear a short flight of stairs, "what then?"

"Then we run like hell," Jones replied honestly, "now
hoist him higher . . . We're almost there."

And the slaves were almost there, a fact not lost on the
stonemaster and his entourage, all of whom watched glumly
as the humans towed Wen-Opp's body into the kill zone
without triggering the structure's defenses.

And they were still watching as the servo-assisted hatch,
the same kind used aboard the Ra 'Na-designed ships,
whirred up and out of the way. Dun-Dar has risked not only
his life, but that of his nymph, and all nymphs to come by
installing a modern door in place of the woody anachronisms
specified in the Book of Cycles. Something of which his

subordinates had no knowledge given the fact that they couldn't read but would be apparent to someone like Hak-Bin.

But Hak-Bin had started to change, or so the rumors claimed, and was in no position to preach orthodoxy to subordinates like Dun-Dar. Not if he wanted to continue his questionable existence. Not if the metal hatch helped keep danger at bay. Except that it *hadn't* kept danger at bay, not in combination with a flawed security system, which meant there was work to do.

The slaves passed through the entryway, there was a dull thud as the door dropped into place, and the Zin gave his order. "Discipline must be maintained. Enter the temple, find the humans, and kill them."

SOUTHWEST OF HELL HILL

Ms. Vosser was waiting for Pas Pol when he approached the sawmill's door. It was chilly, and she wanted to get back inside. "Are you Pas Pol? Excellent. Follow me."

The Ra 'Na followed the towering human into the light lock and from there out into a large room. His nose twitched as strong odors assailed his nostrils, but there was no time for analysis as Vosser took hold of the initiate's arm and pulled him back into some shadows. Her whisper had the force of an order. "Wait here."

Pol nodded and was glad of the opportunity to look around. It was a strange scene indeed. Over to his right a Fon stood dejectedly while a human sprayed sealer onto his brightly decorated chitin.

At the center of the room, the area just in front of him, a makeshift table had been established. Pol saw Dro Rul, was proud to see one of his own seated along with the resistance leaders, and felt a sudden surge of hope. Maybe, just maybe, there was a chance of success.

In the meantime Jared Kenyata, who had been chosen to

rush the Ra 'Na cleric to the meeting, bent to whisper in Blue's ear. The historian nodded, whispered something in return, and turned back to the meeting. Sister Andromeda was in the process of wrapping up a long, mostly self-serving string of lies, and he couldn't wait for her to finish. Here, at *this* meeting, history could be made. But only if the right information was made available at the right time . . . something that shouldn't be left to chance.

Franklin was going to wind up as the coalition's leader, there wasn't much doubt about that, especially given the fact that Rul, Smith, and he had already committed themselves to the politician's candidacy. Now, assuming that just one of the others did likewise, the question of leadership would be settled. So, looking ahead, what Franklin needed was a rallying point, something upon which everyone could agree, and Blue had it, or thought he did. The introduction of Med Tech Shu and the birth catalyst had set the table . . . now to serve the meal.

"And so," Sister Andromeda said with what she hoped was the right amount of dramatic flair, "I wish to nominate Alexander Franklin to be the leader of our coalition!"

There was polite applause as Blue, Smith, and Dro Rul indicated their approval, and Storm joined in.

"I second Sister Andromeda's nomination," Blue said, "and move that we solicit other nominations."

At that point the only other individual likely to make an alternative nomination was Doo-Nol, who, having been humiliated at the hands of slaves, no longer took the process seriously. So, with no other nominations to consider, Blue called for a voice vote and got one. "All those in favor of Alexander Franklin as president pro tem, subject to the laws of the United States of America and to the will of the people as made known through the will of their duly elected representatives, please say 'aye.' "

Dro Rul could have made an objection, could have

pointed out that he and his people weren't citizens of the United States of America, but chose not to. There was a ragged chorus of "ayes," followed by light applause.

Franklin, for whom power had long been something akin to a social aphrodisiac, waited for the rush. It never came. Not after so many deaths, not against such incredible odds, not without Jina at his side.

Blue watched the politician's face, understood what he saw there, and felt a sense of rightness. Franklin had grown a great deal over the last few months. Who knew? Maybe the bastard could pull it off. The historian waited for the applause to fade and was quick to seize the moment. A leader had been chosen now for the focus. "If I could have your attention for a moment . . . Some of you know Pas Pol, the first being to discover the truth about the Sauron reproductive cycle and presently working with what Jared Kenyata refers to as the 'skunk works.' An intelligence organization dedicated to intercepting, translating, and analyzing Sauron communications. It seems there has been a rather interesting development, one which has relevance to earlier discussions and might suggest an area of focus. Fra Pol?"

Though not especially thrilled about the manner in which he had been rousted out of a warm bed, plopped onto the back of something Kenyata referred to as a dirt bike, and subjected to a fur-raising ride through the backwoods, only to be unceremoniously dumped next to a primitive road and forced to march through a swamp, the Ra 'Na understood the importance of the part he was about to play.

What he didn't understand, but was about to learn, was that Med Tech Shu was not only present, but standing in a shadow not fifty feet away. The diminutive Ra 'Na stepped out into a pool of light, heard someone gasp, and staggered as Shu charged out of the darkness. She threw her arms around the cleric, knocked him off his feet, and fell on top of him.

There was a moment of confusion as Manning stepped in to help both individuals to their feet. Shu, thoroughly embarrassed by the scene she had caused, backed away, while Pol was lifted up onto the plywood table. Dro Rul cocked one ear forward in a sign of bemusement. "I'm sure we're all glad to see Fra Pol—but suggest that we defer further demonstrations of affection until *after* his presentation."

Confused and embarrassed, Pol stood frozen at the center of the table. Rul attempted to ease the way. "So, Fra Pol, tell us about your efforts to intercept Sauron communications."

Pol's robe had worked its way upward during the fracas, and he pulled it down. "Yes, eminence . . . Working with others, such as friend Jared, I sought to intercept messages that would help the resistance counter the Saurons.

"There have been numerous successes, but one of the most notable took place not sixteen hours ago. Thanks to a series of intercepted transmissions, we learned that a site near a place called Anacortes has been selected for some sort of new installation.

"The supplies being off-loaded there include tanks, pipes, and a large quantity of chemicals. We also know that some slaves will be sent there, along with contingents of Fon and Kan."

"A factory," Storm said thoughtfully. "The bastards plan to build a factory and spew even more pollution into the Great Mother's bloodstream."

"Not just *any* factory," Deac Smith said feelingly, "but, given the type of materials mentioned, it sounds like a facility similar to what Med Tech Shu described earlier."

"Yes," Franklin agreed soberly. "A place where they can manufacture birth catalyst not thirty miles from the citadel itself."

"Not if we stop them," Blue put in. "*This* is the chance we've been waiting for, the opportunity upon which all of our efforts should be focused. Destroy the factory and we destroy them."

"Yes, but not too quickly," Andromeda put in. "The clock continues to tick. If we interfere *too* early, *too* effectively, the Saurons will build the plant somewhere else. A place we don't know about or can't reach."

"That's an important point," Dro Rul added. "Knowing the Saurons as I do, I can assure you that my people will be ordered to repair the orbital facility."

"Then order them to sabotage it," Franklin said grimly, "or prepare to die."

"I will," Rul responded, "but the odds are against us."

There was a long moment of silence which Cyan, silent until then, finally broke. "But what about what Doo-Nol said? If there are more citadels, ones we don't know about, there could be more catalyst factories as well."

Blue nodded. "Perhaps there are . . . But the fact that they plan to build a new plant at Anacortes, along with the fact that the skunk works team hasn't picked up anything else, would seem to argue against it. After all, why construct a new facility it you can simply increase production at the ones you already have? Still, we should attempt to confirm my hypothesis, lest the bugs hand us another surprise."

"What about the other citadel?" Storm asked. "What can we do about it?"

"Very little," Franklin answered. "Until such time as we can deal with the one on Hell Hill. In the meantime, perhaps Doo-Nol can be convinced to share whatever he knows."

"I'd be glad to have a little chat with him," Storm offered grimly, "since we're such good buddies and all."

That drew a laugh, and Franklin smiled. "Your offer has been duly noted. However, odds are that the very possibility of such a conversation will be sufficient to loosen Doo-Nol's tongue and get us what we need to know.

"In the meantime we need to wrap this session up, get the hell out of here, and prepare to fight. Because meetings like this one are extremely hazardous, Jared Kenyata, Fra Pol, and the other members of the skunk team will devise methods to solicit your views and keep you informed. In the meantime, remember this . . . As Lincoln once said, 'United we stand . . . divided we fall.' The future depends on *you*."

Outside, beyond the metal walls, the Cascade Mountains rose black against the pink dawn, and a new day began.

ABOARD THE SAURON DREADNOUGHT *HOK NOR AH*

Willy had never been on a spaceship before. Hell, truth be told, Willy had never been outside of LA before, except for the trip to Oregon when he was twelve, and that was a long time ago.

So, when the bug named Cam-Hoh ordered him to leave the shuttle, Willy, who no longer feared death, not after surviving so many things he shouldn't have, was happy to comply. He was in a spaceship! Damn! Who woulda believed it?

The girl named Angela sat one seat away, arms wrapped around bony knees, rocking back and forth. She was singing, or moaning, it wasn't clear which. Willy jerked her leash. The six-foot-long strap ended in a chromed choke chain. She struggled to breathe as the noose tightened around her throat. Grubby fingers worked to pull it loose. Willy tugged again. "Come on, bitch . . . it's time to get off this tub and take a look around. Get your butt in gear before the bugs break out the whips."

Angela pulled some slack into the choke chain and managed to stand. Her eyes were red, her nose ran 24/7, and her muscles liked to quiver.

Willy felt nothing but contempt for her. Angela was weak, Angela was stupid, and Angela had been put on Earth to use.

She was pretty, or had been, and still knew how to work it. Her father would have recognized the pout had he been there to see it. "Please, Willy, please? Just one line? I'll give you a blow job—whaddya say?"

The bug named Cam-Hoh clacked his pincers impatiently, and Willy jerked on the leash. "What do I say? I say hell no! Are you crazy? We're on a fucking spaceship for Christ's sake. This ain't no place for a blow job. Now come on before Mr. Hoh has a fucking heart attack. Jesus H. Christ, but you are one stupid fucking bitch."

With both hands on the choke chain, fighting to maintain some slack, Angela allowed herself to be pulled along, only peripherally aware of her surroundings. Only one thing mattered, and that was the white powder in the purple fanny pack belted around Willy's waist. For that powder, and the state it could induce, Angela would do anything.

Half a mile away, in a distant part of the ship, a pair of beings floated side by side. One, no less a being than Hak-Bin himself, was preoccupied by the fact that the nymph he thought of as "the little one" had been rather restless of late, something that caused a great deal of pain. Add the considerable demands of his office, the fact that things were not going particularly well, and there was little to take pleasure in.

Dro Tog, now honored by a position at the Sauron's side, fervently wished he were somewhere else. Especially given the fact that Hak-Bin had been increasingly irritable of late, had frequent bouts of flatulence, and smelled like rotting garbage.

But it was his own fault, the prelate knew that, and cursed his own ambitious heart. Rather than the responsibility-free sinecure that the Ra 'Na had originally imagined, it turned out that the position of Grand Vizier entailed actual work and the need to produce results. Not every day, thanks be to the Great One, but with a certain amount of frequency.

Like most of Tog's better ideas, this one had not originated with him but with one of his subordinates, a rather useful operative named Dio. It had been Dio who, in his capacity of technical adviser, happened to be present when a Kan raiding party stumbled across a colony of human addicts hiding in the ruins of Los Angeles and had the sense to grasp their potential.

Later, in a brilliantly written thesis titled "A program of chemical incentives," Dio had described a plan by which the subslave race could be to motivated to willingly, even joyfully, bear the burdens for which they were so clearly intended.

Yes, the title was rather lengthy, but useful nonetheless, since it provided Tog with nearly everything he needed to know without the tedious necessity of actually reading the report, something the prelate was reluctant to do. Especially if doing so would interfere with his afternoon nap. Now, as the critical moment approached, Tog wondered if it had been wise to put so much trust in Dio's summary and whether there was anything else that he should know.

But the lock opened, a pair of humans tumbled into the compartment, and it was too late for additional research. All the Ra 'Na could do was try to appear confident and hope for the best.

Willy, who had never experienced zero-gee conditions before, and had not been warned to expect them, felt the leash jerk tight as Angela performed an unintentional somersault, slammed into a metal bulkhead, and struggled to right herself.

It took the better part of five minutes for the humans to discover that minimal movements worked best and position themselves in front of the ominous-looking Sauron. Angela, for whom the whole thing was more than a little surreal, wrinkled her nose. "Jeez . . . who cut the cheese? This place stinks!"

Willy, grateful that the addict had not been equipped with a translator, told her to "shut the fuck up," produced the same shit-eating grin that had worked on Miss Cooper in the seventh grade, and eyed the strange-looking twosome that floated in front of him. The black motherfucker was in charge, no doubt about that, and the furry fuck was number two. "Hi! My name is Willy. Which one of you studs goes by the handle of Tog?"

"My name is Tog," the Ra 'Na said with every bit of dignity he could muster. "*Grand Vizier* Tog."

Willy, who had no idea what a Grand Vizier was, said, "Cool. Okay, this is Angela. She's a cokehead."

"A cokehead?" Hak-Bin inquired. "What does that mean?"

"It means she has a Jones for coke. You know, cocaine, crack, snow, flake, or blow. She loves the stuff and can't function without it. So, if you want cooperative slaves, and the Dio dude told me that you do, then feed 'em coke."

It *sounded* good, like the very thing that could solve some of his problems, but Hak-Bin had been lied to before. "Claims are one thing . . . but reality speaks for itself. Look at your cokehead. She twitches like a being possessed. I need slaves who can work—not creatures such as this."

Ironically, the nymph chose that particular moment to stretch, and it was Hak-Bin rather than Angela who produced an involuntary twitch. Willy continued his pitch. "Angela is a bit strung out," the dealer admitted cheerfully, "but that's *without* her blow. Give her what she wants, what she needs, and everything will be different. Watch this."

So saying, Willy withdrew a packet of cocaine from the pouch at his waist. The dose was already sealed in plastic, which meant that by inserting one of the thin red cocktail straws that the dealer often provided to customers, and by sealing the opening with a rubber band, the pusher created a zero-gee delivery system.

Thankful that the pain had started to fade, Hak-Bin watched in fascination as the very sight of the packet seemed to fill the previously despondent addict with newfound vitality. She literally begged. "Please, Willy, please. I'll do anything you want."

"Sure," the dealer said soothingly, "here take this. You'll feel better soon."

Oblivious to the aliens who were watching her, Angela took the rig with shaking hands, stuck the straw up her nose, and made a loud snorting sound.

Willy, who took pride in his knowledge of the products he sold, supplied the narration. "The short term effects will appear in a matter of minutes . . . and last for minutes or hours. Taken in small amounts, say a hundred milligrams or so, the customer feels alert, energetic, and talkative. Then, assuming they receive the correct dose, many people can perform simple physical and intellectual tasks more quickly—which enables them to get by on less sleep."

And indeed, even as Willy spoke, Hak-Bin saw a look of pleasure steal across Angela's face. Her eyelids fluttered, her color improved, and energy seemed to seep under her skin. Then, as if reborn, she smiled and took a look around. "Jeez, Willy, where the hell are we?"

The Sauron was convinced. Here, at the tip of his pincers, was the solution for most of his problems. Once addicted, the slaves would not only do whatever they were told, they would do it better, faster, and with less rest. "Grand Vizier Tog, I am most impressed. I really must congratulate you on bringing this substance to light."

Tog had seen others promise more than they could deliver and ultimately pay the price. He felt a sudden stab of fear. Had he taken the time to read the entire report, he would have been better positioned to gauge the veracity of the human's claims. He cleared his throat. "Thank you, eminence. This, ah, *medication* does show promise. Nothing is perfect, however—as slave Willy will attest."

The statement was a complete shot in the dark, an assumption based on Tog's lifelong experience, but soon paid off.

Willy shrugged. "Sure. Users can experience mood swings, bouts of paranoia, and weight loss, but who gives a shit? We're talking about slaves here."

Hak-Bin was familiar with the cramps by then and knew when they were coming. He waved a pincer. "Slave Willy is correct. The trade-offs are acceptable. The proposal is hereby accepted. The audience is over."

The Sauron waited for the lesser beings to leave, felt the cramps begin, and soon wished he were dead.

NEAR THE MAYAN RUINS OF NAKABE, GUATEMALA

Dr. Maria Sanchez-Jones felt a momentary sense of relief as the heavy metal door closed and the resulting thud reverberated down the temple's long narrow hallway.

Having been a member of the day shift, and never having been inside the temple at night, Jones was unprepared for how spooky the inside of it could be. What light there was emanated from a lichenlike life form that Ra 'Na technicians had sprayed onto the walls. It provided a green luminescent glow. How long would it be until the alien life form found its way outside the walls? And to what effect? Would other indigenous species be forced to fight for their lives as well?

But there was no time for ecological considerations, not with a horde of homicidal Kan warriors to worry about, so Jones waved her companion forward. "Come on! The bugs will come through that door any minute now—and I want to be somewhere else."

Blackley followed. "But what about their promise? Dun-Dar said any slave who made it inside would go free."

"And your mother promised that the tooth fairy would

come in the night," Jones replied sarcastically. "We killed a Kan—what do you expect? A medal?"

Kevin Blackley didn't know what to expect as he followed the academic down the corridor. Jones was jogging, and he did likewise. Did the former beauty queen know what she was doing? He hoped so.

Sheer walls rose to either side. Jones noticed that the "cells," because that's what they resembled, were completely featureless except for some unconnected pipes and what could only be described as a drainage channel that fed the trench located at the center of the main passageway. None of which seemed consistent with a temple, but the Saurons were aliens, so who the hell knew?

Based on previous observations, the social scientist knew that there were no elevators or stairs within the building, just jump platforms that protruded from the interior walls and provided the Saurons with a place to pause prior to the next leap.

The single exception was a spiral ramp located within each tower and presumably placed there so that any Sauron who was unable to jump could shuffle his way to whichever level he chose.

There were many floors, all pretty much alike, except for the fact that the cubicles on the topmost level were slightly larger than the rest. Why? Only the chits knew for sure. But all of that was subsumed as the door opened, a contingent of Kan burst through the opening, and Jones ran for her life.

Dart guns banged, Blackley heard a projectile whir past his head, and realized his body would shield the woman ahead. Was the screening effect intentional? Had Jones *planned* it that way? The academic was more intelligent than he was, the ex-businessman knew that, so anything was possible. Of course he'd been smart enough to align himself with a winner—so he deserved some credit as well.

Jones listened for the sound of an involuntary grunt, the sudden exhalation of air that would signal Blackley's death, didn't hear anything, and was somewhat surprised when she rounded a corner, entered the cul-de-sac, and discovered that her companion was still alive.

"What now?" Blackley panted, looking all around. "Those bastards are two, maybe three jumps away. Where's the exit?"

"Right *there*," Jones replied, pointing to a partially assembled jumble of plumbing.

Blackley followed her finger, saw that one of the pipes stuck straight up out of the floor and was larger than all the rest. A single glance was sufficient to confirm what some part of him already knew. There was no way that he would fit.

Jones was small, *very* small, which was one of the things that he liked about her. Small women were more feminine somehow, or so it seemed to Blackley, and that turned him on. So, while the mouth of the pipe was sufficiently large to accept her tiny frame, it was too small for him, something she must have known from the beginning. He looked from the opening back to her. "You rotten bitch."

There was a double slap as two Kan feet landed nearby. Jones nodded as if in agreement, stepped up onto the pipe, and straddled the hole. She looked him in the eye as she crossed her arms. "Sorry, Kevin, but life sucks."

Then, bringing her heels together, the anthropologist was gone.

Blackley discovered that he still had time to turn, still had time to raise his hands in a futile attempt to ward off the darts, and still had time to object. "No! It isn't fair!"

And it *wasn't* fair, but the Kan fired the t-gun anyway, and something hit Blackley's chest. The human felt his back smack into the wall, wondered where the bright light was coming from, and was suddenly gone.

The Kan, one of Wen-Opp's longtime messmates, took a long slow look around. One slave was dead—where was the other? More warriors arrived, and a noncom stared into the tube. It was pitch-black inside and too small for someone like Blackley. He looked up. "Spread out! Search every level! The soft skin must be found."

Meanwhile, far below the Sauron's flat feet, Jones continued to fall. Unfortunately, the inside of the drainage pipe was not entirely smooth. Ridges marked the places where sections of tubing were imperfectly joined, dents pushed their way in, feeder lines poked into the pipe. The flaws ripped the woman's skin, slammed her back and forth, and threatened permanent injury.

Then, just when Jones became convinced that the torture would never end, it did. The anthropologist fell free of the pipe and had just enough time to recognize the large cavern for what it was before her feet hit the surface of the water. There was an almighty splash followed by the cool wet embrace of the water. The alien lichen, if that's what it was, had been carried down through the temple's storm drains and into the river over which the structure had been constructed. Now, having already colonized the rocky walls, the light-emitting material lit the areas below and above the surface of the water with the same greenish glow.

Jones, welcomed the illumination and kicked with her legs. Her head broke the surface, she sucked warm wet air into her lungs, and looked up. The pipe hung like a long accusatory finger pointed straight at her. There were no signs of pursuit, not that she expected there to be, not given the tube's diameter.

Blackley was dead by then, Jones was sure of that, and felt sorry for him. Sorry, but less than contrite. The truth was that the horny bastard would have died anyway, if not because of her, then for some other woman. That's what Jones told herself at any rate—and heard no objections.

Now, safe for the moment at least, the academic allowed the relatively gentle current to carry her downriver. She saw the point where the water flowed out under the temple's foundation and kicked to center herself on the opening.

Rainwater, some of which had been channeled by the partially completed drainage system, and some of which had found its own way down through natural cracks and crevices, dripped, poured, and gushed from above. It made a splattering noise, thumped the top of her head, and churned the water's surface as Jones passed below.

Then, as she pushed out into the rain, Jones experienced a sudden sense of joy. There was no way to know what lay ahead, but here, now, she was free.

Lightning strobed the horizon, thunder rolled across the land, and the river flowed toward the sea.

4

DEATH DAY MINUS 54

MONDAY, JUNE 8, 2020

Is life so dear, or peace so sweet, as to be purchased at the price of chains and slavery? Forbid it Almighty God!—I know not what course others may take, but as for me, give me liberty, or give me death!

—PATRICK HENRY
Speech to the Virginia Convention, March 23, 1775

HELL HILL

Sex was important to José Amocar, *very* important, which was why he spent so much time preparing for it. First came the period of anticipation, at least three or four days, during which he would intentionally think about sex and abstain. No easy task for someone who liked to masturbate at least once a day—and often took advantage of the cheap blow jobs available in Hell Hill's many alleyways.

Having maximized his desire Amocar would visit one of the hill's many brothels. His favorite, an establishment called the G-Spot, catered to heterosexuals. The person who ran the place, a woman named Flo, knew what Amocar liked: No conversation, no foreplay, and no deviation from his script.

Various women had served the agent—and all reported

the same thing. They would be positioned on hands and knees facing the head of the bed. Amocar would enter the cubicle, approach the prostitute from behind, and drop his trousers. Then, already aroused, he would enter them. Vaginally in some cases—but anally in most.

Occasionally Amocar would lean forward to fondle the woman's breasts, but more often than not the agent was content to knead their buttocks and grunt obscenities.

Most of the prostitutes were happy to follow instructions, but a few simply forgot or sought to pleasure themselves. Deviations of that sort were always met with anger, a slap on the ass, and an admonition to "knock it off."

Flo had a theory about that, about Amocar's need for control, but knew it didn't matter. Not so long as the creep behaved himself and paid his bill.

So that's where Amocar was, just emerging from a session at the G-Spot, when a clutch of five heavily armed Kan dropped off a neighboring roof. The agent saw them, tried to get out of the way, but was quickly hemmed in. The noncom in charge, an individual named Dor-Oll, spoke via translator. "Lord Hak-Bin will speak with you now . . . Come with us."

There were people all around. Some stared openly while others pretended not to see. Would word of the encounter get back to HQ? Yes, of course it would. Amocar pitched his voice low. "Hit me. Do it now."

By the standards of his kind Dor-Oll looked surprised. "Strike you? Whatever for?"

"So the other slaves will believe that you forced me to come," Amocar growled. "Now hit me."

Dor-Oll couldn't grin, not really, yet Amocar would have sworn that the Sauron's lips curved upward at the corners. The back-graspered blow came with unexpected speed. The clublike extremity slammed into the side of the security agent's head and sent him reeling. Amocar stumbled, nearly fell, and barely managed to maintain his footing. He brought a hand up to the side of his face. It came away red with blood. He thought about the .9mm stuck in the waistband of his pants but knew better than to reach for it. *"You bastard."*

There was no way to know exactly how the words were translated, but there was no mistaking the warrior's reaction. The second blow struck the opposite side of Amocar's face, knocked him off his feet, and dumped him to the ground.

Now, as the security agent picked himself up, there was little doubt as to what Manning would hear. The bugs stopped Amocar, shoved him around, and took him into custody. One entire side of his face was swollen, and he had a black eye. That being the case, and with no desire to suffer further, the agent allowed his head to hang while they marched him away.

One brave soul yelled, "God bless you!" but other than that Amocar's journey from the brothel to the nearest observation tower went unremarked.

There was one bystander who watched the byplay with little or no sympathy whatsoever. A woman who, except for her unusual stature, looked like hundreds even thousands of female slaves. She wore a dirty gray scarf over her head, a much-washed dress, and carried a bundle of firewood. She offered it to everyone who passed, hoping that none of them would accept. Her name was Jill Ji-Hoon, ex–F.B.I. Agent Jill Ji-Hoon, and Amocar was her hobby. Besides the fact that the bastard was a misogynist, he was dirty. Not dirt dirty, which he certainly was, but on the take. All she had to do was prove it. Now, as the pathetic piece of crap urged the Saurons to hit him, Ji-Hoon knew she was onto something. Something good. The Kan led Amocar away and she followed.

One of the Taggers had scored the observation tower during the night, and a slave had been assigned to cover the

graffiti. The woman liked the assignment and was determined to make it last. The paintbrush made a slapping
sound as it hit the concrete.

The entryway, which was curved to match the tower's
wall, opened as the party approached. The Kan paused long
enough to allow a Fon-mounted Ra 'Na technician to exit
and gestured for Amocar to enter. The human felt rather
than saw the door close behind him. Meanwhile, unable to
follow Amocar inside, Ji-Hoon found a place on the opposite
side of the street. Assuming Amocar was dirty, he'd be back.

Amocar had never been inside one of the alien structures
before and immediately noticed that the interior light level
was lower than he would have preferred. The warriors morphed from tan to gray as they shuffled onto the semicircular
platform. A buzzer buzzed, the platform seemed to leap up
the shaft, and Amocar felt his knees buckle. It seemed as if
the Kan had been waiting for that because they made sounds
that might have been equivalent to laughter.

The shaft was little more than a vertiginous blur as the
lift carried them upward. The human had barely recovered
from the sudden acceleration when the platform coasted to
a stop. Amocar knew without being told that he had arrived
within the bulbous structure at the top of the tower.

Fear trickled into the pit of the security agent's stomach
as he thought about the impending meeting. Not because
he'd done anything wrong, but because Hak-Bin was a crazy
bastard, and there was no way to know what the geek might
do.

Still, the meeting was at *his* suggestion, and that should
count for something. Especially given the fact that he was
ready to feed the bug some heavy-duty shit. The warriors
escorted the human along one of the spokelike corridors that
connected the tower's core with the outside observation platform.

Amocar's escort, now reduced to only two warriors, ordered him to make a sharp right hand turn. He did so, stepped through an open door, and found himself in a long triangular room. The Kan stayed out in the hallway.

What looked like a Barcalounger occupied the center of the space. A woman of Asian decent stood next to it. She was attractive in a clean-scrubbed sort of way, and Amocar visualized her naked. Her voice was flat and neutral. "Have you been here before? No? Then do as I say. Sit in the chair. Good . . . Now, wait while I place the hood over your head, and slip your hands into the gauntlets."

Amocar recognized the setup as some sort of virtual-reality (VR) rig similar to those in many people's homes. Judging from the cables that snaked back and forth across the floor, the fur balls had found a way to hook the human equipment in with their own. Amocar backed into the chair and sat down. "So, baby, how would you like to sit on my face?"

"About as much as I would like to ram a red-hot poker through my right eye," the woman replied calmly. "Now shut up or I'll wire this backward. The feedback would fry your brain."

Amocar didn't know if such a thing was possible but didn't care to find out. Hak-Bin wasn't planning to meet with him in person, that much was obvious, so the link would be critical. No point in getting his ass in a wringer over a piece of tail.

It took less than a minute for the woman to connect Amocar, check her work, and back out of the room. Amocar lifted the hood, took a quick peek, and discovered he was alone. The agent was about to point out that nothing was happening when darkness rolled over him. The experience was unlike anything the security agent had ever experienced before.

First came a horrible fall into nothingness, like death, or what death might be. Then, just as Amocar thought he was about to throw up, something snapped. Now he was somewhere else. Or *someone* was somewhere else, since he felt a distinct sense of displacement, and the sensory feedback was wrong. Things *looked* different, *smelled* different, and *felt* different. His body was weightless. His vision, which seemed to consist of two slightly overlapping views of the same scene, made him dizzy.

There were lights, two of them, which floated like suns in the blackness of space. Hovering below them, and bathed in blue-green luminescence, floated a badly misshapen mass. Whatever it was spoke, and it was only then, when Amocar heard the voice that he recognized it as belonging to Hak-Bin. "So, human, you wanted to speak with me. Here I am. You look good as a Fon."

Amocar looked down and realized that the virtual him had been rendered as a functionary and knew why everything felt so strange. The aliens had used the modified VR system to momentarily transform him into a bug! He struggled to sound coherent. "Thank you, excellency."

The dark mass waved something that might have been a pincer. "Enough of what you would call 'small talk.' Make your report."

Amocar swallowed, didn't like the way it felt, and launched into a carefully rehearsed account of the sawmill summit. He listed each of the participants, summarized the meeting's contents, and covered the ad hoc election. Franklin had betrayed *his* race . . . and the master race as well.

Hak-Bin listened with a steadily growing sense of anger. His first thought was to round the slaves up, put all of them to death, and complete the citadels without their help.

But as emotionally satisfying as that might be, he knew better than actually to do it. First, because the Fon would never be able to complete the structures in time; second, because any humans who managed to survive would pose a threat to the nymphs; and, third, because something of that sort would signal weakness.

No, brute force was out of the question. What then? The answers, because a number of possibilities presented themselves, were delightfully subtle. They also played into and were consistent with certain plans already in motion. Careful to conceal the extent of his concern from the human spy, Hak-Bin adopted a conspiratorial tone. "This is valuable intelligence. You were correct to bring it to my attention. A female will be delivered to the usual location. Do with her as you will.

"In the meantime, be advised that certain disruptions will occur. A significant number of slaves will be moved from the area where you are located to work on projects nearby. Franklin, and retainers such as yourself, will stay.

"For reasons of no concern to you, the need for individuals such as Franklin will be greatly reduced. Because of that, not to mention the extent of his treachery, you may go ahead and kill him."

Amocar, his mind very much on the woman, licked chitinous lips. They were hard and dry. "No problem, excellency. I'll wait till he goes to sleep, slit his throat, and slip out the back."

"*No,*" Hak-Bin replied emphatically, "you won't. Such a death could be concealed. Others might continue to act in Franklin's name for weeks or even months to come. He must die in public, where hundreds if not thousands can see. Word will spread, and the slaves will do as they are told. Meanwhile, with no one to hold the various factions together, the resistance will fall apart."

"Of course," Amocar agreed lamely, "that's what I meant."

"Good," the Sauron replied. "In the meantime there are other matters to attend to. Start by killing the one called Clan Leader Storm. That should intimidate her peers and cause them to reconsider their flirtation with the so-called resistance movement."

Amocar felt ice water flow into the Fon-body's veins. Locating the eco-nut, and getting close enough to kill her, would be a lot more difficult than offing Franklin. He couldn't say that, however, not to a bug, and specially not to *this* bug. "Yes, eminence, I will do my best. And the other leaders?"

"The others will remain untouched," Hak-Bin replied, "for the moment. Later, after you deal with Franklin, the situation may change. The only thing worse than having resistance leaders is *not* knowing who they are. Do you understand?"

Amocar didn't have the foggiest idea what the chit was talking about, but nodded anyway. "Yes, excellency."

"I'm gratified to hear it," Hak-Bin finished. "You have your orders—now carry them out."

Amocar was about to produce another, "Yes, your eminence," when the connection was severed, his stomach lurched, and he found himself back in his own body. The attendant appeared and disconnected the snakelike black leads. "And a good time was had by all?"

"It couldn't have been better," Amocar lied. "Was it good for you?"

"Not really," the woman replied, "not while you're alive."

Amocar stood, and was about to backhand the woman across the mouth, when a Kan shuffled into the room. She smiled defiantly. "Yes? Was there something else?"

The security agent made a face and followed the warrior outside. The Kan delivered Amocar to ground level and turned him loose.

Still hiding in plain sight, but without the bundle of firewood she had been forced to sell fifteen minutes earlier, Jill Ji-Hoon watched her fellow agent emerge from the tower, blink in the bright sunlight, and hurry away. The fact that Amocar had left under his own power, without so much as a Kan escort, spoke volumes. The question was not *if* he had been spying for the Saurons, but for how long? From the beginning most likely—which meant the bugs knew about the resistance and its plans. Well, there was nothing Ji-Hoon could do about that, but she could sure as hell let them know about Amocar.

Her mind made up, the tall rangy woman left her spot opposite the tower, faded into the crowd, and seemed to disappear.

HELL HILL

Ever since the day on which Sool had come to the Sauron warrior's aid, even going so far as to protect him from the human crowd, things had been just a little bit easier. Not much . . . but a little.

Evidence of the high esteem in which the Saurons held the doctor could be seen not only in the red ear tag that freed her from digging ditches, but in the fact that none of the patients outside her clinic had been rousted since that day and none had been shot at from the observation towers. In fact, a wary sort of friendship had developed between Sool and the Kan who ruled that particular sector of Hell Hill. His name was Nee-Pal, and when Dixie told Sool that the officer was waiting outside, the doctor interrupted an examination to go out and speak with him.

The ever-present queue had migrated as far from Nee-Pal as possible. They watched as the doctor emerged from the clinic, spotted the Sauron, and went to meet him. The alien turned as the Sool approached. "Slave Sool."

Though not exactly collegial—the greeting was polite. Sool inclined her head. "File Leader Nee-Pal."

The bug was all business—and the translation sounded flat. "Be advised that approximately seventy-five percent of the slaves working on this temple will be marched to new locations tomorrow morning. You can remain or go. The choice is yours."

The Sauron waved a pincer toward the clinic. "*If* you decide to go, there is a need to pack your equipment. That is
all." So saying, the chit turned, took a forty-foot jump, and
was gone.

Moments later, back in the clinic, Dixie reacted to the
news. "So, what are we going to do?"

"*We?*"

"Do you need me?"

"Yes, desperately."

Dixie grinned. "That's what I thought. So, 'we.'"

Sool gave the nurse a hug. "Thanks, Dixie, you're the best.
We go where our patients go . . . That's the way I see it.
Better start packing. I'll put the word out. Perhaps some of
our ex-patients will lend us a hand."

The nurse nodded. "How 'bout friends? There's no way
to know who's going and who's staying."

Sool raised an eyebrow. "Is that your way of telling me
to throw myself at Jack Manning's feet?"

Dixie laughed. "In a word, 'yes.'"

Sool sighed. "I screwed up, I admit that, but what's the
point? He has Franklin to take care of—and I have my patients."

Dixie decided to let the matter drop. Perhaps later, after
she had time to think about it, Sool would reconsider. In
the meantime there was packing to do. Lots of it. The
women went to work.

HELL HILL

Even though he was a slave, and working under what he
considered to be primitive conditions, Manning still had
paperwork to do. That's why he was all too happy to put
the current duty roster aside and welcome Jill Ji-Hoon into
his shabby work space. He pointed across the messy desk.
"Kick those boots out of the way, dump yesterday's lunch

into the trash can, and turn that bucket upside down. It makes a passable stool."

The ex–FBI agent eyed the container in question, knew her knees would stick up in front of her face, and shook her head. "I'll stand if it's all the same to you, sir."

"Suit yourself," Manning replied, leaning back in the government surplus chair, "but forget the 'sir' stuff. What's on your mind?"

"It's Amocar, sir. I have reason to suspect that he's working for the bugs."

In spite of the fact that Manning had little to no use for Amocar and would have been delighted to get rid of the slimy slob, alarm bells began to ring. Did Ji-Hoon have the goods on Amocar? The *real* goods? Or was this about the endless shit details *El Segundo* liked to pass her way? Something the security chief had monitored but didn't want to mess with unless he absolutely had to. If she had something solid, then good, Amocar would go down. But, unit cohesion was important, *very* important, and there was no room for vendettas. Manning leaned forward and the chair squeaked. His eyes narrowed. "That's a serious charge, Agent Ji-Hoon—a *very* serious charge. If you have proof, let's hear it. If not, then get back to work."

Ji-Hoon swallowed and stood a little taller. "I followed Agent Amocar to a place called the G-Spot. As he left a group of Kan arrived and escorted him away."

"*Escorted?*" Manning inquired softly, "As in 'let's go have a beer?' Or escorted as in 'come with us or we'll blow your head off?' "

The ex–FBI agent shrugged. "The interaction was friendly at first. Then, realizing the need for a cover story, Amocar instructed the Kan to hit him. They complied."

"Yeah," Manning replied, "I guess they did. I saw the poor bastard about twenty minutes ago and sent him to see Dr. Sool."

Ji-Hoon felt her stomach sink. Trust the little weasel to see Manning first! This was an uphill battle, that much was obvious, but all she could do was see it through. "They got a bit carried away—but the fact remains: He asked for it."

Manning looked her in the eye. "You were close enough to hear that?"

"Well, no," Ji-Hoon answered reluctantly, "but I could read his lips and see his gestures. Amocar *told* the bugs to hit him."

"So, you can read lips?"

"Yes," Ji-Hoon said defiantly, *"I can."*

"Fabulous," Manning said sarcastically. "Well, go on . . . Let's hear the rest."

Well aware that the security chief had already made up his mind, but unable to extricate herself from the situation, Ji-Hoon could do little but continue. The rest of the report sounded more lame than the first.

"That's it?" Manning inquired. "You saw him enter the tower then leave?"

"Yes, sir," Ji-Hoon said stolidly. "I saw him enter the tower, stay long enough to spill his guts, *and leave of his own volition.*"

"So noted," Manning said. "With all due respect to your background, training, and obvious sincerity, I can't hang my number two out to dry on a single person's unsubstantiated testimony. I know Amocar is a jerk. But we're stuck with the creep until we can hang something substantial around his neck. Do you read me?"

Ji-Hoon read him all right. She ground the words between clenched teeth. "Sir, yes, sir." The agent did a military-style about-face and left the office.

Plan A had failed and failed miserably. Well, that's what Plan B is for Ji-Hoon told herself. The boss man needs evidence, so I'll go find him some evidence.

Manning felt mixed emotions as the woman left. Her

story was interesting but lacked substantiation. He'd been right to blow her off. Or had he? Something, he wasn't sure what, wiggled in the pit of his stomach.

ABOARD THE SAURON DREADNOUGHT *HOK NOR AH*

Pinned to the carefully stabilized metal surface by the floating lights, his swollen body laid bare for the other Sauron to examine, Hak-Bin was forced to remain silent while the other Zin poked, probed, and prodded.

His name was Ott-Mar, his title was that of birthmaster, and upon his narrow shoulders rested responsibility for the biological aspects of the great birthing. A role for which he had prepared himself since his own birth hundreds of years before.

It was during those many years of study, those long periods of time when individuals like Hak-Bin had been free to practice their disciplines, that Ott-Mar had nudged the boundaries of racial knowledge and eventually pushed some of them back. All without the knowledge of the egotistical Ra 'Na.

Now, armed with the results of painstaking experimentation, and hoping to advance his line, the Zin had allowed himself to be drawn into the dark netherworld of Sauron politics. A place where once entangled it was almost impossible to escape.

But thoughts such as those were like dangerous gusts of wind—variables that could wreck an otherwise perfect jump. That's why Ott-Mar pushed the errant thoughts away and pulled the black shroudlike garment back into place. Then, with his patient's dignity partially restored, the birthmaster coughed three words into a microphone.

Hak-Bin felt a tremendous sense of relief as zero-gee conditions were restored, waited while Ott-Mar freed his body from the table's surface, and sought an upright position. Then, floating in what were now familiar conditions, the

Zin moved to restore what he saw as the correct interpersonal relationship. One in which it was *he*, not the birthmaster, who controlled the agenda. "So," Hak-Bin said in what he hoped was a lighthearted fashion, "what do you think?"

Ott-Mar, for whom the matter was very serious indeed, made no attempt to respond in kind. "Time is short. We can wait no more . . . You must undergo the treatment within the next few rotations, surrender to the nymph, or accept the cessation of your line. The choice is up to you."

There was silence for a moment as Hak-Bin accepted what he already knew: This was the final decision point. His voice was gruff. "There is no choice, not a *real* one, so let's get on with it."

Ott-Mar, who wasn't sure whether he wanted to trial his theories or escape from them, felt both excitement and fear. But, rather than grant Hak-Bin more power than he already had, the physician sought to conceal his emotions. "Excellent. Appropriate facilities have been established at a place the humans call Nakabe, Guatemala."

Hak-Bin offered the Sauron the equivalent of a frown. "What's the point? I am comfortable here."

"Certain unpleasantries must be dealt with," Ott-Mar replied vaguely, "not to mention the issue of privacy. Besides, what your staff will describe as a planetary inspection tour will help quiet the rumors."

Hak-Bin liked both the idea and the timing. The transfer of slaves from what the humans referred to as Hell Hill, to other locations would serve not only to rip their underground society apart, it would keep his subordinates busy while he underwent the necessary treatments. "It shall be as you say, Ott-Mar. My life, and that of my nymph, depend on you."

The ghosts of birthmasters long dead gibbered in Ott-Mar's ears. "No!" they insisted. "Stop this madness!" But it was too late. The leap had been made, and only the landing remained.

HELL HILL

The sun threw rays of pink light up over the Cascade Mountains as Sauron horns began to groan, searchlights stabbed the streets, and Fon functionaries moved in among the stacks. Some carried Ra 'Na technicians high on their backs while others led packs of human overseers. Their whips cracked, and their heavily amplified voices echoed back and forth among the cubes as they rousted the first shift out of their beds.

Not the *entire* shift, since there had been rumors, and some of the slaves were already up. Not only *up*, but packed and ready to go. It was a gamble, they knew that, since hardly a day went by that some sort of fanciful bullshit didn't make the rounds. "A woman saw Jesus . . . we'll get a day off . . . the Saurons are going to die soon."

There were dozens of rumors a day, and most of them were false. That's why thousands of people ignored the scuttlebutt warning of a major relocation and went off to bed. But others, especially those with an analytical bent, noticed some unusual activity. It seemed as though an unusual number of subtasks had been completed within the last few days, more Kan were evident, and the overseers had been to a lot of meetings lately. That's why some of the slaves put two and two together, came up with four, and were ready to go when the Saurons arrived. They didn't have much, but what they had was precious, and filled their makeshift packs.

Others, those who weren't prepared, were forced to leave without their meager belongings. Some raised their voices in protest, or tried to return home, and were used as examples. The steady pop, pop, pop of t-guns was reminiscent of the Fourth of July, and Franklin, who stood practically nose to nose with a Kan officer, felt as if each dart had ripped through *him*. The first sign that something unusual was about to occur took place when Manning's sentries reported that four files of Kan had taken up positions around the Presidential Complex and sealed it off.

Then, while efforts were under way to make contact with various members of the Sauron command structure, the evictions started. Now, in an effort to be with what he saw as his constituents, Franklin tried to bully his way out. "How dare you block my path! Hak-Bin will hear of this!"

"Hak-Bin gave the orders," the officer replied mildly. "Now return to your quarters. Or would you like me to shoot half a dozen slaves to prove that I'm serious?"

"I could grease him," Manning offered conversationally, his voice pitched intentionally low. "I think we can drop most of the bastards before they know what hit them." The security officer and his team had been on high alert for hours by that time, and all of them were heavily armed. Just one of the reasons why the Kan made no attempt actually to enter the complex.

For one brief moment Franklin toyed with the idea of a balls-to-the-wall breakout. But what then? Once they broke free of the complex additional Kan would be summoned, Manning and his team would almost certainly be killed, and the protest would soon be over. Even worse was the fact that the resistance might very well come apart, the slaves would be slaughtered, and the nymphs would be born. No, he must hold his temper and wait for the right moment to rebel.

Having rejected force, the politician tried another tack. "No, there's no need for additional violence. In fact there's no need for any violence whatsoever . . . Please allow me to talk with the slaves. I'll convince them to cooperate."

"They *will* cooperate," the Kan replied, "or they will die. Now, return to your quarters and take the other slaves with you. Resist, and I will call on air support. A single bomb would be more than sufficient to destroy your pathetic pile of crates."

Asad's 12-gauge made a clacking sound as the operative pumped a shell into the chamber. Franklin waved the agent back. His teeth were clenched so tightly the words barely escaped. "You heard what he said . . . Everybody back off."

The Kan watched impassively as the humans withdrew, waited until they were inside, and turned away. The cordon of warriors remained where they were.

Once inside the residence Franklin hurried up to the heavily fortified roof, where he could look out over the surrounding stacks. Manning followed, and the two men stood side by side as thousands of slaves were forced out of their shelters and into the streets. Dust rose to thicken the air, whips cracked, and people wailed.

Then, like percussion in a symphony from hell, buildings began to explode. Manning counted five such explosions spread out over an extremely wide area, watched the columns of debris fly upward, and wondered what the Saurons were up to. Franklin thought he knew. "Look! Isn't that where Sister Andromeda's first church was established? And over there—didn't she have a chapel there?"

Manning thought so but wasn't sure.

Meanwhile bodies, some bearing packs, many having little more than the clothes on their backs, continued to trickle out of alleyways and join the stream.

The fleshy flood moved quickly at first, but each additional human body added to the congestion, and friction slowed the river to a crawl. That's when black overseers armed with whips and electric cattle prods waded into the crowd. Was that intentional? Yes, Franklin felt very sure that it was, and cursed Hak-Bin with every swear word he knew.

The crowd swirled wherever the African-Americans appeared as they sought to evade the slash of the whips and cried for mercy. Franklin watched a woman stumble, saw her baby fall, and the crowd surge forward. Seconds later, as an opening appeared, he saw the pathetic bundle of rags lying in their wake. "When?" The politician asked himself, unaware that he had spoken out loud. "When will it end?"

"When we kill the bastards," Manning answered grimly. "When every single one of them is dead."

ABOARD THE SAURON DREADNOUGHT *HOK NOR AH*

The lights in the compartment were low, so low that its sole occupant couldn't make out more than the general shape of his furnishings and the occasional bright spot where what little bit of light there was reflected off a memento or two.

But then he didn't need to see to know what his surroundings looked like. Dro, no *Grand Vizier* Tog, had occupied the same quarters for many years. Essentially happy years that looked all the more so when viewed from the perspective of the present.

Fa splashed into the goblet as Tog decided to grant himself a refill.

Not that I haven't been successful, the prelate thought, lifting the wine to his lips. How many Grand Viziers are there? *One*, that's how many, and I am him. Or is it "he"? No, I mustn't allow myself to become distracted. Important matters are at hand, *very* important matters, to which I must attend.

But, even as the Ra 'Na turned his attention to those matters, a more cynical aspect of his persona continued to express doubts. You're on a treadmill, it insisted, and the faster you walk, the faster the belt turns. No sooner did you conceive of and deliver the cocaine concept to Hak-Bin than he demanded more. How long can the process continue before something goes wrong?

Exactly fifty days from now, the Ra 'Na told himself. That's when Hak-Bin will die, and I will come into my own.

Yes, his nymph will take some getting used to, but I deal with the parent, so why not the child?

First you must arrive at that happy moment, the other part of his mind countered, which brings us to the matter at hand. Someone has to die . . . Whom will you choose?

No! the other part of Tog responded vehemently. I have no choice but to obey Hak-Bin's orders. The situation is unfortunate, but this way, with one such as myself making the decisions, the most deserving will live.

The argument *felt* right, and the prelate was quick to reward himself with another sip of wine. Many would have to be sacrificed before the whole thing was over, he knew that, but not yet. No, the immediate problem centered around only four of the many lives entrusted to him. Whom should he choose? Certain skills were required, Ott-Mar had been clear about that, and the choices narrowed accordingly.

Tog touched a button, and the screen near his right hand came to sudden life. Four names glowed there, four profiles sifted out of the thousands that he could call upon. What was the word the birthmaster used? Expendable? Yes, with the possible exception of Fra Pol, the prelate couldn't conceive of individuals more "expendable" than the names on that list.

Two were closely associated with Dro Rul, and therefore corrupt, one had been friends with the traitorous Med Tech Shu, and the fourth had bested Tog in a debate some thirty-two years before. A humiliating moment about to be avenged.

The knowledge of that, the surety of it, should have lifted his spirits. Why did the victory feel so hollow then? And why did the fa, a perfectly good vintage acquired during the siege of Deeth, taste so foul?

The screen glowed, shadows anchored the gloom, and the victor considered his spoils.

NORTH OF HELL HILL

Thanks to the red tag that dangled from her ear, Sister Andromeda had a certain amount of personal freedom, and that being the case, was familiar with Bellingham's waterfront. The once-busy marina had been destroyed early on, and the extent of the devastation could still be seen in the number of masts that poked up through the oily waves. Most of the larger piers had been preserved, however, or even extended the better to meet the Saurons' requirements. Most of the docks were served by long metal ramps that sloped down to floating platforms.

Now, as a steady breeze sent whitecaps chasing each other across Bellingham Bay, Sister Andromeda along with the other members of the long, ragged line shuffled forward. Rather than the random manner in which most of the slaves had been treated, she and her acolytes had been rounded up and marched north to Bellingham, where they, plus a contingent of "blues," were presently in queue.

Up ahead, next to a ramp labeled "(^)," two Ra 'Na technicians could be seen. Both stood on white footstools and held what would have looked like pistols except that black tubes led from the "pistols" to a pair of gray canisters. The devices made a steady ka-thunk, ka-thunk, ka-thunk sound as the slaves passed between them. The question was why? Some sort of inoculation? Andromeda didn't think so. Medical care was not something the Saurons paid much attention to. No, there had to be another more sinister explanation.

In the meantime, and of equal concern, was the mass relocation itself. Thousands of people had been marched toward I-5 while the rest were funneled toward the water. About a 3:1 ratio judging from what Andromeda had seen.

That suggested more than one destination—and more than one fate. What if the date for slave slaughter had been moved up? Andromeda pulled a quick 360 but saw little more than grim resignation on the faces around her. Understandable, since she was one of the few people who knew the truth about the Sauron birth cycle—and the alien plan to kill most of the slaves before the nymphs could emerge. Lacking that critical piece of information, there was little reason for the others to become agitated.

Of course, maybe, just maybe, her worries were for nothing. Many of the people ahead and behind her were members of the Star Com. Did that imply that Hak-Bin was honoring their agreement? And sheltering her organization from whatever fate the other group had been slated for? Yes, she thought, that would explain it.

The line jerked forward. Andromeda found herself standing next to a Ra 'Na technician and felt the alien press the injector against the upper part of her right arm. The cult leader said, "What is that stuff?" The injector went ka-thunk, and a liquid was forced through both the weave of her robe *and* the pores of her skin. The shot hurt, which caused Andromeda to grimace and grab her biceps.

But the discomfort was soon replaced by a sense of euphoria followed by a flood of renewed energy. Andromeda was confused as first, as were the people around her. Then the truth started to dawn—and was soon confirmed by the word that flowed up the line. "Cocaine!" The bugs were shooting the slaves full of cocaine!

The news struck Andromeda as funny. She was still laughing, still enjoying the joke, when she crossed a slippery gangplank onto a barge already half-loaded with people. They continued to laugh as a wave caused the hull to lurch upward and a woman fell down.

Andromeda knew she should be worried but couldn't quite pull it together. Still, her mind seemed unusually sharp, and thoughts flickered through her consciousness like a movie on fast forward. That's when the insight came to her . . . There was a reason for the cocaine, some sort of purpose, and that implied that both she and those around her would be allowed to live! For a while at least. Andromeda gave a whoop of unadulterated joy, grabbed an acolyte, and danced him around.

Meanwhile, watching from the pier above, Willy couldn't help but grin. Business had never been better. The drug dealer jerked on the leash, brought Angela to her feet, and led the addict away. Time was money . . . and he had things to do.

NEAR SEDRO-WOOLLEY, WASHINGTON

It was late afternoon. The sun had started to set, shadows lay long on the ground, and darkness waited to move in. Nal-Uma stood high on the freeway overpass and looked out over the gray, somewhat tattered carpet of human slaves. It covered both the north- and southbound lanes of I-5 and the median in between them. Kan guarded the rear of the column and the flanks as well.

The humans had been walking for the better part of two days, and all of them were tired. Most remained where they were, perched on packs, sitting on wrecked cars, or sprawled on the worn concrete. A few, the optimists among them, had taken possession of territory on the highly prized median strip. One such individual had even gone so far as to start a tiny cook fire. There was something presumptuous about that, and Nal-Uma resisted the urge to march the entire group half a unit down the highway. But *he* was tired, as were his warriors, and the satisfaction he would derive from the exercise didn't justify the effort.

The Kan glanced to his left, made eye contact with a Ra 'Na technical, and knew the sound system was ready. A pair of powerful speakers faced out toward the crowd. Nal-Uma knew that his superiors considered the concept of talking to the slaves, of prepping them for what lay ahead, to be a total waste of time. After all, what did slaves need to know?

But it was Nal-Uma's experience that humans were a

good deal more biddable when they knew what to expect. So, why not take advantage of that fact? Especially if it made his job easier. Confident that he was correct, the Sauron held the microphone in front of the translator clipped to his harness.

Meanwhile, down in the crowd, Sool stared up at the overpass. The Saurons were a capricious lot, which meant that they might be finished for the day or having a break. So, given the fact that neither she nor Dixie wanted to set the clinic up only to tear it down, it made sense to wait. She watched as the Kan shimmered sky-blue and began to speak. "You will camp here for the night. Rations will be distributed upon the conclusion of my comments."

"Then get to the point," a man said crossly, but not loud enough for the Saurons to hear.

Nal-Uma decided that he liked the sound of his much-amplified voice and continued his discourse. "The temple you were working on now nears completion. Once the final stone has been placed my brothers and I will return to space."

That stimulated a few cheers plus a whistle or two. Whips cracked, and discipline was soon restored. Nal-Uma continued unperturbed. "The food, water, and other materials required to sustain our feet have been stockpiled at a place called Everett. Once there it will be your job to load these supplies onto shuttles. That will be all."

At that point the humans were free to make camp. Rations were distributed, and the man with the cook fire grinned. Conversation buzzed as people speculated on what would happen next. Many wanted, no *needed* to believe that the Saurons would pull up stakes and leave, but, thanks to her relationships with Franklin and Manning, Sool knew better. The Saurons planned to leave all right—but *only* after the slaves had been slaughtered. Unless the resistance could stop them—which was far from certain. In the meantime, all Sool could do was keep as many people alive as she possibly could.

Dixie interrupted the doctor's thoughts. "Looks like we have customers."

Sool saw that the nurse was correct. People had already begun to line up adjacent to the medical carts that carried her supplies. She sighed. Her legs were tired, her feet hurt, and the workday had just begun. More than that the knowledge that she wouldn't see Manning, not even from a distance, bothered the medic more than she thought it would. Somehow, there among hundreds of people, Sool felt unaccountably lonely. She forced a smile. "Okay, Dixie, open cart one. You take the blisters—I'll screen the rest."

The nurse nodded. "Will do. So what are you smiling about?"

"I'm smiling because no matter whom we see, and what treatment we decide on, their HMO can't complain."

Both women laughed and Sool felt a little bit better.

HELL HILL

The president had turned the battery powered light off to conserve the battery. His office was lit by three randomly placed candles. They flickered as the door swung open. "Why don't you come on in?" Franklin asked sarcastically, and turned to see who it was.

"Sorry," Manning replied contritely. "I should have knocked."

"Yes, you should have," Franklin agreed with a smile, "but no one else does, so why should you? Take a load off. How did it go?"

Manning dropped into the plastic lawn chair, started to kick his boots up onto the chief executive officer's tidy desk, then thought better of it. "No real problems, sir. The streets are crawling with bugs, and they put guards on every single one of your vehicles, but you can leave the Presidential Complex whenever you want."

"Sure," Franklin replied dourly, "so long as I don't actually go anywhere."

"Yes, sir," Manning agreed reluctantly. "That's the size of it."

"How 'bout the hill? How many people are left?"

"About twenty-five percent give or take. It looks like most of the people were herded onto I-5 and marched south. The rest, maybe three hundred or so, boarded barges. They're headed for Anacortes . . . that's what one of the Ra 'Na told me."

"That lines up with what Pas Pol and Skunk Works came up with," Franklin said thoughtfully. "The chits need slaves to construct the new catalyst factory."

"Yeah," Manning agreed soberly. "I guess they will. I'm waiting for confirmation, but it looks as though Sister Andromeda, and a significant number of her followers were on those barges, and may be in Anacortes by now."

Franklin raised an eyebrow. "They were targeted?"

Manning nodded. "It appears that way. You remember the explosions we saw? Well, you were right. Every single one of the locations was being used by Andromeda's group."

"Hak-Bin is on to us," Franklin said soberly. "He knows who we are, what we hope to accomplish, and how we plan to do it. He plans to neutralize the resistance. First me . . . now Andromeda."

Manning stirred uncomfortably. Was Ji-Hoon correct? Was Amocar dirty? He cleared his throat. "No offense, sir, but that doesn't seem to wash. Why leave you in place? Why not kill you and have done with it?"

"Because the bastard is smarter than that," Franklin replied glumly. "He has a better grip on *our* psychology than we have on his. By leaving some of the resistance leaders in place, but rendering them powerless, he ensures stability. If

I were to be eliminated he fears that someone else would rise up to replace me. Remember, time is on *his* side. Each passing day brings Hak-Bin closer to his goal."

"So what do we do?"

"Good question," the politician answered. "The catalyst factories continue to be the key. Move too quickly and the bugs will build more. Move too slowly and it will be too late. In a few weeks this farce will end. That's when I go underground, the resistance will launch an all-out attack, and the battle will be joined."

The fact that the resistance was about to attack, about to carry the battle to the Saurons, should have come as no surprise to Manning. But, thanks to the nature of his responsibilities, the security officer had a tendency to think defensively. That being the case he was caught off guard. The words spilled out of his mouth before he could fully consider them. "What about the slaves on I-5? What are we going to do about them?"

Franklin searched the other man's face for some sign of what he was thinking. "I don't know . . . Why do you ask?"

Manning shrugged. "Dr. Sool went with them. Voluntarily by all appearances . . . but there's no way to be sure."

Franklin looked into the other man's eyes, saw the concern there, and knew it ran deeper than mere friendship. Manning was in love with Sool and had been for some time. Why hadn't he seen that before? Because Jina was dead. It was she who had reminded him of birthdays and tipped him off to relationships.

But what about the two of them? What of Manning and Jina? A spark perhaps, but nothing more. Not that it made much difference since even on her worst day Jina had been a better person that he was now. The president produced a frown. "I'm sorry to hear that . . . Dr. Sool is the closet thing to a saint either one of us is likely to meet. Perhaps you should check to see what happened to her."

The words belied the expression on Manning's face. "I don't know, sir, it's tempting, but my place is here with you."

Franklin could almost feel Jina's hand nestled in his as he made his reply. "Under normal circumstances I would agree, but Hak-Bin has grounded me for the moment, and the rest of the team can look after my security requirements. Remember what I said though—the charade must end. Get back before it does."

Manning stood. He felt a tremendous sense of gratitude toward the man across from him plus a feeling of urgency. There was no telling what sort of conditions Sool might find herself in. "Thank you, sir, I'll get right on it."

"Not by yourself," Franklin cautioned. "Get some help from Deac Smith."

Manning nodded. "Yes, sir." Then he was gone.

The president watched the security chief go, felt a sense of envy, and sent a thought toward his wife. That was for you, babe, wherever you may be.

Moments later, well after the door had closed, the candles flickered and a gust of air kissed his cheek.

■ ■ ■

A makeshift weight and exercise room had been established in a cube on the ground floor. Like all such places it smelled of sweat. The light such as it was came from more than a dozen candles. Half had been poured to look like Santas—the other half resembled jack-o'-lanterns.

Though far from the sleek vinyl bags she had once been used to, the duct-tape-wrapped duffel bag made an acceptable substitute, and wobbled under Ji-Hoon's repeated attacks. She struck a quick flurry of blows, landed two kicks, and danced backward. That was when she saw Manning. He stood with one boot resting on the wall behind him. He grinned. "Remind me to stay on your good side."

Ji-Hoon shrugged self-consciously. "Just trying to stay in shape."

Manning nodded. "Good idea . . . Listen, about what you said before, it looks like I owe you an apology."

The ex-FBI agent unwound the tape from her left hand. "You nailed him?"

"Nope," Manning replied, "nothing that clean. Let's just say that I have reason to believe that someone sold us out—and he's suspect number one. What I said earlier holds, however . . . we need more than we have so far."

"So?"

"So, get him for me."

Ji-Hoon ripped the last piece of tape off. "I'll do my best."

"*Good*," Manning replied. "I'm counting on it."

NEAR THE MAYAN RUINS OF NAKABE, GUATEMALA

Three Eye, as he was known within the tight-knit group of *sobrevivientes* (survivors), sat motionless next to the river. He'd been there for a couple of hours by then, hunched under the plastic poncho, staring into the darkness. The water gurgled, chuckled, and splashed. Each sound was like a word in a language he almost knew. The *sobreviviente* was afraid to listen too carefully, afraid that the river would pull his spirit out of his body, but there was nothing else to do. That's why Three Eye prayed. To strengthen his bond with God, to suppress the sound of the river, and to hasten the coming of the new day. That's when he could return to the *agujero* (hole), have some breakfast, and get some sleep. Simple pleasures for a simple man.

Three Eye's work-thickened brown fingers had been resting on the vine-braided rope a long time by then. Through it he could feel the river's pulse, the steady thump, thump, thump of its watery heart, and the occasional tug as something small struck the netting, found its way through the oversize holes, and continued downstream.

Some of the things might be edible. If they were, a second net with a much tighter weave was waiting downstream. The *donada* (lay sister) had responsibility for that one, and she was welcome to it. The river was cold, and she would be in and out of it at least ten times during the night. Three Eye's job was to nab the larger items, a considerable number of which were tossed, dropped, or jettisoned into the river. Mostly by the aliens but by slaves as well.

Just during the last couple of weeks Three Eye had snagged a well-sealed first-aid kit marked as the property of the "Navy de Mexico," some soggy MREs from the United States, and, best of all, a semiconscious Fon who had been slaughtered, roasted, and consumed with great gusto. So, when the rope jumped and pulled suddenly tight, the *sobreviviente* knew it was a catch of some magnitude.

The river was too wide to stretch the homemade net all the way across—plus it would have been difficult if not impossible to pull back in. That's why the netting had been stretched over a tubular framework. One end had been anchored near the riverbank while the other was allowed to swing out into the current.

Now, with something in the trap, all Three Eye had to do was pull on the anchor rope. It ran back into the jungle, through a tree-anchored block, and out to the net. It was hard work, but thanks to the leverage provided by the pulley, a single man could haul the trap in. The net resisted at first, as if determined to defy him, but gradually surrendered.

Meanwhile, with the river pushing her against the net, Dr. Maria Sanchez-Jones struggled to free herself. But, just as her fingers found the aluminum frame, the entire structure swung inward, the current dropped away, and the anthropologist was swept into the shallows. Then, while the woman still floundered about, a light hit her in the eyes and a voice said, "You're alive." It sounded just a little disappointed.

"Yes," Jones replied, trying to see past the glare. "Just barely. I escaped from the slave camp."

"Me too," the voice replied as the man placed the light down under his chin. "They shot me," Three Eye said proudly, "but the dart was fired from a long ways off. It drilled a hole through my skull but didn't touch my brain."

Jones wasn't so sure about that but managed to nod agreeably. "You were very fortunate."

"As were you," Three Eye responded agreeably. "Welcome to the *sobrevivientes*."

"*Gracias,*" Jones replied cautiously. "What do the *sobrevivientes* do?"

"We survive," Three Eye replied. "Isn't that enough? Come, the sun is about to rise, and we must return to the *agujero*. The aliens avoid the jungle, but there's no reason to tempt them."

Having nothing better to do with herself, and sensing that her companion was harmless if somewhat eccentric, Jones allowed him to lead her into the jungle's humid embrace. After passing through more than a mile of wet triple-canopy forest, the trail started upward, passing through a labyrinth of rocks and crossing a swiftly flowing stream. But, rather than follow the trail, Three Eye turned to the left and waded upstream. From that point the twosome followed the stair-stepped watercourse upward to the point where it emerged from what looked like solid rock. It was light by then, and Three Eye pointed down at the point where the water issued from the side of the mountain. "You must duck under the ledge, push with your toes, and stand. There's plenty of air on the other side."

The academic checked the man's expression to see if he was serious, decided he was, and waded forward. Then, waist deep in the pool that marked the spot where the stream emerged into the open, Jones ran out of courage. After all she had been through, after all she had survived, another leap of faith was simply too much to take. That's when Jones heard the whine of a Sauron shuttle, knew the aircraft was close, and took the plunge. The water was cold, her toes dug at the gravel, and darkness closed all around.

Then, using her hands to feel for obstacles, the anthropologist pulled and pushed. Her eyes saw light, her head broke the surface of the water, and the ceiling of a cavern arched above. There were holes through which daylight streamed, and just as Jones found a purchase with her feet, she saw a pair of bats swoop into the cave. The night was over, their bellies were full, and it was time to sleep.

Rainwater, still percolating down through the rock above, plopped into the pool around her. Opposite Jones, at the top of a steeply sloping gravel beach, an encampment could be seen. A roof made from leaves had been erected to protect the inhabitants from the interior "rain," and from the bat guano that fell from above. That was the moment when the academic realized that the encampment had been used before, that here, hidden right under her nose, were Mayan ruins. She could see blocks of stone, carvings, and there, over to the right, a guano-obscured statue!

Then, as Jones waded forward, she saw that all manner of boxes, baskets, and net bags had been stacked, placed, and in many cases hung under the thatched roof. None was larger than the underwater hole through which she had passed. A tendril of steam issued from the recently doused fire, and a group of clean if somewhat ragged-looking adult humans watched her approach, while three round-eyed children clung to their mothers' skirts.

That was when Three Eye surfaced in noisy fashion, waved at the people on the beach, and waded toward shore. "Come on! Meet the rest of the family! Then, once you are comfortable, we will look out the window."

Jones wondered what the man was referring to but never got the chance to ask as the *sobrevivientes* crowded in around her. They wanted to hear her story, pump her for news of their relatives, and brag about the *agujero's* various amenities.

It was only then, after Jones had heard them out, that Three Eye showed her what everyone referred to as the *ventana* or "window." It consisted of a three-foot-long horizontal hole in the cavern's east wall. A platform had been erected below the opening so that the *sobrevivientes* could stand and look out.

Jones followed Three Eye up a short ladder and out onto the walkway. Bright sunlight spilled into the cavern, moisture-laden air hugged her shoulders, and the *sobreviviente* raised a cautionary hand. With the exception of the half-healed wound in his forehead, Three Eye was a good-looking if somewhat solemn man. His eyes were dark and intense. "There are rules where the *ventana* is concerned. You must never wear things that could reflect light, make sudden moves, or disturb the vegetation."

Jones nodded, stepped forward, and looked out through the window. Some naturally growing vines and plants helped screen the opening, but there were plenty of gaps. That was the moment when the anthropologist had her first overall look at the alien complex. Thanks to what looked like battlements, and the still dry moat, the temple had a castlelike aspect. To see it there, washed with the early-morning light, was a surprise. But so was how she felt. Much to her own amazement the anthropologist experienced a moment of fierce pride, not only for what she and the rest of the slaves had managed to endure, but for what they had accomplished as well.

More than that Jones found herself thinking about Blackley, about the manner in which she had betrayed him, and felt a sudden sense of sorrow. Tears fell, the citadel shimmered, and the work continued.

HELL HILL

José Amocar was running from something he couldn't see but was deathly afraid of. There were people, lots of people, and they formed a passageway through which he was forced to pass. They pointed at him, made comments about the way he looked, and laughed.

The agent glanced back over his shoulder, but there was nothing to see. The monster was invisible. Amocar could *hear* it, however—and ran even faster. Anything to escape the wheezing sound of its carrion-tainted breath and the steady slap, slap, slap of its enormous feet . . .

Amocar awoke with a jerk. The .9mm was in his hand. Blood pounded in his head, his body felt cold, and his body shook as if possessed by a fever.

The agent managed to sit up, placed his back against a cold metal wall, and examined his surroundings. The cube, one of thousands made suddenly available when the majority of the slaves were marched away, was part of the stack called Flat Top. The light, such as it was, issued from a ceiling-hung battery-powered lamp.

Judging from all the stuff lying around, it appeared as though the previous occupants had been caught by surprise and forced to leave their belongings behind. Then, as sure as night follows day, those who remained looted the place.

Amazingly enough the woman was still alive. She made a noise, or tried to, but the ball gag made that impossible. Amocar had forced the rubber sphere between her jaws and employed a blue bandanna to tie it in place. Her eyes beseeched him, begging Amocar to show her some mercy, but he had seen such looks before and found them easy to ignore.

The woman had been pretty once . . . but not anymore. Hak-Bin had given the female to Amocar as a reward . . . to be enjoyed in whatever way he saw fit. She hung where he had left her, naked except for the tatters of the clothes he had cut away from her body, spread-eagled so that every aspect of her anatomy was exposed. Her hair was matted, her face was bruised, and her hands were blue from loss of circulation. Whip marks crisscrossed her body, her nipples had been removed, and a combination of dried blood, sperm, and urine coated the inside surface of her thighs. The place stank, something Amocar hadn't noticed before, but suddenly found repugnant.

The agent fought a headache as he struggled to his feet. What time was it anyway? Amocar looked at his watch, swore, and stumbled toward the door. Jack-shit Manning was off on some stupid mission or other, which meant he would have to fill in. Not a problem if it weren't for Mr. "this is how we did it in the army" Kell, who would not only watch every move Amocar made, but rat him out the moment the opportunity presented itself. Amocar had his hand on the hatch, and was about to push it open, when he remembered the woman. There was no law enforcement, none at all, but it would be stupid to leave the bitch alive.

The agent turned, drew the hunting knife from its sheath, and returned to his victim. He showed her the blade, saw the fear in her eyes, and laughed. Slowly, so she could have time to think about it, he brought the point down onto the base of her throat.

The woman shivered and tried to pull back.

The knife tip left a thin crimson line as Amocar drew it down over her chest, between her bloodied breasts, and down onto the hard flat plane of her stomach.

Then, with a sharp jab, he opened her up. A length of intestine slithered out, Amocar saw the shock of it hit her eyes, and jerked the knife free.

Amocar had an erection by then, but time was short, so he wiped the blade on what remained of her blouse and left the cube. It fronted on one of the many terraces that stair-stepped their way up the stack's flat top. The agent grimaced as the early-morning light hit his eyes, took a quick look around, and hurried off.

Laundry flapped in the wind, a dog barked somewhere nearby, and the tang of woodsmoke hung in the air. The stack seemed unusually quiet, however . . . like a ghost town dozing in the sun. Ji-Hoon, who had been led to the location by one of the street urchins now in her employ, arrived in time to see the other agent depart. A glance at her watch was sufficient to tell her why. *El Segundo* was supposed to be on duty.

Curious as to what Amocar had been up, to Ji-Hoon slipped her latest ten-year-old operative a pack of gum, cautioned the boy to stay well back, and told him to follow the agent home. Then, confident that she knew where Amocar would be for the next twelve hours or so, Ji-Hoon ducked under a clothesline, nodded to a dull-eyed woman, and approached the cube. Hinges groaned as the wind sought to move the hatch, flies buzzed as if eager to enter, and the smell explained why.

The .9mm filled Ji-Hoon's hand as she pushed her way into the barely lit murk. That's when she saw the woman, the blue-black intestines that dangled from her abdomen, and battled the rising nausea. "You bastard," she whispered hoarsely. "You filthy rotten bastard."

Maybe it was the sound of Ji-Hoon's voice, or perhaps it was the pain, but whatever the reason the woman groaned.

The ex–FBI agent had assumed that the woman was dead and gave an involuntary start. Her first thought was to call 911—but that was no longer possible. Even Dr. Sool was gone.

Ji-Hoon returned the weapon to its holster and forced herself to step in closer. The ceiling-hung lantern provided barely enough light to see by. The agent felt nauseous as she released the gag, pried the saliva-covered ball out of the woman's mouth, and threw it away. The words were so faint they could barely be heard. "Thank you."

"I'll cut you down," Ji-Hoon said, "and go for help."

"*No!*" the woman croaked emphatically, "in the name of God no. You have a gun—I saw it. Please shoot me."

Ji-Hoon looked into the woman's eyes, saw the pain there, and knew she was correct. There was little to nothing that anyone could do for her. "Are you sure?"

The woman managed to nod. "The man who did this . . . will you get him?"

"If it's the last thing I ever do," Ji-Hoon answered grimly. "You have my word on it."

"Good," the woman said. "I'm ready."

Outside, beyond the confines of the metal walls, the shot made a dull thump. Startled by the noise, a bird fluttered into the air. It circled the stack—and flew away.

NEAR MOUNT VERNON, WASHINGTON

The field was flat, open, and right next to the freeway. Just the sort of spot the Saurons liked best. In spite of the gradually warming weather, it was cold at night. That's why the slaves had built more than a dozen large bonfires, all fueled by siding torn from the same barn.

Deac Smith and his fellow reenactors knew that multiple small fires would actually be more useful where heat and cooking were concerned, but were pleased with the large infernos nonetheless. Focused as they were on preventing escapes, and with no external threats to bother them, the Kan had a tendency to look in at the bonfires. Maybe the light would screw with their night vision, and maybe it wouldn't. All a guy could do was hope. He turned to the man at his side. Both lay on their bellies about fifty yards beyond the alien perimeter. "You're sure you want to do this?"

Manning, who had ridden a horse for the first time in his

life, and walked for another ten miles after that, hurt in places he never had before. "Absolutely . . . I wouldn't miss it for the world."

"Then you're just as crazy as I thought you were," Smith replied. "Remember, one hour, that's all we have."

Manning grinned. A camo stick had been used to darken his face, but his teeth gleamed white. "So, what are we waiting for? An engraved invitation?"

Smith chuckled, whispered, "Follow me," and low-crawled in the direction of the encampment. The security chief followed. There were other resistance fighters, roughly thirty of them, hidden out in the darkness. They would provide fire support if that became necessary—but Smith hoped it wouldn't. The whole point of the exercise was to access conditions within the encampment. An attack, if any, would come later.

Careful to keep his head down, the resistance leader followed the edge of an overgrown irrigation ditch in toward the fires. A good way to sneak past humans, but the Kan weren't human. Rather than walk one section of the perimeter the way a human sentry would, the Saurons jumped from point to point, rarely landing on the same spot twice. That made the aliens unpredictable, which was to say dangerous, which was to say scary. Now, as the two men approached the Kan perimeter, Smith paused. Manning, elbowing his way along behind, had little choice but to do likewise.

A gentle breeze sprang up, caused the bonfires to shiver, and blew smoke to the northeast. Smith watched the nearest bug complete a jump, pause to take a look around, and bounce into the air.

Moving quickly in hopes of getting to the next way point before the Kan returned, the ex-Ranger left the protection of the irrigation ditch and squirmed into the open. The earth was relatively soft and gave under his elbows.

Then, with relative safety still a good fifty feet ahead, Smith was forced to pause. The Kan with responsibility for that sector had arrived at the edge of another warrior's turf. He landed, turned, and went airborne again.

Smith knew that if he could see the bug, then the bug could see *him*, especially if he moved. That's why he froze into immobility, hoped Manning would do the same, and felt his heart pound in his chest.

The Kan, an individual named Wob-Ree bounced, and took off again. Like his peers the warrior had been trained to survey the surrounding area from the *apex* of his jump, not from the ground. The fires, which naturally drew his attention, fell away. Then, from a perspective some twenty-five feet up in the air, Wob-Ree eyed the ground below.

Smith watched the alien rise, ran a quick calculation regarding the bug's likely trajectory, and gritted his teeth. Now, based on the way things appeared, and contrary to established patterns, it looked as if the godless spawn of the devil was about to land where he had the last time! Right on top of them! All they could do was wait.

Wob-Ree felt gravity kick in, watched the fires rise, felt his feet hit the ground. His knees flexed to absorb the shock, the Kan scanned the darkness off to his right, but saw nothing. Feral slaves lived out in the woods, everyone knew that, so it was best to be careful.

Smith held his breath. One of the Kan's enormous flat feet was so close that he could have touched it. The radio clipped to the bug's battle harness burped static followed by silence. Then, like an answer to the resistance leader's prayers, the warrior was gone.

Eager to escape any chance of another close encounter of the sort they had just experienced—Smith scuttled his way forward. Manning, who felt at least ten years older, followed.

Then, having passed between the outermost fires, the infiltrators could finally stand. Both men wore blue ear tags and carried handguns beneath their raggedy clothing. The application of two wet wipes apiece was sufficient to remove the camo stick markings.

So numerous were the slaves that they had little difficulty blending in. Most of the people were gathered around the bonfires, and it seemed natural to drift from one to the next. Smith paid close attention to what he heard. There was anger, which beat the heck out of passivity, and a lot of rumors. Some, like those that spoke of a coordinated resistance movement, were even true.

Manning's task was a good deal easier. All he had to do was ask the first person he ran into where Dr. Sool had established her clinic and was directed toward a distant fire. Hearing that, and knowing that Seeko was still alive, filled Manning with joy. Slowly, so as not to draw attention to themselves, the two men edged in that direction.

Meanwhile, not far away, Sool sat on the back of a cart, accepted a cup of tea from an admirer, and nodded her thanks. The ceramic mug was hot, and it felt good to wrap her hands around its warmth. The closest fire, which was about fifteen feet away, crackled and threw a fountain of sparks up into the air.

Strangely, or perhaps not so strangely, the number of people who showed up for sick call had been relatively light. The not-so-pleasant truth was that thousands of slaves had died of various diseases, been killed in construction accidents, or simply murdered by the Kan. Those who survived had a tendency to be young, resilient, and lucky. The net result was fewer people at sick call.

"So," a familiar voice said, "a penny for your thoughts."

Sool felt her heart leap, turned in the direction of the sound, and spilled hot tea on her thigh. She didn't notice the pain. Manning laughed as the doctor dropped the mug, jumped off the cart, and threw her arms around his neck. Their lips met, Sool felt all the things she hoped she might feel, and heard the sound of applause. That's when the kiss ended and the twosome turned to discover that Smith, Dixie, and more than a dozen blues were grinning appreciatively and clapping their hands.

Sool blushed, Manning laughed, and took her hand.

"That's enough," Dixie proclaimed, "let's give them some space."

There were whistles, followed by a catcall or two, but the bystanders obeyed. Slowly, hand in hand, the twosome walked out to the point where firelight surrendered to darkness. "So," Sool said, looking up into Manning's face, "to what do I owe this visit? And how did you get here anyway?"

The security chief shrugged. "I was worried about you, *very* worried, and Franklin allowed me to come. As for the how, well, let's just say that I now know why they invented cars. Horses are a pain in the butt."

Sool laughed. "Now that you're here—how will you get out?"

Manning checked his watch. "You can expect some fireworks in about twenty minutes. That's when the Deacon and I will slip away."

The security chief took her hands in his. They felt small and vulnerable. "Please, Seeko, come with us."

Sool liked the way he said her name . . . as if it were something special. "I'd like to, Jack, I really would, but my duty lies here."

Manning nodded. "I kind of figured you'd say something like that. Okay, how 'bout we break everyone out?"

Sool frowned. "You could do that?"

Manning shrugged. "Timing is important. That's why Franklin put the resistance on hold. Move too early, and the bugs have the time to respond. Move too late, and everybody dies. So why not now?"

"Wouldn't Franklin be upset?"

"Probably, but let's do it anyway."

Sool shook her head. "No, Jack, not for me."

Manning looked back toward the fires. "I'm here because of you, I admit that, but it doesn't change the facts. It would be a lot easier to free these people now rather than later."

"True," Sool admitted, "but the Kan would hunt them down. Many would die."

"Many will die anyway," Manning responded, "on the job, or during the slaughter."

Sool stared intently into Manning's eyes. He was different from what she had always assumed she wanted, yet absolutely right. She raised one of his hands and kissed it. "You may be correct, but your motives are questionable. Put your case to the president. Get *his* agreement, and you'll have mine."

Sool was correct, Manning knew that, and grinned. "You're a pain in the ass . . . did anybody every tell you that?"

"People remind me from time to time."

"I'll bet."

"Kiss me."

Manning kissed her, felt her lips give under the pressure of his, and was suddenly afraid. Now, there in the circle of his arms, he had something to lose. It made him weak and, therefore, vulnerable.

Deac Smith cleared his throat. "Break it off, you two . . . There's going to be one hellacious racket, and we need to be ready."

Manning kissed Sool on the forehead. "Take care of yourself, Doc, and keep your eyes peeled. If the prez green-lights some sort of raid, there will be a whole lot of confusion. Watch for me . . .'cause I'll be there."

Sool smiled. Memories of fear, of gunfire, flickered through her mind. "Yes, I'm certain that you will. Please be careful."

Manning nodded, backed away, and was absorbed by the darkness. The rockets, firecrackers, and other displays went off three minutes later. At least six of the Kan bounced toward the source. No one was there.

The blues cheered, whistled, and danced each other around. Sool watched with arms folded. Dixie seemed to materialize at her side. "Nice work, boss, you got it right this time."

"Thanks," Sool replied. "Some things work better when you don't have time to think about them."

"Amen to that," the nurse said fervently.

Then, as if to underline Dixie's words, a rocket whistled high into the air, where it exploded and showered the slaves with light.

ANACORTES, WASHINGTON

The site for the facility had been chosen for purely pragmatic reasons. The factory would require fresh water and plenty of it. A sizable water main ran next to what had once been a rather pleasant park. By cutting the trees down, and leveling some small service buildings, the aliens freed sufficient ground for their purpose.

The Sauron Book of Cycles didn't include any strictures where the manufacture of birth catalyst was concerned, or that's the way it seemed, as an engine revved, and a team of bright-eyed cokeheads used a crane to swing a pump from one side of the construction site to the other.

Andromeda felt the pain before she heard the crack of the Fon's harakna hide whip. The blow wasn't much as such punishments went, only what the bugs referred to as a "starter," but it would leave an angry weal nonetheless.

Andromeda swore at herself for daydreaming, knew the lapse to be drug-related, and returned to work. She, along with three others, had been assigned to prepare valve assemblies for installation. The necessary parts had been laid out on a series of improvised worktables. Andromeda's job was to snap an injector nozzle into the side of each fitting, grease the threads, and pass the assembly down the makeshift assembly line. Her peers worked in silence.

It had rained earlier that morning, which meant that everything they touched was wet and cold. A fact that would normally generate a considerable number of complaints but didn't.

The simple fact was that the daily injection of cocaine had changed the way the slaves viewed the world. Now, as their bodies grew increasingly dependent on the drug, it moved in toward the very center of their lives. Cocaine was more important than their loved ones, more important than food, and more important than anything but the worst sort of pain. Even more horrible was the fact that Andromeda *knew* what the Saurons were doing to her and was still powerless to stop it.

Each day was the same. A restless night during which the hours seemed to crawl by. Then, as light appeared in the east, the anxiety would begin. Would the dose arrive on time? Would it be strong enough? Did the bugs have enough blow to supply the entire workforce?

That's when Andromeda's hands would begin to shake, when some of her fellow slaves became dizzy, and others started to hallucinate.

Then, after a breakfast which they were forced to eat, the slaves would rush to queue up. Everyone wanted to be first—especially since the chits had a consistent tendency to come up five doses short. Not *every* time, since that would introduce an element of predictability, but every third or fourth day, so as to keep the addicts on edge and at each other's throats.

Most of them understood that, *understood* the manner in which they were being manipulated, but found that the knowledge made no difference. The drug was in charge, and they were unable to intervene.

So, thanks to the leverage provided by the cocaine, construction was actually *ahead* of schedule. Something which, thanks to her knowledge of Sauron plans, Andromeda knew could hasten the slave slaughter.

In fact, throwing all caution to the winds, she had even gone so far as to tell others what she knew in hopes that she could garner some support. Some people believed her and others didn't. It made no difference. Once hooked on cocaine only the most rebellious of souls had sufficient strength to fight back—and they were few and far between. That's why Andromeda, in an effort to sabotage the facility, had been forced to act entirely on her own.

Most of the parts were crudely made, a fact that made perfect sense to anyone who understood that while the processing plant had to function, it wouldn't have to last for long. Clearly defective parts, like plugged injectors, were supposed to be identified by Fon inspectors prior to delivery. But a few made it through—and whenever Andromeda came across a clearly defective part, she was careful to install it.

What was it that her mother used to say? "The devil is in the details?" Yes, that was it, and the phrase seemed to fit. Soon, very soon, the Saurons would crank up their processing plant only to discover that it didn't work. All hell would break loose, the problem would eventually be fixed, but time would be lost in the interim. Precious time that could save lives.

But what about her need for cocaine? If the plan worked, and the Saurons lost, she would go into withdrawal. That struck Andromeda as funny. She laughed out loud. No one even turned to look.

NEAR THE MAYAN RUINS OF NAKABE, GUATEMALA

The temple complex shimmered in the late-afternoon heat as the black manta-ray-shaped shuttle circled, began to lose altitude, and came in for a landing.

The artificial lake had been constructed using slave labor. It was oval in shape and exactly the right length for medium-sized vessels to land on. The shuttle pancaked in, sent waves racing toward the opposite shore, and coasted toward a long finger-shaped jetty.

The reception party, led by Dun-Dar himself, was already in place. Pendants hung limply from poles, and a horn groaned, as mooring lines were made fast. That's when double rows of inspection-ready Kan snapped to the Sauron equivalent of attention and the main hatch whirred open. Two human slaves, attired in identical smocks, rushed to slide the metal gangplank into place as the first of the visiting dignitaries emerged from the ship's lock.

The hot, humid air hit Dro Tog like the breath of some horrible beast. It was heavy with the odor of rotting vegetation, the stench of untreated sewage, and the tang of ozone. It was not the sort of place where someone covered with fur would want to spend much time.

The cleric blinked into the harsh afternoon sun, wondered how such a hellish environment could give rise to intelligent life, and stepped onto the gangplank. It gave slightly as the portly prelate made his way onto the pier.

A Ra 'Na technician was there to greet Tog. His name was Isk, and he looked considerably older than he had on the day when he bested the future Grand Vizier in a debate and unknowingly signed his own death warrant. Isk had orange fur flecked with white and matted by the heat. "Welcome, eminence. All is ready."

Tog took a long slow look around, assured himself that the specially constructed sedan chair met specifications, and nodded his head. "Good work, Isk. Rest assured that I will remember your many accomplishments."

Unaware of the irony involved, Isk bobbed his head in return. "Thank you, eminence."

Eager to get his charge ashore and retire to his air-conditioned quarters, Tog turned back to the shuttle. A Fon stood waiting. "Please inform his excellency that everything is as it should be."

As the functionary departed to convey the good news, Tog walked past the custom sedan chair to the point where Dun-Dar stood waiting. "Greetings, eminence. Lord Hak-Bin will come ashore within the next few minutes."

Dun-Dar regarded Tog with the contempt he felt for all such individuals. To his mind the entire notion of setting one slave over another was little more than an obscene farce. "Thank you for stating the obvious. Now get off my dock before I give you some *real* work to do!"

Frightened, and more than a little taken aback, Tog hoisted his robe and waddled toward shore. The incident served to remind the Ra 'Na of the extent to which he was reliant on Hak-Bin's patronage and how important the Sauron's good health continued to be. Until the nymph emerged and the existing relationship would continue. Or so the prelate hoped and assumed.

There was a stir as Ott-Mar's sedan chair arrived at the foot of the pier and the birthmaster backed his way out of the internal sling. He, at least, was glad to see Tog and greeted the prelate with the familiarity that one conspirator reserves for another. "Our patient? How is he?"

"A little out of sorts," Tog answered cautiously, "but otherwise normal."

"That bad, eh?" the Zin replied dryly. "Well, the surgical suite is ready, and we'll soon have him on the table. The anesthetic should shut him up even if nothing else will."

Afraid to agree, Tog kept his mouth shut. The decision

was validated when Hak-Bin's heavily swathed body appeared in the hatch and Ott-Mar took to the air. He traveled the length of the dock in two well-calculated jumps.

Unable to see how he could help, and worried lest he somehow get crosswise with Dun-Dar, Tog was left to watch as two sturdy-looking Fon functionaries assisted their master across ten units of open dock, helped him maneuver his badly swollen body into the reinforced sling, and ignored the nonstop abuse to which they were subjected.

"Keep your incompetent graspers off me!" Hak-Bin ordered, as a Fon brushed an especially sensitive section of badly displaced chitin. "What are you trying to do? Kill me? Ott-Mar . . . where have you been? Did you see that? I want the idiot shot."

The functionary in question looked understandably concerned, but the physician waved him away. "I'm sorry, eminence," the Zin said soothingly, "but the worst is over. You're on the surface of Haven now, and the pain will soon be over."

"You're sure?" Hak-Bin inquired eagerly. "The operation will succeed?"

"Yes," Ott-Mar lied, "I'm sure. Now settle in and try to relax while the slaves take you to surgery."

The words seemed to have the desired effect because the pain seemed to abate for a moment, and Hak-Bin looked nearly normal. "Yes, thank you. And one more thing . . ."

Ott-Mar tried to conceal his impatience. "Yes, my lord?"

"I would like to introduce File Leader Kat-Duu . . . He will accompany me into surgery."

Because of the large number of bodies crowded around the sedan chair, the physician had failed to take notice of the Kan until then. Now, as the warrior stepped forward, Ott-Mar recognized him as the much-decorated veteran in charge of Hak-Bin's bodyguards. A harakna hide eye patch concealed his left eye socket, whorls of metal "death" studs covered both his shoulders, and his battle harness was festooned with what seemed like an excessive amount of weaponry. The physician allowed himself the Sauron equivalent of a frown. "There's a limited amount of space, my lord, and I have the required number of assistants."

Hak-Bin waved a pincer. "You fail to take my meaning Ott-Mar. Rather than assist you, Kat-Duu has been assigned to *kill* you, should something go wrong. Isn't that right, Kat-Duu?"

The warrior made no reply, nor was there any need to. The hard implacable stare said it all. "Is the situation clear?" Hak-Bin demanded, his eyes fever-bright.

"Yes, my lord," Ott-Mar replied, as something heavy seeped into the pit of his stomach. "The situation is very, very, clear."

NEAR CONCRETE, WASHINGTON

The helicopter generated a steady roar as it followed Highway 20 east toward the town of Concrete. Given the fact that a barricade had been placed across the road just beyond Lyman, plus an infestation of feral humans, the Saurons preferred to avoid the area. And why not? Especially since slavers could be dispatched to harvest workers, thereby reserving the hard-pressed Kan for other more important tasks.

Human-manufactured aircraft were a rarity by then, so the sound of the Chinook's rotors, plus the self-confident manner in which the big helicopter flew up the Skagit River valley was sure to attract some attention. Eyes peered up through a maze of evergreen branches, binoculars tracked the aircraft's progress from a lookout station positioned high on a hillside, and the volume of CB radio traffic increased.

The resistance leader named Storm was busy weeding her vegetable garden when word of the visitation arrived. The boy was ten, and true to the name he had taken for himself, ran like the wind. He cut across the assembly hall's sod roof, leaped a swiftly flowing creek, and dashed across open ground. "It's coming! The helicopter is coming!"

"There's no need to yell," Storm said gently. "The sound of your voice can carry a long ways."

Wind knew she was correct and did his best to look contrite. "Sorry, Storm. I got excited that's all."

"No problem," Storm replied, gathering her tools into a bucket. "We have to be careful . . . Especially in the forest. The habits we establish here will serve us there. Tell Strength that I'm on my way."

Full of his own importance, and eager to deliver the new message as quickly as possible, Wind nodded and ran back the way he had come.

Five minutes later Storm entered the underground command center, dropped the galvanized bucket by the door, and established eye contact with her chief of staff. He was a wiry little man who had acquired his moniker by virtue of that which lay within rather than the size of his body. "So, it's true? Franklin is on his way?"

Strength shrugged and gestured toward the once-elegant dining room table. A variety of communications equipment covered its much-abused surface. A woman sat in front of the table listened via earphones and took notes as the reports filtered in. "Everyone's telling Sparks the same thing . . . A Chinook helicopter is eastbound up the valley. The registration numbers match the one Franklin has used in the past. There's no sign of Sauron activity down here . . . although we have no way to know what's happening in orbit."

"The bastard has balls," Storm replied, "you have to give him that. I wonder what sort of cock-and-bull story he told the bugs in order to justify the trip? Oh well, it hardly matters. Whatever it was worked. Come on—we'd better get going."

The old Honda Four Trax Foreman ES didn't look like much, but it ran pretty well. Of even more importance to

Storm and the rest of her community was the fact that the ATV could pull a trailer, produced a minimal heat signature, and was easy on gas. Storm preferred to drive, so it was she who swung a leg over the gas tank, and settled behind the controls. Strength hopped on behind.

The 433cc engine roared as Storm advanced the throttle, spewed gravel out from under four knobby tires, and flew up the ramp. It felt good to enter the sunlight, to skid into the first turn, and accelerate away. A party of woodcutters waved as the twosome passed. Storm waved back. Then, having applied just the right amount of brake, the ATV burst out of the tree line, skittered onto the old two-lane highway, and accelerated toward the west.

By prior arrangement the helicopter was supposed to land in the open area out front of the old Alpine Motel. Knowing that it pays to be paranoid, especially with the bugs in control, the Sasquatch warriors had been ordered to secure the entire area. Both of the group's 120mm light mortars had been pre-registered on the LZ, heavy machine guns were sited in predug pits, and no fewer than forty members of the self-styled "eco-army" were hidden in the surrounding area.

Now, as the ATV approached the rendezvous point, Storm heard the steady whup, whup, whup of the Chinook's giant rotors over the sound of the Honda's engine and steered for the center of the motel's weed-infested parking lot.

Both of them dismounted, and Storm shaded her eyes as the enormous helicopter banked and circled the old motel. "They're checking us out," Strength said levelly. "Looking for any sign of a trap."

"Makes sense," Storm commented. "That's what we would do. How 'bout those mortars? Any chance they could be misinterpreted?"

"I don't think so," Strength replied, "especially considering the fact that we warned them we would have some fairly heavy stuff scattered around the area. Agent Amocar said he understood."

An artificial wind tugged at their clothing as the helicopter circled again. It was lower by then—only fifty feet off the ground. "Agent Amocar?" Storm yelled. "Who's he?"

"One of Manning's people," Strength replied. "The short guy who walks funny."

Storm had a vague memory of a man fitting that description preceding Franklin into the sawmill summit. She nodded. "Good . . . We wouldn't want some sort of misunderstanding. Lord knows we have enough problems already."

Strength squinted into the swirling dust, wondered why the Chinook continued to hover toward the far side of the parking lot, and saw that something had been mounted at the center of the open hatch. It looked familiar, like something he'd seen during his hitch in the air force, although it was difficult to be sure. Still, even the remote possibility of such a thing was sufficient to cause Strength to turn and take a step in Storm's direction.

But 20mm slugs move quickly, and even though Strength was already in motion, they hit Storm before he could make contact.

Not willing to entrust such an important task to a bug, or another human for that matter, Amocar had chosen to act as his own gunner. Careful to allow for the helicopter's motion, he steered the metal hailstorm across the parking lot and onto the primary target.

Storm was just starting to understand, just beginning to comprehend, when the first slug blew her right leg off, the second smashed her pelvis, and the third blew a grapefruit-sized hole through the center of her chest.

Still diving, still determined to save Storm from the fate she had already suffered, Strength entered the line of fire.

The slugs from the minigun ripped his body to shreds, drifted sideways as the Chinook started to pivot, and raked the front of the motel. Wood shattered, glass exploded, and the old-fashioned neon sign disintegrated as the 20mm slugs tore the place apart.

Now, having recovered from the initial shock of seeing their most important leader murdered right in front of their eyes, the ecowarriors opened fire.

Mortar rounds wasted themselves on the gore-splattered pavement, a .50-caliber machine gun chugged as the operator chased the helicopter, and small-arms fire came from every direction.

Amocar fell over backward as the minigun cycled empty and the Chinook turned toward the west. Then, with slugs punching bright holes through the helicopter's thin skin, Amocar yelled: "Go! Go! Go!" and the pilot applied full military power.

His name was Hernandez, he had been brought in from the Sauron complex in Guatemala, and he didn't give a shit why the helicopter's original registration numbers had been changed, why Amocar wanted to grease one particular woman, or why the *bichos* (insects) were willing to go along with it.

All *he* wanted to do was get out of the firefight alive, put the *helicóptero* back on the ground, and collect the *etiqueta rojo* (red tag).

Meanwhile, to the rear of the otherwise empty chopper, Amocar listened to the sound of automatic weapons fire fade, nodded approvingly, and planted his butt in a fold-down seat. The mission had gone well, better than expected, and Hak-Bin would be pleased. So pleased that it might be possible to request a bonus of some sort. Two women perhaps? Yes, that would be fun, now wouldn't it?

And why not? Especially since he had not only eliminated the woman called Storm, but done so in a manner that would cast suspicion on Franklin, thereby weakening the entire resistance movement.

Amocar fumbled under the seat, located the six-pack of Dos Equis, and popped the cap. It was warm, *too* warm, but wonderful nonetheless.

The helicopter droned, the beer went down, and Amocar allowed himself to dream.

NORTH OF EVERETT, WASHINGTON

The sun had set, the fires had died down, and most of the humans were fast asleep. From Nal-Uma's perspective, seen through the combat goggles that he wore, they looked like blobs of light scattered across the open field. In the distance, spaced evenly along the perimeter of the camp, other blobs jumped from point to point. Not only had his warriors had less sleep than the slaves—they had been on the bounce since the night before.

The problem started with the fireworks set off during the previous dark cycle—and continued throughout the succeeding day.

First came the messages spray painted across freeway overpasses. Though unable to read them himself, Nal-Uma knew the glyphs had significance from the way the humans reacted. Those near the front of the column read the words, exchanged secretive glances, and sent a shiver back through the crowd.

Being no fool, and curious as to what the ferals were trying to tell their more domesticated brethren, Nal-Uma forced one of the slaves to translate. The woman was frightened and had a tendency to stutter. "The wwwords say, 'Fffreedom is at hhhand,' master, but I didn't write them."

"No," the Kan replied thoughtfully, "you didn't. Stay close . . . I may have need of you."

Then, addressing the column from the top of a half-slagged semi, Nal-Uma attempted to put the matter away.

His voice was amplified, and Sool, who along with Dixie was standing toward the rear of the crowd, had no difficulty hearing it.

"I will say this once and only once . . . Pay no attention to empty words written by pathetic creatures who live in the forest. Look around you . . . Is 'freedom at hand'? No, I think not. Freedom, when it comes, will be granted after the temples have been completed. Remember that, and walk quickly, knowing that the sooner you arrive, the sooner you will finish. That is all."

The Kan's words acted to quiet the crowd, for a while at least, but the psychological warfare continued.

Nal-Uma put flankers out. The warriors had seen combat on other worlds, knew what it was to fight under strange circumstances, and weren't easily shaken. Or so the file leader believed until the same warriors began to report a variety of strange phenomena and were clearly concerned about it. Ferals were sighted—but always in the distance. Horrible wailing sounds could be heard, which according to his human interpreter, came from something called bagpipes.

Objects were left where both the Kan and the slaves would see them. A cluster of small red, white, and blue flags that fluttered in the breeze, a Sauron skull, mounted on a pole, and hundreds of Hershey bars scattered across I-5.

The net result of all this activity was a tendency for the flankers to stay in close—and thereby cede everything else to the ferals. Not an especially good thing to do. Nal-Uma *knew* that, but lacking additional troops was powerless to do anything about it. So, knowing that his brethren were stretched thin, and that reinforcements were unlikely at best, he resolved to work with what he had.

The column, which normally stretched out to occupy half a unit or so, was compressed into half that distance, overseers were encouraged to mete out punishment for even minor offenses, and orbital fire support was called on to police the areas just beyond Nal-Uma's flanks.

First came the pressure of suddenly displaced air, then the crack of what sounded like lightning, followed by the roll of artificial thunder. Yet in spite of the way the strikes served to bolster morale and keep the ferals at bay, the very fact that such a step was necessary served to keep Nal-Uma on edge.

Now, after a long stressful day, the fall of darkness meant the possibility of more harassment. Or, and this was what the file leader hoped for, the ferals had called it quits. There had been absolutely no sign of them for the last couple of units, and that augured well.

And so the day went, until night fell, and the Kan were forced to remain on high alert. To do so was consistent with the Sauron doctrine of dynamic defense, which stemmed from the mobility natural to Kan warriors. Because the Saurons remained in motion, rather than hunkering down behind static defenses, there were no strong points on which potential enemies could focus. To attack the Kan "was to attack the air," or so the saying went, and Nal-Uma knew that it was true. Still, for reasons the Sauron couldn't quite put his pincer on, he felt a sense of foreboding. An ancestor gibbered inside his head, and he tried to ignore it.

Now, as the file leader kept watch, shadows began to shift as Deac Smith and his resistance fighters began to move in. Where the previous night had been about flash and psychological impact, this was the real thing. Nal-Uma had twenty-three warriors to call upon plus a cadre of human overseers. Four of the Kan lay dead before the file leader knew the battle had begun.

Among the arsenal of weapons Deac's Demons could call upon was the traditional Native American longbow, except that these bows were made out of high-tech laminates instead of wood, and were equipped with wheels, cams, cables, stabilizers, and light-intensifying 2X scopes.

Tests had been conducted using a captive Sauron, and based on the results of that endeavor, Deac Smith knew that the black carbon arrows would not only fly straight and true, but the handmade "bug points" would shatter Kan chitin and drive deep within their bodies.

The signal consisted of three clicks on his radio. There were six soft thumps as the bowstrings were released, four cracking noises as the arrows found their targets, and a bleating sound as a badly wounded warrior crashed to the ground.

The dead sentries were all from the same quadrant of the defensive line, which opened a gap. Manning, along with fifteen of Deac's Demons, had belly-crawled to within thirty feet of the Sauron perimeter. He came to his feet, brought the Mossberg 12-gauge to port arms, and charged the newly created breach.

Then, on a signal from George Farley, who had command of that particular group, the infiltrators came together into an evolution so venerable that a Roman legionnaire would have instantly recognized the formation for what it was: the infantry square. And that's where they were, all facing outward, when Nal-Uma did exactly what Deac Smith had predicted the Kan would do . . . he attacked.

Manning, one of those assigned to the area within the center of the square, checked to ensure that his safety was off and closed his eyes. That was important, *very* important, as Popcorn Farley had emphasized more than once. "Keep 'em shut," he admonished, "or pay the price when the flares go off. 'Cause if you're blinded when the bugs fall, we are ski-rewed. Do you read me?"

Everybody read him, and most obeyed. But it was difficult, *very* difficult to close ones eyes when the enemy was about to attack, which was the reason why Harv Bodine failed to do so. He watched all four of the flares go off, saw them bathe the landscape with harsh white light, and struggled to see.

Then, as the initial intensity of the flares started to fade, and they drifted slowly toward the ground, Farley gave the order. "Open your eyes! Watch for silhouettes! The bastards are in the air by now!"

And the Kan *were* in the air, as Nal-Uma could clearly see via his computer-assisted night goggles. He watched the color-coded blobs, *his* blobs, fall toward the red blobs, and felt a rising sense of excitement. Now, finally, the ferals would learn their lesson. And not just learn it, but learn it here, where the domesticated slaves could watch.

Like Dixie, Sool was rolled up in a pair of blankets, lying beneath one of the medical carts. The "pop" of the flares, the sudden wash of white light, and unexpected wail of bagpipes was more than enough to wake her. She shook the nurse. "Dixie! Wake up! It's them!"

Subsequent to the nighttime visitation from Manning, the two women had prepared packs containing what few personal items they had, the set of surgical instruments that Sool had pieced together, and what few pharmaceuticals were on hand.

Now, rolling out from under the cart, they were already dressed and ready to go. All they had to do was grab the packs, sling them on their backs, and figure out which direction to take. All the slaves were up by then, standing in confused clumps, unsure of what to do.

That was when the gunfire erupted on the far side of the encampment and men and women dressed in buckskins and other outlandish attire seemed to materialize among the newly awoken slaves. "Follow me!" they yelled. "This way!" and proceeded to fade back into the darkness.

Some of the slaves followed, but many, conditioned by months of captivity hesitated, afraid to enter the unknown.

Sool waved them forward. "Come on! Do as they say! This is our chance!"

And such was the doctor's credibility, and such was her personal following, that the doubters followed. And other people followed *them*, and still others followed *them*, until a flood of humanity streamed off the field and vanished into the surrounding murk.

The mass exodus was very visible to Nal-Uma, just as *he* was very visible to Deac Smith, who had been stalking the Sauron for more than fifteen minutes by then.

In fact the file leader had just begun to absorb the nature of the feral plan, and appreciate the manner in which all of his forces had been sucked toward a single spot, when a human-shaped blob stepped into the space before him and the file leader realized the extent to which his own personal security had been ignored. Not only had he remained stationary in order to assess the situation, but he had neglected to sweep the area behind him. The t-gun was not only holstered, but tabbed in, which meant the human had the advantage. He was alive, however, remarkably so, which suggested a desire to parley. Silly really, since there was nothing to discuss, but why not? Especially if he could seize some sort of advantage.

Now, as Nal-Uma moved the goggles up and out of the way, the Sauron saw that the intruder had blackened his face, as if to imitate his betters, and held an ugly-looking submachine gun cradled in his hands.

Smith's voice was level and calm. Nal-Uma heard the words via his translator but couldn't make sense of them. " 'He leadeth me in the paths of righteousness for his name's sake.' That's from the Holy Bible, Psalms 23:3." The words might not mean much, but there was no mistaking the subtle movement of the weapon's barrel.

The Sauron sent a message to the muscles located in his powerful hindquarters. They bunched just as they were supposed to, but at the very last second, just as the pent-up energy was about to be released, a burst of .9mm slugs tore his belly open, blew green gore out through Nal-Uma's back, and silenced his line forever. Meanwhile, unaware of the sudden loss of leadership, the Kan pressed their attack.

Still blinded by the flares, Harv Bodine heard weapons fire all around him, and fired his as well. The bullets missed an incoming warrior by a good three feet and were lost in the night sky.

The Kan fired his t-gun twice. Both darts hit Bodine, and the combined explosions blew him in half.

Manning felt something warm splatter the back of his neck, heard the distinctive thump as a pair of enormous feet hit the ground, and spun to his right. The Kan was turning, too, only to the left, which made it a race. The first being to complete the turn, and acquire a target, would win.

The security chief heard himself scream some sort of incoherent war cry as the shotgun came around, and he squeezed the trigger.

Only half of the double-ought buck hit the Kan's thorax, but that was enough to throw the warrior off-balance and send his darts wide. A man in buckskins took the projectiles in the back, staggered as they blew his spine out through his chest, and flopped facedown. Manning worked the Mossberg's slide, felt more than heard the next shell slot itself in the chamber, and jerked the trigger.

This load of lead was dead on. The slugs, each the size of a .38 pistol round, tore the left side of the warrior's throat out. His head seemed to wobble, toppled over sideways, and his body followed it down.

Now, ready to kill, and keep on killing, Manning jacked another shell into the weapon's chamber and pulled a 360. But there was nothing to shoot at. Only half a dozen beings remained standing and all were human. They looked at each other as if surprised to discover that they were still alive.

Another set of flares went off and threw a ghastly pall over the circle of crumpled bodies as Farley bent over a fallen Kan, jerked the bowie knife free from the alien's chest, and returned it to its sheath. Then, turning to his troops, Farley did what so many leaders had done before him. He put his grief on hold, gathered the living, and led them away. "All right! Time to pull out! Or would you like to be here when the shelling begins?"

As if to punctuate the ex-Ranger's words, what sounded like a runaway freight train roared over their heads, something hit the center of the mostly emptied field, and a column of dirt mixed with abandoned belongings rose high into the air.

The debris was still falling, still raining down, when the survivors started to run.

In the meantime, off to the east, the mass exodus continued. The moment a group of slaves cleared the field and entered the tree line, they were divided into groups of twenty-five and led away. Sool and her companions were a good half mile into the woods, following an overgrown maintenance road, when the orbital bombardment began.

She felt the earth jump beneath her feet, listened to the successive explosions, and thought about Manning. He'd been there, she'd *felt* it, somewhere in the fighting. But where was he now? Lying on his back? Dead eyes staring at the stars? Or running for his life? No, for *her* life, or what her life could eventually be were the insanity to end. The slaves walked for the better part of two hours before being ushered into a musty-smelling farmhouse and herded down into the basement.

Food was waiting, along with makeshift bedrolls, and a half dozen smiling faces. A woman stepped forward. She had warm intelligent eyes, a buxom figure, and dark brown skin. "Hello! My name is Amanda Carter, and I'm a member of the resistance. Please allow me to welcome you home."

With the exception of those having darker-colored skin, most if not all of the newly escaped slaves had been abused by black overseers at one time or another, and some viewed Carter with open suspicion. The silence stretched thin.

Sool took two steps forward, opened her arms, and met Carter's gaze. "Hello, Amanda, my name is Seeko, and it's a pleasure to meet you."

The two women embraced, the tension seemed to drain from the room, and both groups merged. Somebody handed Sool a piping hot mug of Campbell's Bean and Bacon soup. She thanked them, found a place in a corner, and placed her back against the concrete wall.

The soup was good, the mug was empty, and the doctor was asleep by the time Dixie found her ten minutes later. The nurse looked up at the man who stood at her side. He looked tired and blotchy with someone else's blood. "She would want to see you . . . I'll wake her up."

Manning shook his head. "No, she needs her sleep. We all do. If you don't mind, I'll just sit down and take a load off. We can talk when she wakes up."

Dixie said that would be fine and left to get some soup.

Manning meant to wait for her, intended to remain awake, but soon started to fade.

And that's where Dixie found them, side by side, both dead to the world. The man and the woman . . . the doer and the thinker . . . the killer and the healer. You are one strange pair, the nurse thought to herself as she looked down on the couple, but these are strange times. We're going to need both of you.

Slowly, gently, Dixie pulled a blanket up around their shoulders, extinguished a nearby candle, and tiptoed away.

5

DEATH DAY MINUS 41

SUNDAY, JUNE 21, 2020

The tree of liberty grows only when watered by the blood of tyrants.
—BERTRAND BARE'RE DE VIEUZAC
Speech to the National Assembly, 1792

NEAR THE RUINS OF NAKABE, GUATEMALA

The temple complex shimmered in the hot afternoon sun. Thousands upon thousands of slaves, along with contingents of Kan, Fon, and Ra 'Na, lined both sides of the gently curving road. If any of them thought the situation unusual, or wondered about the oversize sedan chair, they gave no sign of it. There was the drone of insects, the momentary snap of an otherwise languid pennant, but little else was heard. Just the slap, slap, slap of slave feet, the rasp of their breathing, and the thump of Tog's heart as it pushed blood into his head.

Never one to spend time in close physical proximity to Saurons when he didn't have to, the Dro would have been happy to catch a ride on a human-drawn cart, or even waddle up the road had that been a choice. Unfortunately, as part of what Ott-Mar no doubt considered to be an act of kindness, the Zin insisted that Tog ride atop one of the Fon.

Like most of the clergy, Tog had been so honored before, but that was back in his younger days when his body had been more flexible, and a good deal lighter to boot.

Much to the cleric's embarrassment the Sauron functionary even mumbled something about "fat fur balls," but not so loudly that Ott-Mar could hear. Then, with help from two human slaves, the paunchy prelate was loaded into the saddle and left to his own devices.

Now, swaying like a ship at sea, Tog battled to maintain his seat and keep his lunch down. The single bright spot, and the Grand Vizier gave thanks for it, was the fact that owing to the ceremonial nature of the procession his none-too-happy mount was reduced to a slide-step shuffle and unable to bounce. The landscape lurched, the sun beat down, and there was little to do but endure.

Roughly fifteen units forward of the point where Tog bobbed and swayed, Hak-Bin looked out through gauzy curtains and held communion with his nymph. "Can you feel them, little one? Trying to find you with their eyes? Conscious of the gulf that separates you from them and wondering why? Yes, I know you can. Well, your turn will come soon enough. But first, so I can ensure your safety, certain precautions must be taken.

"Yes, that means a delay, but a relatively brief one. You are early, after all, *very* early, and that is part of the problem."

The ensuing movement, followed by a moment of exquisite pain, left no doubt as to the nymph's lack of sympathy. The next member of the line wanted to be born sooner rather than later.

Hak-Bin bit down on a corner of fabric, waited for the pain to subside, and reacted as he would to any surly subordinate. "You'll pay for that . . . My life continues. The power you hunger for is *my* power . . . and will continue to be my power for forty-one more days."

The unborn Sauron didn't like that, not one little bit, and

did its best to punish its progenitor. But Hak-Bin had been injured many times during his long life, had withstood "the cleansing by pain," and knew that he could take it.

The procession had arrived at the edge of the moat by that time, and those who watched the heavily curtained sedan chair pass could not possibly have imagined the battle of wills that raged within. Most, to the extent that slaves considered such matters, imagined that a Zin lolled within, his body supported by a mountain of cushions, eating the Sauron equivalent of grapes. Would they have felt even a shred of sympathy had they known the truth? No, Hak-Bin supposed, probably not. But they should have.

Feet thumped on raw wood as the slaves carried their burden into the temple, the sedan chair shook as Hak-Bin locked his pincers onto the interior framework, and Dr. Maria Sanchez-Jones watched from the hill high above. What the hell were the Saurons up to anyway? The sedan chair vanished, the door closed behind it, and there was no way to know.

SALMON NATIONAL FOREST, IDAHO

With the exception of the scouts out in the forest, and the Hammer Skins assigned to guard Racehome's perimeter, everyone else listened as Raymond Dent, self-styled "Lion of the Airwaves," returned to the air.

Everyone who was anyone, and that included both Jonathan and Ella Ivory, were crammed into the underground studio as a self-important assistant delivered the cue, and Dent, still recumbent on his flower-strewn stretcher, started to speak. The radio personality had a wonderful voice, even Ivory was forced to admit that, and a delivery to match. Every word he said sounded as though it came straight from Yahweh's mouth. "Good evening, this is Raymond Dent, the Lion of the Airwaves, speaking to you from a secret location hidden somewhere in the western part of what used to be the United States of America. But that nation perished, my friends, eaten from within by the Zionist Occupational Government, soiled by the pre-Adamite muds, and burned by the Saurons.

"Now, even as the days grow dark, a new nation is born. A *Christian* nation, an *Aryan* nation, a new *Israel*. No, you cannot come here, not yet. Satan's children, the sons of Belial, are too strong for that. But what you can do is prepare your mind, body, and spirit for the glory ahead. A time when Amerika will be pure again. When the white race will live free of miscegenation, when no trace of mosque or synagogue can be found on our fair land, when our culture, the *white* culture, will rise like a tower of hope and bathe the land in its light. Until then you must remain where you are, grow strong, and prepare for the final cleansing.

"Look to those around you, even to those with whom you sleep, or to those who manifest themselves as children. Are they pure? Or are they servants of the beast? Waiting to pull the new society down?

"Every garden has weeds my friends—and every gardener must be vigilant. If you are a Soldier of God, a *true* Aryan warrior, you will understand my meaning.

"Now, even as Satan's beasts become aware of this broadcast, and start the search for our transmitter, the final battle begins. Tell others what you heard, and monitor this frequency, especially between 9:00 P.M. and 3:00 A.M.

"May Yahweh bless and protect you . . . This is Raymond Dent, the Lion of the Airwaves, signing off."

A switch was thrown, the onlookers started to applaud, and the self-important assistant thumbed a stopwatch. "One minute and fifty seconds," he said proudly, "which puts us well under the two-minute mark."

Like everyone else in the room Ivory knew Dent and his followers were trying to keep each broadcast under two minutes in hopes that doing so would extend the period of time before their haphazard network of transmitters were located and destroyed. By sending the signal through what remained of the telephone network, and routing it to transmitters located hundreds of miles away, the Dent heads believed they could insulate Racehome from the possibility of Sauron retribution.

Nice in theory, but hard to believe, especially given the level of technology that the aliens possessed. But, except for Ivory, the only person in the community actually to live under the whip, the Saurons were something of an abstraction. As with tuberculosis, they knew about the disease, understood how dangerous it could be, but didn't believe that such a thing would ever happen to them. The reality of that caused Ivory to be depressed rather than elated. Ella squeezed his arm. "So, will you do it?"

"Do *what*?" Ivory asked, wondering what he had missed.

"Why, the interview of course," his wife answered easily, "what else?"

Ivory realized that the room had grown quiet, that all eyes were on him, and that a trap had been sprung. His opposition to the radio show was fairly well known—but most of the community thought the broadcasts were a good idea. By inviting Ivory to take part in the program, Dent was forcing the military leader publicly to oppose the show, and thereby isolate himself, or participate, and thereby add to its legitimacy. The racialist forced a smile. "An interview? Of course . . . Nothing would give me more pleasure."

There were cheers, renewed clapping, and high fives all around.

Dent, who was more than satisfied with the evening's work, fell back against the pillows. The wink was directed at Ella . . . and the smirk was for Ivory. "I won," it seemed to say, "and you lost."

Ivory discovered that his hand had somehow drifted to the butt of the .9mm handgun holstered at his side. He ordered it to fall, summoned a stare, and aimed it at Dent. Eyes locked, wills clashed, and events were set into motion.

HELL HILL

The temple was all but complete by then, its secrets safe within thick limestone walls, its towers thrusting brazenly toward the morning sky. Manning, who still had difficulty walking after the return journey on the back of a horse, turned his back to the complex and looked out over the area below.

Like everything else about the Sauron complex, the semi-circular plaza and the spire that marked its center was huge. But then it would have to be in order to accommodate a million Saurons. Even if they were packed into tiny cells. That being the case there was more than sufficient room for the roughly one thousand slaves expected to attend Franklin's speech. Not just *any* speech, but the first speech in which the politician would openly advocate rebellion, and therefore the last speech on behalf of the Saurons.

Now, as the whips cracked, and the pathetic remainder of the once-burgeoning slave population was herded up toward the top of the hill, Manning considered the task before him. Protect the Big Dog even as he committed the equivalent of suicide, get him off the hill before the Saurons could react, and pull a world-class fade. No small task on a peninsula swarming with Kan. Manning sensed movement at his elbow and turned to find Franklin at his side. "Sir, I really must . . ."

"Don't lecture me on risks," Franklin said good-naturedly, "not after the I-5 raid. Who led that attack by the way? It wasn't me."

"I didn't *lead* it," Manning replied. "I only took part in it, after *you* gave permission."

"And it's a good thing I did," Franklin said dryly, "since you would have gone ahead regardless of what I said."

"Not true," the security chief said sheepishly, "not after Seeko said 'no.' "

Franklin laughed. "You're a lucky man, Jack. Take good care of her . . . Women like that don't come along every day."

The comment caused both men to think about Jina, which neither of them wanted to do. Manning placed his body between the president and the plaza. "Please leave the platform, sir. I'll call you when things are ready."

The politician took one last look around, made a face, and complied. Kell, along with Alaweed, hustled the chief executive away. Though vulnerable to any number of things, the black SUV was a safer place to wait.

With Franklin under wraps, Manning could turn his attention back to the task at hand. A well-conceived security zone should resemble a well-set table, having a place for everything and everything in its place. A quick check confirmed that Wimba, Dylan, Lu, and Amocar were all where they should be. Wait a minute . . . Amocar? On duty? And actually doing his job? Now, *that* was unusual . . .

But wait a minute—somebody was missing. Manning pulled a piece of graph paper out of the inside pocket of his jacket and checked to ensure that he was correct. The security chief swore under his breath. The plan called for an operative to be posted on the north side of plaza. That particular slot had been assigned to Jill Ji-Hoon, and the agent was nowhere to be seen.

Though not gifted with physical beauty, or a lightning-fast intellect, Amocar had one quality that set him apart. He was lucky. Call it ESP, intuition, or a sixth sense but whatever it was often served to warn him when danger threatened. Amocar felt a featherlike touch, looked up toward the platform, and half expected to meet Manning's gaze. But the security chief was turned to the right and looking off toward the north side of the plaza.

Amocar followed the other man's gaze, saw the gap in the line, and felt ice water enter his veins. The rotten, dirty, filthy bitch was gone! There was only one possibility . . . Somehow, some way, Ji-Hoon knew about the hit! More than that, she was on her way to stop it!

Manning turned to his left, started to speak into the voice-activated boom microphone, and stopped. Amocar had disappeared.

Meanwhile, not far away, preparations were under way. Farkas had been a cop. Not an especially good one, but a cop nonetheless, which was how he came to know a state trooper named Horsky. The same Horsky who worked as a slaver. Now, having been seconded to Amocar, and given what he considered a plum assignment, Farkas was in an extremely good mood.

For reasons known only to the Saurons, the ceremonial horns that groaned with such monotonous regularity nearly always did so from inside an enclosure called a kak. The kak consisted of colorful fabric stretched over metal frames, which were connected together via simple pin-style fasteners to create a four-foot-by-twelve-foot room. Or, as Farkas thought of it, a hide similar to the ones his uncles used for duck hunting.

Yes, the fact that three Fon were inside with him, blowing bass notes through huge tripod-mounted animal horns was a bit distracting, but every job has its downside. Kind of like being the only cop in Guthrie, Washington. Did the aliens approve? Disapprove? There was no way to tell as the horns groaned and Farkas went about his business.

The kak had been positioned on the third level of the temple facing west. That put the enclosure above and behind the temporary speaker's platform from which Franklin would address the crowd.

The task was relatively simple. Lock the .300 Winchester onto its rest, center the crosshairs on the back of the politician's head, and squeeze the trigger. The 176-grain Sierra bullet would handle the rest.

There were details to consider of course . . . The wind that blew in from the southwest, the deflection involved, and the persistent need to pee. But those things could be compensated for, *would* be compensated for, and the certainty of that made Farkas feel good. Horsky would owe him, his position within her organization would thereby be strengthened, and his rep would grow. One of the few things worth having anymore. The Fon blew air through their wide flat mouth pieces, the horns groaned, and the assassin made his final preparations.

Jill Ji-Hoon heard the horns, knew the seconds continued to tick away, and felt completely helpless. Yes, she could have approached Manning, could have told the security officer about her suspicions, but to what end? Would he believe her? Or pooh-pooh the whole thing as he had before? There was no way to be sure—and no time in which to find out.

Ji-Hoon knew what she had seen through her binoculars, however. While off on what he described as "a health break" Amocar had escorted a suspicious-looking man into the temple. She lost sight of them after that, and was surprised to see the twosome appear on the third-level terrace, and stroll toward the kak. That was the point when the ex–FBI agent noticed the long, cylindrical package tucked under the stranger's arm and guessed what it might contain. Shortly thereafter, Amocar left, and the stranger entered the fabric-enclosed kak. The perfect place from which to shoot Alexander Franklin.

Unsure of what support she might or might not receive, Ji-Hoon left her post, pushed through the steadily growing crowd, and sought one of the temple's side entrances. Now, having arrived, the agent found herself face-to-face with a belligerent Kan. He saw that Ji-Hoon was armed and placed a pincer on his t-gun. His voice had a grating quality. "Slaves are not allowed."

"Master Har-Dee sent me," Ji-Hoon extemporized. "An unauthorized human was sighted on level three, and I was sent to investigate." It was a good bluff, or so it seemed to her, but unbeknownst to Ji-Hoon, the Zin named Har-Dee had been killed in a shuttle accident just two weeks before. On top of that, the Kan had been a member of the ceremonial guard that carried Har-Dee's body to its final resting place and took part in the jump dance that followed.

Convinced that the slave was lying, the warrior started to pull his weapon. It was only halfway out of its holster when Ji-Hoon fired a single shot from her .9mm Beretta. The slug passed through the lens of the alien's left eye, nicked the bottom of his brain, and severed his spinal cord. He dropped like a sack of potatoes.

The agent turned, weapon raised, prepared to die fighting.

But the side entrance was hidden within heavy shadow, and the sound of the single gunshot had been lost in the groaning of the horns, the crack of the overseers' whips, and the crowd noise.

Her heart racing, and her breath coming in short adrenaline-fueled gasps, Ji-Hoon struggled to get a grip on the insectoid body. The Kan was heavier than he looked, and it soon became apparent that none of the carries she'd been taught was going to work on the insectoid body, so the ex–FBI agent used brute strength to drag the Sauron in through the door.

Once inside Ji-Hoon felt the temperature drop, wondered where the strange green glow was coming from, and heard water gurgle as it flowed through channels located along the base of the sheer walls. What looked like cells lined both sides of the passageway. They were small, and there were thousands of them. Ji-Hoon managed to drag the corpse into the second cubicle on the right. The Sauron's chitin made a grating sound as it scraped along the limestone floor.

Ji-Hoon gave an involuntary jump as the voice boomed through her radio. "Snake One to Snake Seven . . . Where the hell are you? Over."

A lump formed in the back of the agent's throat, and it was a struggle to swallow it. Manning was pissed . . . and she could hardly blame him. Should she answer, and be drawn into a lengthy explanation? Or push forward? And save the justifications for later? The decision was relatively easy. The radio was clipped to her left shoulder strap. Ji-Hoon squashed the "transmit" button and spoke into her boom mike. "This is Seven. Condition red, I repeat *red*, man with a gun. I'm on it. Over."

"You're on it?" Manning demanded. "On *what*? On *where*? Report damn you."

But Ji-Hoon was on the move by then, satisfied that she had given the security chief enough information to work with and determined to reach the assassin located above.

Amocar heard the transmission, swore, and hurried up the steps that led to main entrance. The words came in hasty spurts. "This is Snake Two . . . Ji-Hoon deserted her post. I'll take care of it. Cancel condition red. Over."

Ji-Hoon started to reply, thought better of it, and sprinted for the other end of the corridor. Manning was smarter than that—she hoped so anyway—and would take appropriate steps.

Meanwhile, down on the plaza, the last of the slaves were poked, prodded, and pushed into position. Kell, who had responsibility for the agents around the president, listened to the transmissions, and turned toward the SUV's open window. Sandi Taglio, a cigarette drooping from the corner of her mouth, raised an eyebrow. "So what's it gonna be, Kell? Shit? Or get off the pot?"

"Get off the pot," the ex-Ranger replied, "and I mean *now*. Get the Big Dog outta here."

Franklin, who continued to monitor developments with a rising sense of apprehension, chose to intervene. He opened the door and jumped to the ground. "Sorry, Vilo, I know you mean well, but I have a speech to give . . . Not just *any* speech, but the most important speech of my life."

Kell made as if to move forward, as if to remove the politician by force, but Franklin raised a hand. "Hold it right there, Vilo . . . Am I your president? Your *real* president? Or a way to avoid hauling stone? If I'm the real president, then you will respect both my judgment and my wishes. This speech is more important than my life."

Kell could have pointed out that Franklin wouldn't be able to give the speech, not if he were dead, but thought better of it.

A Kan chose that particular moment to land not ten feet away. He pointed a pincer at Franklin. "The slaves are ready. You will speak now."

Franklin allowed himself a grin. "See what I mean? Even the Kan want to hear my speech."

Like Manning, Kell had once harbored doubts about Franklin's motives and sincerity. But that was then, and this was now. The two men locked eyes. "I don't have a president, sir, but our country *does*, and I'll do whatever he asks."

Those few words, coming as they did from a man like Kell, were like an infusion of strength, hope, and courage. The president extended his hand, the soldier shook it, and they walked out onto the platform together.

Farkas saw the target enter the killing zone, licked his lips, and removed the safety. Questions flickered through his mind. Why go to all this trouble when the bugs could off Franklin anytime they chose? Why were the Fon blowing into those goddamned horns? What would happen if he missed?

The crowd, many of whom had a burgeoning respect for Franklin, produced a reedy cheer, the crows cawed from corpse-hung crosses, and the assassin's questions went forever unanswered.

Conscious of the manner in which the seconds continued to tick away Ji-Hoon turned, ran the length of an unexplored hallway, and nearly missed the dark spiral ramp. It had been a while since she had worked on the complex and things were different. Heartened by the discovery she followed the path upward, her boots thumping against tightly laid stone as she passed the first exit, and emerged on the top floor. Like the floors below, tiny cells lined both sides of the hall. Ji-Hoon looked left, then right, and saw where bright sunshine splashed on the floor. A doorway out onto the terrace! The agent started to run.

Franklin had jumped out of a plane once. Not because he had to but to see if he could. He'd been frightened, very frightened, but managed to pull it off. Now, as he stepped out onto the crudely built platform, the politician felt the same way he had on that day many years before. Scared, but proud, and filled with a sense of excitement.

People cheered, some did anyway, which suggested that they believed in him. Light winked off the chrome-plated mike stand. A breeze touched his left cheek. Horns groaned from above. His voice was amplified and rolled over the crowd. "My fellow Americans, rather than write a new speech, I thought I would rely on some existing text. Maybe it has been a while since you had an opportunity, or a reason to study this particular document, but I assure you that it will be time well spent. Perhaps *you*, like *me*, took these words for granted. Perhaps, all of us should consider them again."

Then, his eyes roaming the crowd, Franklin began to recite: "We hold these truths to be self-evident, that all men are created equal, that they are endowed by their Creator with certain inalienable Rights, that among these are Life, Liberty, and the pursuit of Happiness . . ."

There was silence at first, followed by what sounded like a growl, then a roar of approval as the slaves came to sudden life. Farkas shook his head in amazement and started the long slow squeeze. The crosshairs were where he wanted them to be, on the back of Franklin's head, and the bullet would follow.

Ji-Hoon emerged from the terrace, yelled something incoherent, and charged the kak. The framework collapsed, fabric tore, and Farkas went down under her weight. Though not armed with a handgun, the ex-cop liked to carry a knife, and managed to pull it out.

Ji-Hoon, the .9mm still clutched in her hand, rolled to the right. She was on her back, sun spearing her eyes, when the would-be assassin jumped to his feet. The knife was already on its way down when the agent pulled the trigger. Two slugs slammed into the ex-policeman's chest, and Farkas collapsed on top of her.

That's the way things were when Amocar arrived. He saw the metal framework topple, saw the Fon back away, and heard Franklin's voice. ". . . That whenever any Form of Government becomes destructive of these ends, it is the Right of the People to alter or abolish it, and to institute new Government, laying its foundations on such principles and organizing its powers in such form, as to them shall seem most likely to effect their Safety and Happiness . . ."

Amocar knew there was no way Hak-Bin had approved the speech, knew all hell would break loose when the bugs figured it out, and knew who would take the fall: *him*. He had one chance and one chance only. Kill Franklin or die on a cross.

The .300 Winchester lay where it had fallen—still attached to the makeshift rest. Amocar rushed across the terrace, pulled the weapon upright, and brought the stock to his shoulder. The stand came with it, and the extra weight made the weapon difficult to hold. Precious seconds passed while Amocar took his stance, found the target, and placed the crosshairs where they were supposed to be.

That's when Manning came out through the door, brought the .40-caliber Smith & Wesson up, and fired six times in quick succession. Brass casings flew through the air, bounced off limestone, and tumbled away as slug after slug pounded Amocar's back. But the agent wore a Kevlar vest under his shirt—and the bullets lacked the velocity required to punch their way through.

Amocar staggered, allowed the rifle to fall, and went for his pistol. Manning first—*then* Franklin . . . Hak-Bin would be very . . .

Ji-Hoon, still pinned beneath Farkas, brought her hand up. The handgun bucked, the .9mm slug disconnected Amocar from his body, and darkness pulled him down. He screamed, but no one heard.

". . . And for the support of this Declaration," Franklin intoned, "with a firm reliance on the protection of divine Providence, we mutually pledge to each other our Lives, our Fortunes, and our sacred Honor." The crowd, which had been silent for a while roared, the crack of whips was heard, and heavily armed Kan jumped into the middle of the crowd.

Kell looked for Manning, wondered where the boss man was, and gave the necessary orders. "Snake Three to Snake Team . . . Plan A, execute. Over."

People swarmed around Franklin, doors slammed, and Taglio put the SUV in gear. The vehicle jerked forward, swerved to avoid some slaves, and took to the air as it cleared the top of the hill. The Suburban hit hard, bounced, and kept on going.

Slaves scattered as Taglio leaned on the horn, sent an empty tea stall spinning off a fender, and gave a whoop of unrestrained joy. The windows were open and a country-metal band pumped bass as the driver braked into a hairpin turn, applied power, and sent gravel spewing out the back. The Saurons were monitoring the SUV by then, tracking the vehicle's progress from above, determined to punish Franklin for his perfidy. In fact, the only thing that prevented the Kan from destroying the vehicle right off the bat was a desire on the part of the local sector commander to cover his posterior.

Not really required, but advisable, especially when dealing with a Zin like Hak-Bin. The only problem was that the Kan had been unable to get in touch with the supreme one. It seemed no one could find him, not the stonemaster down in Nakabe, nor Hak-Bin's staff on the *Hok Nor Ah*. So, with the humans clearly bent on escape, and no orders to the contrary, the sector commander was free to indulge his own wishes: "Destroy the human vehicle . . . Do it now."

Taglio jerked the wheel to the right as an orbital cannon opened fire and blew an elephant-sized divot out of the road ahead. Dirt and gravel rained down on the Suburban's roof as it sailed through the falling debris, skidded into a turn, and continued to roll. The windshield was cracked but remained intact.

Taglio figured the energy weapon was computer-controlled. Assuming that was correct then each shot would be calculated to allow for atmospheric conditions, the rotation of the planet, and her rate of speed. That's why the driver stood on the brakes, counted to five, then stomped on the accelerator. The SUV took a nosedive, skidded, then took off again.

The next energy bolt missed by the equivalent of a city block. In the meantime Taglio knew the computer was analyzing random stops, searching the route ahead, trying to predict what she would do next. That's why Taglio brought the vehicle to a stop, aligned the nose on the gate below, and hooked preanchored bungee cords onto the steering wheel. Once that was accomplished it was a relatively simple matter to put the Suburban in motion, activate the cruise control, and throw herself out through the door.

The SUV lurched forward, picked up speed, and was doing fifty miles per hour by the time it hit the main gate. That's when the Kell's homemade bomb went off, when the four-wheeler exploded into a thousand pieces, and the sentries were cut to shreds.

The debris was still falling, and black smoke had started to boil up into the sky, when the last energy bolt touched down. Taglio, who had paused to watch the results of her handiwork, never felt a thing. There was light, a strong desire for a cigarette, but none to be had.

Franklin heard the SUV roar away, felt hands pull at his clothes, and did the things they told him to do. Then, with the crowd still swirling around him, Manning suddenly materialized with Ji-Hoon at his side. "This is your whip, Mr. President . . . I suggest that you crack it occasionally and shout some orders. Agent Wimba will cover your six while the rest of us will force a hole in the crowd."

Having already approved the escape plan, Franklin might have been insulted by the instructions but wasn't. The truth was that he *needed* a reminder, a way to connect with the new reality, and nodded as he accepted the whip. "I've been waiting a long time for this."

Manning grinned. "Yes, sir, I'm sure you have. Make it look good because plan B really sucks."

Franklin laughed, knew it was the wrong expression, and adopted a frown. Then, herding his security detail in front of him, the president of the United States started down the side of the hill.

Chaos reigned all around as the whip-crack sound of the orbital bombardment began, *real* overseers tried to restore order, and Sauron fighters circled the hill. Sharpshooters, located high in the observation towers, added to the confusion. Each slave that they shot was like a raindrop hitting the surface of a pond. Concentric rings of fear rippled out through the crowd. People turned uphill in an effort to escape, only to encounter the slaves coming down. Fights erupted, people screamed, and a woman was crushed.

Kan, none of whom had been trained for what amounted to riot control, added to the confusion by jumping from point to point, issuing contradictory orders, and even arguing with each other. That's when the SUV exploded, the watch commander mistakenly assumed that the hill was under attack from the surrounding forests, and ordered his troops to rally around Observation Tower ^–[]. This error in judgment proved to be a godsend for Franklin and his security team, who passed the crater where Taglio had died, down through the still-smoldering main gate, and out into the relative freedom beyond.

That's when Franklin tossed the whip aside, turned, and looked back at Hell Hill. There were more fighters now—circling like flies above a dead corpse. The chief executive turned toward Manning. His voice was hard and cold. "Any word from Deac Smith? Is he ready?"

"Yes, sir. Ready and waiting."

Franklin nodded. "Tell him to fire."

Manning passed the order, twenty seconds passed, and fifteen man-portable FIM-92C Stingers leaped up out of the surrounding forests, located the heat they were searching for, and took off in hot pursuit. Alarms sounded within the alien fighters, but the pilots hadn't encountered any resistance in a long time, and precious seconds were lost while they double-checked their systems.

Two of the heat-seekers suffered malfunctions and never connected with their targets. Three missiles chose the *same* target and blew it out of the sky. The rest of the Stingers went one-on-one with the manta-ray-shaped fighters, and with the exception of a single aircraft that managed to limp toward the east, the rest were destroyed.

The security team applauded and Franklin nodded in agreement. "What was it my daddy used to say? 'It ain't over till it's over'? I think that pretty much sums it up."

Those close enough to hear chuckled, Manning waved the group forward, and the government of the United States of America melted into the forest.

NEAR THE MAYAN RUINS OF NAKABE, GUATEMALA

The storage room was large, *very* large, which was the reason why Ott-Mar had chosen it for use as his makeshift surgery. The walls were lined with floor-to-ceiling metal-faced drawers. There were thousands of them, and each was large enough to hold a few personal effects. Later, as each nymph emerged from his cell, inherited memories would push themselves forward and each newly born Sauron would visit the storage room to collect his particular inheritance.

The nature of such bequeathments would vary. Some would consist of ancient artifacts, brought from the home world and carried through space. Others would include items looted from conquered worlds, tools peculiar to that particular line's area of expertise, and, though somewhat rare, scholarly works authored by two or even three generations of progenitors.

Now, filled as it was with the harsh glare of stand-mounted work lights, the specially constructed operating table on which Hak-Bin lay, banks of life-support equipment, backups for the life-support equipment, a back table loaded with surgical instruments, a console dedicated to anesthesia, and three strange-looking suspension frames, the room seemed a little smaller.

Or that's the way it seemed to Grand Vizier Tog, who, contrary to what he imagined to be good medical practice, not to mention his own personal preferences, had been ordered to be in attendance. The reason for this travesty was too apparent. Hak-Bin, who remained conscious and lucid in spite of the heavy-duty preoperative medications administered by Ott-Mar, wanted all those having shared responsibility for his physical well-being to be present during the operation so that it would be easier to kill them if anything went wrong.

That's why Hak-Bin's chief of security, the murderous Kat-Duu, stood on the far side of the room. He wore two perfectly matched t-guns in black thorax holsters and seemed to be enjoying himself.

It was a horrible situation, the worst Tog had ever managed to get himself into, which accounted for the sudden flurry of prayers. There hadn't been much to ask for, not since Tog's elevation to the Droma, but the present circumstances provided sufficient motivation.

Would the Great One respond? There was no way to be sure, of course, but not having requested anything in quite a long time, the prelate imagined that his request might go to the head of the line, where it would be acted on with a degree of urgency consistent with his lofty rank.

In the meantime Ott-Mar sent for the donors. The Fon, each selected because of a near-perfect health record, and surreptitiously tested to ensure that they were free of all the chemicals, hormones, and enzymes associated with the change, had been summoned to the temple under false pretenses. The functionaries had no idea what awaited them until the moment when they entered the operating room and were seized by specially trained Kan. Understandably surprised, not to mention frightened, the unsuspecting Fon kicked and squealed as they were transported from one side of the room to the other, locked into metal frames, and gagged.

The Kan were still in the process of wrapping tape around their snouts when Hak-Bin addressed them from his place on the operating table. "Please allow me to apologize to you and your respective lines. Like warriors in a battle, it is now necessary to sacrifice your lives so that the race can live. I now add your names to those that shall be passed to my nymph and from him down through eternity. Thank you."

If the Fon were impressed by the signal honor thus bestowed upon them, there was no sign of it in the way that their eyes bulged, their limbs strained to break free, or their excrement soiled the floor.

Like outsiders caught in the midst of a family dispute, all four of the Ra 'Na technicians assigned to assist Ott-Mar did the best they could to ignore the manner in which the "donors" had been treated, little suspecting the fate already in wait for them.

But Tog *knew*, and not only knew, but had chosen them with that reality in mind. It wasn't something the prelate liked to focus on, however—so he forced his mind away.

Satisfied that he had done the right thing where the Fon were concerned, Hak-Bin gestured to Ott-Mar and surrendered himself to the fates.

Well aware of the operation's purpose, and the way it would impact him, Hak-Bin's nymph went on a rampage, only to discover that certain medications had been used to limit the extent of his movements. The reality of that made the nymph furious. In spite of the fact that Ott-Mar would escape into death, Hak-Bin's nymph swore that the physician's offspring would suffer in his place, and do so for a long, long time.

Now, as both the Sauron and his nymph lost consciousness, the operation began in earnest. A saw whirred and fine black dust was sucked away as Ott-Mar removed sections of Hak-Bin's badly distorted chitin. Drills whined as the Ra 'Na medical technicians bored holes through donor exoskeletons, gained access to key blood vessels, and inserted the necessary catheters. Pumps came on-line, were tested, and hooked to lengths of clear plastic tubing.

Eventually, as the initial preparations were completed, Tog lost track of which tube led where, but understood the basic architecture of Ott-Mar's plan. Once the tubes were connected, and certain medications had been administered, Ott-Mar planned to remove every single drop of Hak-Bin's enzyme-polluted blood, replace it with fluids obtained from one or more of the donors, and thereby stabilize his patient long enough to get through the next thirty-five days.

Assuming things went well, and they would have to if the birthmaster wanted to live long enough to die properly, the high-nymph would continue to develop albeit much more slowly, and Hak-Bin, made a good deal more presentable as a result of cosmetic surgery, would be free to coordinate the final days. Unless something went wrong, in which case everyone, with the possible exception of Kat-Duu, would die almost immediately.

And so it was that Tog, along with others in the room, watched the green fluid surge through the clear plastic tubes and hoped that the procedure would prove successful. The process took time, however, and it was more than a full unit later before Ott-Mar announced that he was pleased with the results and ordered that the single surviving donor be put to death. Then, as the anesthesia was terminated, and Ott-Mar waited for his patient to awake, came the moment that Tog had been dreading.

Suddenly, at a nod from Kat-Duu, the Ra 'Na med techs were seized and shackled together. Tog tried to merge Kan-like with the background, but it didn't work. Kat-Duu wore something similar to an evil grin as he grabbed the prelate and dragged him out into the adjoining courtyard. The condemned were already in place—their backs to freshly dug graves. A group of humans, shovels in their hands, cowered against the back wall. "How do you want them killed?" the

Kan demanded. "A dart in the head? Slit their throats? Slow strangulation?"

The med tech named Isk sought Tog's eyes. The prelate saw the anger there and turned away. "You knew?" Isk demanded. "You *knew* they would kill us?"

"Don't be silly," Kat-Duu interjected. "Of course the Grand Vizier knew . . . Now, where were we? Ah, yes, the question of methodology. So, your furry eminence, what will it be?"

"Darts," Tog replied, his eyes on the floor.

"What did you say?" the Kan demanded. "Louder please . . . I couldn't hear you."

"Darts," the prelate reiterated, praying that the misery would end.

"Oh, *darts,*" Kat-Duu responded agreeably. "That's very generous of you. Much less painful . . . Well, come on then, I'm sure you'll want to be present, and there's no point in waiting around." That being said, the Kan walked down the line and shot each slave in the head. Isk was last, and no mattered how long he managed to live, Tog knew he would never forget the contempt in the technician's space-black eyes.

Then the eyes were gone as Isk's body toppled backward into the grave. That was the moment when Kat-Duu turned, aimed the t-gun between Tog's eyes, and produced something akin to a grin. The prelate, sure that Hak-Bin had forsaken him, wet himself.

Kat-Duu laughed, restored the weapon to its holster, and waved a pincer at the humans. "Fill the hole with dirt or jump in yourselves. It makes no difference to me."

The humans rushed forward, hurried to do the Sauron's bidding, and soon melted away.

Finally, after everyone else had left, Tog remained. The prelate felt an overwhelming sense of loss, grief, and shame. Regardless of the fact that the limestone was damp with his own urine, Tog dropped to knees. And it was then, after more than forty years of self-concerned twaddle, that the Great One finally heard a genuine prayer.

SALMON NATIONAL FOREST, IDAHO

The gravel road wound along the side of the gently rounded hill like a snake squeezing its prey. Ella's pregnancy was more visible by then, and Ivory took it slow, easing the old pickup through the potholes.

The trip to the top of the hill was something of a luxury, both in terms of the fuel that it would consume and time stolen from other activities. But it was important, so important that Ivory was willing to risk a daylight journey, and to hell with the consequences. Besides, for reasons the racialist could only guess at, Sauron activity had been rather light lately, almost as if the aliens were busy elsewhere.

Though not identified as such on maps of the area, the wide spot had long been used as a scenic outlook, a place for lovers to park, and a pull-out for local hunters. Proof of that could still be seen in the broken glass that crunched under Ivory's boots, the shell casings that littered the ground, and the old picnic table someone had left.

Ella was waiting when Ivory rounded the front of the truck, allowed herself to be lifted down to the ground, and turned her face up for a kiss. "This was a nice idea, Jonathan . . . Who would have guessed that you would be such a romantic?"

Ivory kissed her, drank in the soap-clean smell of his wife's hair, and took her hand. "Come on, I want you to see the view."

Together the couple walked over to the badly weathered picnic table, sat on the top, and placed their boots on the sole surviving bench.

Ella had been there on previous occasions, but not for a couple of years, and had forgotten how beautiful the view actually was. There were trees, thousands of acres of second- or third-generation forest, all of it gold with buttery sunlight. And there, not far beyond, lay Howther Lake. The water was so clear she could see logs lying at the bottom, and, had they been down closer, might have seen trout swimming near the banks. The lake had belonged to her grandfather at one time, but that was before the federal government forced him to sell it, and added one more grievance to an already long list. Still, the lake was beautiful, and Ella said as much.

"Yes," Ivory agreed, as if waiting for that very comment. "The lake *is* beautiful—and very, very dangerous. That's where the Saurons will land, right where your grandfather liked to go fishing, not two miles from Racehome.

"Then," he said, pointing to the northwest, "the chits will follow the old trail up toward the complex, break through the perimeter, and enter the mine. The rest won't be very pretty."

Ella started to say something, but Ivory raised a hand. "Don't get me wrong, we'll kill some of the bastards, hell, we'll kill a lot of them, but not enough. The simple fact is that they have aircraft, and we don't, which means we're going to lose."

Ella searched her husband's face. "That's what you brought me all the way up here for? To tell me we're going to lose? Why now, Jonathan? Why didn't you say these things before?"

Ivory could feel her pulling back, could feel the growing anger, but bulled ahead. "Because we weren't advertising our presence before . . . Every time Dent goes on-air it's like a poke in the eye. The Saurons won't put up with that forever."

"The transmitters are located a long ways off," Ella said levelly, "you know that. This is about Dent isn't it? You're jealous."

"No," Ivory lied, "this isn't about Dent. It's about my wife and baby. Racehome isn't safe. There's no way I can make it safe. Please allow me to move you, your mother, and your personal staff to a better location. I'll stay here and do everything I can to protect both Dent and Racehome."

The expression on Ella's face seemed to soften. "Your concern means a great deal to me, Jonathan . . . but I could never agree to that. What about those who stay? It would appear as though we were ready to sacrifice them."

I *am* ready to sacrifice them, Ivory thought to himself, but knew better than to say it out loud. "I figured you would say something like that."

Ella raised a carefully plucked eyebrow. "So?"

Ivory shrugged. "So, I'm going to insist."

Ella heard the crunch of gravel and turned in time to see four members of Ivory's elite Hammer-Skin unit emerge from the surrounding brush. They wore camouflage and full combat gear. There were women as well, a physician's assistant, and an LPN. Neither women was willing to meet her gaze. Ella turned to her husband. Her eyes were narrowed to slits, and her mouth made a hard, straight line. "You'll pay for this."

Ivory sighed. "Yes, I suspect I will."

ABOARD THE SAURON DREADNOUGHT *HOK NOR AH*

It was dark inside the passageway, *very* dark, and packed with small furry bodies. Their leader, none other than the now-legendary Fra Pol, checked the device on his wrist. Another five units, that's how long he and thousands of others would have to wait. It was important for every group to attack at exactly the same moment.

Dro Rul, acting in the role of general, had gone to great lengths in order to emphasize that. "First comes the advantage of surprise . . . Though powerful, this weapon fires but a single shot, so it should be used to maximum effect. Then we must divide them," the Droma continued, "and thereby reduce their strength. Should one of our teams attack prematurely, and go down to defeat, the Kan thus freed will rush to defend other parts of the fleet.

"Finally," Rul cautioned, "there is the matter of our allies. Even as we attack the Saurons in space, the humans will do likewise down on the surface."

It made sense, Pol knew that, but the waiting was hard. Somebody began to pray. Not too surprising since most of the officers and noncoms were members of the clergy. Would the Saurons hear? Probably not, but it was best to take no chances. The initiate called for "silence" and such was his credibility that not one of the often querulous Ra 'Na took exception to the order.

One of the commandos grinned. "So, Fra Pol," he whispered, "are you glad to be back?"

"Thrilled," Pol responded, remembering the furtive manner in which he had been smuggled aboard. "I left in a garbage disposal unit—and returned in a grain bin. It would be nice to ride in a seat for a change." The commando chuckled, as did others close enough to hear, and the seconds ticked away.

Will the revolt work? Pol wondered. And how many of us are about to die? Not that it makes much difference since every single one of us is slated to die in any case.

Pol looked at his wrist chron, confirmed that only one unit of time remained, and checked his weapon. After experimenting with a variety of human-manufactured guns, and determining that most were too large for the average Ra 'Na, and produced excessive recoil, the research and development team worked to produce small but serviceable .22-caliber submachine guns. The only problem was that the relatively low-velocity slugs had a tendency to bounce off simulated chitin.

This issue was resolved by upgrading the ammo to .22

Magnum, substituting specially hardened "bug killer" rounds in place of the soft lead slugs, and equipping the "grease guns" to fire three-shot bursts. The fact that the .22 ammo fell well short of the velocity required to punch holes through hull metal was an added bonus.

One last look confirmed what Pol already knew—it was time to attack. This particular maintenance way, one of many that the Ra 'Na had managed to delete from the vessel's memory banks over the years, passed directly over the ship's bridge. There was very little doubt that the Saurons would be surprised when furry bodies began to tumble into the control room, but could they get a sufficient number of bodies through the hatch before the bugs were able to respond? To do so was critical, which was the reason why Pol had drilled his team in secret.

Pol made contact with his second-in-command, a female name Lin Mok, and saw the way her ears were laid back against her skull. He nodded, and having already checked to make sure the hatch was unlocked, Mok jerked it up and out of the way. She was the first one through—immediately followed by Pol.

Strangely enough the bridge of a Sauron starship was one of the few places where all three castes worked together. In keeping with a requirement for literacy, not to mention political control, commanding officers were drawn from the ranks of the Zin. War officers, those in charge of the vessel's weapons systems were Kan, and systems officers, those responsible for everything from life support to garbage disposal, were Fon functionaries.

Or course the *real* work, not to mention technical savvy, was supplied by Ra 'Na slaves, some of whom were aligned with the resistance and some of whom were not. Even sympathetic technicians had intentionally been left in the dark lest they inadvertently give warning.

Son-Das, the Zin who had the misfortune to be on duty

at that particular time, was resting in the command sling, scanning the latest readiness reports, when Ra 'Na resistance fighters began to pour out of a hole not five units from his head. There was barely enough time to recognize one of the intruders as Lin-Mok, a female assigned to no less a personage than Lord Hak-Bin, when the formerly respectful slave raised some sort of weapon and fired a burst at his head.

Three of the .22-caliber slugs hit the target, punched holes through the Sauron's skull, and blew brain tissue out through the back of his head. The others spanged off the bulkhead beyond, buzzed like enraged bees, and slammed into an equipment rack. Other guns chattered, the weapons officer collapsed, and the systems officer was wounded.

Pol, who had intentionally withheld his fire in order to focus all of his attention on the responsibilities of command, shouted, "Hold your fire!" even as a ricochet whined past his right ear. The commandos obeyed and looked around the room in stupefied silence. Every single one of them had been exposed to violence since birth, but always directed toward *them*, never the other way around.

Now, to see dead Saurons, killed by their own hands, was both wonderful and amazing at the same time. The fact that other Saurons had survived, and stood helpless before their guns, was equally wondrous. The Ra 'Na were still absorbing that, still processing it, when Pol issued the next set of orders. "Mok, put the surviving Saurons in a corner and post a guard on them. That includes our people . . . Maybe they support us and maybe they don't. We'll sort that out later. The rest of you safe your weapons. We have enough problems without someone shooting themselves in the foot.

"Da Dwa . . . Get on the com. I want to know how things went in the Fire Control Center, the Propulsion Pods, and down on the Launch Deck. Once that's out of the way, put a call in to Dro Rul. He'll want a report."

Dwa slipped into a recently vacated seat, touched some

keys, and met with immediate success. Video appeared. A bloody bandage had been wrapped around the technician's head and his voice was filled with pride and determination. "This is the Fire Control Center of the Ra 'Na vessel *Liberty*. How can I assist you?"

Dwa couldn't help but smile in response to the manner in which the ship had already been renamed. "This is the bridge . . . please report."

The resistance fighter at the other end of the call nodded grimly, said "Thanks be to the Great One for your victory," and plucked the camera out of the console in front of him. Then, holding the device at arm's length, he panned the compartment. Pol, who had taken up a position that allowed him to look down over Dwa's shoulder, saw what looked like utter devastation.

Unlike the bridge, the Fire Control Center had been staffed by Kan. Even after no less than three human-manufactured flash grenades had been dropped into the compartment from a ventilation duct, quickly followed by a homemade gas bomb, the Kan *still* put up a fight. And, judging from the chaotic sprawl of both Sauron and Ra 'Na bodies, had nearly won. In fact, judging from the video, no more than six of twenty-six Ra 'Na commandos survived, and half of them were wounded. "Did you take any prisoners?" Pol inquired. "If so, what kind of shape are they in?"

The commando restored the camera to the console in front of him. His features were hard and grim. "There are no prisoners," he said flatly, "none whatsoever."

"No Ra 'Na?" Pol persisted.

"The collaborators died defending their masters," the commando replied, his eyes daring Pol to take exception.

Though opposed to what amounted to summary executions, the cleric understood. He nodded. "My name is Pol, Fra Pol, and I am in temporary command of this ship. Lock yourselves in, make repairs if that's possible, and don't allow anyone to fire the vessel's weapons without my authorization. Is that understood?"

The commando, who had been forced to memorize the name and face of every officer who might wind up in command, nodded. "Understood."

"Good," Fra Pol concluded, "and there will be no more executions. We are Ra 'Na—not Saurons. Pol out."

■ ■ ■

The attack on the *Hok Nor Ah*'s port propulsion pod was a fiasco from the start. P'ere Slas, the cleric in command, had little if any aptitude for things military, and, typical of the church services for which he had responsibility, launched his attack ten units after he was supposed to.

As a consequence of that, and the fact that the Fon in charge of Propulsion Pod Two had been warned by that time, a dozen Kan were ready and waiting when the Ra 'Na made their move. The slow-moving Slas was killed within seconds of emerging from the deck-level air duct. The second Ra 'Na to enter the engineering space did manage to fire a single burst, however, and as luck would have it, hit a bulkhead-mounted fire extinguisher. It went off, fell to the deck, and spun like a top.

The distraction provided just enough time for three additional Ra 'Na to enter the compartment, two of whom used their weapons to good effect.

A Kan warrior staggered under the unexpected onslaught, threw his pincers into the air, and died. But there were *more* Kan—and they wasted little time revenging their brother's death.

Given her status as a medic, Shu was one of the last commandos to emerge from the air duct and had little choice but to step on her leader's dead body. Not counting a clutch of Fon functionaries, who watched in stunned silence, only two defenders remained. The first, a fearsome-looking Kan,

lifted a struggling Ra 'Na over his head and threw the resistance fighter down. There was a sickening thud, as the
little body smacked into the metal deck and lay motionless.
Shu threw herself forward. The Kan staggered as the medic
landed on his back, attempted to shake the Ra 'Na off, and
failed.

The weapon, a small off-the-shelf Teckna survival knife,
rose and fell. Thanks to illicit dissections Shu helped Pol
perform on dead Saurons, the medic had a better-than-
average understanding of their anatomy. She aimed the
dagger-shaped blade for the crevice where the warrior's neck
armor came into contact with his thorax and rammed it
home.

Blood spurted, the Kan howled in pain, and fell as a damage control ax bit into the side of his right leg. The warrior's
most recent assailant, a normally mild-mannered brother
named Yath, recited the death hona as he broke the blade
free from the Kan's exoskeleton and took a second swing.
The ax cut all the way through this time and lopped the
extremity off. Blood spurted, and Shu managed to jump
clear just as the Sauron fell.

Both Ra 'Na were prepared to resume the attack, but the
Kan grabbed his stump, said something incomprehensible,
and departed to join his ancestors. That was when the med
tech took a look around, heard the intercom go off, and
heard a familiar voice. "Propulsion Pod Two? This is the
bridge. Report."

She stepped over the body of a fallen comrade, made her
way to the com console, and found Pol looking back at her.
He saw the blood on her clothes and gave thanks for the fact
that all of it was green. "Shu? Are you all right?"

The medic nodded, thanked the Great One for keeping
Pol alive, and made her report. "Yes, I'm fine, but most of
the team weren't so lucky. P'ere Slas launched the attack
late—and the Kan were waiting for us."

Pol nodded his understanding. "Propulsion Pod One remains under Sauron control—as does the Launch Deck. Both attacks failed. Odds are that one of the two locations managed to warn the staff in Pod Two."

"And you took the bridge?"

"Yes, we did, and the Fire Control Center as well."

"Which means?"

"Which means we must hold," Pol said thickly. "And hold, and hold, and hold. We don't control the ship—but neither do the Saurons. So secure the hatches, disable the servos, and prepare for a counterattack."

Shu looked at Yath, and he nodded. "The hatches to Pod Two have been secured. How 'bout the rest of the fleet?"

"Reports are still coming in, but it looks like at least twenty-five percent of the fleet is ours."

Shu placed a finger on the screen. Pol knew that anyone with access to a com screen could see—but decided he didn't care. "I love you."

"And I," the initiate replied, "love you."

Elsewhere aboard the *Liberty*, and dozens of other ships, the battle continued to rage. A blow had been struck—but the war raged on.

NEAR THE MAYAN RUINS OF NAKABE, GUATEMALA

Lord Hak-Bin had been moved from the makeshift operating room to more pleasant quarters, where he could recover from the effects of the anesthesia and the operation itself. In fact, unlike the indigenous structures that most Saurons had little choice but to take advantage of, the lodge with the high-peaked roof, removable walls, and generous floor plan had been constructed with Sauron comforts in mind.

The fact that the quarters had previously been occupied by Dun-Dar, who was now forced to wait in his own antechamber, added to that individual's growing sense of frustration. News, all of it bad, continued to pour in. Not only had there been some sort of slave revolt at the citadel located north of the equator—the fleet was under attack as well. Was Hak-Bin aware of that? No. Why? Because Ott-Mar had given instructions that his patient should not be disturbed. So now, as Dun-Dar was forced to await admittance to his own lodge, the Lord high-idiot lolled within. Or so the stonemaster assumed.

In that regard, however, Dun-Dar was wrong. Far from lolling about, Hak-Bin was not only up, and on his feet, but he stood admiring himself in a full-length mirror. In spite of the fact that his body was still somewhat swollen, and the manner in which stainless-steel sutures had been used to hold certain sections of chitin together, he looked much more presentable than before. So much so in fact that the Zin wouldn't hesitate to appear in public. Not nude, of course, but swathed in one of his new custom-made black togas, and hung with the ornaments of office.

Of far more importance than how he looked was how Hak-Bin *felt*. Not only had the transfusion cleansed his blood of change-related toxins, it effectively put the increasingly demanding nymph on hold and infused his body with energy. So much so that the Zin shuffled over to the door, threw it open, and was about to take a walk when he found himself snout-to-snout with a startled Dun-Dar. The stonemaster managed to recover his composure and gestured respect. "Lord Hak-Bin . . . Ott-Mar said your health was much improved. I'm pleased to see that his report was accurate."

Hak-Bin took note of the manner in which the word "health" had been used as a stand-in for his actual condition and gave the normally blunt stonemaster credit for some tact. "Thank you, Dun-Dar, I feel much better. My apologies for usurping your quarters. Please allow me to assure that I will withdraw by day's end."

The mere mention of the manner in which he had been

inconvenienced went a long way toward improving Dun-Dar's mood. "It was nothing," the stonemaster lied. "I'm sorry to bother you during your convalescence, but I have news to impart."

"None of which will be good," Hak-Bin responded, catching a whiff of the pheromone the other Sauron had emitted and correctly assessing the stonemaster's body language. "Well, come in, make yourself comfortable in your own quarters, and tell me the worst. I'm back now—and ready for most anything."

But Hak-Bin *wasn't* ready, not for the news that Franklin had escaped a well-deserved death, that the human resistance fighters had gone so far as to attack Sauron fighters, that a group of ferals were making regular radio broadcasts, that a large number of formerly placid Ra 'Na were in open revolt, that fully half of the *Hok Nor Ah* had come under their control, that more than a quarter of the fleet was now in their hands, and that a large number of Zin were after his head. It was a lot to absorb—but Hak-Bin managed to do so. Dun-Dar watched in wonder as the other Zin not only withstood the onslaught of negative news but seemed energized by it. If ever there had been evidence that Hak-Bin had been born to lead, here it was.

"Disturbing though the situation is, it could be worse," Hak-Bin allowed thoughtfully. "Based on your report it sounds as if the citadels are intact, both catalyst factories remain under construction, and seventy-five percent of the fleet is under Sauron control."

Dun-Dar could see the manner in which the other Zin was already at work weaving the facts into a story that the Council of Clans might accept—and was amazed by the other Sauron's brazen effrontery. "Yes, lord, your points are well taken. How can I and those under my command be of service?"

"Keep the slaves under control," Hak-bin replied. "Finish

the citadel, complete the necessary preparations for the great day, and save a cell for me. It will be an honor to die here with leaders such as yourself."

This was high praise indeed, and even though Dun-Dar suspected that the other Sauron was trying to manipulate him, he couldn't help but feel flattered. "I will see to it myself, lord. My nymph is pledged to yours. May I ask where you will go from here?"

Hak-Bin looked surprised. "Why, up into orbit . . . The fleet falls under my authority does it not?"

Dun-Dar bowed formally. "Yes, eminence, I feel confident that it does."

NEAR BELLINGHAM, WASHINGTON

The house had been rather nice at one time, but that was before the owners were forced into slavery, looters trashed the place, and the birds moved in. Now, with the exception of the single room in which the meeting was being held, the place was a mess.

Still, while not as nice as it had been, a little cleanup work had been sufficient to restore the dining room to something like livability. The heavily scarred dining room table, which had once been the center of family dinners, was now laden with maps, binoculars, a pistol belt, and multiple cups of instant coffee. Professor Boyer Blue blew the steam off the black brew and raised the mug into air. "To the president of United States . . . A free man at last!"

Franklin grinned. "Maybe not *free* . . . but out and about."

Deac Smith took a ceremonial sip of coffee. "We'll take what we can get."

"I'll second that," the man called Patience added, "although the Sasquatch Nation regrets the fact that Sauron fighters were allowed to crash into the fragile waters of Puget Sound. Who knows what sort of pollutants have leaked out to poison the water?"

Franklin would have been happy to see five hundred Sauron fighters dive into Puget Sound, but nodded dutifully and gave thanks for the fact that Blue had been able to bring the greens back to the table after Amocar assassinated their leader. The fact that the onetime bodyguard had been killed while trying to shoot the very man he was pledged to protect had gone a long way toward placating them. "Yes," Franklin replied, "I'm sure we all look forward to the time when we can work on a global cleanup. In the meantime the battle continues—and I would like to introduce P'ere Nec who agreed to sit in on behalf of Dro Rul."

The Ra 'Na sat level with everyone else with the aid of two telephone books. He had dark, nearly black fur, streaked with rust and gold. Like most of Dro Rul's inner circle, the cleric had an ascetic bent and wore plain brown robes. His beady brown eyes darted from one face to the next. "Dro Rul sends both his regards and his apologies but knows you will understand. Our people launched their attack on the oppressors approximately twelve units ago. Dro Rul felt it was important that he be with our people."

Blue nodded. "Yes, of course. Thank you for making the long dangerous journey to the surface."

"There are dangers," the cleric conceded, "but conditions continue to improve. I came here from a Ra 'Na-controlled factory ship, on a Ra 'Na shuttle, with two Ra 'Na fighters for protection. A wondrous moment indeed."

"Absolutely," Franklin agreed. "But while I have no wish to understate our joint accomplishments, it's my duty to focus on the tasks that lie ahead. So, if no one objects, I would like to discuss item number two on the agenda."

Having heard no objections, the chief executive officer nodded. "This particular issue has more relevance to those of us who happen to be human—but would have an impact on our alliance with the Ra 'Na should anything happen to me."

"Which it darned near did," Smith said heavily.

"Yes, there was something of a close call," Franklin admitted reluctantly, "but, thanks to the folks on my security team, I'm still around. The next attempt could be successful, however, which is why we need a vice president. I believe that Professor Blue is an excellent candidate—and hereby nominate him."

Blue raised an eyebrow. "Regardless of his wishes?"

"Yes," Franklin answered decisively. "I can't *force* you to accept my nomination—but I hope your conscience will. The requirements of the people, and of our alliance with the Ra 'Na, leave little room for personal preference."

"Motion seconded," Smith said firmly.

Given the fact that only one potential candidate remained, all heads swiveled toward Patience. He was a big man with a round face and a bushy beard. He raised both hands palms outward. "Oh, no you don't . . . I hang drywall with the best of them, play a little banjo, and sing in the choir. But a politician I'm not, and, assuming this thing goes our way, that's what you're going to need."

All eyes returned to Blue. The historian had already passed on the presidency—for what he thought were excellent reasons. But now, with no other takers, the academic couldn't find it in his heart to refuse. "All right . . . if that's what you want me to do. But only till proper elections can be held."

"Done," Franklin replied. "The nomination has been made and seconded. No other nominations were put forward. All those in favor of Professor Boyer Blue for vice president of the United States say 'aye.' "

There was a chorus of "ayes."

Franklin nodded. "Let the record show that Professor Blue was named vice president by acclamation, to serve until regular elections can be held or until this body shall determine otherwise."

There were cheers, followed by another toast, and the historian made history. There had been other African-American presidents, but this was the first time that African Americans had held *both* of the country's top political positions, and was something to be proud of if they lived long enough to celebrate.

"Now," Franklin said, "let's tackle the next item on the agenda. While we attacked the Saurons—another group attacked *us*. I refer to the so-called Society of the White Rose—a group that seeks to spread hatred via regular radio broadcasts. If I'm not mistaken, this is the same group of so-called 'racialists' who murdered my wife. If we ignore the bastards, they could not only draw support away from our cause—they could use racism to destroy any chance of putting American society back together when this is over."

Manning, who stood at the back of the room, winced. Not only had he been in love with the president's wife, but his sister had been an enthusiastic member of the organization under discussion and directly responsible for Jina's death.

"An excellent point," Smith commented softly. "Were the FBI and Secret Service still functional, they'd go after the scumbags full force."

There was silence for a moment. When Patience spoke his voice was hesitant—as if unsure of how his words would be received. "No offense, Mr. President, them having killed your wife and all, but is this the right time to go after them? We don't have a lot of resources as it is . . . Can the resistance fight on two fronts and win?"

It was a practical question and deserved a practical answer. Franklin raised his estimation of the self-described drywall hanger by a full notch. "Patience makes a good point. I can't even pretend to be objective. What do the rest of you think? Should we go after the White Rose? Can we afford to do so? And where are they anyway?"

P'ere Nec cleared his throat self-consciously. "Their head-quarters are located in the area you call Idaho. Our technicians noticed the facility sometime ago, but, as with so many other things, they forgot to report it to the Saurons."

There were chuckles all around. Blue was first to speak. "Yes, I think we should go after them, but no, we can't afford to do so. Not in the conventional sense anyway."

Franklin leaned back in his chair. It made a creaking sound. "Your comment seems to suggest that a nonconventional means might exist. Do you have something specific in mind?"

"Yes," Blue replied carefully, "I do. It's kind of Machiavellian, however—and wouldn't look very nice in the history books."

"Screw the history books," Franklin said pragmatically. "Unless we manage to win, there won't be any history books. What's your idea?"

"Well," Blue began, his delivery unconsciously shifting to cadences once used in the classroom, "thanks to our Ra 'Na allies we know where these people live. That being the case, we could feed the information to the bugs and let *them* handle the problem."

Franklin gave a long low whistle. "That *is* Machiavellian. But I like it . . . How 'bout the children? What happens to them?"

Blue was amazed to discover that he hadn't thought about the possibility of children. Had he changed? Become hardened by months of ruthless occupation? Yes, it seemed that he had. Horrible though it was, he was willing to condemn children to death in order to achieve what he saw as the greater good. Just like so many of the historical figures he had once lectured about. When Blue spoke it was as if the voice belonged to a stranger. "I wish there was some way to protect them, Mr. President, but I don't see how."

The room was silent for a moment, and Franklin bowed

his head. "No, I suppose there isn't. You were correct, Boyer, this won't look very pretty in the history books, but I feel we have very little choice. We need to put everything we have into fighting the Saurons. So, how would it work? Why would the Saurons listen to us?"

P'ere Nec spoke with downcast eyes. "I am ashamed to say that not all of my kind support the resistance. They have been slaves for such a long period of time that some identify themselves with the Saurons. One, a collaborator named Dro Tog, would be happy to convey the news to his masters."

Franklin allowed the front legs of his chair to hit the hardwood floor with a loud thump. "Brilliant! Let's make it happen . . ."

The resistance leaders moved on to the next agenda item after that, but Boyer Blue, who had seen his own daughter die on a live television broadcast, soon lost the thread. *More children would die*—and the responsibility was his.

DARK SIDE OF THE MOON

Three fighters, all of which had been liberated from the ship *Nu Mor Ga (Memory of Ancestors)*, during the revolt, and now belonged to the newly formed Ra 'Na navy, lurked just off the dark side of Earth's moon. They were undetected so far, and the Great One willing, would remain so long enough for Tra and his two companions to complete their mission. Lord Hak-Bin had vanished from sight for a period of time, but now, judging from the com traffic that raced back and forth between the citadel near Nakabe, Guatemala, and the dreadnought *Ib Se Ma (Taker of Worlds)*, the big bug was about to reappear.

It could be something else, of course, since the Sauron transmissions had been encrypted using code generators developed by the Ra 'Na themselves, but the pattern looked promising. There was quite a bit of evidence that Hak-Bin had been holed up in the citadel at Nakabe . . . and the *Ib*

Se Ma was one of the few major warships not sabotaged, damaged, or somehow compromised during the revolt.

So, assuming that Ra 'Na intelligence was correct, and Hak-Bin was about to lift off, the mission was relatively simple: intercept the Sauron shuttle and destroy it.

There were problems, however, not the least of which was the fact that neither Tra nor his fellow pilots had been trained to fly anything other than shuttles and other unarmed craft. Yes, Ra 'Na pilots had flown combat missions in the distant past—the fact that interceptors even existed was proof of that fact—but unlike his Kan counterparts, who were born with inherited skills, Tra had none of *his* ancestor's skills to guide him.

Not only that, but given the fact that only a handful of interceptors had been converted for use by Ra 'Na pilots, there was every likelihood that the three-person attack force would be outnumbered as well. The knowledge of that weighed heavily as the newly minted fighter pilot sat in the recently converted seat, his face plate retracted, trying to ignore the coppery smell of Kan body odor that still permeated the cockpit. He was frightened, *very* frightened, but happy to be where he was. *If* they could pull the mission off, *if* they could kill Hak-Bin, the odds would be greatly improved. Momentarily leaderless, the Saurons would squabble amongst themselves, and Dro Rul would capitalize on that.

Tra checked the hastily converted control board, wished the waiting was over, and stared out into the blackness of space. Perhaps someday his people would return home. Where was the much-storied Balwur anyway? Straight ahead? Somewhere astern? If the stars knew, they refused to answer.

ABOARD THE SAURON SHUTTLE *OR SU,* (USEFUL)

The shuttle had cleared Earth's atmosphere and was on course to land aboard the *Ib Se Ma,* when the warning arrived. The pilots received it, checked to make sure the fighter escorts had as well, and sent word to Hak-Bin via a Fon named Ath-Dee. He shuffled down the aisle, bowed, and delivered the news in the slow, ponderous style he considered appropriate for intercourse with members of the Zin caste.

"I'm sorry to disturb your eminence, but it seems that the slaves seized some of our fighters, three of which are positioned on the far side of the moon. Based on their location, and the fact that they have already started to accelerate, there is a strong possibility that they intend to attack this shuttle. The pilots believe that we can outrun them. Please check to ensure that your safety harness is secured . . . and notify me if there's anything else I can do."

Hak-Bin occupied a thronelike passenger sling that took up a disproportionate amount of the cabin. Ott-Mar rested within a standard sling toward the front of the compartment, and Tog, who wished he was somewhere else, occupied a bolt-down seat on the far side of the main aisle. Hak-Bin looked up from a swing-out data screen and regarded the Fon with the Sauron equivalent of a frown. "We have a fighter escort?"

"Yes, your lordship. Five of them."

"Who is in command of this shuttle?"

"Pilot, Hol-Zee, your lordship."

"Go forward. Tell Hol-Zee that Saurons don't run from slaves and to reduce his speed by twenty-five percent. The slaves will attack, our escorts will slaughter them, and the fur balls will learn a lesson. Understood?"

Ath-Dee swallowed hard. Hol-Zee wasn't going to like the message and might very well take it out on him. Why couldn't the two of them communicate via the intercom? But the functionary, who was secretly teaching himself to read, already knew the answer. Because by forcing him to carry their messages back and forth they formalized the caste system and kept themselves in power. Ath-Dee said, "Yes, eminence, right away, your eminence," and shuffled toward the cockpit.

Meanwhile, sitting where he could hear the entire interchange, Tog felt his bowels begin to loosen. There had been rumors on the ground but nothing he could put a finger on. Now it seemed apparent that Dro Rul and his cadre of fanatics had gone so far as to stage a revolt of some sort! More than that, they were intent on killing Hak-Bin himself! Not to mention the poor souls who might be with him. The essential unfairness of that made the prelate angry—and thoughtful. What if the lunatics actually managed to win? What then?

Tog remembered the murders, the mass grave, and felt a sudden sense of panic. Maybe, just maybe, he could change Hak-Bin's mind. Tog cleared his throat. "Excuse me, eminence—but I couldn't help but overhear . . . Might I offer a comment?"

Hak-Bin looked up from the screen just as the shuttle started to slow. The Sauron had little but contempt for most of the Ra 'Na race, but Tog was consistently useful. The occasional indulgence would cause no great harm. "Yes, Grand Vizier?"

Tog had come to dislike the title, especially in light of the revolt, but didn't dare say so. "The plan you outlined made perfect sense . . . But what if something were to go wrong? How would the Sauron race, not to mention humble servants such as myself, fare in the event of your premature death? I urge you to reconsider."

"Yes," Ott-Mar put in, "I certainly didn't operate on you only to have the results of my efforts destroyed by rebellious slaves."

Such was the extent of Hak-Bin's ego that he actually believed both individuals cared about his safety. "Your concern for the well-being of the race does both of you credit,"

Hak-Bin replied gravely. "However, please consider the larger context. Assuming that the threat assessment is accurate, and the slaves are gunning for me, eyes on both sides of the conflict are waiting to see what we will do. Should we run, that sends one kind of message—if we don't, that sends another.

"Besides," Hak-Bin said confidently, "once the slaves come within range our escorts will annihilate them. So sit back, relax, and the entire matter will soon be settled."

Tog wasn't so sure. In spite of the fact that the Ra 'Na pilots were not only gullible enough to be swayed by Dro Rul, they *were* Ra 'Na, which meant that their technical savvy was superior to that possessed by their opponents. He couldn't say that, of course, so the prelate offered a bow and was forced to await his fate.

■ ■ ■

Triggered by an order from the Ra 'Na-controlled *Nu Mor Ga*, and guided by tracking data supplied by the Fire Control Center aboard the very same ship, the fighters emerged from cover and began the long run in toward their intended target. Tra frowned as the target vessel slowed. Why would it do that? Shouldn't they apply power rather than reduce it? Not if they *wanted* the Ra 'Na to attack. That's when the Ra 'Na saw that three of the five delta-shaped symbols on his display had turned to fight. Now it was clear that two of the interceptors had been assigned to remain with the shuttle—presenting still another screen of protection through which he and his companions would have to pass. It was a smart move and proof that the Kan knew what they were doing.

Tra scanned the control board, released his safeties, and touched the center of his chest for luck. The amulet his mate had sewn for him formed a lump under the fabric of his flight suit. Then, ears laid back under his helmet, teeth bared in an unconscious snarl, Tra pressed the attack. There were three things the Ra 'Na had promised himself he wouldn't do: He wouldn't break off, he wouldn't fire early, and he wouldn't shit in his flight suit. That's why Tra held the little ship steady, watched the oncoming fighters grow larger, and bore down on his sphincter. One of them, the interceptor in the center, was his.

The oncoming Kan fully expected the middle fighter to turn and run. After all, what fur ball in his or her right mind would face a Kan? That, plus the fact that a stern chase would make his job that much easier, caused the Sauron to withhold his fire.

But the incoming interceptor *didn't* turn . . . and the Kan felt his heart start to pump a little bit faster as he directed a message to his left pincer. It never arrived.

Lacking the confidence to use his weapons in a selective manner Tra fired all of them at once. All manner of offensive electronics came on, missiles lanced out from beneath stubby wings, and nose-mounted energy cannons burped coherent light.

The totality of the onslaught, plus the Kan's failure to act quickly, produced catastrophic results. The Sauron fighter exploded. A new sun appeared, was snuffed from existence, and took its place at the center of its own solar system.

Tra's fighter had already passed through the debris field, and emerged from the other side, by the time the truth dawned on him. He'd gone one-on-one with a Kan and won! A war whoop formed itself in the back of the fighter pilot's throat, but died as Tra eyed his screens. The Kan had destroyed the other two ships, turned back toward Hak-Bin's shuttle, and were hot on his trail.

Now, with two Saurons in pursuit and two waiting up ahead, Tra knew his fate. He was going to die. The only question was how many Kan would die with him. More confident now, and determined to make his death count, the Ra 'Na bored in.

Ing-Ort, the senior of the two pilots left to guard the shuttle, was disappointed by his brother's untimely death, but not entirely surprised. The planetary attack had been a one-way affair—and pilots like Gon-Por had grown somewhat complacent. He had warned them against such a possibility, but they knew better, or thought they did, and the results were plain to see. Slowly, almost casually, Ing-Ort brought his onboard electronic countermeasure equipment on-line, released his safeties, and applied power.

Tra was still a good distance away when the pursuing ships peeled off to either side, and suddenly he knew why. They had been herding him! Withholding their fire lest they inadvertently hit the shuttle!

Ing-Ort fired a pair of missiles, made an adjustment, and fired two more.

Tra saw the first set of tracks appear on his heads-up display, turned to avoid them, and placed himself right in front of missiles three and four. That's when the Ra 'Na realized that the opposing pilot had intentionally launched the first missiles at less than maximum speed—a possibility that never even occurred to him. It was a lesson learned, *and* a lesson lost, as the second pair of missiles struck their target and Tra was killed.

Seconds later, aboard the shuttle Tra had tried so hard to destroy, the Fon named Ath-Dee delivered the good news. He saw no reason to mention the loss of a fighter escort and therefore neglected to do so. "The rebel fighters were destroyed eminence—and full power has been restored. We should arrive aboard the *Ib Se Ma* eighteen units from now."

Hak-Bin looked up, said, "Of course," and returned to his screen.

Ott-Mar felt relieved—and Tog gave a prayer of thanks.

The deaths were unfortunate, but all too predictable, and the result of Rul's folly.

Meanwhile, in a last desperate attempt to hit the shuttle and kill its passengers, the *Nu Mor Ga* opened fire. But Sauron-controlled vessels responded in kind, other ships joined in, and the shuttle was able to escape.

Dro Rul, watching the battle from afar, bowed his head in prayer. The ship shuddered as its defensive screens neutralized most of the incoming fire but passed a little of the energy along. It seemed liberty had a price—and the price was very, very high.

ANACORTES, WASHINGTON

It was late evening, almost nighttime, as the small outboard pushed the boat in toward land. There was some chop as the wind blew waves in from the Strait of Juan De Fuca. The whitecaps hit the *Sunshine*'s metal hull, threw a smattering of spray up over the bow, and reluctantly gave way as the boat cut them in two.

Darby, worried lest the sound of the 20 hp motor give them away, gestured at the figure huddled in the stern. Though frequently contentious, and more than a little annoying, Chu was the only Crip that Darby had brought along. Though missing an arm, the young woman was otherwise intact and capable of returning on her own should that become necessary. "Back off the power a bit . . . the last thing I need is a reception committee."

"Yes, Admiral, whatever you say, Admiral," Chu responded sarcastically, but too low for the ex–petty officer to hear. The *Shine* moved sluggishly through the water as the twosome rounded Cap Sante and made their way toward the west. Thanks to orbital photos supplied by the Ra 'Na resistance movement, Darby knew the catalyst factory was located in what had been Volunteer Park, at Fourteenth Street and H Avenue.

But knowing where the facility was, and knowing what kind of conditions prevailed, were two different things. What about security? How many Kan had been stationed there? Where were the slaves quartered? How would the catalyst be stored?

Deac Smith needed answers to those questions and needed them badly if he and his forces were to launch an attack on the facility. That's why he had approached the Crips—in hopes they could obtain the information he needed.

Darby, who was, to the best of her knowledge, all that remained of the United States Navy, felt she had no choice but to agree. Especially now that Franklin had cut his ties to the Saurons—and irrevocably committed himself to the role of president.

The bow smacked a wave, the *Shine* bucked, and Darby pointed toward the city. Lights had appeared, *Sauron* lights, marking the factory's location for anyone who cared to see. And why not? The aliens were in charge—and had yet to take the resistance seriously. Chu nodded, angled the bow in toward the land, and applied a touch more power. The waves were hitting the starboard side of the boat by then— and threatening to spill over the top.

The ex–petty officer stared into the gloom. Had the Kan posted sentries all along the shoreline? Was she entering a trap? Or were they farther back? Wrapped around the factory? There was only one way to find out. Darby gestured again. "All right, this is far enough. Bring the bow into the waves. I'll meet you in ten hours. In the event that I fail to show up, come back in two hours. If I still fail to show up get the hell out of here. Understood?"

Chu had heard it before. She nodded and did her best to steady the boat as Darby moved to port. Then, the ex–petty officer sat on the boat's side, adjusted her face mask, and fell backward into the water.

Chu threw the motor into reverse and took a cupful of

water in over the stern as she backed away. It was hard to tell where Darby was, and the last thing Chu wanted to do was cut her with the prop. Then, sure that she was clear, Chu motored away. There were piers, plenty of them, each with a nice dark cave below.

The water was cold, even with the wet suit, and the desire to escape it propelled Darby toward shore. The ex–petty officer kicked with her fins, took occasional bearings on the Sauron lights, and closed with the shore. Then, while still fifty feet off from the shoreline, Darby paused to check for sentries. In spite of the fact that it was difficult to see, what with the up-and-down motion of the waves and the water droplets that dotted the surface of her mask, it appeared as if the shoreline was deserted.

Careful to make as little noise as possible, Darby completed her swim. Given the debris and charred wood that littered the waterfront, it appeared that the Saurons had strafed the shoreline during the initial days of the attack.

Darby paralleled the shore for a time, located the place where the remains of an old dock tilted down into the water, and made her way in. A wave slammed Darby into a half-submerged beam and attempted to suck her out. She kicked with her fins and sought some sort of handhold. The wood was slick and didn't offer much purchase. Then, having been pummeled for a second time, the resistance fighter managed to hook her fingers over a two-by-four cross-cleat, pulled herself up, and was free of the water.

Then, having removed the mesh-style pack, Darby traded her fins for a pair of canvas slip-ons, removed the .38 Magnum from the waterproof bag, and stuck it into the nylon shoulder holster already in place under her left arm. Darby knew the pistol wouldn't offer much protection against a file of Kan, but she might be able to kill one or two, and there would be some satisfaction in that.

Moving carefully the ex–petty officer made her way up

the ramplike surface, slipped between two half-burned buildings, and found herself on a street littered with all sorts of debris. A lamppost had fallen from one side of the thoroughfare to the other, a UPS truck had crashed into the side of a building, and dog-ravaged bones lay scattered about. Careful to keep to the heaviest shadows, and pausing frequently to listen, Darby worked her way toward the west. Lights appeared and disappeared as the resistance fighter made her way past what remained of once-proud houses.

Then, after a block or two, Darby came across a badly bent street sign and risked a quick hit from her penlight in order to read it. The sign said "H Avenue," which, according to the briefing materials, should take her south toward the factory.

Now, moving with the utmost care, the ex-sailor eased her way along H Avenue, following it toward the lights. She hadn't gone far, no more than a block, when the sound of voices acted to freeze her in place. The first belonged to a woman. "That's mine! I found it."

Now, as Darby came closer, she saw what looked like a Dumpster backlit by a fire.

"So?" a male voice demanded. "It ain't no good. Not without electricity."

"I don't care," the first voice responded. "I want to hold it. Give it here."

Darby placed a hand on the .38 and continued to ease forward. None of it was the way she expected it to be. Where were the Kan? How could feral slaves gather around a fire without being discovered? And why would they do so?

Borsky made a face, handed the implement to his friend, and watched Ellis pretend to dry her long, scraggly hair. Her face had been attractive once, but that was before the effects of malnutrition, too much sun, and the cocaine had their way with her. Still, something about the dryer, and the way it connected Ellis to the past, seemed to restore a little of her former beauty. "You remember how it was?" she asked dreamily. "Back before the bugs? We had it good, *real* good, but didn't know it. I used to worry about how I looked . . . Can you fucking believe that? Damn, I was stupid."

Borsky was about to say something soothing when he heard the crunch of broken glass and spun to his left. The piece of rebar wasn't much, just a space age club, but it was all he had. "I know you're there . . . step out into the light."

Darby obeyed. The .38 lay against the side of her right thigh. Borsky saw the ex–petty officer's horribly disfigured face and took a step backward. "Who the hell are you?"

"A member of the resistance," Darby answered truthfully. "The name's Darby."

"So, it's true then," Ellis said, the dryer still aimed at her temple. "The resistance movement actually exists."

"Oh, it's true all right," Darby admitted, "and we need your help. What can you tell me about the factory? What happened to it?"

Borsky shrugged. "Nothing." He hooked a thumb back over his shoulder. "It's back where the lights are."

"Right," Darby said disbelievingly, "and I'm the tooth fairy. If the factory is *there* . . . how come you're *here*?"

Borsky looked at Ellis. "She doesn't know."

Ellis lowered the dryer. "No, I guess she doesn't. Look, honey," Ellis said, shifting her gaze to Darby, "are you familiar with Hell Hill?"

Darby nodded. "Sure, I used to trade stuff with a woman who called herself Sister Andromeda."

Borsky spit into the fire. The spittle made a hissing sound. "The bitch . . . this is *her* fault."

"Maybe," Ellis allowed, "but that's beside the point. What I'm saying is that things are different here. The Kan guard the factory—but the slaves are free to come and go."

"We ain't free," Borsky said bitterly, "not by a long shot."

"He's right about that," Ellis admitted. "I didn't mean 'free' as in *really free*, I meant 'free' as in able to leave the factory when our shift is over."

"But we'll be back in the morning," Borsky added. "The bugs made sure of that."

Darby, who didn't relish the notion of hanging around the fire any longer than absolutely necessary, allowed her impatience to show. "No offense, but I don't have a lot of time. Please get to the point."

"Here's the point," Ellis replied, pulling a sleeve up. "They used to keep us inside the fence but discovered they didn't have to. Not so long as we get our daily dose of cocaine."

Darby peered at the dirty skin, saw the badly ulcerated sores, and suddenly understood. The bugs had a new way to force compliance. "I'm sorry."

Ellis nodded. "Thanks. So are we. What would you like to know?"

"Sister Andromeda . . . Where can I find her?"

"Same place as always," Borsky replied, "sitting around talking to the people stupid enough to listen to her bullshit."

Ellis got to her feet. The dryer clattered against the pavement. "You'd better keep a low profile. There's some who would turn you in for an extra hit of coke. Stay here, and I'll bring her back."

Darby raised an eyebrow. "How do I know I can trust you?"

"Tell you what," the woman replied, "how 'bout I leave Borsky on deposit?"

Ellis thought her joke was funny, cackled gleefully, and was soon lost in the surrounding murk.

"No need to worry about Ellis," Borsky put in. "She'll keep her word, now if it was me, well, that might be different."

"Thanks for the warning," Darby said dryly, as she stepped back out of the light. "Stay where you are . . . I'll be watching."

Borsky shrugged, added wood to the fire, and held his hands toward the warmth. "Whatever turns you on. It ain't like I have anyplace to go."

The next ten minutes took what seemed like an eternity to drag by. Borsky continued to crouch there, the firelight illuminating his face, while Darby lurked in the shadows. Her nerves were stretched wire tight. It was dangerous there—and the primal part of her knew it. "Run!" it shouted, "Hide!" but the petty officer refused to listen. Right or wrong, like it or not, Andromeda qualified as one of the resistance movement's leaders. *If* she could make contact, *if* they could talk, the cult leader could theoretically provide a wealth of information regarding the factory and the situation in general. Finally, after what seemed like an hour, a rock clattered across the pavement. Borsky looked up from the fire. "It's Ellis—she's coming in."

Darby lowered the .38, allowed herself to breathe, and heard the scrape of footsteps. Andromeda shuffled into the circle of light followed by Ellis. Darby was shocked to see the manner in which the formerly fastidious woman had been transformed into a dirty, disheveled, old hag. The resistance fighter took a moment to listen before stepping out into the light. Andromeda heard the movement and turned to see. "Darby? Is that you?"

"Yes," the former petty officer replied, "it's me all right. Who else would wear a face like this one?"

Andromeda's eyes brimmed with tears. "It looks wonderful to me." And with that the cult leader gave Darby a hug. It was unexpected, from Darby's perspective at any rate, and she felt awkward. Especially when it was over. It was Ellis who broke the ensuing silence. "Come on, Borsky, they want to talk."

"It's *our* fire."

"So, fucking what? There's enough wood around her to start a thousand fires . . . Besides, I need some shut-eye. Let's go."

Borsky spit into the fire as if that might put it out. He came to his feet. His eyes locked with Darby's. "She's a lying bitch. Keep that in mind."

Then, with Ellis leading the way, the two of them were gone.

Andromeda shook her head sadly. "He hates me, and I don't blame him. I know it sounds stupid, but I actually believed the Saurons would lift humanity up. Even worse is the fact that I managed to convince people like him that it was true. Now look at us. We're nothing but a bunch of coke addicts waiting for a fix." Andromeda's head fell, and her entire body seemed to radiate a sense of helplessness.

"We all made mistakes," Darby said soothingly, "but that's in the past. This is *now*. I was sent to learn everything I can about the factory. They told me you already know about the plans to attack it. What you might not be aware of is the fact that Franklin left Hell Hill and took the government underground. Right about the same time the Ra 'Na rose up and took part of the fleet."

Andromeda's head came back up. Something like the old fire burned in her eyes. "The Ra 'Na did *what*?"

Darby raised her eyebrows. "They took some of the fleet. About twenty-five percent if what I heard was true."

"Don't you see?" the other woman demanded. "There's the answer! Tell Deac Smith that the actual complex is very well guarded. Tell him that the best thing to do is attack from the air. Some of those manta-shaped fighters could do the job—or an attack from orbit. Yes! That would be ideal."

"But what about the slaves?" Darby inquired pragmatically. "At least some of them would be killed. Probably more."

"The more the better," Andromeda said, her eyes flashing. "Anything would be better than this misery. Just tell me where the first energy bolt will fall, and I'll be there."

"I understand," Darby said gently, "but people like Borsky and Ellis might feel differently."

"Only because they're deluded," Andromeda said sternly. "Even if we escape the Saurons, there's no way to escape the cocaine. Death would be a blessing."

"I'll pass your opinions along," Darby promised, "or maybe you'd like to come in person. There's room in my boat."

The passion seemed to leak out of Andromeda like air from a balloon. "No, much as I would like to, I lack the strength. I want the next hit more than I want my freedom."

Darby nodded, fumbled for the notebook, and pulled it out of her pack. It was sealed in a Ziploc bag and the folks at S. C. Johnson & Son would have been proud of the fact that it was still bone dry. "Sorry to do this to you—but Deac gave me a list of questions."

Andromeda said she understood, answered all the questions put to her, and gave Darby another hug. Then, alone with the fire, the cult leader considered what she had done, or *not* done, since the crime was one of omission rather than commission.

None of Darby's questions addressed the possibility of sabotage—and Andromeda failed to mention the manner in which some of the injector assemblies had been plugged. The question was why? Because there was a good possibility that her efforts to disable the plant would be discovered? Or because she wanted fire to flash down from the sky? There was no way to know. Andromeda began to cry—but her sobs were lost in the crackle of the flames.

ABOARD THE SAURON CRUISER *IB SE MA*

Though not as large as the *Hok Nor Ah*, the *Ib Se Ma* was a formidable ship nonetheless. She was half a mile long, more than five hundred feet wide, and normally carried a crew of approximately ten thousand Saurons and their slaves.

But now, large though she was, the Sauron vessel was horribly crowded. Some Saurons had been captured by the mutinous slaves, and were still being held, but others, literally thousands, had managed to escape. The refugees came on shuttles, tugs, and in at least one case aboard a garbage scow. And the only things most brought with them were their appetites, unrealistic expectations regarding the manner in which they would be accommodated, and a deep-seated anger. Slaves attacking Kan? Ships under Ra 'Na control? Humans running amok? The fleet frozen in place? Ships sniping at each other? Fon graffiti on bulkheads? The entire situation verged on madness.

And if the Fon were unhappy, and the Kan were angry, the Zin were absolutely furious. They knew about the change, how very few days remained, and how vulnerable the race would be should any of the preparations fail. More than that they knew, or believed they did, that Hak-Bin was a changeling, that he had taken unfair advantage of his position, and worst of all failed to execute his duties.

Now, as those who could filtered in from throughout the fleet, they found their sedan chairs trapped in fleshy traffic jams. Peeking out through closely drawn curtains, the Zin saw grim-looking Kan stationed at each intersection and Fon who had been forced to camp in the hallways. Such Ra 'Na as there were had been chained to hastily welded U-bolts to prevent them from fleeing into the heretofore secret passageways that riddled the ship.

Now, as a phalanx of Fon struggled to make holes through which the sedan chairs could pass, some of the council members became even more angry, while others were frightened. Politician that he was Hak-Bin had not only anticipated the way his brethren would react to the experience, but stood ready to capitalize on it. Rather than wait for the council to arrive and settle into the relative comfort of their slings, Hak-Bin was there to greet each Zin as he entered the chamber. This was so unusual, and Hak-Bin was so respectful, that many of the clan leaders found it difficult to remain angry and were somewhat mollified by the time they entered their respective cradles.

Others, those less susceptible to flattery, continued to be angry. However, rather than use the time to rally others to their cause, they were forced to sit and glower as Hak-Bin saw to the needs of the council's more malleable members, even going so far as to bring snacks to some of them.

There was some carefully modulated conversation, however, most of which centered on the fact that Hak-Bin looked a lot better than the rumors suggested he might, which left the real question unanswered. Had he started to change or not? Many wanted to ask Ott-Mar, who, along with Grand Vizier Tog and some other retainers, stood at the rear of the compartment, but none dared do so.

Finally, after all of the council members had been seated, a series of three tones were sounded, and Hak-Bin opened the meeting. Something he wanted to do as quickly as he could. A series of images popped into existence. They seemed to hover in midair. Hak-Bin shuffled from one to the next. "These pictures are live . . . Here's the citadel in the northern hemisphere . . . And here's the citadel in the southern hemisphere. Please note that both are not only intact—but in the final stages of construction.

"Now, please direct your attention to *this* feed. Construction of the orbital catalyst factory is now complete, and, while the one on the surface is two days ahead. The point," Hak-Bin continued, "is that in spite of the so-called revolt, none of the preparations for birth-death day have been compromised thus far."

"Tell that to our dead brethren," a Zin named Mal-Hiz said angrily. "Tell it to Mon-Oro. You told him everything would be fine, and the fur balls killed him while he slept in his sling. Take a look around this chamber, my lord . . . *Five* cradles are empty. Approximately one-third of the fleet has been lost, and more ships may fall. Many of the vessels that remain in our graspers have been damaged or neutralized because of our inability to repair or operate them. Meanwhile, down on the surface, the human resistance movement has grown so strong that the ferals make regular radio broadcasts! How dare you come before this body and tell us that everything is fine?"

At least half the council stomped their feet in agreement.

It was an excellent summary, and Hak-Bin was actually grateful to Mal-Hiz for being so articulate. The accusations not only served to vent some of the pent-up anger, they set the stage for the rest of Hak-Bin's presentation. A response which skillfully skirted the situation in orbit to focus on the surface below.

"Mistakes were made . . . I admit that and assume full responsibility," Hal-Bin replied, his eyes roaming the chamber. "But there is no need to panic. In fact, corrective measures are already under way. Thanks to information obtained by Grand Vizier Tog, and subsequently passed on to me, the radio broadcasts Mal-Hiz referred to are about to end. By the time you return to your respective quarters, the humans responsible for them will be dead."

Tog was careful to stare straight ahead as some of the Zin looked in his direction. The fact that he was there, privy to their private deliberations, was both a sign of how far he had come and how vulnerable he was. The latest coup, made possible by information from an anonymous source, further cemented his relationship with Hak-Bin. Something he now wanted to downplay in case the rebels won.

"So," Hak-Bin continued lightly, "all that remains is to retake the vessels now under Ra 'Na control, put the troublemakers to death, seal the ships for use by our nymphs, and begin an orderly withdrawal. Does anyone have any questions or comments?"

Some of the council members had clearly been swayed by Hak-Bin's decidedly upbeat message. Others, individuals like Mal-Hiz, were a good deal less sanguine, but found themselves with a limited number of options. They could call for a vote of no confidence and hope to force a change of leadership, but what if they lost? Now, as birth-death day loomed ever closer, Hak-Bin had the power to grant some very important favors. Which clans would be transported to the surface first? Which citadels would they be assigned to? And which levels would they occupy?

Thanks to memories inherited from their ancestors, the Zin knew that such seemingly trivial matters could have a material effect on nymph mortality, especially now, and were therefore hesitant to give offense.

Besides, there was the question of how the Fon and Kan would react to a change in leadership. Rumors were rampant, literacy had continued to spread, and it was difficult to gauge how much support each Zin could command. That being the case, opposition was limited to muttered comments, hostile stares, and negative pheromones that leaked into the air.

Hak-Bin understood the quandary that the council members found themselves in and, more than that, had counted on it. All that remained was to close the meeting and return to his new quarters. "Given the fact that there are no questions or comments, I suggest that we return to our various ships, continue to work through the issues that confront us and prepare for the great day."

The Zin left after that . . . but Tog remained. He had been assigned quarters so nice they had formerly been occupied by a Fon. Females were his to command. Food, no matter how exotic, was a com call away. So why did he feel so lost? So extremely empty? So dead inside? There was no one left to ask.

SALMON NATIONAL FOREST, IDAHO

By the time the bugs finally came and launched their attack on Racehome, Jonathan Ivory no longer thought they would. After all, the broadcasts had been taking place for awhile now, with no reaction.

It was a gray day, the kind that threatens rain, but never seems to deliver. That in spite of the fact that the fire danger was high, and the more religious members of the community had prayed for precipitation. Ivory wasn't among them, however, since the whole notion of an all-knowing, all-seeing, all-powerful God, even a white one, made him feel nervous.

Besides, there were plenty of things to claim his attention, not the least of which was the urgent need to deal with the steady stream of people brought in via Dent's radio broadcasts. Much as he hated to do so, Ivory was forced to admit that the self-proclaimed Lion of the Airwaves had recruited a lot of new members to the cause.

By including semicoded directions in his broadcasts, messages like "men and women who wish to join us should gather in the city of Smith on such and such a day," the on-air personality brought all manner of survivalists, racialists, and just plain whackos out their hidey-holes and out into the open. Then, once assembled at an appropriate location, Ivory's "shepherds" would appear, sort the wheat from the chaff, and march the "anointed" to Racehome.

In spite of the fact that the steady stream of newcomers had a tendency to look to Dent for inspirational leadership, all the able-bodied men were automatically inducted into Ivory's Hammer-Skins, which meant there wasn't much that the Lion could do without Ivory's buy-in.

The result was a de facto alliance, which, in the absence

of interference from the Saurons, had actually started to prosper. So much so that by the time the bugs launched their attack Ivory had concluded that Ella had been correct where the broadcaster was concerned and, had the baby been born, might have moved her back to Racehome.

The first indication that an attack was under way came when the orbital bombardment began. Thunder rolled as energy weapons fired, blew two-ton divots out of the surrounding forest, and a hand-cranked siren began to wail.

The command bunker was located just outside the entrance to the mine. Ivory felt the earth shake, knew instinctively what the cause was, and rose from his chair. Conscious of how his demeanor could effect those around him, the racialist walked outside, accepted a pair of binoculars from one of the sentries, and scanned the area in front of him. All over Racehome well-drilled men, women, and children ran for their preassigned battle stations. There were plenty of weapons—and everyone over the age of ten had one.

Farther out, beyond the central compound, gigantic explosions marched across the land. First came a sound similar to the roar of a freight train, then the earth-shaking whump as the energy was released, quickly followed by the pistol-shot-like crack of shattered trees, the clatter of falling rock, and the rainlike patter of loose soil.

Ivory watched a fountain of dirt and rock soar upward, saw a seventy-foot fir tree launch itself skyward, and spoke from the corner of his mouth. "Order all units to hold their fire. This is the preliminary bombardment. Judging from the way the explosions march back and forth, the weapons are computer-controlled. The *real* attack will begin when this one ends. The bugs will land on Howther Lake. Order the units there to wait until at least *two* shuttles have landed before launching the SLMs."

Ivory's orders were relayed to racialist forces via a network of CB radios. Weapons were readied, children under the age of ten were herded down into the mine, and Racehome was ready for war. Or thought it was, and would have been, except for one critical miscalculation.

Rather than land on Howther Lake as Ivory had assumed they would, the Saurons employed a different kind of airborne attack. The battle platforms, which the Saurons had stolen from the Arnth more than a hundred Earth-years before, had a tendency to be temperamental but were otherwise perfect for the occasion. Or such was the opinion of Centum Commander Dor-Une, a no-nonsense veteran and the Kan in charge.

There were rumors, *persistent* rumors, that the current generation was about to die, giving way to another. This was secret, or *had* been secret, due to the endlessly arrogant Zin belief that the lower castes would panic if faced with their own mortality.

Contrary to their opinions, however, was the fact that not only Dor-Une but thousands of other Kan and Fon not only believed in the rumors, but found a sort of solace in them. And why not? They had lived long eventful lives, each would produce a near replica of himself, and the ancestors awaited.

The only problem, and one which Dor-Une had been careful to take into account, was the fact that no one who had heard the rumors and decided to believe them would want to die *before* his nymph could be born. One of the real reasons why the Zin decided to withhold the reproductive information? Yes, quite possibly.

So, in an effort to ensure that his warriors would not only suffer as few casualties as possible, but would know that the odds were stacked in their favor, the Centum insisted on what amounted to an overwhelming force augmented by the impact of an aerial bombardment and the element of surprise. Each of the circular battle platforms could carry twenty Kan for a distance of twenty human miles at anything up to a hundred feet off the ground. Then, emptied of all but two pilots, and the gunner located in the weapons blister just beneath their feet, the combat disk would provide close-in fire support.

Now, as the compound came under fire from orbit, and dozens of battle platforms swept in over the surrounding treetops, Ivory felt something horrible slither into the pit of his stomach as the Kan infantry dropped and bounced up into the air. They shimmered, went out of focus, and came back again. Gunfire lashed up to meet them, a few turned somersaults as slugs hammered their chitin, but most survived. Though trained to fight an enemy who could leap into the air, the Hammer Skins weren't prepared to deal with something like this, and there was only one person Ivory could blame: himself.

And so it was that the Saurons fell on the humans like a plague of locusts, their t-guns firing with the regularity of well-strung firecrackers while heavier weapons yammered and a hailstorm of armor-piercing slugs tore buildings apart, blasted through concrete walls, and penetrated bunkers.

Faced with an enemy that was a great deal more mobile than they were, and unable to reinforce each other without coming under a withering fire, the racialists had little choice but to hunker down and fight a hundred Alamos.

Though forced to withdraw into the entrance to the mine, Ivory could still see some of what was happening and monitor the rest by CB radio. There was nothing he could do as clusters of Aryan warriors, most of whom were oriented to the lake, found themselves surrounded, were hosed with automatic weapons fire, and blown to bloody rags by the Sauron equivalent of rocket-propelled grenades.

Oh, there were victories all right, like the SLM that struck one of platforms, exploded, and sent the burning disk into the tinder-dry forest where an entire grove of trees burst into flame. But moments such as that were few and far between. Many of the Hammer Skins ran, or tried to, but were cut down in heaps. The eventual outcome was clear to see. Ivory thought about his family, felt a pang of regret, but was glad that Ella and the unborn baby were safe.

The racialist turned to a grim-faced aide, issued a set of orders, and turned back in the direction of the compound. An explosion shook the ground as an ammo bunker blew. Tracer fire stuttered upwards as a .50-caliber machine gun found one of the battle platforms and punched holes through its hull. Flames appeared, the disk tilted, and slid into the ground below. Earth rose in a wave. There were no explosions just a crash and the shriek of tortured metal. Then, like so many airborne sharks, additional battle platforms were drawn to the scene. They formed the corners of a rectangle, put coordinated fire onto the pit from which the .50-caliber continued to fire, and tore the crew to shreds.

Ivory wanted to run, knew that the earlier more cynical version of himself *would* have run, but somewhere along the line he had come truly to believe in the cause and now stood ready to die for it.

The racialist heard a disturbance and turned to discover that an outraged Dent had been deposited at his feet. The Lion of the Airwaves had been strapped onto his stretcher and was accompanied by four heavily armed Hammer Skins. Dent's face was so suffused with blood that it had a purplish hue. His eyes darted from side to side, clawlike hands tugged at the belt strapped across his bony chest, and spittle flew from his lips as he spoke. "How dare you! Release me immediately! You'll pay for this!"

"Some of the geeks who work for him were trying to take his highness out through the escape tunnel along with the women and children," a Hammer Skin said disgustedly. "The chicken-shit bastard."

"And the geeks?"

"Dead."

Ivory nodded. "Well done."

The fighting was closer by then, so close that slugs had started to ricochet off the rock face that surrounded the mine's entrance, and they could hear the screams as members of the Home Guard were cut down. "Lift my stretcher!" Dent commanded. "Carry me away! We must live to fight again!"

Ivory shook his head sadly. "That would never do. A legend will soon be born. A legend that tells how the leaders of the White Rose died to defend Racehome. A legend that will live long after we are dead. Give the coward a weapon."

Someone dropped a .9mm handgun onto the broadcaster's chest. Dent brushed the pistol aside.

Ivory sighed, bent to retrieve the weapon from the dirt, and released the safety. "Okay, asshole, have it your way," he said, and shot Dent twice in the chest.

"Now," the racialist said, turning to the Hammer Skins, "let's buy some time for the women and children. Once that's over, well, heaven wouldn't be heaven without beer, and I'm buying."

The skins laughed, turned toward the Kan, and vanished, as an energy bolt struck the entrance to the mine. Rock fell, sealed the tunnel, and gave the noncombatants an opportunity to escape.

Meanwhile, in a cabin not far away, a baby waited to be born. She would be white, like the rose for which she would be named, and a vessel ready to be filled.

6

DEATH DAY MINUS 20

SUNDAY, JULY 12, 2020

Behold a pale horse: and his name that sat on him was Death, and Hell followed with him.

—HOLY BIBLE
Book of Revelation 6:8

ABOARD THE RA 'NA VESSEL *LIBERTY*, (FORMERLY THE *HOK NOR AH*)

Having just entered the crisp cold waters of Puget Sound, Pol was about to propel himself out over a richly populated clam bed, when the biosupport tech shook his shoulder. "Fra Pol . . . it's time to wake up."

Suddenly snatched from the Ra 'Na equivalent of heaven Pol found himself back aboard the *Liberty* with only a blanket between his body and the hard cold deck. The U-shaped passageway located just aft of the ship's bridge made a convenient if somewhat unlikely dormitory. There were other quarters, but none so close, and Pol wanted to stay nearby. Two technicians, both asleep, lay to the initiate's right. The lights had been dimmed to make the space more comfortable.

Pol checked the chron strapped to his wrist, confirmed

that Umar was correct, and rubbed his eyes. Two units of sleep, that's what the initiate had allowed himself, and it wasn't enough. There was no time for self-pity, however, not with a partially liberated starship to command, assuming he could actually command it, which remained in doubt. Pol sat up, stretched, and accepted a mug of tea. "Status?"

Having taken orders from Saurons all of his life, Umar struggled to accept the new reality. Taking direction from a Ra 'Na initiate, especially a disreputable individual such as Pol, was a novelty indeed. "Things are pretty much the same . . . The Kan control the Launch Deck and the starboard propulsion pod, but the rest of the ship is ours."

Pol took another sip of tea. It was piping hot and served to lubricate his thoughts. "You haven't heard from the Kan in Propulsion Pod One yet? That's a surprise . . . The bugs tend to allocate two units for nearly everything they do. Patch the hull, mop the deck, it makes no difference. So, given the fact that it has been two hours since our last attempt to break in, they should have reacted by now."

Umar was about to say no, that he hadn't heard from the Saurons and doubted they were quite that predictable, when a com tech named Spon spoke over the intercom. "Commanding officer to the bridge please . . . The Saurons in Pod One would like to speak with him."

Umar watched in wonder as Pol finished his tea, put the mug aside, and came to his feet. "Tell Spon to put them on hold. I need to pee."

Umar watched the initiate waddle away. Not only had Pol correctly predicted what the Saurons would do next . . . he had put the master race on hold! Here was a cool customer indeed—and one which the biosupport tech was increasingly willing to follow.

Pol fancied he could feel Umar's eyes on the center of his back as he made his way down the corridor, past the lavatories set aside for the Zin, Kan, and Fon, to the hatch marked "slaves."

Once inside, the initiate checked to ensure that he was alone and heaved a sigh of relief. The truth was that he *did* need to pee, but more than that to integrate who he was with who he was *supposed* to be, the steely-eyed commander of an extremely powerful warship. Lacking any Ra 'Na military leaders on which to model himself, Pol hoped to emulate Dro Rul's self-possessed surety and the casual, sometimes humorous style demonstrated by humans like Deac Smith and "Popcorn" Farley.

That's the persona Pol *hoped* to present anyway, although the outcome was anything but certain. Would he be able to enter eyeball-to-eyeball negotiations with a Sauron and hold his own? Or would he be reduced to little more than a puddle of subservient slave slime? Because in spite of the initiate's iconoclastic ways, and the acts of defiance for which he was now famous, the Saurons scared the shit out of him.

That was the real reason he had gone down the hall, not only to relieve the pressure on his bladder, but to summon the courage necessary to face a member of the master race. Associated as they were with so much pain and suffering, the words "master race" caused a sudden surge of anger. Pol recognized the emotion for what it was, managed to seize control of it, and used the feeling to cement his resolve.

The Ra 'Na washed his hands, left the lavatory, and strolled down the corridor. A female passed, and Pol nodded politely. She, like most of her peers on the *Liberty*, knew who the rumpled initiate was and hurried to tell her friends.

Com tech Spon was waiting when Pol entered the control room, claimed one of the recently installed chairs, and offered a smile. "Sorry about that, but like the humans say, 'when you gotta go, you gotta go.' What's up?"

"It's the Kan in Propulsion Pod One, sir, they want to parley."

Pol heard the "sir," wondered if such an honorific was seemly, and decided that it was. Most of Deac Smith's subordinates called him "sir," and none of them were slaves. "Military courtesy," that's what Farley called it, and insisted it was necessary. "Okay," Pol responded, "put the bug on."

Spon, who had never been to the planet's surface and had no idea what a "bug" was, said "Yes, sir," and made the necessary connection.

Lit-Waa, the ranking Sauron in Pod One, heard the com tone and took one last look at his surroundings. The attempt to seize control of the starboard propulsion pod had failed, but only barely. Suddenly, with no warning, Ra 'Na slaves had boiled up out of a heretofore innocuous access panel, opened fire with miniature weapons, and killed three of his brethren in less time than it would take to hop from one foot to the other.

In fact, had it not been for the fact that one of the intruders died as the result of friendly fire, and fell backward into the hatch, the two surviving members of his file would have been killed as well. However, thanks to the temporary blockage, the Kan had time to draw their weapons and slaughter the rest of the rebels as they fought their way up past the corpse. Once that was accomplished, it was a simple matter to seal the maintenance hatches and call for reinforcements. The only problem was that no reinforcements had been forthcoming, and Lit-Waa was reasonably sure that they never would.

That being the case, the Kan had little choice but to take the situation into his own graspers and try to escape. The dead Saurons had been piled out of camera range over in a corner, while the Ra 'Na bodies had been bound with tape and arranged to make it appear as though they were still alive. Would the fur balls fall for it? Yes, the Kan thought that they would. There was no way to be sure, however—

and a small but persistent emptiness claimed the bottom of the Sauron's stomach.

Now, as Lit-Waa turned his snout toward the camera, the *real* test began. Regardless of which slave the fur balls sent to negotiate with him, he or she would be frightened. The key was to use that fear, to seize the initiative, and get what he wanted. Careful to look as intimidating as possible, the Kan opened the circuit. "Yes? What do you want?"

Pol saw a tough-looking Kan, some damaged equipment, and a row of Ra 'Na laid facedown on the deck beyond. They had been bound hand and foot, and it appeared as though the entire assault team had been taken alive. Good news and bad news all at the same time. Good because they were alive—and bad because the Saurons would try to use the captives for leverage. First things first, however—which meant putting the Kan in his place. "You're wasting my time, bug face . . . Umar, pump the atmosphere out of Pod One." So saying, Pol broke the connection, and the screen went to black.

Startled by Pol's order, and unsure of what to do, Umar looked up from his console. The entire bridge crew, some twelve individuals in all, looked on as well. "There were at least eight Ra 'Na laid out on the deck," Umar said. "Surely you don't mean to . . ."

"I *mean* what I said," Pol answered firmly, "and please make note of the fact that as commanding officer of this vessel, I require unquestioning obedience. Should we have to take this ship into battle, the Saurons are unlikely to offer time for debate. Now, execute my order."

Umar, his ears laid back against his skull, touched a series of controls. Elsewhere, at the opposite end of the ship, a pump started. Moments later air, one of the few things that Saurons and Ra 'Na had in common, was sucked out of Pod One and stored against future need.

Lit-Waa was still trying to deal with the slave's unexpectedly confrontational response, still trying to settle on a course of action, when a subordinate pointed toward a console. "Look! Our air! They're pumping it out."

Lit-Waa confirmed that the warrior was correct and had little choice but to reevaluate his approach. The fur balls were willing to sacrifice the hostages. That was a surprise. He reopened the link. The same Ra 'Na he'd seen before appeared again. "Yes?"

"You made your point. Restore the atmosphere."

"Say, 'please.' "

The entire bridge crew watched in amazement as the Kan was forced to swallow his pride. "*Please* restore the atmosphere."

Pol nodded. "Umar, you heard the bug, *please* restore the atmosphere."

The rest of bridge crew laughed, but more than that, learned something about their new relationship with the Saurons. A relationship in which *they* gave orders—and the so-called master race had to obey them.

Lit-Waa heard the hiss of air as it entered the compartment.

"So," Pol said lazily, "what can I do for you?"

"My brothers and I wish to leave the ship," Lit-Waa responded. "Send a shuttle or similar craft to the Pod One airlock."

"And the hostages?"

"The slaves will remain unharmed," Lit-Waa lied, "which you can monitor via this com link."

The offer had much to recommend it. Not only would Pol regain full use of Propulsion Pod One, and restore the ship's full maneuverability, he would free the resistance fighters. Yes, three Kan would escape, but so what? Three bugs wouldn't make any difference one way or the other. So, why hesitate? What, if anything, was wrong? Then it occurred to him . . . During the time the com link had been open, not one of the hostages had moved. Were they truly alive?

The initiate's first impulse was to ask Lit-Waa—but a second possibility came to mind. Still on the com, and still in eye contact with Sauron, Pol issued an order. "Umar, the bug assures us that our friends remain unharmed. Let's see if that claim is true . . . Analyze the environment in Pod One to see if oxygen consumption is consistent with the number of individuals visible on the screen."

The biosupport technician was mystified, but said, "Yes, sir," and went to work.

Meanwhile, in Propulsion Pod One, Lit-Waa cursed the slave technologies and wondered why his race was so much less capable. Had they performed all of the work themselves, had all of the castes been taught to read, perhaps . . .

Umar looked at the readings, checked to make sure he was correct, and felt a sudden wave of sorrow. "Oxygen consumption rates are consistent with what three Saurons would require. Slightly elevated due to stress . . . but otherwise normal."

The finding was the one Pol expected to be given—but the realization brought him no pleasure. His voice was hard and cold. "I hereby call upon you and your companions to surrender."

Lit-Waa, embarrassed by the way in which a mere slave had been able to best him, and furious at the consistently disrespectful manner in which he had been addressed, spit defiance at the screen. "Come and get us, slave! Or do you lack the courage?"

Pol touched a button. The screen faded to black. His voice seemed to echo between the control room walls. "Remove the atmosphere from Pod One, wait fifteen units, and pump it back in. Send a burial crew, a damage-assessment team, and some propulsion techs. I want *both* engines back on-line as soon as possible."

Umar complied, readings began to fall, and the com started to chime. The sound continued until Spon killed it. No one answered the call.

ABOARD THE SAURON DREADNOUGHT *IB SE MA*

Hak-Bin stood in front of an enormous expanse of armored plastic and looked at the planet below. In spite of the fact that Hak-Bin had spent a significant part of his life aboard Ra 'Na ships, and in close contact with the Ra 'Na, he knew he would never fully understand them. The propulsion system, yes, that was necessary, as were controls, life-support systems, all manner of other mechanisms.

But why, given all the effort involved, had the Ra 'Na decorated so many bulkheads with bas-relief artwork? Or set aside spaces for non-food-related plants? Or constructed blisters like the one he now stood in for the sole purpose of simply looking outside?

Ah well, the Sauron thought to himself as he turned back toward his desk, if the slaves were logical, they wouldn't be slaves.

Denied the comforts of the *Hok Nor Ah*, the Zin had been forced to find new quarters, and the observation dome had been converted to his use. Much to his own surprise, Hak-Bin discovered he didn't miss the things left behind. Was that because he had already accepted a noncorporeal existence? Yes, the Zin mused, that would explain it.

And it was true, because even as Hak-Bin entered the sling, and the U-shaped desk that seemed to embrace, he did so with a sense of joyful anticipation. He had problems to solve, resistance to overcome, and nothing was more pleasurable than that.

A single glance at his desktop screen was sufficient to confirm that his first appointment of the day was with Centum Commander Dor-Une, a levelheaded sort who had distinguished himself by locating the feral complex from which the unauthorized radio broadcasts emanated and reducing it to ruble. A truly fine piece of work for which both the Kan and his line would be recognized.

Hak-Bin touched a large pincer-sized button, saw the hatch open, and waited for the Kan to shuffle forward. Dor-Une was a warrior's warrior. His chitin shimmered gray, his battle harness gleamed, and his posture radiated confidence. The Centum even *smelled* strong! Here at least was an individual the Zin could count on. "Centum Commander Dor-Une . . . Thank you for coming."

The Kan offered a stiff bow. "The pleasure is mine, eminence."

"Please," Hak-Bin said, gesturing toward one of the sling chairs arrayed in front of his desk, "take a seat."

The officer accepted the invitation, slid his torso into one of the guest cradles, and wondered what sort of dra lay in store for him. There was a saying among the Kan: "Make a mistake and pay once. Win a battle and pay twice."

Now, with the supposedly secret birth-death day on the horizon and Hak-Bin up to his snout in problems, the Kan felt sure he would pay. The question was how.

"First," Hak-Bin said congenially, "please allow me to congratulate you regarding your recent victory. One of many I might add—stretching back more than a hundred units."

Dor-Une couldn't remember the victories Hak-Bin referred to—but he could *feel* them. "Thank you, eminence," the warrior replied cautiously. "My brethren fought bravely."

"Yes," Hak-Bin agreed, "I'm sure they did. And now, as the ferals continue to make trouble, we have further need of their valor."

Here it comes, Dor-Une thought cynically, the well-sharpened stick. "Of course, eminence—we live to serve."

"Excellent," Hak-bin said, "I think you'll like this assignment. Rather than hunt the ferals down, as you were previously required to do, this group will come to you. The Fon are about to complete work on a factory, a very important factory, and it's my belief that the so-called resistance will attempt to destroy it.

"However, rather than destroy the factory, it is *they* who will suffer, since you and your brethren will be lying in wait."

"The factory will function as a trap then."

"Precisely."

"We have troops in place?"

"Yes, but not very many. Highly addictive drugs have been administered to keep the slave population under control."

"I can call upon whatever resources I deem appropriate? Take whatever measures I think necessary?"

"Of course," Hak-bin said soothingly. "Give me a victory . . . the rest is up to you."

"Thank you, lord," Dor-Une responded. "I will do my best. Is there anything else?"

"No," Hak-Bin replied, "just a sense of urgency. It's my guess that the humans will attack soon."

"Understood, eminence," the Kan replied as he backed out of the sling. "You can rely on the Kan."

"And I give thanks for it," Hak-Bin said sincerely. "And one more thing . . ."

"Lord?"

"You'll find a slave outside. Please send him in."

The Centum said, "Yes, excellency," and backed away.

Meanwhile, just beyond the metal hatch, Tog sat waiting. Waiting and sweating. Once again he had been summoned, once again he had no idea why, and once again he feared for his life. There was a good deal of irony in that, especially since he had cast his lot with the Saurons in order to *avoid* fear. He had survived so far, but a certain amount of that had been luck, and how long would the good fortune hold?

Tog's thoughts were interrupted as the hatch hissed open, a fierce-looking Kan emerged, and fired words like darts from a gun. "His eminence will see you now."

Tog mumbled his thanks, scurried through the opening, and heard the hatch close behind him. "Grand Vizier Tog!" Hak-Bin proclaimed expansively. "It's good to see you! Please, take a seat."

Warmed by the Sauron's greeting, and hopeful regarding the nature of the visit, Tog sat in the single Ra 'Na chair. It was small, and the desk was large, which meant the Zin towered above him.

"So," Hak-Bin began, "how is morale among the slaves?"

Tog, cognizant of how important it was to walk the line between the truth and politically expedient fiction, chose his words with care. "Locally, which is to say aboard the *Ib Se Ma*, morale is fairly good. Elsewhere, especially on other ships, it's my understanding that problems persist."

Hak-Bin gestured his agreement. "Yes, I would agree, which has everything to do with our visit. You, more than any other slave, have proven your loyalty to the Sauron race. And now, much as I would like to see you sit back and relax, there is one more favor that I must ask."

Tog felt a series of conflicting emotions. Resentment where the word "slave" was concerned, pleasure in the un-alloyed praise, and a growing sense of dread. What sort of "favor" did the Sauron have in mind? The anxiety continued to build. "Thank you, eminence. How can I be of service?"

"Let's talk about the 'problems' you referred to," Hak-Bin began. "It seems that most, if not all the difficulties can be traced to a certain Dro Rul. The two of you know each other?"

"Yes," Tog replied hesitantly, "though not especially well. While both of us served in the College of Dromas— but there was very little on which we could agree."

"And a good thing," Hak-Bin said sternly, "since this Rul person has been sentenced to death."

Tog, mind racing, felt ice water trickle into his bloodstream. "Death, my lord?"

"*Yes,*" the Zin answered emphatically, "which would go a long way toward bringing this mutiny nonsense to a speedy conclusion."

"Of course," Tog replied cautiously, "it's unfortunate, but discipline must be maintained."

"Precisely," Hak-Bin agreed. "Now, given the fact that we agree, the only question is how the execution should be carried out. And that my friend, is where *you* come in."

"*Me,* my lord?" Tog asked, as he fought to maintain his composure. "Pardon me for saying so—but I lack even the most basic of qualifications."

"Ah, but that's where you are wrong," the Sauron replied smugly. "In order to kill Rul, the would-be assassin must first get near to him—and who better than another Dro? The rest is simple . . . You aim the weapon, pull the trigger, and 'bang!' The troublemaker is dead."

"But Rul would refuse to see me," Tog said desperately, "and I have no weapon."

"Oh, Rul will see you all right," Hak-Bin said reassuringly, "especially if we give him reason to believe that the Grand Vizier is about to join the rebel cause. And, as for the weapon, well, I took the liberty of having one made. Here, take a look at this."

So saying, the Sauron reached into one of the desk's many recesses, found what he was looking for, and removed a lacquered tray.

Tog had little choice but to stand, move forward, and accept the offering. The object that lay on the tray looked as though it was sculpted from white clay. Though inert, it looked dangerous nevertheless.

"Go ahead," Hak-Bin said earnestly, "pick it up. Be careful where you point that thing though . . . We wouldn't want any accidents."

Tog's mind churned as he wrapped his fingers around the carefully contoured handle. What did the comment mean? That the gun was loaded? That he could shoot Hak-Bin in the head, leave the compartment, and make a run for it? The rebels would welcome him, and his safety would be assured.

But what if the comment was some sort of test? What if he pointed the weapon at Hak-Bin, pulled the trigger, and nothing happened? The ensuing punishment would be long and painful. Tog turned the weapon so it was pointed at planet Earth. He was surprised by how natural it felt . . . like an extension of his hand.

Hak-Bin nodded. "It feels good, doesn't it? To hold death in the palm of your hand. As well it should. That weapon was made with your mission in mind. The entire mechanism was manufactured from an extremely strong ceramic material that can pass through metal detectors without setting them off. It contains two bullets, both of human manufacture, either of which will do the job. All you need to do is get into close physical proximity and fire both barrels. Then, minus their most important leader, the Ra 'Na rebellion will collapse."

Tog turned the weapon over in his hands. His chest felt tight, and it was hard to breathe. "Yes, eminence, but what happens to me?"

Hak-Bin made sounds which Tog knew to be laughter. "An excellent question! We will choose the meeting place with extreme care. A team of specially trained Kan will be in hiding nearby. Once the weapon has been fired you will use this to send them a signal."

Hak-Bin produced what looked like a short length of rod. It was made from the same material as the gun. Tog accepted the device and found that it was cool to the touch. "You'll notice that one end is protected by a cap," the Sauron added pragmatically. "The button is underneath. Don't press it until the moment comes. A Kan named Lim-Tam is in charge. Call him prematurely, and he won't be amused. My staff will help arrange the meeting—and handle your transportation requirements. Any questions?"

Tog had questions, lots of them, but knew better than to ask. Hak-Bin had what he wanted, and the meeting was over. "No, eminence, I have no questions."

The Ra 'Na had backed toward the hatch, and was just about to leave, when Hak-Bin called his name. "Grand Vizier Tog . . ."

"Yes, eminence?"

"See Kat-Duu on your way out. *He* has the bullets for your weapon."

Tog remembered the moment of temptation, swallowed the lump that formed in his throat, and bowed.

Hak-Bin watched as the Ra 'Na withdrew and the hatch closed. It felt good to laugh.

A SHOPPING MALL NORTH OF MOUNT VERNON, WASHINGTON

Darby heard the president of the United States before she actually saw him. The muffled thump, thump, thump of semiautomatic gunfire grew steadily louder as the resistance fighter followed Jill Ji-Hoon down the littered corridor toward the source of the noise. The mall had been looted more than once, repeatedly vandalized, and part of it burned. Half-dressed mannequins stared from shattered storefronts, a blackened barbecue, and a large pile of trash marked the spot where someone had lived for a while, and a momentary breeze sent a fifty-dollar bill skittering down the edge of the walkway. Neither woman sought to pick it up.

Two heavily armed guards waited up ahead. Ji-Hoon paused to speak with them, laughed at something the male said, and turned to Darby. "So, how 'bout it? Are you packin'?"

Darby nodded. "A .38 and a pocketknife."

"Please remove both items, place them on the table, and assume the position. No offense—but the pat-down is SOP."

Darby shrugged. "None taken."

Once the search was completed, Ji-Hoon led Darby through a large pair of double doors and into what proclaimed itself to be the Bon Marché. It was a big store, but a largely empty one, with little more than the odd scrap of clothing on the nearly empty racks, tables, and shelves. The gunfire had stopped by then, and as Darby followed Ji-Hoon back through menswear, she saw that a rough-and-ready firing range had been established on the far side of the store. Mannequins served as targets, and one of them, minus the left side of her face, had sustained multiple hits to her torso.

In spite of the fact that Darby had never met Franklin face-to-face before, she had seen the "talkies" that the Saurons had dropped, and recognized him right away. Franklin saw her approach, holstered his weapon, and extended a hand. "Hi! My name is Alex, and this is Jack Manning. He's my chief of security."

Manning gestured toward the mannequin. "You've seen him shoot . . . He needs all the security he can get."

Darby felt a sudden stab of pain, knew it meant she was smiling, and made note of the fact that neither one of the men had reacted to her face. Not visibly at any rate—which was all she could hope for. "It's an honor, sir, my name is Darby."

Franklin nodded and released her hand. His voice was solemn. "I know . . . Thanks to you, and the other volunteers, five Sauron ships were destroyed in what future historians will refer to as the Battle of Bellingham. Assuming we beat the bugs, and assuming I'm alive, it will be my pleasure to hang the Medal of Honor around your neck.

"In the meantime, in my capacity as chief of the armed forces, I hereby commission you a full lieutenant in the United States Navy. Come on, let's have some coffee."

Manning grinned, and Darby, literally speechless as a result of the unexpected praise, followed the president over to a large display table. The clothing that had once been stacked there was gone, but a sign said "Sale!" in bright red letters, and harkened back to happier times. Deac Smith was there—and rose to give Darby a hug. Then, having been introduced to Boyer Blue, Patience, and the Ra 'Na named P'ere Nec, the newly commissioned naval officer took her seat at the table. It was littered with maps, coffee cups, and other odds and ends.

"So," Franklin said deliberately, "I hear you took a little swim . . . At the rate you're going we'll run out of medals."

"Chu went with me . . . and the Kan never knew I was there," Darby said modestly.

"Still," Franklin insisted, "based on the synopsis from Deac, I'd say what you did took a whole lot of guts. Let's hear the full report."

Darby laid it out, starting with a description of her landing, the conversations with Borsky and Ellis, followed by the visit with Sister Andromeda. There had been rumors, but nothing solid, so the use of cocaine as a way to control the slave population came as something of a shock.

Franklin, who had never been especially fond of Andromeda, was still saddened to hear about the deplorable state she was in. He shook his head sadly. "You have to give the bugs credit. They've done an excellent job of identifying our weaknesses and coming up with ways to exploit them."

"That's for sure," Blue said soberly. "So, what should we do? It sounds as if Andromeda wants an air strike . . . Is such a thing possible?"

All heads swiveled toward Nec. The Ra 'Na cleric sat on

a tall stool. "Theoretically it is," Nec replied, "or will be, as soon as the situation in orbit becomes clear. Many of our ships, which is to say those in which Ra 'Na forces occupy the control room, remain infested with Saurons. Rooting them out involves compartment-to-compartment fighting. Soon, within a matter of days, I should be able to provide a better assessment of our offensive capabilities. Perhaps, if things go well, we will have an opportunity to attack the factory."

"Great," Patience put in sarcastically. "In order to save our people, we plan to incinerate them from orbit. What could be better?"

"I understand your point of view," Franklin said carefully. "More than that, I sympathize with it. But this is the Sauron catalyst factory we're talking about. Were we to leave the facility untouched, a new generation of Saurons will be born—and any humans who survive will do so as slaves. Besides, I'm no expert on things military, but doesn't the orbital thing cut two ways? If the Ra 'Na can fire on the area around the factory so can the Saurons."

"Which brings us to the possibility of an old-fashioned infantry assault," Smith said pragmatically. "Based on the intelligence Darby brought back, it looks like the factory is only lightly defended. Given the element of surprise, we might be able to break through the defensive perimeter, set some demo charges, and amscray before the orbital weapons come into play . . . Especially if P'ere Nec and his folks can keep the Sauron fighters off our backs."

"We would certainly try," the cleric responded. "Realizing our pilots lack combat experience."

"They're gaining more with each passing day," Franklin said grimly, "and something is better than nothing."

"Let's say the attack is successful," Blue said skeptically. "How would Deac and his troops deal with a bunch of cokeheads? Imagine trying to move those people cross country while they enter withdrawal."

"The vice president has a point," Patience admitted. "The assault force will need to carry some coke to tide the slaves over—and we'll need a detox program at the other end."

Franklin sighed. In a situation where it was tough to provide free humans with enough to eat, the notion of a drug rehabilitation program seemed to verge on the ridiculous. Still, there didn't seem to be much choice. "Okay, let's go around the table . . . Boyer?"

The ex–history professor nodded. "If Deac thinks he can pull it off, then I'm for it."

"Patience?"

"An infantry assault beats the hell out of an orbital assault. My people will accept responsibility for the detox program."

"Excellent. Thank you. P'ere Nec?"

"The Ra 'Na will support you in every way that we can."

"And we appreciate that . . . Deac?"

"Lord willing, we'll pull it off."

Franklin nodded. "I hope he or she is paying close attention. We'll need all the help we can get."

ABOARD THE *BALWUR*, (FORMERLY KNOWN AS THE *NU MOR GA*)

The drop bay, originally intended as an area in which mines could be armed and launched from an area near the ship's stern, was brightly lit. *Too* brightly lit for the task at hand. The coffins, each stamped with the occupant's name, were lined up on a conveyer belt. Each was about four feet long, rectangular in shape, and made of gleaming metal. There were sixty-seven of them. Some had been sent to the *Balwur* from other ships, but many of the casualties had been suffered aboard the cruiser herself, during the final battle for control. And there were more casualties, *thousands* more, most of whom had been unceremoniously dumped from the ships that remained under Sauron control.

Now, as the belt paused, then started up again, Dro Rul continued to pray. The prelate's words, combined with those uttered by hundreds of relatives and friends, created a dirge so powerful that the ship's fittings began to vibrate, as if the *Balwur* herself mourned the loss of those who had served her.

The full hona consisted of more than a hundred stanzas, each of which would normally be sung by a member of the clergy, but this was war, and there was no time for such niceties. That's why a toth, or shortened version of the prayer, was used instead.

Each time the line of coffins paused, and a member of his flock was ejected into the cold blackness of space, a little bit of Rul's heart went with it. Most of the possibilities the naysayers had warned him about had indeed come true. Thousands of Ra 'Na lay dead, the majority of the fleet remained under Sauron control, and preparations for birth-death day continued. *Some* of the Ra 'Na vessels had been freed, however, the *Balwur* among them, and that provided Rul with reason to hope.

A Klaxon sounded as the last coffin was ejected from the dispersion tube, the toth came to an end, and the mourners started to leave. Rul wanted to follow them, to return to his quarters for some much-needed sleep, but that wasn't to be. His aide, a hyperefficient cleric named P'ere Dee, seemed to materialize by his side. As usual, the younger Ra 'Na's attention was directed to the palm comp that linked him to computers throughout the liberated portion of the fleet. "Sorry to intrude, excellency, but if you still wish to attack the citadels prior to the strategic withdrawal, it will be necessary to do so soon."

Rul sighed. The so-called withdrawal was tantamount to a full-blown retreat. Not what he wanted—but there was very little choice. Most of the shipboard battles would end fairly soon. Based on the most recent reports, it appeared as though the majority of the fleet would remain under Sauron control until the change forced them into the citadels. That being the case, the master race would quite naturally attack any vessel known to be under Ra 'Na control. Some of those attacks would be clumsy, especially those launched by vessels crewed solely by Saurons, but others, those having Ra 'Na collaborators, would be quite effective.

So, given the fact that the newly liberated ships were not only badly outnumbered, but lacked a reliable command and control structure, it seemed advisable to pull them out of orbit and regroup beyond the planet's gravity well. Then, with a command structure in place, the "free" navy would be better prepared to fight.

Would the Saurons follow? No, few of Rul's advisers thought so. First, because there were only so many Ra 'Na willing to help them; second, because the Saurons lacked the technical know-how required to operate the ships completely on their own; and, third, because too little time remained to them. Birth-death day was coming up fast, and thanks to efforts made by the humans, the master race was running behind schedule.

That was the theory in any case, and emotions to the contrary notwithstanding, Rul had agreed to act on it. But not before one last act of defiance. An attack on the citadels that would not only bring additional hope to the humans, but force the Saurons to spend precious time and energy trying to make repairs. Rul, cognizant of the coffins now orbiting Earth, gave a nod. "Thank you, P'ere Dee. Notify the bridge . . . I'm on the way."

Elsewhere aboard the ship, down on the Launch Deck, a single cleric emerged from a shuttle, passed through the lock, and offered his credentials to a pair of heavily armed guards. A bandage concealed what remained of his left ear, another bandage protected the wound on his left arm, and he walked with a strange bowlegged gait. One of the sentries, an individual named Niss, examined the holo doc. "Your name is Has?"

"Yes, *P'ere* Has, assistant to Grand Vizier Tog."

Nis growled deep at the back of his throat. "You work for 'turd' Tog? The collaborator? We should put a bullet through your head."

"The Grand Vizier is a true champion of the people," Has answered defensively, "and sent a message to Dro Rul. I have that message in my possession and wish to deliver it."

"So, hand it over," Niss replied. "I'll pass it on."

"No," Has replied stubbornly, "the message is for Dro Rul. Please notify him that I have arrived."

Niss made a face and turned to his companion. "Put a message in to P'ere Dee—he'll know what to do. Meanwhile, let's put the collaborator in holding tank two."

"I'm *not* a collaborator," Has said indignantly, but it made no difference and they took him away.

Meanwhile, in spite of efforts to restore the *Balwur*'s bridge to pre-Sauron conditions, the lighting was too low and many of the fittings were too large. Still, it was nice to see Ra 'Na-style seats where slings had recently been, and to know that the Saurons who remained were under heavy guard.

Rul, careful not to usurp the authority of the vessel's newly named commanding officer, stood to one side as the ex–power tech prepared the ship for battle. Her voice was calm and steady. "Pods One and Two—both engines ahead one-third. Energy cannons two, four, six, and eight, stand by to fire on target one. *Balwur* to the fleet . . . may the Great One protect you . . . commence firing."

HELL HILL

His name was Sko-Mor, and as chief overseer, and assistant to the resident stonemaster, it was his responsibility to see to the workforce, and ensure adherence to the work schedule. Had the Fon bothered to familiarize himself with the human system for tracking time, he might have known that it was exactly 6:00 P.M. when the shift ended and the slaves streamed down off the hill. A common occurrence witnessed many times before.

What Sko-Mor *failed* to notice, however, not until it was too late, was the fact that as the slaves streamed down *off* the hill, the next shift failed to move *up*. Then, just as the discrepancy began to dawn on the overseer and the wheels had started to turn, artificial lightning flashed down out of the clear blue sky, struck Observation Tower ^–[], and cut the structure in two. The top half was still falling, still many feet from the ground when a loud crack was heard, and thunder rolled across the bay.

Now the Fon understood. The slaves had been warned about the attack in advance . . . and that's why they remained at the bottom of the hill! The humans would pay for that, and pay dearly, the moment the bombardment ended.

Thanks to his position on the roof of the citadel's north tower, Sko-Mor had an excellent position from which to view the ensuing destruction, or would have, if the next bolt of energy had been directed somewhere else. Unfortunately for the overseer, the next shot touched down not ten units away, incinerated his body in less than one one-hundredth of a unit, and damaged the tower's roof.

Meanwhile, many miles above, the crew of the *Balwur* gave a reedy cheer. Not for long, because the cruiser came under almost immediate fire from Sauron-controlled vessels all around them, but long enough. Blood had been drawn— and even the normally dour Rul was forced to release a satisfied smile. Then, with covering fire from Pol's *Liberty*, the *Balwur* and the other ships of the newly reconstituted Ra 'Na navy broke orbit and withdrew into space.

Has had the holding cell all to himself. Like the rest of the Ra 'Na the cleric had been born and raised in space. That being the case, he recognized the tremors that ran through the ship's hull for what they were. The ship was under attack! And, judging from the way it felt, the *Balwur* was fighting back.

Has felt the gentle tug as the ship powered its way out of orbit and escaped into space. The reality of that produced mixed emotions. On the one hand, Has was proud of what his people had been able to accomplish against seemingly impossible odds. But what about his mission. Would Rul agree to see him? And what if he didn't? But there was nothing the cleric could do except worry, and finally, once the battle-induced tremors had subsided, drift off to sleep. And that's what Has was doing when the hatch hissed open, two members of the newly formed Ra 'Na constabulary entered, and one nudged him with a boot. "P'ere Has? Get up. Dro Rul wants to see you."

Has rubbed his eyes, allowed the second constable to help him to his feet, and was herded out into the corridor. The cleric had served aboard the *Balwur* during his younger days and knew the vessel well. That being the case, he had a pretty good idea of where they were taking him and could direct most of his attention to the sights and sounds around him. Perhaps most noticeable was how happy members of the crew were as they shouted greetings to each other, and even went so far as to hold hands and dance in circles. And that in spite of the bandages many wore, the bulkheads splattered with Ra 'Na blood, and the informal memorials that marked places where major battles had been fought. Also worth noting was the complete absence of Saurons— and the resulting absence of fear.

It was heady stuff, *wonderful* stuff, so much so that by the time Has was shown into Rul's ascetically barren chambers, the envoy had serious doubts regarding what Tog liked to refer to as ". . . the loyalist cause." Loyal to *what*? The Sauron who had applied a red-hot iron to his genitals? To slavery? To fear? None of it made sense. Still, the fact that Tog sought to enter into some sort of dialogue raised the possibility of racial reconciliation, and that was good. Or so it seemed to Has.

The compartment was already filled to near overflowing with all manner of individuals, both ecclesiastical and secular, all of whom wanted to obtain Rul's advice, permission or an indulgence of some sort. But first it was necessary to get past P'ere Dee, better known to many as "the iron gate," who, for better or worse, was empowered to decide who would be allowed to see Rul, and in what order.

And so it was that Has was suddenly plucked from the obscurity of the outer waiting room and escorted into Dro Rul's study. The cleric went to one knee, bowed his head, and was about to offer further obeisance when the prelate touched his shoulder. "I know you mean well, P'ere Has," Rul said, "but the time has come to ask ourselves whence such traditions came? From the planet on which we originated? Or from the race that took it over. Do we kneel to the person? Or to the Great One whom that person represents? All of us must find time to meditate on such questions. So, until such time as we come up with answers, I would ask that you forgo such rituals and greet me as you would anyone else. Here . . . sit by my side . . . Now, P'ere Dee tells me that you were entrusted with a message."

"Yes," Has replied eagerly, accepting the proffered chair. "The Grand Vizier, that is to say Dro Tog, would like to meet with you."

Rul's ears rotated forward. "For what purpose? There is very little upon which we agree."

"That's just it," Has replied earnestly. "I think he's coming around."

"He said that?"

"Sort of," Has extemporized. "Dro Tog admits that the Saurons have grown increasingly abusive, and based on that, a rebellion is justified."

Having just returned from an errand, P'ere Dee arrived in time to hear the last part of the exchange. He gave a snort of disbelief. "No, offense, P'ere Has, but the so-called Vizier not only qualifies as a collaborator but may be guilty of greater crimes. Why listen to him?"

"I believe the message was directed to *me*," Rul put in, gently asserting his authority. "The book of tides tells us that no transgression is so great that a soul should be abandoned to darkness. Moreover, there are practical considerations. Were Tog to shift his allegiance, many of those who still cling to the old reality would come over with him. The cause would be strengthened and the conflict shortened."

Dee clearly disagreed but managed to keep his mouth shut.

"So," Rul continued, "where would this meeting take place?"

"There is an asteroid," Has replied, "currently used for storage. Realizing that you may have concerns regarding security, Tog suggests that you search the planetoid prior to the meeting and bring a force of bodyguards. He will come alone."

"Why not meet us out here? Beyond the planet's gravity well?" Dee inquired suspiciously. "Even if the asteroid is clear, Dro Rul could be intercepted on his way to or from the meeting."

Has replied with a shrug. "For all I know, the Grand Vizier, I mean Dro Tog, would have agreed to such a proposal. Please remember that he had no way to know that you would break orbit."

"P'ere Has has a point," Dro Rul said diplomatically, "as do you. Let's settle the matter with an agreement to meet on the asteroid. The two of you can work out the details. Let's hope something good comes of it.

"Now, if you will excuse me, I must attend the first meeting of the free Dromas. I'm not sure what I fear most," Rul said wryly, "the Saurons or my peers. I fear there will be as many opinions as there are tongues to articulate them. Wish me luck."

Both of the clerics did, Rul withdrew, and the planning got under way. Maybe, just maybe, something good *would* come out of the meeting.

ABOARD THE SAURON DREADNOUGHT *IB SE MA*

The *Ib Se Ma*'s cavernous Launch Deck had been temporarily sealed and pressurized. Thousands upon thousands of Saurons stood shoulder to shoulder waiting to hear what many already knew: All of them were about to die.

Slave labor had been used to erect scaffolding with a platform on top. A ramp led upward but Hak-Bin, eager to prove that his health was intact, made the journey in a single leap. Once on top of the structure and gazing out over the assembled multitude, the Sauron took a moment to admire the symmetry arrayed before him. The Zin stood at the front of the assemblage—like black jewels gathered around his feet.

Those Kan not on guard duty around the perimeter of the Launch Deck, or down on the planet's surface, stood in precisely aligned ranks. Their chitin shimmered as it sought to match the dull gray metal beneath their feet.

Behind the warriors, their numbers far greater than the Zin and Kan combined, stood the Fon. Many looked up toward the platform with what could only be described as implacable stares. Some had taught themselves to read, that's what the intelligence reports said anyway, and the very thought of it served to chill Hak-Bin's blood. What if that capacity were passed to their nymphs? Such knowledge could destabilize the entire social structure. For example, had all of the Fon been able to read, and troubled themselves to access the computerized data available to the Zin, they would know about the damage inflicted on the citadels, the manner in which thousands of rebellious Ra 'Na had escaped into space, and the fact that the human resistance continued to grow stronger. Angered by what they would no doubt see as his failings, who knew what the functionaries might do?

Fortunately, thanks to the memories that *his* nymph would inherit, the Zin felt confident that his descendent would be cognizant of the danger and take the steps necessary to deal with it.

Warmed by that thought, Hak-Bin stepped forward. Three globe-shaped cameras, all held aloft by a technology the Zin would never understand, shifted in response. Hak-Bin knew that the images produced by them would be beamed to similar assemblages within other Sauron-controlled ships, the citadels on the planet below, and to hundreds of Kan outposts. Individuals not free to watch the feed would have access to recordings. The words had been memorized and came easily. "Greetings . . . We have come a long ways since our ancestors seized the first ships and made their way out into the vastness of space. During the succeeding years we have survived journeys through seemingly endless night, swarms of meteorites, and battles with implacable foes. All to advance our race toward the final destination: a planet known as Paradise. Have we arrived? No, as any of you presently located on the surface of the planet can attest."

The joke stimulated laughter, not only among those watching the feed on the planet below, but from those on the Launch Deck. Thus encouraged, Hak-Bin continued. "No, the planet we call Haven is just that, a place where the race can rest and regenerate. Not only in the figurative sense, but in the *real* sense, prior to resuming our epic journey."

Hak-Bin paused there, waiting for the words to sink in, ready should the Fon, or even members of the Kan, react in a negative manner.

But no one moved or broke the ensuing silence. Unsure of whether that was good or bad, Hak-Bin had little choice but to go on. "Yes, the time has come for the present generation to move on, through the veil of death, and into the next world. That's where our ancestors, the same beings who have watched over us throughout our long lives, wait to greet us. Unlike slaves, who live in eternal fear wondering whether there is some existence after the change called death, each of us has been in communion with our forefathers since birth, and *knows* that life goes on. Once we enter the next world our victories will be enumerated, our lives will be celebrated, and we shall live in peace.

"But first, before we can claim that reward, the next generation must enter *this* plane of existence. The moment when the vast majority of our descendants will arrive is only nineteen days away, and many of you, myself included, have already felt the beginning of the change. Do not fear such sensations, but welcome them, knowing that a new version of yourself is about to be born."

There was a reaction this time as the crowd stirred, comments were exchanged, and perimeter guards went to the highest level of alert. They had been briefed six units before—and those who found the situation hard to accept had been relieved of duty. But the stir had more to do with a sense of relief than one of anger, as hundreds of Saurons learned that the symptoms they had experienced of late had a legitimate cause.

"Yes," Hak-Bin said understandingly, "there can be some discomfort. However, thanks to a substance that will be made available to you in the very near future, the transitional process will be made easier.

"Now, here's how it will work . . . Each one of you has been assigned to a citadel. The *true* purpose of these citadels is to protect you and your nymph during the birth process. Over the next nineteen days, those of you not already on the surface will be transported there. Those of you who are on the surface will withdraw to the citadels. Shortly after your arrival you will be shown into a preassigned birth chamber, provided with appropriate medications, and left to make the journey in peace.

"The fleet, meanwhile, plus a cadre of carefully selected breeder slaves, will await the arrival of your progeny. Once they have emerged and had a chance to acclimate themselves, the journey to Paradise will continue."

"What about the prisoners held aboard rebel ships?" a Fon yelled. "And what's to keep the humans from killing us while we give birth?"

The Fon would have said more, as would others scattered throughout the crowd, but a single shot from a Kan assault rifle served to silence them. The dart, fired by a warrior stationed in the girders above, punched a hole through the top of the functionary's head and traveled down through his brain, into his throat, and from there to his left lung. He fell in a heap. No one moved.

"You have questions," Hak-Bin said calmly. "I understand that. And your questions will be answered. Not here, but in smaller groups, where members of the Zin can respond to specific concerns." And eject you from a lock, the Zin thought to himself, should you threaten the rest of the race.

"So," the Zin concluded, "please return to your duties secure in the knowledge that the situation is under control, that your new lives will soon begin, and your nymphs will inherit all the knowledge, wisdom, and experience gleaned during your long productive lives. That is all."

There were no cheers, just the shuffle of feet and a heaviness of spirit as the Saurons left the Launch Deck.

Finally, after everyone else was gone, only one Sauron remained. His name was Aut-Tuu—and he was dead.

ANACORTES, WASHINGTON

Centum Commander Dor-Une stood on the foundation of a razed building and looked out over the ruins of what had been Anacortes, Washington. It was evening, the sun had smeared the western horizon with reddish orange light, and another day was about to end. Not just *any* day, but one of only a few that remained to him, spent as most of them had been, doing his duty. Or so the Kan assumed.

Sadly, especially now, Dor-Une could remember no more than two standard years back, and could do little but speculate as to prior events. It wasn't fair, not to his mind at any rate, though many of his peers seemed to pay little if any attention to the matter. Their lack of introspection, especially in the wake of Hak-Bin's announcement, was nothing short of amazing.

Yes, some of them had expected something of the sort, thereby lessening the shock, and yes, they were in constant if somewhat unclear contact with their progenitors, but the overall level of acceptance seemed to hint at something deeper, a preprogrammed response that enabled his brethren to prepare for the next generation's imminent arrival without regard for their own departure from the physical world.

There might have been more such thoughts had Sub-Centum Ome-Tur not chosen that particular moment to intrude. Like the rest of Dor-Une's command, he was exactly the same age as his superior officer and had the same amount of experience. Their perceptions were different, however, since where Dor-Une saw the sunset, and the manner in which it served to symbolize the ever dwindling number of days available to him, his second-in-command saw little beyond the mechanics of purpose. "It will be dark in a few units."

Dor-Une gestured agreement. "Yes. The humans will attack at night, if not this one, then the next, or the one after that. Odds are that they will arrive by boat. Remind the pickets of the plan . . . Fire, fall back, and fire again. Then," the commander said, opening a pincer by way of illustration, "we will close the trap."

The pincer made a clacking sound as it closed—and Ome-Tur made a note to use the same device when passing the orders along.

Meanwhile, some sixty miles to the east, three helicopters sat in the center of a small field, their engines roaring as rotors started to turn. George "Popcorn" Farley stood in the door of Dragon One while Deac Smith yelled up at him. "Watch your six, George . . . the bugs can be tricky."

"Roger that," the ex-Ranger responded. "It shouldn't be difficult since my six is a lot larger than it used to be!"

Smith laughed, waved, and backed away. Engines roared even louder as the Vertol CH-48 Chinook helicopters lifted off and nosed toward the ragged strip of orange light that still served to split day from night.

Up front, in Dragon One's cockpit, Vera Veen handled the controls while her copilot, John Wu, eyed the jury-rigged screens that some Ra 'Na technicians had wired into the already cluttered instrument panel. The original plan had been to attack the catalyst factory from the sea, but then, after giving the matter some additional thought, Farley had changed his mind. Given that the humans had not launched any sort of airborne assault in the past, the ex-Ranger reasoned that doing so would provide his team with the element of surprise. Assuming the Chinooks managed to reach the LZ unharmed, that is . . . which was where the Ra 'Na came in.

On orders from Fra Pol, four flights of three fighters each

had been launched from the newly liberated *Liberty* just prior to the moment when that vessel broke orbit. Then, taking advantage of the ensuing confusion, the rebel fighters landed on a body of water known as Lake Washington, where they scooted under the high-rise portion of the I-90 floating bridge, and immediately powered down. Now, thanks to the newly installed com gear ranked in front of him, Wu could communicate with the fighters, and the *Liberty*, should that be necessary.

The copilot checked to ensure that the Ra 'Na fighters were aloft, verified that they were, and gave a sigh of relief. Sauron fighters, that's what he feared most, and it was up to the Ra 'Na to keep them at bay. Could the fur balls do it? What with their lack of experience and all? Maybe, and maybe not. But what they could do was buy the choppers some time. And it was Farley's hope that the fighter cover, plus the relatively short flight time, would enable the pilots to put the assault team on the ground *before* the orbital bugs were able to intervene. Then, with the humans right on top of their objective, the Saurons would be forced to put a hold on the heavy stuff or risk destroying the factory themselves.

"How are we doin'?" Veen inquired, her face lit from below, and nearly obscured by the night-vision rig.

"We're cooler than a hog in a wallow," Wu answered, adopting what he fancied to be a hillbilly accent, "and ready to raise some serious hell."

"Roger that," Veen acknowledged cheerfully, "watch out, bugs, 'cause here we come!"

The warning from orbit and the sound of primitive aircraft engines reached Centum Commander Dor-Une within units of each other. He cursed his brethren for their negligence, cursed himself for assuming the humans would attack from the sea, and cursed the stomach cramps that threatened to distract him. Damn the nymph anyway! Even a warrior unborn should know better than to interfere at a moment such as this.

But, like the professional he was, Dor-Une managed to push all of those concerns aside and focus his attention on the enemy. He activated his radio. There was no time to pass orders down through the chain of command, so he took advantage of the command override built into the Ra 'Na-designed com system. "This is Dor-Une . . . Prepare for an airborne assault. It's impossible to say where the ferals will land, so be attentive. Once they touch down report the location and concentrate your fire on their aircraft. I repeat, concentrate your fire on their aircraft—*not* on their troops.

"Then, once their means of escape has been snatched away, you will herd them into the killing zone established as part of the original plan. The rest will be easy. Dor-Une out."

Farley stood toward the front of the chopper and looked back at the combat-equipped truck drivers, insurance salesmen, schoolteachers, sushi chefs, business executives, and construction workers who comprised his forty-eight-person platoon. It was a mixed group all right, but every one of them had fought the bugs before and knew what to expect. None were planning to stay—so each member of the team carried a full combat load consisting of an assault weapon or light machine gun, a handgun, combat knife, at least fifteen magazines of ammo, 40mm grenades, plus water, flares, body armor, com equipment, and med kits. Once on the ground, Farley's team, plus an identical unit led by a retired gunnery sergeant named Waller, would attack the factory.

The third platoon, which included the SAMs, mortars, and heavy machine guns, would set up as quickly as they could and provide fire support.

It was a hairy mission, probably the worst Farley had participated in, and the knowledge weighed on his gut. He was getting too old for this sort of bullshit and should have been home sitting on the porch. That was when Wu came on the intercom, announced that they were "one minute out," and welcomed his passengers to "bug city."

Farley ordered his team to release their seat belts, reminded them to check their weapons, and braced himself against the impact. There hadn't been much AA fire, not that he could see, and that boded well. Maybe, just maybe, the bugs were napping.

There was a distinct thump as the gear touched down, and Farley jumped to the ground. Confident that his troops would follow, the ex-Ranger raced across the onetime parking lot and took cover behind a burned-out van. Others joined him one by one. That's when the Saurons opened fire—and armor-piercing darts stitched holes along the Chinook's fuselage.

Veen bit her lip as the platoon deassed the chopper, chanted, "Come on, come on, come on," and felt the ship shudder as alien projectiles ripped through it. Helicopters have a lot moving parts—which means there are plenty of things that can wrong even under normal circumstances. Now, with enemy fire pounding the Chinook, the situation was anything but normal. Finally, the last soldier was off, her crew chief yelled, "Go!" and Veen resumed her mantra as she fed fuel to the twin turbine engines. "Come on, come on, baby, you can do it."

And the helicopter *did* do it, lurching into the air just as a Sauron SLM flashed through the space just vacated, and Dragon Two settled into the LZ. The second ship wasn't so lucky. Men and women were still spilling out of the helicopter's belly when a second SLM struck the aircraft's tail, destroyed both engines, and ignited the onboard fuel. The resulting fireball lit the night.

Farley watched the assault team bail out, gave thanks for the fact that most of them appeared to have made it, and got on the radio. "Red Dog One to Dragon Three . . . The

LZ has been zeroed . . . repeat zeroed. Break it off and back around. We could use some fire support. Over."

Dragon Three, under the control of an ex-army pilot by the name of Dawkins, who gave thanks for the reprieve, banked to starboard. The turn, and the resulting tilt, provided the door gunner with the chance she'd been waiting for. Her name was Izu, and though only five feet tall, she was all warrior. The 7.62mm minigun whined as if eager to begin its task, began to roar, and spit thousands of rounds per minute at the enemy below.

Dor-Une, still gloating over the manner in which the slaves had rushed into his trap, felt a sudden sense of alarm as the helicopter was transformed from a troop delivery system into a platform for an extremely nasty offensive weapon. Guided by Izu's gentle hand, the 7.62mm slugs found the Kan and ripped them to pieces. The Centum Commander screamed into the com. "Destroy that aircraft! Do it now!"

The Sauron warriors were nothing if not obedient. Half a dozen SLMs lanced upwards, sought heat, and locked in. Some went for the flares that Dawkins triggered, but some didn't. The interval between the warning tone and the sound of the first explosion was so short that one blended into the next. Dawkins, Izu, and the rest of the heavy weapons platoon were gone in a flash of light.

The debris from Dragon Three was still falling when Farley waved the first and second platoons forward. "Red Dog One to Red Dog Team . . . Are you people paid by the hour? Let's get a move on."

The Kan fell back into a series of prepared positions, fired just enough to maintain contact, and waited for the slaves to enter the kill zone.

The factory lay one city block to the west . . . and the defensive fire was lighter than Farley had expected. On the other hand, *nothing* was as he had expected. Either Darby had her head up her ass—or the place had been reinforced subsequent to her visit. Either way the outcome was the same. There were a lot more bugs than there were supposed to be, and if the Saurons were surprised, it was sure hard to tell.

Lead elements of the assault team came under fire from the Sauron equivalent of a light machine gun. The first platoon silenced the weapon with a volley of 40mm grenades and continued to push forward. The catalyst factory, which was inexplicably lit, appeared up ahead. Farley paused, scanned the facility with a pair of light-intensifying binoculars, and tried to make sense of what he saw. Either the bugs were stupid, a definite possibility, or they were smart and . . .

The ex-Ranger's thought process was interrupted as Dor-Une ordered his mortars to fire. A series of explosions marched their way across the ground to Farley's rear. The human knew he'd been boxed, knew he wouldn't make it home, and gave the only order he could. "Assault team, advance!"

And the assault team *did* advance right into the carefully planned cross fire that Dor-Une had worked so hard to prepare for them. But even as alien tracer fire cut the night into slices of darkness, and his team members continued to fall, Farley made one last call. "Red Dog One to Dragon One . . . over."

Vera Veen, still circling well clear of the firefight, was quick to reply. "This is Dragon One . . . go."

"It was a trap . . . Execute Plan B. Red Dog out."

Veen swore bitterly and turned to Wu. "You heard the man . . . make the call."

"Are you sure?"

"That was an order goddamn it! Make the call!"

Wu made the call.

Twelve fighters circled thousands of feet above. The Ra 'Na flight commander, an ex–shuttle pilot named Yad, swore as the transmission came in. Now, just as a swarm of Sauron fighters were making their way down through the atmosphere, the humans were in the mood to talk. He had no notion of human radio procedure and his voice was terse. "Yes? What do you want?"

Wu forced himself to ignore the other pilot's tone. "Execute Plan B. Over."

Yad checked one of the screens arrayed in front of him. Each member of Farley's team had been provided with an electronic locator beacon. Each individual appeared as a green dot. There were surprisingly few of them, and they were clustered within the very area he had just been ordered to attack. "Have you lost your mind? If we attack the factory, your ground forces will be slaughtered."

Wu heard his own voice as if it came from a long distance away. "Roger that Strike One . . . but they're going to die anyway. You have your orders . . . carry them out. Over."

Yad felt something hard settle into the bottom of his stomach. He said, "I understand," and opened a link with the rest of his command. "Flights two and three will engage the Saurons. Flight one will follow me down. Arm bombs and missiles. This target is critical. We can't afford to miss."

There were a variety of replies, all affirmative, and the battle was joined. As flight one dove—flights two and three started to climb. Some envied flight one. At least they wouldn't have to face Kan pilots one-on-one. Not yet anyway.

Meanwhile, down on the ground, Farley was down to ten effectives. They lay on their backs feet together, weapons aimed upward. "All right," the ex-noncom said, "let's make the bastards pay."

The Kan jumped after that, their momentarily gray bodies nearly invisible against the night sky, weapons winking red. Counterfire lashed up to meet them, alien bodies turned somersaults in the air, and blood fell like warm rain.

But more Kan jumped, and *more*, until the sky was full of them. And each time they jumped the warriors met less resistance until there was hardly any at all. And finally, just as the Ra 'Na fighters made their first run, the last member of the assault team died. His name was George "Popcorn" Farley, he'd been a Ranger once, and now, by all accounts, he still was.

Dor-Une felt the ground tremble as the incoming fighters started to unload their ordinance. It didn't seem fair. He'd done *his* part . . . but the half-wits in the air arm had failed to do theirs. Still, there was hope, especially in light of the low-quality forces that opposed him. Not one of the Ra 'Na pilots had ever dropped a bomb before, so it wasn't too surprising that none of them were able to hit the intended target.

Yad, who was no better than the rest, swore when he saw that his last bomb was hung up. He started to toggle the emergency release, thought better of it, and banked to the left. "All right, slaves—the master race awaits! Put all of your missiles on the factory."

Like most of the slaves assigned to the day shift, Sister Andromeda was well clear of the factory by the time the assault began. But she had seen the influx of Kan, knew a trap had been laid, and hurried to warn someone. The assault force moved quickly however, and by the time Andromeda had traversed a section of burned-out ruins and arrived on the scene of the fighting, the battle was mostly over. The Saurons launched flares. They soared into the air, went pop, and drifted downward. The harsh green light cast an eerie glow over the ravaged landscape.

The cult leader stepped over an eviscerated Kan and into the circle of death. The humans lay like the petals of a dead flower—their weapons clutched in lifeless hands, or inches from dead fingertips. Andromeda felt a terrible sense of grief bubble up from deep within. Sobs racked her body, and she made no attempt to control them. The Ra 'Na fighters passed over her head, made a long slow turn, and began their second run.

Andromeda recognized Farley and knelt beside his body. The Ranger's hand was sticky but warm. She clasped it to her chest. Now, as she waited for the final release, the words that came to the onetime cultist's lips were from a religion that predated hers. "The Lord is my shepherd; I shall not want. He maketh me to lie down in green pastures: He leadeth me beside still waters . . ."

Yad lined his fighter up on the catalyst factory, caught the explosion from the corner of his eye, and knew his wingman was dead. Although the pilot did not regard himself as especially religious, the hona seemed to chant itself. "From the ocean we came . . . and to the ocean we shall return. For I am but a drop in the sea of life, carried by currents unknown, and cast up where the Great One will have me."

Sister Andromeda heard the rhythmic pom, pom, pom of the Kan AA batteries, the shriek of outgoing SLMs, but never looked up. "Yea, though I walk through the valley of the shadow of death, I will fear no evil: for Thou art with me . . ."

Yad fired his final pair of missiles, toggled the emergency bomb release, and felt his fighter rise as the thousand-unit bomb fell away. There was just enough time to get off a burst from his nose cannon prior to pulling up and out of the dive. Moments later he was climbing, thrilled to be alive, and amazed to find that he and his wingmates owned the sky.

A missile hit the ground not ten feet from where Andromeda knelt, exploded, and set her free. There was light, a feeling of weightlessness, and an enormous sense of relief.

Dor-Une never saw the bomb, it was too dark for that, but somehow knew that death was on the way. Death for not only him but the nymph within. He met it the same way he had encountered life: head up, eyes open, feet planted firmly on the ground.

The bomb struck, the catalyst factory exploded, and 204 slaves were killed. However, 416 Saurons died in the same blast, not to mention those who would die because they lacked birth catalyst, and those who would never be born.

Vera Veen knew that, knew she was lucky to be alive, but somehow wished that she wasn't. Officers weren't supposed to cry, not in front of subordinates, but the pilot didn't care. Tears rolled down her cheeks as she turned the helicopter toward the east. The engines droned, and the survivors, all three of them, were carried home.

NORTH OF MOUNT VERNON, WASHINGTON

Franklin looked upward. The skies were clear, and, without the glare produced by the cities of the past, the stars twinkled like diamonds. Points of light in what appeared to be an otherwise dark galaxy.

Yes, there was beauty, if you had a telescope powerful enough to see it, but there was horror as well. Not in the stars themselves—but in the life forms they could produce. Why would an all-seeing, all-knowing, all-powerful god produce a race like the Saurons? Yet what, come to think of it, had the aliens done that humans had not? Bomb cities into rubble? You bet, plenty of them. Enslave thousands of sentient beings? Been there, done that. Practice genocide on a massive scale? Sure, and there were ovens to prove it. So, it came down to a matter of free choice, and what sentients did with it.

There was the rustle of clothing, and a familiar voice said, "I thought I might find you out here."

Franklin turned to greet Dr. Sool. Light spilled from an open door. It lit the left side of her face. It was beautiful, and her skin reminded him of Jina's. The medic offered the politician a cup of coffee. He took it. "Jack sent you."

Sool smiled. "And what if he did? He cares about you . . . We all do."

"Not those who are dead," Franklin said bitterly. "Not Popcorn Farley, not Sister Andromeda, not the rest of them."

Sool took a sip of tea. "All of us are going to die, Mr. President, the only question is when. Thanks to the sacrifice made by people like Farley, the Saurons lost fifty percent of their birth catalyst plus the capacity to make more. That's equivalent to killing half their nymphs in a single blow. No small accomplishment. The job needed to be done. They agreed to do it. End of story."

Franklin tried the coffee. It was hot and warmed the pit of his stomach. "So you have a degree in psychiatry as well."

Sool shook her head. "No, the truth is so obvious anyone could see it . . . Anyone but you."

"So, do you think we can win?"

The medic shrugged. "Maybe, though it's far from certain. I know one thing, however . . ."

"What's that?"

"We have the right leader."

Franklin raised his mug. "Thanks, Doc. Perhaps you aren't a shrink . . . but you're the next best thing."

Sool grinned. "Don't speak too soon . . . Wait till you see my bill!"

ABOARD THE RA 'NA CRUISER *BALWUR*

Until very recently the compartment had been used as a sort of lounge by the Fon. Now, by virtue of the fact that all of the vessel's previous owners had either been wounded, killed, or locked away in one of the ship's holds, it had been transformed into an assembly hall. As such it was packed to overflowing with small, furry bodies. Contravening voices filled the air, ears lay flat against sleek skulls, and arms flailed wildly as a multiplicity of debates raged throughout the room.

Rul sat on a bench off to one side and watched in wonder. Slavery was horrible, but the chaos before him was nearly unbearable, especially to one who admired order in the way that he did. Yet, based on secret documents handed down through the Ra 'Na priesthood, the dro knew that such settos had been a common occurrence back during pre-Sauron days, and were in fact a hallmark of democracy.

True to the time-honored institutions of the past, the new government would include a secular chief executive officer, an upper house comprised of senior members of the clergy, and a much larger lower house in which the various guilds would attempt to build coalitions, block each others' initiatives, and ram their agendas through. The very process taking place in front of him . . . except that debate centered on a single issue.

Now that the Ra 'Na dominated ships had withdrawn into space and were free to do as they pleased, some of the newly freed slaves wanted to depart for the now nearly mythical planet of Balwur.

Others, Rul among them, felt that to leave would amount to cowardice, and an unforgivable betrayal of both the Ra 'Na who remained on Sauron-controlled ships and the humans on the planet below.

"Nonsense," the runners responded, insisting as they did that most if not all of the Ra 'Na who remained on Sauron vessels did so voluntarily, and that the humans could take care of themselves. Some even went so far as to refer to the humans as clath, or "furless ones," a racial slur that reflected the extent to which they had been influenced by Sauron society.

All of which was necessary if not especially attractive, since public debate had been silenced since the fall of Balwur and must necessarily resume. The only problem was that the Saurons were about to reproduce, lives were being lost, and time was running out. That being the case, Rul signaled

P'ere Dee . . . and came to his feet. As with so many other things, Dee had anticipated the moment and equipped himself with the Ra 'Na equivalent of a bullhorn. "Silence!"

Hundreds of standard units earlier, prior to the fall of Balwur, such an order would have been greeted with insults, rude noises, and outright rebellion, since no one but the chief executive could issue such an order, and then only in the most dire of circumstances. But all of those present had been slaves and were used to following orders. The silence was total. Rul took control by simply moving to the front of the compartment, scanning the assembly with his laser-like gaze, and projecting his considerable personality.

"Debate is a necessary and time-honored component of democracy. Later, when the present crisis has been resolved and the Sauron menace has been forever put aside, there will be ample opportunity for talk. But *here, now,* deeds must substitute for words.

"Some say that we have suffered enough, that we should run, and leave the collaborators behind. I say they are wrong. With perhaps the exception of a few rebels, brave souls such as Fra Pol, every single one of us functioned as a collaborator in one way or another. Whom should we leave? By what test will you sort them out? And who is so innocent that they qualify to make such judgments?

"Some say that the humans should be left to fight their own battles. I say they are wrong. Who struck the *first* blows? Who destroyed the *first* Sauron ships? Who showed us the way?

"Some believe that we are somehow superior to both humans *and* Saurons because of our technological know-how. Well, I am here to tell you the Great One cares not for technology, nor the nature of the material that covers our bodies, but for the quality of the being within. Choose wisely my friends . . . or take the first steps down the same path that the Saurons followed so long ago."

There was silence after that as the vast majority of those present stared down at their feet and looked embarrassed. Finally, Sel San, leader of the Power Tech Guild, cleared his throat. "I would like to thank Dro Rul on behalf of the Power Tech Guild—and move that we call for a simultaneous vote by both houses. All those in favor of staying say 'aye.' "

The response reverberated like thunder. "AYE!"

"And those opposed?"

Silence.

San turned toward Rul, delivered an old-fashioned bow, and smiled. "I know it's hard to believe—but it seems the entire assembly is in agreement."

There was laughter—and the Ra 'Na were truly free.

NEAR THE MAYAN RUINS OF NAKABE, GUATEMALA

It was night, and moonlight made a path across the river as it rushed, gurgled, and splashed its way toward the sea. Three Eye claimed that it spoke to him, or tried to, but either the river had no interest in Jones or she lacked the necessary talent because all she heard was the sound of water rushing by.

The *donada* was ill—and the anthropologist had volunteered to replace her on the second net. Partly because their little community was so dependent on the tidbits that the Saurons dumped into the river—and partly because she was bored.

Though relatively safe, the subterranean cavern where the *sobrevivientes* lived was more than a little stultifying. There was no Internet connection, no books, and no one with whom Jones could have a truly intellectual conversation.

So, why am I still here? the academic asked herself for the thousandth time. Why haven't I left? Made my way out of here? Surely there were others, people who evaded capture and managed to survive.

But what sort of welcome would she receive? Men liked her—but that cut both ways. Men like Blackley would allow themselves to be used. But others, and there were plenty, would simply take what they wanted.

Jones shivered. Was it the coolness of the night? Or the thought of winding up as some postapocalyptic alpha male's sex toy? So that's what it came down to . . . The cave was boring, but it was safe, and that's why she stayed.

Something hit the net, sent a shock through the hand rope, and broke the academic's train of thought. She started to react, to pull the trap in, but felt *another* object hit the webbing, and *another*, until the combined weight exceeded what Jones could hold. That's when she was forced to let go, the rope whipped through the block back among the trees, and was sucked into the river as the net released its load.

Curious as to what she had caught, then immediately lost, the academic waded out into the river. There was an eddy there, a place where the current liked to park things, prior to snatching them away. The water was warm, blood warm, and caressed her knees. Something bumped into the anthropologist's leg—then quickly disappeared. But there were *more* blobs, dark somethings that bobbed up and down while waiting for their turn.

Jones waded out a little bit farther, managed to get her hands on one, and almost let it go. The object was soft, *too* soft, and wore some sort of clothes. That's when she turned the body over, saw the Ra 'Na's dimly lit face, and knew the truth. The Saurons were murdering their slaves. Not just a few, as some sort of punishment, but, judging from the number of blobs, hundreds or even thousands.

As if to corroborate the anthropologist's theory another corpse spun into the eddy, paused for a moment, and was soon sucked away. More followed, became tangled up with each other, and started to form what amounted to a logjam.

Jones backed away. Part of her felt sick, but the other part, the academic part of her personality, wanted to know why. Had the citadel been completed? And would the aliens actually leave? The river tried to tell her, but Jones couldn't hear, and the bodies continued to accumulate. Whatever the answer, the academic knew one thing for sure . . . Something was going to happen.

HELL HILL

The president of the United States crouched among the burned-out remains of a half-million-dollar summer home and peered through his binoculars. Hell Hill, which lay to the south on the other side of Pleasant Bay, shimmered in the sun.

Seen from a distance the citadel, which sat castlelike atop gradually rising tiers of pastel cargo modules, looked like a medieval town perched high above the Mediterranean. Only the observation tower, which lay where it had fallen, and the badly scorched citadel gave lie to the illusion.

The politician gave an involuntary start as a Sauron shuttle whined over the partially collapsed house, circled, and landed out on the bay. Another had pulled away from one of the floating docks and was ready to take off. Thousands of Saurons had landed during the last two days, and there was no end in sight.

Even now, while hundreds of slaves worked to repair the damage done to the citadel's roof, a long column of Fon could be seen marching up the dirt road, past the rows of crow-picked crosses, and into the limestone complex where the birth chambers awaited them.

The politician lowered his binoculars and turned to the soldier crouched at his side. Deac Smith had taken Popcorn Farley's death especially hard—and deep circles underscored his eyes. But he was determined, not to mention angry, and Franklin knew it would go hard with any Sauron that Smith happened to encounter. "So, you still feel good about a day-light break?"

Smith nodded. "Yes, I do. We're going to take casualties no matter what we do . . . Once the demo charges go off, the slaves will start to run every which way. Directing them down through the wall will be hard enough during the day. At night, with no orbital mirror to provide extra illumination, the whole thing would be impossible. People would fall off cliffs, run the wrong way, and Lord knows what else. Besides, the last thing the bugs will expect is a daylight attack."

Franklin was familiar with the arguments, having formulated some of them himself, but felt reassured nonetheless. No one knew when the Saurons planned to kill their slaves—but there was little doubt that the day would come soon.

Rather than wait for that day, and the slaughter that would follow, the resistance had resolved to engineer a massive breakout. A lot of slaves would die, there was no way to avoid that, but at least they'd have a chance. Franklin checked his watch. "Okay, Deac, make it happen."

The ex-Ranger nodded, waited for the last few seconds to tick away, and spoke into his radio. The first thing that happened was that the stripped-down pickup truck, better known to the residents of Hell Hill as Cappy's Meat Wagon, blew up.

Cappy wasn't near the vehicle when it exploded, nor were the slaves assigned to pull it. They had been excused and sent elsewhere when the meat wagon's rear axle failed earlier that morning, leaving the vehicle stranded by the main gate.

Had the Kan assigned to guard the entrance been less preoccupied with the aches and pains that plagued them, and had one or more of them been willing to penetrate a virtual cloud of flies and look through the pile of bodies stacked in the back of Cappy's truck, they would have discovered the massive demo charge and still had sufficient time to disarm it. But such was not the case, which meant that the guards, the bodies, and the main gate simply vanished as 250 pounds of military-grade C-4 was detonated from a position half a mile beyond the wall.

The subsequent explosions were spaced along the entire length of the landward perimeter at points easily accessed from the hill's eastern slope. Little bits of wood and stone were still raining down when Manning, closely followed by a group of volunteers, charged through break number three. The "moles," as the sappers liked to refer to themselves, had spent days driving tunnels in under the base of the wall. Carefully shaped charges, detonated on cue, handled the rest.

Now, as Manning waved his self-designated Pathfinders forward, and gave something analogous to a rebel yell, he questioned his own sanity. A lot of Smith's best people had died during the Battle of Anacortes, which meant the resistance was short of officers. That was part of it, but there was more . . . Somewhere along the line the security officer had crossed the line from neutral professional to full-blown patriot. A transformation that came as more of a surprise to the security chief than those around him.

But then, as an SLM slammed into one of the observation towers, and Kan swung into the action, the time for thinking was over. All over Hell Hill specially trained volunteers emerged from hiding, ran into the streets, and yelled the exact same words: "Leave everything behind! Run down the *east* side of the hill! Leave everything behind! Run down the *east* side of the hill!"

Most of the slaves obeyed, running as if their lives depended on it, which they certainly did. A group of Fon overseers, backed by human collaborators, emerged from a side street and attempted to turn the would-be escapees. They shouted orders, cracked their whips, and blocked the path. Those at the front of the crowd hesitated, and some managed to stop, but only for a moment. More and more people arrived with each passing second, and those toward the rear pushed from behind. Unaware of the confrontation ahead, they pushed from behind. Suddenly, like a dam bursting under pressure, the mob rolled forward.

Whips cracked, and some of those in the first few ranks fell under the lash, but most kept their feet. Those who went down were quickly trampled into red mush. A few of the Fon managed to jump clear, but the rest were overwhelmed and torn apart the moment the crowd came into contact with them. Human collaborators, or those *perceived* to be collaborators, fared no better. There were screams as they were subsumed by wave after wave of flesh.

Now other volunteers appeared. They provided the next set of instructions. "Run toward the orange smoke! Run toward the orange smoke! Run toward the orange smoke!" The slaves looked, saw pillars of orange smoke, and ran toward them. Once they were close enough, more monitors urged them to move through whichever break they had chosen and out to freedom. Guides met the fugitives, formed them into groups, and led them into the protection of the surrounding woods.

That's how it was *supposed* to work, at any rate, although plenty of things could go wrong, not the least of which was the fact that the Kan didn't approve of exploding walls, incoming SLMs, *or* escaping slaves.

In spite of the fact that the nearest observation tower had already sustained two hits from SLMs, it not only remained standing, but provided the Sauron gunners with the ideal platform from which to fire on the slaves below. Some of the warriors functioned as snipers, choosing each target with care, while others hosed the hillsides with automatic weapons fire, happy to kill anything that moved. A poorly conceived strategy that effectively did away with slaves, collaborators, and Fon alike.

The steady rattle of automatic weapons fire, the whoosh of incoming SLMs, and the screams of wounded slaves created a hellish symphony as Manning and his team fought their way up the same slopes others were streaming down. The goal was to establish enough resistance to slow pursuers down and buy time so that as many slaves as possible would be able to escape.

Someone yelled, "Here they come!" and opened up with an automatic weapon. Manning looked up to find that at least a dozen Kan were leapfrogging down the hill, firing both from the apex of their jumps *and* when they touched down.

Manning bellowed, "Spread out!" and lifted the 12-gauge riot gun to his shoulder. The trick was to lead the bastards, to put the double-ought buck where the bug was *going* to be, and let the Kan run into it. Simple in theory, but damned hard when the target not only morphed to match the sky, but insisted on shooting back.

The security chief followed a momentary shimmer, got out in front of it, and squeezed the trigger. The shotgun slammed against his shoulder, and Manning worked the slide. The shimmer was still there, still falling, obviously unharmed.

The weapon made a clacking sound as a shell seated itself in the chamber and a solid boom! as it fired for the second time. The slugs hit the warrior just as he was about to land, tore the head off his shoulders, and sent a fountain of green gore gushing into the air. What remained tumbled down the hill. Manning looked for more targets, couldn't see any that were close enough to do anything about, and turned to check his team. Two were dead, one was wounded.

A group of slaves came downhill, leaped to clear some of the bodies, and skidded in an attempt to slow their progress. Manning waved his arms and pointed toward the casualty. "Hold it! Take him with you!"

The first man looked uncertain, but the sight of the 12-gauge seemed to help make up his mind. He and another man grabbed the Pathfinder under the armpits, snatched him off the ground, and carried him downhill.

Darts pinged off the cargo modules to Manning's right as a sniper opened fire on the pathfinders from above. "The tower!" Manning yelled. "Head for the tower!"

Then, obeying his own command, he ran. Four SLMs had hit the structure by then. Each left a wound, through which a latticework of metal reinforcements could be seen. Smoke oozed from the holes like black blood. But, in spite of the damage the red-orange wink of gunfire from high on the observation platform testified to the fact that the objective remained a threat.

Some of the team members questioned Manning's sanity, since charging such a strongly held objective seemed suicidal, and stayed where they were. Others, those who understood, or simply believed that the security chief knew what he was doing, continued to follow him. They were the lucky ones because no sooner had they scampered to higher ground than a well-aimed energy bolt flashed through the planet's atmosphere to obliterate those who had stayed behind.

The ground shook, the resulting shock wave knocked half a dozen still-fleeing slaves off their feet, and more explosions followed as the orbital shelling continued.

Heart pumping and lungs on fire, Manning rounded a corner and charged up a heavily rutted street. A dog barked from a doorway, the remains of a shattered street stall lay scattered in the street, and laundry flapped over his head.

Up ahead, a woman, her hands raised as if to defend herself, backed out of a cargo module, then staggered as half a dozen darts ripped through her body. Manning yelled, "Grenade! HE!" and heard a solid ka-chunk as a 40mm grenade arced into the cargo module. There was a flash, followed by a hollow boom, as still-morphing chitin sprayed out onto the road.

Satisfied that the way was clear, Manning turned his attention to the tower, which loomed ahead. As the security chief and his team made their way up onto the level area at the spire's base, they encountered the spot where an incoming SLM had decimated the Kan assigned to defend the main entrance. The remains of their badly mangled bodies were scattered all around the blackened crater.

"Bring the C-4!" Manning shouted. "Pack it into the entrance!"

Now, as what remained of the original team approached the tower's gore-splattered base, they realized that the manner in which the observation platform projected from the structure's side served to protect the area directly below. That didn't prevent the warriors from dropping the Sauron equivalent of grenades, however, many of which exploded prior to impact, and sent shrapnel screaming through the air. Manning heard one of the devices go off, heard something zing past his ear, and bellowed at the top of his lungs. "Set the C-4 and let's get the hell out of here!"

"It's ready, sir!" an army reservist yelled.

"Who has the remote?"

"*I* do, sir," the reservist replied.

"All right then," Manning answered. "Stay with me! Give the team thirty seconds to get clear of the area and let it rip. Come on everybody, let's go!"

So saying, Manning ran out and away from the tower, heard darts ping off the modules on the left side of the street, and dashed toward the relative safety of a heavily shadowed alleyway. That's when he heard someone say, "Damn!" turned to see the reservist go down, and saw the remote skitter across the hard-packed dirt.

Bodies pushed past as Manning turned, made for the remote, accidentally booted the device away, swore a blue streak, ran the device down, and returned to get the reservist. He was lying on his back, holding a handgun with both hands, and firing up at the observation platform. The dark splotch on his camos showed where a dart had ripped through his thigh. "Here," Manning said, dropping the remote on the man's chest, "I think you dropped this." Then, scooping the reservist up, darts stitching a line past his boots, the security chief ran for cover. He was halfway there when the weekend warrior punched the button, the C-4 detonated, and a giant explosion rocked the hill.

Franklin heard the boom, saw dust rise around one of the few spires that remained, and held his breath. Nothing seemed to happen at first. But then, with the dignity of a giant redwood falling in the forest, the column started to topple. Dots, which might have been Kan, could be seen spilling off the observation deck as the spire fell. A fraction of a second later it struck one of the stacks and broke into three sections. One burst into flames.

The ground shook as the tower hit, Manning felt a wave of heat wash across the back of his neck, and was thankful when another team member offered to carry the reservist. Together the two men ran, stumbled, and skidded down the side of the hill as a trio of Sauron fighters screamed in from the south. The pilots had orders to stay well clear of the citadel, but everything else was fair game.

The high-rise stacks made the easiest target, and the Kan pilots went after them first. Missiles slammed into Big Pink, exploded, and sent cargo modules spinning through the air. Some of the humans, those who happened to be inside when the break began, or those who believed that safety lay in staying put, had been hiding in the metal containers. Many died where they were, but a few survived the initial pass and skittered down the hill.

Nor was the surrounding countryside spared as the woods came in for an orbital bombardment followed by more than

a dozen strafing runs. But that contingency had been anticipated, intermediate shelters had been dug, and most of the
slaves were huddled together below ground when the energy
bolts started to fall.

Some were not so lucky, however. Manning, escaping
with the five remaining members of his team, had the reservist across his shoulders again as they entered the tree
line, saw a woman wave, and ran in her direction. It was
only after Manning had half dived, half fallen into the crude
log bunker, and the woman had collapsed on top of him,
that the security chief realized that the small body belonged
to Seeko. She kissed him, he kissed her, and they held each
other tight as the ground shook. Many people had died . . .
but those who survived were free.

ON ASTEROID 0^ 2103

The Sauron shuttle slid along the flanks of a massive destroyer and thereby provided Tog with an opportunity to
look out through the view port and gape at the damage done
to the vessel during the recent conflict. Difficult though it
was to believe, his fellow Ra 'Na had attacked the vessel and
blown a large hole in the side of its hull! It was madness,
pure madness. Still, in spite of the fact that he disapproved,
the prelate couldn't help but feel a burgeoning sense of
pride. Having never paid his race the respect they deserved,
the Saurons had paid for their arrogance.

The shuttle dove into the gap between a pair of darkened
factory ships, turned to starboard, and started to decelerate.
Tog felt the tug and knew what it meant. Soon, within a
matter of units, he would be face-to-face with Dro Rul.
That's when he would remove the custom-made weapon
from his sleeve, point it at the other prelate's body, and pull
the trigger. Then, before Rul's staff could react, Lim-Tam
and his fellow Kan would emerge from hiding. Or would
they? The possibility that they wouldn't, that Hak-Bin

would allow him to be killed, had kept Tog awake during the last two sleep cycles.

But what choice did he really have? If he failed to make the assassination attempt, Hak-Bin would kill him for sure. No, all he could do was carry out the plan and hope for the best.

More than a hundred units before, Asteroid O Λ 2103 had been equipped with external engines and mined. Then, after all the useful minerals had been extracted, the interior surface had been sealed and filled with water. An extremely valuable substance during long journeys between the stars. Nearly empty now, the asteroid awaited a new supply of H_2O for use by the next generation of Saurons. Assuming that Hak-Bin was able to restore order, and had sufficient slaves to carry out the work, none of which was certain.

Rather than mate with one of the huge intake ports, the way a tanker would, the shuttle nosed into one of two open docking stations. The pilots, both of whom were Ra 'Na collaborators, established lock-to-lock contact and killed power. The copilot released his harness, got up, and left the control room. He half expected to find that his passenger was up and waiting next to the hatch, but such was not the case. Tog remained strapped into his seat. "We have arrived, excellency . . . You can disembark whenever you choose."

Tog nodded. "Thank you." It took all the strength the prelate could muster to release his harness, come to his feet, and shuffle toward the lock. Air hissed, pressures were equalized, and Tog passed through the surface station and into the asteroid's interior. Countless layers of pale yellow paint had been applied to the walls of the main passageway. It ramped downward and curved at the same time. A neatly painted sign commanded Tog to follow the illuminated line in case of a fire, power failure, or pressure leak.

The deck, which consisted of duracrete rather than metal, had been buffed to a high sheen. There were what appeared to be skid marks, barely noticeable lines that might or might not be consistent with slip-slide movements Saurons made whenever they were forced to walk. Did that mean that the Kan were where they were supposed to be? Waiting to bail Tog out? Or did that amount to wishful thinking? There was no way to be sure.

Because the main chamber was practically empty and had been undergoing maintenance prior to the rebellion, it was readily accessible via thick metal doors. These opened inward, so that when the chamber was full, water pressure would act to seal them against the walls of the reservoir and prevent any chance of a potential blowout. Why Hak-Bin and his staff had chosen this particular venue for the meeting was not only a mystery—but one Tog was unlikely to solve.

The prelate paused outside access hatch six, took a look around, but saw nothing out of the ordinary. That being the case, there was nothing to do but step inside.

The main chamber was huge. Roughly spherical in shape, like the asteroid itself, the walls of the reservoir consisted of native rock covered with gray spray-on sealant. The storage tank's floor was somewhat irregular, which meant that pools of water remained below the central column and the lowest set of water intake pipes. The central part of the structure was comprised of a metal pillar intended to strengthen the asteroid and hold it together. Winding their way around the supporting member and climbing toward the roof above was an ivylike maze of pipes, pumps, and platforms. Powerful work lights, rigged for the benefit of the maintenance crews, bathed the interior with harsh white light.

Tog felt very small as he stepped out onto one of six causeways that connected various access doors with the central pump column. Metal clanged as the Ra 'Na made his way out toward the center of the chamber where, by the terms of the agreement, the meeting was scheduled to take place.

Once there Tog experienced something akin to an anticlimax since there was no one to talk to and nothing to do. The next fifteen units passed slowly. Water dripped from somewhere high above, hit the pool below Tog's feet, and sent ripples out to the edge of the pond. A pump started up, ran for a few moments, and shut itself off.

Then, just as Tog was starting to believe that Rul wouldn't come, he heard a distant clang. Then, a few units later, a hatch opened, and Rul stepped out onto the same causeway Tog had made use of earlier. Consistent with the terms of the agreement, two bodyguards followed the prelate out toward the center of the tank. However, much to Tog's amazement, both were human. Had Hak-Bin anticipated such a possibility? Or were the Kan counting on smaller, less threatening adversaries? Assuming they were present at all. Tog felt his heart pump a little faster.

If Rul was frightened, or intimidated by the Grand Vizier's presence, there was absolutely no sign of it as the prelate arrived on the central platform and stopped a few units away. As always his robes were plain and bereft of any ornament. The greeting was polite but cool. "Greetings, Dro Tog . . . you look well."

Tog inclined his head. "As do you. Thank you for coming."

"P'ere Dee insisted that I bring bodyguards," Rul continued apologetically. "The female is called Jill Ji-Hoon . . . and the male is named Vilo Kell. The entire area was searched a few units ago—but they want to scan you too."

Tog nodded to the humans. The female nodded in response, stepped forward, and produced a paddle-shaped device. She wore a translator, and the words had a formal quality. "Hold your arms away from your body please."

The prelate did as he was told and held his breath as the metal detector was passed over each surface of his body. The woman nodded, said, "Thank you," and returned to her previous position.

"So," Rul said, "P'ere Has indicates that you are ready to join the resistance . . . Is this true?"

Tog slipped both hands into opposite sleeves, found the weapon with his right, and wrapped his fingers around the handle. Hours had been spent pulling the gun out of the arm holster, and the prelate felt confident that he could manage it. The rod, the one he would use to summon help, was clutched in his left hand. The trick would be to thumb the button *prior* to pulling the pistol.

"Yes," Tog replied, "I am. I still favor order over disorder, but the slaughter must stop." And it was then, as Tog mouthed the words, that a face appeared in front of his eyes. The face belonged to Isk, one of the four Ra 'Na who had witnessed Hak-Bin's surgery and subsequently been put to death.

Suddenly, deep within, something broke loose, rose to the surface, and blocked the prelate's throat. Words refused to come, muscles wouldn't respond, and tears streaked his fur. Part of him wanted to thumb the button, to pull the weapon, but another part resisted. The result was *no* motion whatsoever.

That was the moment when Lim-Tam, consistent with the considerable latitude granted him by Hak-Bin, decided it was time to intervene. A team of Ra 'Na had searched the tank earlier but failed to find him. The humans were something of a surprise, but they were outnumbered two to one, and that advantage would suffice. He signaled his companions and they dropped straight down.

Kell sensed the movement above before he actually saw it, drew both handguns, and was firing before the Kan had dropped more than twenty-five of the fifty feet that separated the pump platform from the ground. The human knew it was iffy, knew he'd be lucky to hit one of the warriors before their feet touched down, and resolved to monitor his ammo. Once the Kan were down it would be damned embarrassing to stand there clicking at them.

Alerted by Kell, Ji-Hoon fired as well, empty casings arcing away to plop into the water below. One of the Kan did a half somersault and smashed his head onto the causeway. A second screamed, managed to land upright, but died with two bullets through his thorax.

Perhaps it was the gunfire, or a previously unknown reservoir of strength, but whatever the reason, Tog discovered he could move again. The prelate looked up, saw the blur of falling bodies, and drew the specially designed weapon. Then, for reasons Tog wouldn't have been able to articulate, the cleric pushed Rul off the causeway.

The other Ra 'Na was still falling, still breaking the surface of the water, when the third Kan landed. As luck would have it his big flat feet hit metal almost directly in front of the Grand Vizier's position. Tog pointed the weapon, squeezed the trigger, and was rewarded with a loud bang. The slug punched a hole through the Sauron's throat. It was difficult to say who was the more surprised, Tog, or the warrior himself. Blood sprayed front and back. The Kan collapsed.

Astounded by the enormity of what he had done, Tog dropped the gun and turned as the fourth Kan landed on the platform. He tried to explain. "It was an accident! I didn't meant to shoot but the . . ."

Lim-Tam put a dart through the slave's head, swung his weapon to the left, and staggered under the impact of three .9mm slugs. The Kan ordered his pincer to squeeze, couldn't get the message through, and fell backward into the water below. There was a splash as both bodyguards slammed fresh magazines into their respective weapons. "Is that all of them?" Kell asked, scanning the structures above.

"Looks like it," Ji-Hoon said, nudging a body with her

boot. "If there were more, we would have heard from them by now."

"Probably," Kell agreed, "but I see no reason to linger. I'll grab the padre—you scout ahead."

Ji-Hoon headed for the other end of the causeway as Kell pulled Dro Rul out of the bloodstained water. The prelate shook himself like a dog, and water flew in every direction. "Thank you."

Kell shrugged. "You're welcome. Come on, let's get out of here before the reinforcements arrive."

"Yes," Rul agreed, "that makes sense . . . There's something I must do first, however." So saying, Dro Rul walked over to the place where Dro Tog had fallen and knelt next to his body. Then, forcing himself to ignore the fear that urged him to run, the prelate recited the same death toth he had so recently administered to hundreds of others.

Finally, coming to his feet, the cleric uttered the only eulogy Tog was likely to receive. "Glutton, liar, and collaborator. Brother Tog was those and more . . . But finally, in spite of his many failings, Tog was a patriot. May his soul find everlasting peace." Then, still clad in his soaking-wet robes, Rul left the platform. The day was only half-over, and he had work to do.

7

DEATH DAY MINUS 7

SATURDAY, JULY 25, 2020

Freedom suppressed and again regained bites with keener fangs than
freedom never endangered.

—Marcus Tullius Cicero
De Officiis, 44 b.c.

**ABOARD THE SAURON SUPPLY SHIP *AK TA BE, (WORLD
LIFTER)***

The birth chamber would have been an exact duplicate of
those on the planet below had it not been for the fact that
the walls were completely transparent—providing a clear
view of the Fon who squatted within. His name was Nis-
All, and unlike most early changers, certain substances had
been administered to the functionary to not only jump-start
the birth process, but produce an entirely new result. One
that could not only rescue the Sauron race from at least some
of the difficulties it faced—but vault Ott-Mar and his entire
line into a position of prominence. All subject to Hak-Bin's
approval of course.

Rather than locate his laboratory on one of the larger,
more important vessels, where it was likely to attract un-
wanted attention, Ott-Mar had chosen to place the facility
on a humble supply ship. Not only that, but by way of
further ensuring the laboratory's continued security the Zin

had even gone so far as to insist that the ship be crewed almost entirely by Saurons. That being the case, it had been a simple matter to eliminate all five of his Ra 'Na technicians immediately after the start of the rebellion, thereby ensuring that no word of his highly sensitive experiments leaked to the resistance. But now, with the experiment nearly complete, it was time to share his findings with others. Assuming that Hak-Bin honored his promise to come. That's why Ott-Mar felt a profound sense of relief when the Fon spoke over the intercom. "Lord Hak-Bin has arrived . . . and is on his way to the laboratory."

For his part the subject of Ott-Mar's concerns felt anything but relieved as he followed a slightly swollen Fon down the supply ship's main corridor. No matter how carefully Hak-Bin's plans were conceived, no matter how well they were executed it seemed that all of them turned to dra. Recent examples included the manner in which the catalyst factory had been destroyed—and the botched assassination attempt. Not only would the surviving factory be unable to meet demand, but the rebellious Dro Rul had consolidated his power and was using it to launch raids against Sauron assets.

Now, just as Hak-Bin was preparing to shift his headquarters from orbit down to the southern citadel, Ott-Mar had requested that he stop off on one of the fleet's least distinguished vessels. In fact, had the request originated with anyone other than the birthmaster Hak-Bin would have ignored it. But Ott-Mar knew him, knew the kind of pressure he was under, and was unlikely to waste his time. Or so Hak-Bin assumed as the servile Fon opened a hatch labeled, "Storeroom, Saurons Only," and ushered the Zin inside.

The lights were extremely bright, and Hak-Bin blinked as he looked around. He saw pumps, ventilators, and life-support modules, tubes that ran every which way, and there, at the very center of the tangle, a transparent box. However, before Hak-Bin could examine the misshapen mass that squatted within, Ott-Mar was there to greet him. "Welcome, my lord, thank you for coming." The scientist looked a bit bloated—and had clearly entered the change.

"I can't say that it's a pleasure," Hak-Bin replied, "not with all the problems I have, but my presence speaks volumes. You asked that I come, and here I am."

"And I'm grateful," Ott-Mar said sincerely. "Very grateful . . . Now, knowing how busy you are, I'll come straight to the point."

"I'd be grateful if you would," Hak-Bin replied, peering into the experimental birth chamber. "Who, or what, is *that*?"

"His name is Nis-All," Ott-Mar answered carefully, "and he's about to give birth."

"Any idiot could see that," Hak-Bin said impatiently, "but so what?"

"No offense," Ott-Mar responded, "but thousands of our brethren have been murdered by the slaves, and now, with only one catalyst factory still on-line, hundreds of thousands will die without successfully giving birth. In fact, based on my projections, it appears as though up to fifty percent of the race is at risk."

"So?" Hak-Bin demanded harshly. "What is, *is*."

"True," Ott-Mar agreed diplomatically, "but unusual situations call for unusual solutions. If you would be so kind as to wait one moment, I will demonstrate what I mean." So saying, Ott-Mar stepped over to a jury-rigged control panel, released a carefully calibrated dose of birth catalyst, and watched the liquid surge through a length of plastic tubing.

Hak-Bin saw the creature that had been Nis-All jerk in

response to the sudden influx of chemicals, heard the functionary's chitin crack as it gave under pressure, and watched the dark glistening birth sac billow out onto the floor.

Nis All screamed, a long mournful sound that served to remind Hak-Bin of the pain *he* had experienced prior to the recent operation. He turned to Ott-Mar. "Is there something you can do for him? He's in pain."

"Not anymore," the other Zin replied. "Nis-All has gone to be with his ancestors. Now, watch the birth sac. This should be interesting."

Hak-Bin forced himself to look even though the sight of it made him feel dizzy. Fluid continued to pulse through the braided umbilicals as Nis-All's body transferred what remained of his life force to the next generation. The podlike sac shivered, parted as razor-sharp teeth sliced through the translucent tissue, then shivered *again*. Hak-Bin watched in amazement as not one, not two, but *three* new Saurons entered the world. He turned to Ott-Mar. His voice was filled with awe. "Will each be different?"

"Each nymph is an exact replica of its parent," Ott-Mar answered proudly, "but, thanks to variations in experience, will develop separate personalities."

"So, you can apply this process now? To *our* generation?"

"I can apply it to those who have access to birth catalyst," the other Zin answered carefully, "thereby increasing the number of Saurons who are born. As for those who lack the catalyst—I'm afraid their lines will come to an end."

All three of the nymphs were visible by then, busily consuming what remained of the nutrient-rich birth sac, and occasionally pausing to nudge each other.

Hak-Bin took a moment to consider Ott-Mar's words. Thousands of lines would come to an end. That was unfortunate, but thousands would be strengthened as well. The main thing was that the race would not only survive but prosper. He offered a gesture of respect. "You did all of the research yourself?"

"Not entirely," Ott-Mar admitted modestly. "Some of the knowledge I needed was resident in the Ra 'Na archives . . . and the rest came from the humans. The *application* of their theories . . . that was mine."

"The race owes you a considerable debt of gratitude," Hak-Bin said sincerely. "I will instruct my staff to provide whatever materials you may require. Given that the second citadel continues to be more secure than the first, I suggest that you start your efforts there."

Ott-Mar bowed. "It shall be as you say, excellency."

Hak-Bin started to leave, paused, and turned back. "And *my* nymph? How many will there be?"

"One, my lord, since your nymph was nearly mature when you made the decision to intervene."

Hak-Bin took note of the manner in which responsibility had been assigned to him, knew it was fair, and nodded. "And yours?"

"There will be three Ott-Mars, excellency . . . assuming you approve."

Conscious of the fact that there was very little he could do to stop the scientist, not given the present situation, Hak-Bin could do little but agree. "The more Ott-Mars the better," he heard himself say, but couldn't help but wonder. How much power was he ceding to the scientist anyway? And how would his nymph keep three such minds in check?

Ah well, the Zin concluded as he shuffled down the hall, *I* had *my* problems, *you* must deal with yours. The nymph, well on the way toward recovery by then, answered with a jab from his elbow. Hak-Bin grunted, boarded the shuttle, and waited for the vessel to depart.

Meanwhile, a machine no larger than the dot over an "i," crawled down off the Zin's shoulder, made it to the deck, and scurried away. It would take a while to reach the shuttle's cockpit and the tiny docking station hidden there, but the effort would be worth it. Once ensconced in the bay, the robot would purge its memory banks, absorb some much-needed power, and go to standby. As for what happened to the data so recently gathered, well, that was for some other entity to worry about. Its function had been fulfilled—and that was all any machine could reasonably ask for.

ABOARD THE SAURON DESTROYER *NA GA, (THE RAVAGER)*

The *Ravager* had been under Sauron control when, during the height of the Ra 'Na mutiny, she was erroneously attacked by a Sauron dreadnought and two cruisers. Such was the weight of the incoming fire that by the time the mistake was rectified, and the attack was terminated, the smaller vessel was little more than an orbiting wreck. That being the case, and having received no communications to the contrary, the Saurons assumed that the entire crew was dead and wrote the vessel off.

But the entire crew *wasn't* dead. Had anyone cared to investigate, they would have discovered that while injured, the ship's Ra 'Na pilot still clung to life. Something of a miracle considering the fact that the rest of the individuals in the control room had been killed when a missile opened a thirty-unit gash in the side of the hull and thereby released most of the ship's atmosphere into the surrounding vacuum.

Strangely enough, Kas owed her continued existence to the ship's commanding officer, a Zin named Bri-Mor, who had just ordered the pilot to suit up and inspect the repairs made to the forward heat deflector two units earlier. That's why she was dressed in space armor when the attack began— and why she was the only individual to survive the explosion.

The impact hurled the diminutive Ra 'Na across the control room, where she smashed a rack packed with electronics. Then, as if the fates were determined to find and kill her, the external vacuum tried to suck the pilot out through the crack in the hull. The gash was too narrow however—and her suit refused to pass through it.

Finally, as if tired of playing with her, the pressures equalized and Kas was left to drift in circles. The pilot awoke from time to time, or thought she did, but wasn't completely sure. It was hard to tell where dreams ended and reality began. Still, the one thing both states had in common was the pain in her head and the taste of blood in her mouth. It was the pain, plus the incessant beep, beep, beep in her helmet, that finally brought Kas around. The pilot was horrified by what she saw. Bodies, some of which belonged to friends, drifted through constellations of blood droplets. Others remained strapped into their chairs.

The mind-numbing shock of the scene nearly robbed Kas of her capacity to reason, but the beep, beep, beep meant something and served to focus her mind. First the pilot realized that her oxygen was gone, or *nearly* gone, having already sustained her for days. Then she noticed that at least half of the control room's indicator lights continued to glow, suggesting that one of the vessel's two engines had survived the attack and remained on-line. And that was the moment when Kas found her purpose, a reason to live, and forced her body to comply.

The movement made Kas's head swim, but she refused to give in and managed to push-pull herself over to the place where the hull had been holed. The sealant, squirted into the gap on orders from the ship's computer, had the appearance of gray fat. The Ra 'Na's helmet continued to beep at her as Kas struck the substance with her gloved fist, confirmed that it was solid, and turned toward the hatch. It was closed, just as it should be, which meant the compartment should be airtight. With the emphasis on *should*.

Conscious of the fact that she had five, ten units at most, in which to pump air into the control room, Kas launched herself toward the main control panel. There were handholds, designed with that situation in mind, and the pilot grabbed one. Quickly, forcing herself to concentrate, the Ra 'Na tapped a sequence of keys. The buttons changed color, a screen flickered, a blue bar began to creep downward, and the pilot knew air was entering the compartment. But would it enter quickly enough? Or would she remove her helmet only to die of asphyxiation?

The beep extended itself into a long steady whine, Kas started to choke, and had to release her neck seal. A half twist to the left was sufficient to release the helmet. The Ra 'Na attempted to breathe but discovered that the atmosphere was too thin for comfort. Her breath came in quick little gasps as her body fought to oxygenate her blood. Then, as more air entered the room, breathing became easier, and the blue bar hit the bottom of the screen.

Kas was forced to pause. She tried to vomit, failed to bring anything up, and wondered why her head hurt so badly. But the pilot had a job to do and was determined to do it. The key was surprise, because once the ship started to move, an attack was likely to follow.

Quickly, lest her own body betray her, Kas pulled herself over to the pilot's position, released the thing that had once been her lover, and allowed it to drift away. Then, having strapped herself into the gore-drenched seat, the Ra 'Na let her hands play the keyboard. Here, in her greatest moment of need, habit took over. Computers checked, systems reported, and the situation became clear. Assuming everything held together for a sufficient period of time, and assuming no one managed to blow the *Ravager* out from under her, the plan might actually work.

Slowly, so as not to stress the single surviving engine any more than was necessary, Kas punched the appropriate coordinates into the navcomp, checked to ensure that they were correct, and handed control to the ship's main computer. It considered the order, discovered a programming conflict, and kicked it back. Kas entered the code required for an override, and the *Ravager* broke orbit.

Many of the Sauron vessels had been emptied by then, but a few remained active, and immediately took notice. Com calls were made, visual signals were sent, but there was no acknowledgment. That being the case, safeties were released, weapons brought on-line, and warnings given.

Still receiving no response, energy cannon fired, missiles flashed through space, and the *Ravager* shuddered as her screens flared. Kas, still strapped into her chair, watched dully as ship-to-ship torpedoes tracked across her screens. Some came close but none of them actually struck the destroyer, partly thanks to luck, but partly because of where she was headed: down into the planet's atmosphere.

Vessels like the *Ravager* were the largest ships that could successfully negotiate Earth's atmosphere. Now, as the warship nosed down through the exosphere, thermosphere, and mesosphere, the destroyer was tracked, predictions were made, and the efforts to destroy her doubled.

Alerted by the Sauron's activities, and certain that anything the slave masters objected to amounted to something they would approve of, the Ra 'Na fleet opened fire. Having little choice but to defend themselves, the Saurons had to return fire, thereby reducing the number of weapons directed at the *Ravager*.

And so it was that the ship, along with its sole living occupant, passed through the stratosphere and entered the troposphere, where it leveled out and began the final run. There was sufficient time for a warning, although there was very little that most of the Saurons could do beyond listen to the Klaxons and hope someone would deal with the problem.

There were witnesses, of course, humans assigned to watch Hell Hill from the woods to the east, in preparation for the assault scheduled for the following morning. They saw a flash of light as artificial lightning tried to spear the vessel from above, heard the resulting boom, and spotted a dot low on the southern horizon. A dot that quickly grew, resolved into a spaceship, and screamed over Samish Bay.

There was no way to know how fast the *Ravager* was going when she hit the south side of Hell Hill, but an ex–airline pilot put her speed in excess of a thousand miles an hour, and there was no reason to doubt him. The resulting explosion knocked many of the witnesses off their feet.

The citadel was destroyed on impact, the north face of the hill crumbled into Pleasant Bay, and a series of explosions marched through the ruins.

As Kas died more than a quarter million Saurons died with her, or twice that number if one counted their nymphs. It was a victory for which she would never be credited—but which gave the humans a chance. Not a surety, but a *chance*, for which Boyer Blue was thankful. Though not one of those fortunate enough to witness the destruction of Hell Hill, he arrived less than forty minutes later, before the fire had burned itself out, and the back half of the *Ravager*'s hull could still be seen protruding from the hill's south slope. The sight of smoke billowing up out of the wreckage should have made him happy, the historian knew that, but he couldn't find the joy that seemed to fill those all of those around him.

What was it that Wellington supposedly said to a dinner companion? "Madam, there is nothing so dreadful as a great victory—excepting a great defeat." Yes, Blue thought to himself as he looked out over the devastation, Wellington understood.

ABOARD THE RA 'NA DREADNOUGHT *LIBERTY*

The compartment was packed with small furry bodies—as were similar compartments throughout the Ra 'Na fleet. Screens had been rigged so that the audience could watch the proceedings and learn from what took place. Because *soon*, within a matter of hours for some, they too would be asked to board one of the Sauron-held vessels, pad down empty corridors, and murder every member of the master race that they could find.

Dro Rul walked out onto a raised platform, and Shu felt her pulse pound just a little bit faster. Everyone cared about the boarding party and hoped their mission would go well, but no one knew the team's commanding officer as well as she did, nor cared as much about his personal safety. The last thing the med tech wanted to do was witness her lover's death, yet that was exactly what might occur as Fra Pol took a boarding party aboard the Sauron dreadnought *Ib Se Ma* in an attempt to find any changers who remained hidden aboard the ship. Something none of the Ra 'Na in the room had been trained for. By watching Fra Pol's team, the rest of them would learn what worked and what didn't.

The screens flickered into life. Each camera was mounted on a marine's shoulder and showed that individual's name under the shot. Shu sought out the frame labeled "Fra Pol," and knew she was seeing what *he* saw. She wanted to be there, had *requested* to be there, but the request was denied. By Rul? By Pol? Or by someone else? There was no way to know. All she knew was that her stomach ached, her mouth felt dry, and the video made her dizzy.

Rul looked down from the screen to the audience. His words were direct and to the point. "As you know the change has begun. Many of the Saurons, I daresay *most* of the Saurons, are on the surface or en route.

"Once there, they intend to spawn a new generation of

slave masters, reassert their dominance over our race, and reclaim the fleet. Something they will be better able to accomplish if at least some of them are born in space. Especially since their plan to maintain and breed a population of collaborators failed.

"In order to cement our freedom and ensure that any Saurons who manage to survive are trapped on the planet below, it's important that we control *every* ship in the fleet."

P'ere Dee was seated in the front row. He nodded approvingly. If all went well, the humans would eradicate the Saurons and thereby reclaim not only their planet but their freedom. However, should the furless ones fail, the Ra 'Na would be free to depart for Balwur, confident in the knowledge that the Sauron menace had been effectively contained.

"So," Rul continued, blissfully unaware of his subordinate's line of thought, "the *Liberty*'s commanding officer, Fra Pol, volunteered to lead the boarding part, which will show us how it's done. Please pay close attention, as many of you will soon have an opportunity to take part in such missions yourselves.

"Now, as Fra Pol and his brave crew near the *Ib Se Ma*, please join me in prayer . . . 'From the ocean we came . . . and to the ocean we shall return . . .' "

Though aware of the fact that his every deed would be witnessed by thousands of his fellow Ra 'Na Pol couldn't hear Dro Rul and wouldn't have wanted to. Not with the *Ib Se Ma*'s enormous bulk looming ahead and no idea of what to expect. The fact that the shuttle he rode on remained unharmed was a testament to the fact that most of the ship's crew had departed for Earth, but that was the extent of his knowledge. What if he and his crew were walking into a well-prepared trap? The training video would be short indeed.

But there was no further time for doubts as the shuttle made contact with one of the dreadnought's rarely used emergency locks. The entry point was driven by two considerations: the fact that the hatch which provided access to the ship's Launch Deck was closed, and the hope that *if* a trap had been laid, the Saurons were waiting at some other location. Of course, Pol knew that if *he* could conceive of such a strategy, the Saurons could too, which left him where he had started. There was no way to know what awaited them.

Considerable progress had been made where Ra 'Na military gear was concerned, and as Pol made his way back toward the lock, he was pleased to see that all of his marines wore hastily manufactured body armor, combat harnesses, and were armed to the teeth. The small .22-caliber submachine guns used during the mutiny had proved extremely effective and now served as the standard assault weapon for all Ra 'Na forces. Small two-shot .22 Magnum derringers obtained from the humans served as backup weapons—as did the newly released vibro blades.

"All right," Pol said, his words echoing throughout the Ra 'Na fleet, "you know the drill . . . We blow the exterior hatch, enter the lock, and check to ensure that the ship is pressurized. Then, assuming it is, the first file will enter, secure the immediate area, and wait for files two and three. Once everyone is aboard, we search the ship, kill any Saurons still aboard, and seize control. Once that's been accomplished, the Launch Deck will be reopened, the new crew will board, and we return home for lunch. Not just *any* lunch . . . but oysters from the planet below."

Shu smiled as the boarding party cheered, knew nobody else would have thought to provide an inducement like that one, and knew that others would do likewise in the future. Pol gave a lighthearted bow, and the camera bowed with him.

Then it was down to business. A team of space-suited environment techs entered the shuttle's lock, used a probe to access the hatch's control mechanism, bombarded the security system with ten thousand codes per second, waited for one of them to hit, and opened the door. Then, happy still to be alive, they entered the dreadnought's lock.

A quick check was sufficient to establish that the ship remained pressurized. That being the case, the technicians withdrew, Pol entered, and the boarding party followed. The interior of the ship was dark, much darker than usual, which added to the gloom.

Used as he was to the *Ib Se Ma*'s sister ship, Pol recognized the steady whir of air as it passed through a vent over his head, the faint tang of ozone, and the slight, almost imperceptible, vibration, which meant her engines remained on-line. Not because they *needed* to be on-line—but because the Saurons didn't know how to shut them down.

But there was something else as well—a feeling that might reflect reality or be the product of Pol's hyperactive imagination. Perhaps it was the total absence of foot traffic when the Ra 'Na stepped out into the normally busy corridor, the brooding silence, or the creak of steadily cooling metal as the dreadnought entered the Earth's shadow. Whatever the reason, Pol found himself whispering as he directed his marines to take up defensive positions and wait for the rest of the boarding party to catch up.

It was then, while the Ra 'Na positioned themselves to defend their only line of retreat, that one of the thousands cameras located throughout the ship made a fractional movement and zoomed in. It was difficult for Sel-Nam to see, especially given what the change had done to his eyesight, but there was no mistaking the identity of the small bipedal bodies or the nature of their mission. The hunted had been transformed into hunters. Well, hunt away, the Zin thought to himself, because I have a surprise for you!

It was difficult to concentrate, and each movement brought pain, but finally, after what seemed like a heroic effort, the Sauron managed to grasp the remote, squeeze the side grips, and activate the alien machine. Originally employed by a race called the Lopathians, thousands of such machines had battled the Kan some 157 years earlier and been destroyed.

Now, having discovered a score of such mechanisms moldering away within one of the fleet's asteroids, and having very little faith in Hak-Bin's ability to carry out his duties, the Zin forced a Ra 'Na computer technician to reprogram one of the robots and subsequently put the slave to death.

Metal clawed on metal as the long-dormant eight-legged robot came back to life, took its place between the Sauron and the hatch, and waited for something to kill.

The fleet watched as Pol checked to ensure that the entire thirty-six person team was in place and properly oriented. Then, taking advantage of the fact that all of them were familiar with the *Ib Se Ma*'s layout, the Ra 'Na boarders turned toward the core of the ship. A single Ra 'Na took what humans often referred to as "the point," followed by Pol, two fire teams armed with automatic weapons, a group of technical specialists, more marines, the team's second-in-command, and the individual assigned to the drag position. It was his task to ensure that nobody was able to slip up behind the group—a responsibility that forced him to walk backward half the time.

There were places where, judging from the pockmarked bulkheads and bloodstained decks, intense battles had been fought. Battles which the Ra 'Na had lost. Pol felt as if the ghostly crew members were there, looking over his shoulder as he padded down the corridor, waiting for their revenge. Not a pleasant sensation and one he rid himself of by focusing his mind on the task at hand.

The team's first stop was in front of a seemingly innocuous access panel. One of the boarding party's specialists, an enviro tech named Slas, used a special key to open the box, punched a code into the key pad, and watched a three-dimensional diagram populate the screen. Apparently satisfied with what he saw, Slas tapped more keys, watched the visual morph slightly, and pointed to a series of bright green dots. Thanks to the camera mounted on his body armor, thousands of enviro techs could listen in. "We have five hits, sir, four of which are consistent with Sauron physiology."

Pol frowned. "And the fifth?"

"That's one of ours, sir. He or she is on the move, with blip three in hot pursuit."

All over the fleet ears went back as the audience imagined how that would feel. To be the only one of your kind, on a nearly deserted ship, pursued by a murderous foe. Many of them shivered.

Conscious of the fact that everything he did was being broadcast, Pol thought rather than said some of the swear words he had learned on Earth. It was tempting to intervene—but was that the right thing to do? He had the mission to consider—not to mention the boarding party itself. Mind racing, the cleric eyed the screen. Outside of Three, who was clearly intent on following Five down a corridor two grids over, One, Two, and Four remained stationary. An icon flashed on and off beside blip one. Pol pointed to it. "What's that?"

Slas shrugged. "It's hard to say, sir. The icon signifies that electromechanical activity is taking place within that compartment but doesn't specify what kind. It could be anything ranging from a robo sweeper to some sort of malfunction."

Pol nodded. "How many of the Saurons can be handled from the bridge?"

Slas looked. "Two and Four. Three is on the move, and it appears as if One either knew how to enter a command override or forced someone to do it for him. See the delta-shaped symbol here? That means the environmental controls for that particular compartment are locked. No password, no access. You won't be able to pump that one from the bridge."

"Sounds like a Zin," Pol said thoughtfully. "Some of them actually know a thing or two."

Slas, mindful of the life-and-death scenario being acted out not far away, cleared his throat. "Sir? What about blip *Five*?"

Pol looked, saw that Five had lost some of his or her lead, and started to issue orders. "Hars, take three triads, plus the techs, and secure the control room. Once that's accomplished lock Two and Four into their compartments and pump the air out. The rest of the team and I will go after blips Three and One in that order . . . Any questions?"

All over the Ra 'Na held fleet, newly minted officers and noncoms took note of the brisk, efficient manner Pol used to brief his troops and made plans to do likewise.

Shu, her eyes locked on a shot of Pol provided by the camera labeled "Slas," bit her lower lip. Why couldn't Pol lead the team headed for the bridge? Where a person of his rank belonged? Well away from whatever dangers still lurked in the *Ib Se Ma*'s darkened passageways? But she knew the answer . . . Pol was determined to go where the greatest danger lay because that was his nature—and because that's the way he believed leaders should lead.

"All right," Pol said, "there's a Sauron on the loose. Let's find the misbegotten sinner and send him to his ancestors."

Aware as he was that the somewhat wayward cleric had never been one to worry about rules, religious or otherwise, Dro Rul smiled and gave thanks for sinners.

With the possible exception of Pol himself—the rest of the boarding party was extremely fit. Bare feet padded on metal decking as they cut from one corridor to the next, turned toward the bow, and ran full out.

Unaware that he was being pursued, and intent on catching his prey, the Kan named Bla-Mas shuffled forward. He was different, very different, in that rather than change early the way it was rumored that some of his peers had, it seemed that *his* body was determined to change late if at all. That being the case, Bla-Mas saw no point in being herded into one of the citadels and hooked to a bunch of tubes.

So, taking advantage of the considerable confusion that surrounded the ship's evacuation, the Kan hid. Then, having emerged, it wasn't long before the Sauron discovered that rather than being alone, at least one other being roamed the same corridors that he did. A Ra 'Na who, judging from its size, remained a juvenile and had somehow managed to survive the recent slave slaughter. Well, not for long, Bla-Mas told himself, not for long.

Nom paused to listen, thought that she could hear the soft shuffle-step-shuffle made by the pursuing Kan, cursed herself for a fool, and ran as best she could. The leg, which had been broken in a fall, slowed her down. Worse yet, assuming she could gain access to the secret passageways that crisscrossed the ship, the fully inflated splint was likely to impede her progress. The passageways were her best hope, however—which was why Nom was headed for one of the access points her parents had shown her.

The very thought of them brought tears to Nom's eyes, and she sniffled as she limped down the corridor. They had known, had seen what would happen, and hidden her away. "Stay here," her father ordered, "stay here until *all* of the food and water is gone."

But there was lots of food and water, her mother had seen to that, and the hidey-hole was boring. *Very* boring, which was why she had ventured out too early and was presently running for her life.

Nom limped around a corner, glanced around, and realized she had taken a wrong turn. This was a dead end, and in order to correct her mistake, the teenager would have to return the way she had come. Nom turned, heart thumping in her chest, and limped toward the main corridor. The leg had started to ache by that time and the youngster whimpered as she turned the corner.

Bla-Mas saw the slave up ahead, uttered a shout of triumph, and drew his t-gun. That's when Pol shouted, "Hit the deck!" and hoped the teenager would obey.

Nom processed the words, heard a loud bang, and threw herself forward.

Though surprised to hear a voice coming from the rear, Bla-Mas was a warrior and reacted swiftly. He turned, the t-gun coughed, and a dart plucked a marine off his feet. The boarding party opened fire, and the audience watched as a swarm of .22-caliber bullets devoured their target.

"Hold your fire!" Pol yelled. "Hold your fire!" as what remained of Bla-Mas collapsed in a heap. The staccato bark of the small submachine guns ended as fingers came off triggers.

"All right." Pol said, "someone grab the youngster and let's . . ."

Neither the boarding party nor the fleetwide audience ever got to hear whatever it was that Pol planned to say next. A hatch whirred open, the Lopathian battle bot emerged, and the boarding party started to die. Energy bolts, each of which seemed to know exactly what path to follow, found their targets.

Shu heard herself utter an audible yelp as the camera labeled "Argo" swiveled in the direction of the noise, jerked uncontrollably, and toppled over backward.

Pol cursed himself for getting caught up in the chase, turned toward the machine, and opened fire. Sparks flew as the small .22-caliber slugs bounced off the machine's armor, struck bulkheads, and buzzed away.

That was when a marine named Foth ran forward,

launched himself toward the robot, and slid along the deck. Thousands watched via Pol's camera as the brave Ra 'Na arrived under the robot's curved belly, triggered the demo pack, and blew the construct three units up into the air. It crashed on top of Foth's remains, showered the area with sparks, and finally went limp.

Having been opened from within, it was a simple matter for a triad to enter the compartment where Sel-Nam lay hidden and do what needed to be done.

Then, with the situation back under control, Pol turned his attention to the Ra 'Na bodies. There were six of them, laid out side by side, as if at attention. His head bowed, and tears streaked his fur. Shu, who better than anyone knew what Pol felt, wished that she could hold him.

THE MAYAN RUINS OF NAKABE, GUATEMALA

Dr. Maria Sanchez-Jones had a front-row seat as the final days elapsed. The fact that she was there, standing at the cavern's *ventana* (window), was no accident. Shuttles had been arriving for days. At first they belly-flopped onto the surface of the artificial lake, disgorged orderly files of Zin, Kan, or Fon and took off again.

The initial groups of newcomers were met with organized jubilation. Drums pounded, banners waved, and the newcomers were marched toward the waiting citadel. Well, not *marched*, since many moved with considerable difficulty, but shuffled as best they could.

Then, as time wore on, the tenor of the arrival process seemed to change. In place of the orderly groups already down, the shuttles started to disgorge what appeared to be a random assortment of individuals from every caste. Not only that, but many of what Jones thought of as "the second wave" seemed to be in worse physical condition than those who had arrived earlier. Some were carried into the citadel on slings.

Finally, after what seemed like endless around-the-clock landings and departures, the flow started to slow. As much as an hour would pass during which there were no arrivals, followed by a flurry of activity as a half a dozen aircraft circled, and took turns crashing into the already crowded lake. Many of the latecomers sank, but some survived, as shuttles piled on shuttles.

Jones hated the Saurons with a passion, but even she felt something approaching sympathy as sickly Zin, Kan, and Fon pulled themselves out of the wrecks, hopped from ship to ship, and finally made it to shore. Some lacked the strength to continue and collapsed at the side of the road, while others shuffled on past. The question was *why*? Why build the fortress to begin with? Why were so many of them ill? And why slaughter the slaves?

The anthropologist had a theory, but theories must be tested, and she laid plans to do so. Three Eye, whom Jones wanted to recruit as her assistant, was something less than enthusiastic. "Please, *senorita,* consider what you ask. . . . To go down there, to examine one of the sky creatures, such an idea is madness."

But somehow, in spite of all the hard work and the damage that the sun had inflicted on her skin, Jones continued to be attractive. A great deal more attractive than the other female *sobrevivientes* were, and that, combined with the fact that Three Eyes was a man, combined to seal his fate.

And so it was that the two of them waited till night, left the relative safety of the *agujero* (hole), and made their way down to the area adjacent to the lake. Reasonably confident that the Saurons who had fallen next to the roadside didn't represent much of a threat, Jones made liberal use of a carefully hoarded flashlight. Three Eye, who regarded the expenditure of such a valuable asset to be something approaching a *pecado* (sin), was beside himself with angst.

But Jones, a rag held to her nose in a futile attempt to

mitigate some of the stench, barely heard the steady stream of complaints. Nearly her entire attention was focused on the bodies that lay scattered about and the fact that, based on the noises she heard, at least some of the Savrons were alive!

Careful, lest she enter some kind of trap, the anthropologist approached what had once been a Fon. Now, well into the change, but without any birth catalyst, the Sauron resembled nothing so much as a pile of putrid meat. Still, there was a sort of rasping sound, as if something was attempting to breathe, and the gurgle of fluids as they traveled from one organ to the next. The anthropologist held out her hand. "Give me the spear."

Three Eye, who had worked long and hard to mate the sliver of metal to the aluminum shaft, hesitated. First the *professora* led him here, to the place of the *muerto*, now she wanted the most valuable tool he owned. Was there no end to the woman's insanity?

"The spear," Jones insisted. "Give it here."

Slowly, reluctantly, Three Eye parted with the spear.

Careful to put as much of the shaft as possible between the corpse and herself—Jones poked one of the bodies. There was no reaction.

Slightly more confident, the academic moved closer. Now, thanks to the splash of oval light, Jones could make out the sort of details not visible from high above. Based on the manner in which the alien's chitin had separated down the center of its thorax, some sort of suture line existed there. What amounted to a seam that had parted under pressure exerted from within. Fascinated by what she had seen, Jones moved even closer. There, within a translucent sac, something continued to pulsate. Was that the source of the rasping noise? Yes, she thought that it was. Now, bending over, the anthropologist directed the light directly into the sac. Something burst through the tissue and teeth snapped just shy of her face as Three Eye jerked Jones back and out of the way.

Then, snatching the spear out of her hand, the *sobreviviente* stabbed the nymph. It made a horrible screeching sound, gave up a fountain of green blood, and collapsed.

"So," the peasant said, stepping back from his handiwork, "what do you think now, *professora*? Was Three Eye correct?"

"Yes," Jones said, her eyes drifting toward the place where the citadel acted to block out the stars, "Three Eye was correct. But we learned something, *mi amigo*, something important."

Three Eye looked quizzical. "We did?"

"Yes, we did. The sky creatures are about to give birth."

Three Eye frowned. "*All* of them?"

"Yes," Jones replied, "I'm afraid so."

"Shit."

"Yes," the academic agreed, "that pretty well sums it up."

ABOARD THE RA 'NA SHUTTLE *NOMATH, (SEABIRD)*

It was a bright sunny day, and the shuttle threw a vaguely delta-shaped shadow over the land below. It seemed to undulate as the aircraft followed the Columbia River downstream past Umatilla, Oregon, the Dalles, and along I-84 into Portland. "You see what I mean?" Boyer Blue demanded, pointing to the river below. "There they are!"

The shuttle banked to port and started to circle. The president of the United States had to scrunch down in order to peer out through the Ra 'Na-designed view port. Sure enough, three Sauron shuttles were moored to the same pier. They looked strange in such close proximity to the few pleasure craft that remained afloat. More evidence that the Ra 'Na were correct. Those Saurons fortunate enough still to be in transit *prior* to the destruction of Hell Hill had to go somewhere, and now, as the change claimed their bodies, spacecraft had started to land on any body of water the pilots could find.

Some, based on images captured from orbit, seemed to be carrying red gasoline cans, clear plastic jugs, and anything else they could use to transport some sort of liquid. Were such containers filled with birth catalyst? Collected from the orbital factory? Yes, there was a good chance that they were.

Now, over Manning's strenuous objections, both the president *and* vice president were in the same aircraft over what the security chief considered to be enemy-held territory. He couldn't stop them, but he could sure as hell intervene, which he didn't hesitate to do from the rear of the aircraft, where he, along with four members of his team, was seated. The pilots, both of whom were Ra 'Na, had grown used to the human by then, and were far from surprised when his voice came over the intercom.

"Hey, Lam, how many times do you intend to circle left? There's all sorts of folks down there, many of whom are armed, and can't tell the difference between a shuttle piloted by Ra 'Na and Kan. Hell, there's plenty of them who don't even know there's a difference. That being the case, let's turn to starboard, zigzag, or do something to throw the bastards off."

Lam, who had rather taken to the breezy informality typical of human interactions, was about to give the security chief what humans referred to as some "lip," when an SLM zigzagged into the air, and he was forced to take evasive action. The Ra 'Na pilot fired flares, rolled, and climbed. The maneuvers were ultimately successful, and Franklin, thankful still to be in possession of his lunch, attempted to restart the previous discussion. "So, the Saurons are going to ground. What should we do?"

"If we had the whole thing to do all over again, I would recommend that we allow the Saurons to enter Hell Hill's citadel, *then* attack it," Blue responded. "By doing so we could have kept all of the bastards in once place. However, thanks to the fact that a good Samaritan leveled the hill, I suggest we work with the Ra 'Na to locate the Sauron aircraft, put hunter-killer teams down at those locations, and root the bastards out of their hiding places. Once on the ground many of those teams will run into locals who may or may not be friendly to the cause. Political liaison officers will accompany each combat group in an attempt to bring such groups into the fold."

Blue, in his role as interim vice president, had been assigned to survey as much of the United States as possible, contact any groups that he might encounter, and start the long, laborious process of reconstruction.

Though not very far into the process the ex–history professor had already encountered four putative presidents, none of whom had qualifications that even began to approach Franklin's, a couple of would-be dictators, one theocracy, a group of racialists similar to those calling themselves the White Rose, and any number of experimental governments, many of which espoused philosophies similar to that of the Sasquatch Nation.

Some had refused to acknowledge Franklin as president, but most, impressed by the fact that he was an ex-governor, and by his accomplishments so far, were quick to sign aboard. Especially when assured that an election would be held three months after the Saurons were defeated.

Franklin considered the vice president's proposal. The process the ex–history professor laid out made sense but would be damned hard to implement. What if some of the more recalcitrant groups refused to cooperate? And inadvertently provided the Saurons with an opportunity to reproduce? Or, worse yet, actually *sided* with the Saurons the way Sister Andromeda had in the past? How long would it be before a fresh generation of Kan warriors swarmed up out basements, sewers, and subways in an attempt to retake the planet? The prospect made his head ache. Franklin rubbed his temples. "Okay, Boyer, what you say makes sense. Let's get on it . . . But what about the *other* citadel? The one down in Guatemala?"

"That's an entirely different situation," Boyer replied thoughtfully. "Remember what I said about Hell Hill? And the way we *should* have handled the place? Well, here's our chance to do it right. The key is to let the bugs settle in, wait for them to enter, and tear the place apart. Assuming you agree, I recommend that we build an assault team with that mission in mind and put in a request for the aircraft required to transport it."

Like most residents of Hell Hill, Franklin was well acquainted with the citadel, the thickness of its walls, and the multiplicity of defensive weapons systems that guarded the approaches. Odds were that hundreds if not thousands of his countrymen and women would die while throwing themselves at the fortress in Guatemala. But it had to be done. The Saurons would reproduce otherwise, and now, weakened as it was, the human race was vulnerable. "What about an aerial attack?" Franklin asked hopefully. "The Ra 'Na could bombard the place from space . . . or drop one of our nukes on it."

"Good questions," Blue acknowledged, "but you won't like the answers. I tested the second idea on Patience, and he went ballistic. *No* nukes, or *no* support, and that's final. Any harm to what the greenies call the Great Mother and they pull out."

The Sasquatch Nation comprised an important part of Franklin's base of support—especially now that other eco-minded organizations were being uncovered. Yes, he could simply ignore them, but what about later? When he and others tried to rebuild? A schism like that would be hard to overcome. "And the orbital attack?"

Blue shrugged. "It's doable . . . but probably pointless.

The bugs built the place to withstand anything up to and including an assault using their *own* weapons. Kind of the way medieval noblemen built their castles to withstand catapults—the most powerful weapon of the day."

Franklin sighed. "Okay, it looks like the United States of America will have to invade Guatemala."

Blue grinned. "Just wait till some clown reinvents the United Nations . . . The General Assembly will love that one!"

INSIDE THE CITADEL AT NAKABE, GUATEMALA

Tradition held that an entire centum of Kan would give up their right to procreate in return for having their lines forever memorialized in the chant of honor. Now, having received the chemicals required to abort their nymphs weeks earlier, they stood in long straight lines. Intricate patterns had been painted onto their chitin, thereby setting the warriors apart from their brethren. To inspect them, to shuffle the length of the evenly spaced ranks, was to acknowledge the extent of their sacrifice.

Individual rays of artificial light crisscrossed each other as they streamed down to illuminate the floor below. Thousands of onlookers, many so swollen that they appeared ready to burst, lined the birthing galleries. Those who could stomped their feet in unison, and the sound reverberated off the damp limestone walls as Hak-Bin shuffled from one end of the assemblage to the other, thanking each Kan on behalf of the race.

Then, when the review finally came to an end, it was time for one last meeting. The location was the oversize birthing chamber reserved for Hak-Bin's personal use. The cell was located on the very top floor, as befitted the Zin's rank, but the honor paled when compared to the effort required to get there. No longer able to jump, the weary Sauron had no choice but to shuffle up what seemed like endless ramps until, nearly exhausted, he entered the rectangular room. The last part of the physical world that Hak-Bin would see. Those waiting to receive the Zin included Dun-Dar, the local stonemaster, Ott-Mar, his personal physician, and a Fon named Lon-Nar, who, in spite of his own needs, was expected to make the Zin comfortable prior to seeking a lesser space far below. He gritted his teeth and hoped that the torture would soon end.

"So," Dun-Dar began, giving his superior time to recover from the long strenuous climb, "all is ready."

Hak-Bin struggled to breathe. "How many—were able to make it inside—before the doors were sealed?"

"Exactly 851,457," the stonemaster answered confidently, "or eighty-two-point-four percent of capacity."

"And the citadel to the north?"

"Communications were severed about six units ago," Dun-Dar replied. "But we assume things went well."

Hak-Bin wanted to say that the stonemaster should assume nothing—but knew such a comment would be pointless. The failures were his, not Dun-Dar's, and all of them knew that. Even assuming that a similar number of his brethren had been able to take refuge in the northern citadel, something he was starting to doubt, that would leave approximately three hundred thousand individuals unaccounted for. A disaster of nearly unimaginable magnitude.

Soon, once he crossed over, the punishment would begin as *his* ancestors, supported by the untold thousands for whom there would be no nymph to carry on, would subject him to a tidal wave of well-deserved abuse. Fortunately, there was no way to die once you were dead. They would have crucified him otherwise. The one bright spot in all this, the one thing from which Hak-Bin could take a modicum of comfort, was the fact that *his* nymph would rule what remained. "And *your* responsibilities?" Hak-Bin inquired, turning his gaze to Ott-Mar. "What of them?"

"Each and every individual who made it through the doors will receive a sufficient amount of catalyst," the physician said proudly, "and many will give birth to multiple nymphs."

"Excellent," Hak-Bin replied. "I wish to thank both of you for all that you have accomplished. My nymph will accord your nymphs the full weight of honor and respect earned through your efforts. Please pass into the next world knowing that thanks to your accomplishments your line was advanced, your names forever recorded in the minds of my descendants, to be sung for all eternity."

Deeply honored, and at least momentarily appeased, both of the Zin bowed their way out of the chamber.

Lon-Nar, who saw the exchange as the worst sort of dra, was happy to see them go. Still, his nymph would soon be vulnerable to Hak-Bin's nymph, which meant it paid to be careful. That being the case, the Fon adopted his most obsequious manner while he invited the Zin to lower himself into the concave recess centered in the middle of the floor, inserted a needle into the appropriate vein, and released the intravenous drip. Then, hoping that the other Sauron was satisfied, Lon-Nar backed out of the room.

Hak-Bin watched the other Sauron withdraw, felt the nymph stir as the catalyst found its way down into the birth sac, and allowed himself to relax. That's when the next him surged into the now-emptied space, took control, and started to scheme. Hak-Bin felt a sense of pride, welcomed the new mind, and allowed himself to fade. Three units later the Sauron was gone.

NEAR THE CITADEL AT NAKABE, GUATEMALA

A tropical storm had moved in over the lush green jungle below. Rain poured down in sheets, pattered against millions of leaves, and dripped to the ground. Puddles fed already swollen streams, which merged with heavily loaded rivers that roared toward the sea.

The engines made a smooth humming sound as the aircraft nosed its way toward the southeast. The interior of the Ra 'Na lifter wasn't all that different from the cargo compartment of a Chinook helicopter, except that the H-shaped aircraft had two such compartments located side by side. The starboard hull was rigged to accommodate troops. The port hull was loaded with supplies. Fold-down benches had been installed along both sides of the interior.

The president of the United States, flanked by members of his bodyguard, sat with his back to the outboard side facing inward. The windows were low by human standards, and it was necessary to scrunch down in order to look outside. Not that there was anything to see beyond a thick layer of clouds. Franklin turned toward Manning. "I hope our friends know where they're going."

Now, with the skies pretty much to themselves, it was a relatively simple matter for the Ra 'Na to ferry the allied assault team in from the assembly point near Bellingham, Washington. The lifters, which could make vertical takeoffs and landings, were considerably slower than shuttles but boasted a much greater payload. Manning frowned. "The pilots seem pretty competent to me . . . It's what we're going to face on the ground that you need to worry about."

Franklin sighed. "Look, I know you're pissed, but this is something that I have to do."

"I don't see why," Manning answered grimly. "What if you get yourself killed? What then?"

"We've been through this before," Franklin insisted. "Blue would take over, that's what vice presidents are for."

"No disrespect to the vice president," Manning replied evenly, "but it's *you* that people look up to. Besides, you don't have anything to prove. You risk your life every time you get up in the morning."

Franklin nodded. "Thanks, Jack, that means plenty coming from you . . . But the fact is that I *do* have something to prove, both to the people who still believe that I'm a collaborator and to *myself*. Besides, given the way that you and your team take care of me, what's the worst that could happen? A hangnail? A mosquito bite? Some damp clothes?"

Manning chuckled in spite of himself, as the lifter banked to the right and started its vertical descent. A voice came over the intercom. It belonged to a Ra 'Na pilot and sounded stiff. "We have arrived over the landing zone. There may be a need to take evasive action. Please check your safety harnesses."

Comfortable in the knowledge that Ra 'Na fighters had already flown through the LZ, drawn fire from computer-controlled surface-to-air missile batteries, and destroyed them, Manning checked his laptop computer. The screen showed a flight of fifteen lifters, each represented by a red delta, each five minutes apart. The plan called for Lifter One to land, off-load its troops, and take off.

Then, assuming the LZ was reasonably secure, the second lifter, the one that carried the president of the United States, would make its approach. Once the "Big Dog" hit the ground, the security team would throw a second ring of protection around him while Lifter Two dumped its containerized cargo. The arrangement was far from ideal, since Manning would have preferred to bring the president in on the last ship, but it was the best deal he'd been able to negotiate.

Franklin, eager to catch a glimpse of the landing zone, turned to peer out through the window. Mist consumed the aircraft, raindrops streaked across the window, and the lifter lurched as the increasingly choppy air battered it about. Then, just as the president began to wonder if the clouds went all the way to the ground, the jungle appeared. The Sauron fortress slid into view a few moments later. The first thing Franklin noticed was that the Guatemalan citadel was the virtual twin of the one near Bellingham. Or what the one on Hell Hill looked before the spaceship plowed into it. There were three towers, all in a cloverleaf pattern, and connected by short, sturdy wings. Blackened areas indicated where the Ra 'Na continued to take potshots at the complex from orbit.

Now, as the aircraft lost more altitude, the president noticed two features that the northern site lacked, a water-filled moat and what appeared to be an artificial lake filled to overflowing with black, rain-slicked hulls.

In fact, having looked a bit closer, Franklin thought he could see where a few shuttles had attempted to land on *top* of those already down, creating pileups and triggering at least one fire. Of course there were lifters too, aircraft identical to the one he was on, parked helter-skelter all around the citadel's perimeter. That meant the pilots would need to land farther out, well away from the complex, which suited Assault Force Commander Deac Smith just fine. The ex-Ranger was concerned about the possibility of booby traps, computer-controlled weapons emplacements, and who knew what else. That's why his sappers would go in first, search for booby traps, and clear a path to the fortress itself.

The first lifter was down by that time. There had been no opposition, which meant that Smith, a platoon of his best troops, plus a heavy weapons platoon, had secured the LZ. Franklin knew he shouldn't be scared, not surrounded by his bodyguard, but felt that way anyway. When the others went through a weapons check he did likewise, pulling the .9mm out of its shoulder holster, ejecting the magazine to ensure that it was full, and slamming it back into place.

Manning watched the president from the corner of his eye, hoped the politician wouldn't shoot himself, but knew better than to say anything. The practice had paid off, and while something less than an expert, Franklin could hit the broad side of a barn. Which, assuming the security team was on the ball, he would never need to do.

Lifter Two descended through the rain, swayed as a gust of wind hit the twin hulls from the southeast, and squatted twenty feet from the welcoming orange smoke. Vilo Kell, who had been a Ranger himself and understood how Smith wanted things done, led a heavily armed team consisting of Jonathan Wimba, Garly Mol, Rafik Alaweed, and Gozen Asad out into the downpour, where they formed a secondary ring of protection within the existing perimeter. Manning waited for the go-ahead to come in over his headset, nodded to Franklin, and followed the president out into the rain. Orvo Orvin, the security team's com specialist, and Jill Ji-Hoon followed behind.

Franklin felt a spatter of rain hit the top of his unprotected head, felt it stop as Asad produced an umbrella, and wondered if he should object. No one else was equipped with an umbrella so why should he have one? But, based on the ear-to-ear grin plastered across Asad's face, Franklin suspected the agent had thought to bring the implement himself. The kind of thing people always tried to do for Jina. He nodded to the young man, said "Thanks, Goz," and saw the grin get even wider.

The lifter's engines wound up, the aircraft lifted off, and another came in to land.

"So," Franklin said, addressing his comment to Manning, "what now?"

"Now we wait," Manning said calmly, rain pouring down off his bush hat. "There's no way to know what kind of stuff the bugs left for us to stumble over . . . Smith will let us know when it's safe to move."

Franklin, who had imagined himself being among the first to arrive at the citadel, managed to hide his disappointment. Maybe Manning had been right, maybe he should have agreed to come in last, rather than stand there in the rain. Still, this was where the action would soon take place, and there was no way that he could bear to miss it.

The minutes ticked by, *more* lifters landed, and *more* troops hit the ground. Most of them were human, but a contingent of Ra 'Na marines arrived as well, all led by a now familiar face. Franklin bent at the waist in order to shake Fra Pol's hand. "It's good to see you again, Fra Pol, but I'm surprised Dro Rul allowed you to come."

Water ran off the Ra 'Na's fur, and he grinned. "No offense, Mr. President, but look who's talking! Besides, I forgot to ask him."

Franklin laughed. It was clear that no matter who ended up in charge, Pol would continue to ignore them. A true revolutionary through and through.

The conversation was interrupted when one of Deac's Demons materialized out of the downpour. He wore camos and clutched an assault rifle to his chest. The name "McKay" was hand-lettered on his helmet cover. He'd been a cop, and it showed. "An adult female approached the perimeter, sir. She knows how to get inside the citadel, sir, or that's what she claims. Deac Smith is out with the sappers. Would you care to speak with her?"

Glad to have something to do, Franklin nodded. "Sure, bring her in."

Manning spoke into his mike. "Snake One to Snake Four . . . Accompany Trooper McKay, check to make sure the woman is clean, and bring her in. Over."

Mol had been facing west with her back to the president. She said, "Roger that, One. I'm on it. Four out," and jogged in from where she'd been stationed. That created a hole, which the other agents covered by pulling back.

When it came, the boom was so muted by distance and the muffling effect of the rain that Franklin looked to Manning for confirmation. "Was that some sort of explosion?"

The security chief nodded and turned to Orvin. "Got anything?"

The com specialist was monitoring Smith's command channel. He nodded. "The advance party encountered some obstacles. They're making a path."

There were more explosions and Manning wondered what "encountered" meant. Had the obstacles been detected ahead of time? Or "encountered" as someone died? He shivered and hoped for the former.

Franklin was chatting with Pol, learning the latest on the effort to sanitize the fleet, when Mol returned from her errand. The president turned to discover that although the woman who accompanied her was a good deal smaller, and dressed in what could only be described as rags, her personality was considerable indeed. It seemed to fill the space around her. Not only that, but the woman was pretty, *very* pretty, with perfectly even features, a nice figure, and big brown eyes. They stared at the politician with a strange sort of intensity—as if determined to make an impression.

"This is Dr. Maria Sanchez-Jones," Mol said dryly, as if there was something about the woman she didn't particularly like, "and she's clean. Dr. Jones, this is Alexander Franklin, president of the United States."

Franklin summoned the sort of smile once reserved for influential business people, religious leaders, and foreign dignitaries. "Good morning! Please, step under the umbrella, it's wet out there!"

It had been a long time since anyone had treated Jones in the manner to which she had once been accustomed— and the courtesy was sufficient to produce a pageant-quality smile. "Thank you, Mr. President. I can't tell you how happy I am to see you and your troops. Does this mean that the Saurons have been defeated?"

The woman was close now, *extremely* close, and for the first time since Jina's death Franklin felt a strong sense of attraction. He shook his head. "No, Dr. Jones, there's been some progress, but we're a long way from total victory. In fact, based on recent intelligence, it appears that the bugs came up with a way to increase the number of nymphs produced by some members of their population. Just another reason why it's so important to destroy the complex."

Jones liked the man. She moved fractionally closer. "My friends call me, Maria. That's why I came—to help you get inside."

"I'm all ears," Franklin responded. "Please proceed."

Jones hooked a thumb back over her shoulder. "As you know by now, the aliens forced us to construct the citadel *over* a river, which flows down under the towers and exits from the far side. They made use of the flow to fill the moat, create the artificial lake, and provide the slaves with drinking water. They also used it as a way to rid themselves of waste. Pipes stick straight down and empty into the river. In fact that's how I escaped . . . I dropped through a pipe, fell into a pool, and the water carried me downstream."

Franklin listened with interest and respect. The woman had guts, that was for sure, and he felt a growing sense of respect. "So, what are you saying? That we could go downstream, work our way back up, and access one of those pipes?"

"No," Jones replied honestly, "*you* couldn't. The pipes are way too small . . . but *he* could."

Both Franklin and Manning turned to see that the doctor was pointing at Pol. The Ra 'Na, still standing in the rain, saw their eyes turn his way. "Who? Me?"

"*Yes*," the anthropologist answered emphatically, "assuming that you could devise a way to reach the pipes from the water below, then work your way up through them, it should be possible to cut your way out."

"All it would take would be a few of them," Manning

said thoughtfully, "and they could open the doors from the *inside*."

The entire group turned in response to the distant pop, pop, pop of automatic weapons fire. Orvin pressed the earphones in against his ears. "The advance party ran up against some automatic weapons emplacements, sir. They took casualties but continue to probe the Sauron defenses."

The mention of casualties caused Manning to look across the rainswept clearing to the point where an army-issue field hospital had been established. The self-erecting shelter bore a large red cross. Sool would be in there, along with Dixie and a team of Ra 'Na med techs. He felt a sudden yearning but managed to push it away.

"Damn!" Franklin said enthusiastically. "That sounds promising. What do you think, Fra Pol? Would such a climb be possible?"

The cleric shuddered, hoped no one would notice, and imagined what such a venture would entail. The human hadn't mentioned how far off the water the pipes were located—but there were ways to close that kind of gap. No, the real horror would begin the moment that some poor fool entered a pitch-black pipe, and painstakingly worked their way upwards. And eventually, once they made it to the top, what then? It would be necessary to cut their way out, sneak through darkened passageways, and access the front door. Not a pleasant prospect and one that scared the dra out of him. But there was only one answer that could be given, so he gave it. "Yes, sir, assuming that we find everything pretty much the way she described it."

All eyes returned to Jones, and she shrugged. "There's no way to know . . . I haven't been back."

"Okay," Franklin said, "I think it's worth a try . . . Orvin, get a message to Smith, explain what we're up to, and tell him we'll stay in touch."

The com tech nodded, and the message went out.

■ ■ ■

Deac Smith ducked as another automatic weapon opened up. Darts stitched a line along the ground only one foot in front of his position, threw tiny fountains of water into the air, and exploded like firecrackers. Not *big* explosions, the kind a grenade would make, but smaller explosions that could still do damage. Someone screamed, and Smith uttered an uncharacteristic swear word as a trooper low-crawled in beside him. "I have Snake Three on the horn, sir . . . The Big Dog is on the move."

Activated by who knows what, hundreds of self-propelled mines surfaced from somewhere below the surface of the muck and started to move outward. A machine gun opened up, detonated half a dozen of the devices, and shrapnel whined through the air. A piece of it hit one of the troopers in the head. His head fell forward, and it appeared that he was asleep.

"Damn the man," Smith replied crossly. "The last thing we need is a politician running around loose! Tell the Big Dog that I would *prefer* that he remain where he is . . . Order Bone Three to put additional fire on those mines . . . What's he waiting for? One to crawl up his leg?"

The radioman spoke into his mike, and another machine gun opened up. It cut a swath through the army of oncoming explosives, but more continued to surface. That's when someone shouted, "Look! They're opening the door!" And a group of six Lopathian attack bots spidered out to join the fray. "I need mortars!" Smith yelled. "Hit those suckers before they can disperse! And put some rounds on those doors! Maybe we can jam one!"

But the order came too late. The heavy metal doors closed without difficulty, and, by the time the 4.2-inch mortar shells started to fall, the machines had separated. Gouts of mud shot up into the air, one of the war bots exploded under a direct hit, but the rest opened fire. Bolts of bright blue energy stabbed the misty murk. A woman screamed as a hole the size of a saucer appeared at the center of her armored abdomen. There was barely enough time to take a look at it before she keeled over dead.

"Fall back!" Smith ordered. "By the numbers!"

The troopers obeyed, each platoon falling back through the ranks of the one stationed to the rear, until a good fifty yards separated them from the oncoming land mines. "Okay," Smith shouted to his com specialist, "call the Ra 'Na! Tell them I want artillery support! And it had better be accurate!"

And it *was* accurate, since every single member of the assault team had been equipped with a beacon, and the Ra 'Na knew exactly where each one of them was. Artificial lightning flashed as destruction rained down from the sky. Smith watched in satisfaction as an assault bot vanished, half-ton divots of rain-soaked mud flew high into the air, and entire sections of self-propelled mines were detonated.

Finally, when the bombardment ended, a strange sort of silence settled over the area. Those mines not destroyed settled into the mud. The computer-controlled weapons emplacements went to standby. That's when Smith realized that the advance team had mapped the boundary beyond which the citadel no longer felt a need to defend itself and were momentarily safe. He turned to the radioman. "Call the Big Dog . . . tell him I want to report."

The com specialist murmured something into his mike, looked surprised, and looked Smith in the eye. "Sorry, sir, but he's unavailable."

"Unavailable? Where the hell is he?"

The radioman spoke into his mike, shook his head in disbelief, and made eye contact with Smith. "It doesn't make much sense sir, not given the situation, but Snake Three claims that the whole lot of them went swimming."

■ ■ ■

It was Three Eye who led the group out and around the citadel, down to the river, then upstream along its banks. It was swollen now, fat with the runoff from the tropical storm and loaded with debris. High water made it difficult to walk. More than once the heavily loaded party was forced back into the jungle. Rain cascaded from leaf to leaf, dripped from branches, and made their lives that much more miserable. It was dark under the canopy of foliage, but the river sang to their right, and Three Eye never failed to bring them back.

At one point, where trail and river met, they saw where two shuttles had been both run up on a sandbar. Unable to land on the artificial lake, and with nowhere else to go, the pilots chose the river. But there were currents to contend with, not to mention some tight turns, and both attempts failed. Were they still in there? Strapped into their seats? Or had some of the passengers managed to escape? There was no time to stop and investigate.

The river roared as it passed over the last of three falls. None was particularly high, but Jones remembered how it felt to be swept downstream, not knowing what lay ahead, and feel the bottom drop out from under her body. Then came the momentary feeling of relief as she fell into the first pool, only to be dragged over the next ledge, and the *next*, prior to being swept downstream. The experience had been terrifying. So why go back? When she could have remained hidden? Because there was no choice. The Saurons had to be stopped, and this was the only way she knew to help.

Having assigned himself the drag position, Manning came to regret it as he attempted to walk backward, tripped over tree roots, and repeatedly fell down. Not that point was a walk in the park. Kell had to watch for booby traps, land mines, *plus* homicidal Saurons.

The trail disappeared over a rise. The security chief took a run at it, lost traction, and swore. His boots slipped, he fell, and swore again. Then, having pulled himself up the slope with the assistance of a vine, he hurried to catch up.

The easternmost tower loomed above as lead elements of the party topped another rise and got a glimpse of the point where the river emerged from a curtain of vegetation. The vertical wall was reminiscent of a castle. Automatic weapons opened up on them almost immediately. They pulled back, used laser pointers to mark the defensive positions, and called on the heavy artillery. Bolts of energy screamed down through the atmosphere, blew chunks of limestone out of the walls, and the eastern defenses were silenced.

Now, free to approach, the allies followed the river up to the citadel itself. The water, so active below, oozed out from under the citadel, swirled as if to gather its strength, and swept over the first ledge. Pol felt a sense of relief. Earlier, while listening to Jones, he had feared that the river might gush out from under the fortress, making it difficult to travel upstream. There was no way to tell if the rest of the plan would work, but now, having seen it, there was very little doubt that his team could enter the cavern.

The trail dipped after that, took a sharp turn to the right followed by a meandering left. Then, as hundreds of birds took to the air, and the party passed the lower pools, they saw that bodies littered the riverbank. Ra 'Na mostly, since humans were too large to drop through the pipes; there was a pile of larger bodies as well. Men and women forced to jump from the tower above to land on the rocks below. Birds had picked the top layer of corpses clean, but more waited below, and the stench was incredible. Franklin swore, and someone gagged, and Pol murmured a prayer.

The next half hour was spent sorting out the equipment the allies had brought with them. Most of it had been carried by the humans, who, as the small aliens knew, made excellent beasts of burden.

Based on the description the human had provided, Pol estimated that the pipe through which Dr. Jones had fallen ended approximately fifteen units above the surface of the water. But that was low water, and this was high water, which, based on unofficial historical data provided by Three Eye, would cut the gap by as much as a third.

That being the case, Pol's marines believed it would be relatively easy to shoot a spike into the overhead, climb a line, and rig a platform below. Then, careful not to load themselves down with too much gear, a team comprised of three volunteers would wedge themselves into the tube, press their backs against one side, position their feet on the other, and push-slide toward the top. That was the relatively easy part. As for the rest, well, that would be more difficult.

Now, as the gear was sorted, then loaded into inflatable rafts, an argument broke out. Franklin wanted to accompany the Ra 'Na up into the cavern, Manning objected, and so did Pol. The Ra 'Na had enough problems without one or more humans to care for.

Finally, having no support for his position, the president was forced to back down. Therefore, there was little he could do but watch as the Ra 'Na transported their rafts up to the highest pool, launched them into an eddy, and pushed their way through a curtain of rich green foliage. They disappeared after that, and the humans waited to make sure their allies had been successful.

Jones' offer to accompany the marines had been refused. Now, as she stood at the president's side, she was struck by the extent of his presence. It was obvious from the way he watched the Ra 'Na depart that Franklin not only cared about their mission, but about *them*. The anthropologist remembered the cold-hearted manner in which she left Kevin Blackley to die and felt a sudden sense of shame. Then, as if aware of her distress, Franklin took her hand. He smiled. "I guess there isn't much we can do here . . . so it's time to hike up into the landing area."

Jones looked up, nodded wordlessly, and felt sorry when the president let go.

. . .

It was warm within the citadel—warm and humid. Partly because of the weather outside and partly because there were so many bodies packed into one place.

Now, as each Sauron went through the same process, the demarcations of caste fell away. Kan warriors, some of whom had sustained terrible wounds during past campaigns, discovered pain worse than anything they had ever felt before. Zin intellectuals, their bodies bursting from within, screamed with the same fervor as Fon functionaries.

Meanwhile, as more and more of the old generation died, *new* voices were heard. The nymphs, hundreds of which were only a few units old, clicked, popped, and snapped as they broke free of the sacs in which they had been imprisoned. The triplets, many of whom seemed more aggressive than the rest, were loudest of all.

The screams, overlaid with semimeaningless babble of newborn nymphs and punctuated with the occasional boom, as rebellious slaves attacked the citadel created a cacophony of sound which, when combined with the stench of dead bodies and the hot humid air, turned the interior of the fort into an unspeakable hell. A hell that Centum Commander Nis-Sta and his warriors had promised to defend.

Now, as the officer patrolled the corridors and tried to ignore the horrors around him, morale was the Kan's foremost concern. Rather than go out and engage the enemy directly, his warriors were under orders to remain inside and listen to the screams.

And, making a bad situation worse, in spite of the fact

that Nis-Sta and his warriors would escape the agonies of birth, their bodies were old, *very* old, and increasingly tired. That's why the officer shuffled from post to post, engaged the troops in conversation, and tried to keep their spirits up. Most responded, which was amazing given the circumstances, and for which Nis-Sta was thankful. Old Saurons continued to die, new Saurons were born, and the warriors remained loyal to both.

■ ■ ■

Alien lichen bathed the cavern in a sickly green glow. The water, which appeared black and glassy, eddied out toward the river below. Bats, resentful of the manner in which powerful lights had been aimed up at the ceiling, continued to swoop and soar. One of them swept past Pol's head. The cleric flinched, the rope swayed, and the Ra 'Na struggled to hold himself up. Both of his arms ached, the insides of his calves were raw, and he wanted to let go. *Would* have let go had he been alone—instead of on display for everyone to see.

Finally, after another desperate heave, the platform came level with his head. Hands reached down, Pol was hoisted up, and the platform swayed dangerously as he grabbed a supporting line. "Good work, sir," File Leader Quas said encouragingly. "Just hang on while we get things organized."

The other member of the team, a technician named Twan, nodded respectfully, and the two of them went to work. Pol couldn't remember when he had decided to lead the team himself. All he knew was that when he called for volunteers he requested only two. Every single marine in his party had offered to take part, but these two, both in top physical condition, seemed like the best choice.

Because Pol was the weakest link, and knew it, he assigned himself to the number three position. If he became stuck, or was otherwise unable to complete the climb, the others would continue unimpeded. The arrangement was questionable, since the size of the cleric's waistline dictated that someone else should lead the effort, but Qwas and Twan lacked leadership experience, a shortfall that could prove critical.

So, contrary to the dictates of common sense and in spite of the fear that claimed his belly, Pol prepared to do the very thing he would most likely fail at: climb a vertical pipe and enter an enemy-held fortress.

"Okay," Qwas said, helping the cleric into the specially adapted combat vest, "the pockets are loaded with the usual stuff, including extra ammo and a couple of grenades. Not much, though, or it would get in the way. A special nonslip surface has been glued to the back. Keep your assault weapon tight against your chest, place your back against the wall, and push with the rubber-soled boots. Once I get to the top I will cut my way out, deal with any Saurons who happen to be in the area, and give Twan a hand. You come next. Any questions?"

The file leader made the whole thing sound so easy that Pol felt silly for having any doubts. The cleric shook his head, watched the marines duck under the pipe and soon disappear from sight. Then it was his turn. Pol stooped under the opening, then stood. Alien lichen had colonized the inside surface of the pipe, which when combined with their headlamps, would provide sufficient illumination. The cleric couldn't see the upper reaches of the tube, not with two bodies in the way, but that was just as well. What he couldn't see couldn't scare him.

A hand reached down, and Pol was grateful. Twan hoisted the initiate upward and waited while he wedged himself in place. Then, satisfied that his commanding officer was off to an acceptable start, the technician hunched his way upward.

The light from his headlamp soon started to fade. Pol followed.

It was difficult at first, *very* difficult, but the initiate made progress. He learned that his elbows could be useful, adding as they did to the downward push, especially where one length of pipe joined another. Because of the process used to manufacture them, each joint was marked by a small ridge, an imperfection for which Pol was thankful, since it provided extra purchase *and* a place where he could indulge in a moment of rest.

That's when Pol would look upward, see the distant lights, and realize the extent to which the other two were ahead. Frustrated by his own weakness and anxious lest he fall even farther behind, the cleric would push off and try to make better time.

There were obstacles, however, not the least of which was the fact that the pipe was a *pipe*, and placed there for a reason. The first downpour came when a holding tank filled, a relay closed, and a valve opened. The mixture of rainwater, birth catalyst, and waste matter entered the pipe *below* the point where Twan happened to be, fell unimpeded on Pol's head and shoulders, and gushed down between his legs. It was warm, it stank, and the unexpected weight of the liquid nearly dislodged him. In fact, had it not been for the fact that the cleric happened to have one foot planted inside the opening to *another* pipe, he would have fallen.

Pol threw his arms out to increase the amount of contact with the walls, had the presence of mind to hold his breath, and waited for the flood to pass. Finally, after what seemed like an eternity, it did. Then, fighting for a purchase on the now-slippery walls, the journey continued.

■ ■ ■

The rain had stopped, but the air remained heavy with moisture. Everything was wet, and a heavy mist floated just off the ground. In spite of the fact that the towers were intact, more than a dozen black splotches marked the points where heavily concentrated fire had succeeded in silencing most if not all of the computer-controlled weapons emplacements. Now, with those out of the way, or most of them out of the way, the allies were intent on entering the citadel itself. The main entryway seemed to sparkle as the latest volley of SLMs wasted themselves on the heavy hull metal. Finally, after no fewer than fifteen missiles had expended their combined energies on the now-blackened barrier, the attack ended.

Franklin lowered the binoculars and handed them to Smith. "I see what you mean . . . that stuff is damned hard. How 'bout an attack from orbit? Maybe one of the ship-mounted weapons could do the job. They were pretty effective over on the east side of the citadel."

Smith sighed. Franklin meant well, he knew that, but the need to respond to his frequently naive suggestions was hard to take at times. Especially when he was tired, hungry, and generally pissed off. "We considered that, sir. But an orbital bombardment would destroy the bridge over the moat. That would force us to not only build another one, but to do so while taking fire, which would result in hundreds of casualties."

Franklin frowned. "Good point . . . I wonder why they left it there?"

"So those spider-shaped robots could cross the moat," the ex-Ranger explained patiently. "Plus, it may be rigged to blow. If so, we'll probably lose it, but a guy can hope. Maybe Pol will succeed."

"How would you rate his chances?"

Smith looked at the ground. "Not very good."

"And if he fails?"

"We go to Plan B."

Franklin raised both eyebrows. "The spaceship idea?"

"Why not? It worked on Hell Hill."

"Yeah, but most if not all of the slaves had escaped. There could be hundreds or even thousands of slaves locked inside those towers."

Franklin shrugged. "Dr. Jones doesn't think so, but you're right, there's no way to know for sure. So what do we use for Plan B?"

"A miracle," Franklin said, slowly. "What we need is a miracle."

■ ■ ■

Qwas hunched his shoulders, pushed with his feet, and watched the blob of light slide upward. That was his marker, the measure of his worth, and the object that he lived to elevate. Earlier in the climb, back before his shoulders had started to ache and before he'd been drenched with a liquid so foul that there were no words to describe it adequately, the file leader had paused to look upward every now and then. Not anymore. Minimal though it was, that effort consumed too much energy.

No, the best thing to do was remain in a sort of trance, put everything he had into the climb, and ignore all else. Push, hunch, push. That was the story of his life, the purpose for being, the . . . The top of Qwan's head hit something solid, and he swore.

Then, tilting his head back, he allowed the light to play across the surface above. There it was! The very thing he had been striving for . . . A valve assembly or something similar. Now, how to deal with the obstruction? Would a small quantity of explosives be best? Or should he use the power tool strapped to the front of his vest? The first option would be faster—but the second would cause less commotion. The file leader whispered into his mike. "Fra Pol? Can you hear me?"

"Yes," the cleric replied, "and so can anyone else who cares to monitor this frequency. No names, remember? So, what's up?"

"Sorry," Qwas replied contritely. "I forgot. Objective one is now in sight."

"Excellent," Pol replied. "Good work."

"So," Qwas continued, careful lest he commit another gaffe, "which *tool* would you suggest?"

Here was a decision that Pol dreaded. Either choice could be wrong. The explosives would make noise, no doubt about that, but the power tool would take a long time. He went with what the humans referred to as his "gut." "Use the faster of the two alternatives—and be careful."

Qwas fumbled with one of his pockets, located the block of C-4, broke a chunk off, and rolled it between the palms of his hands. Then, once he had a "snake," it was time to place it. As he leaned backward, the marine's entire body shook from the resulting strain. The Ra 'Na fed the plastic explosive into the recess around the valve, pressed it into place, and pushed the wireless detonator down into the charge. Some of the explosion's force would be directed down, rather than up. The question was how much? Would the valve come loose? Or simply sit there? The file leader wasn't sure.

Then, shoulders aching, he forced himself to check his work. Satisfied that everything was as it should be, Qwas allowed himself to return to what he now considered to be a more natural position, and activated the radio. "I'm coming down. Prepare for falling debris." Thus warned, both Twan and Pol did the best they could to lock themselves in place and protect their heads.

Reluctant to descend too far, lest he have difficulty climbing back up, Qwas stopped. Then, careful not to drop it, the marine removed the remote from one of his pockets, prayed that everything would work, and pressed a button.

The charge made a dull thump as it went off, sent the

valve assembly up through the limestone floor, and showered Qwas with bits of debris. He waited, looked up, and saw a new source of light! Scared, but thankful to be alive, the marine hunched his way upward.

Now, cleared of all obstructions, the pipe served to conduct sound. The marine heard long, bloodcurdling screams, waves of unintelligible click speech, and wondered if the explosion had gone unnoticed.

But the sound of the C-4 had *not* gone unnoticed. As luck would have it a warrior named Tze-Gas was passing chamber 2,456 just as the charge went off, the valve assembly flew into the air, and fell on the triplets below. One of the nymphs died instantly and the others produced a storm of incomprehensible gibberish.

Well aware of the fact that the citadel suffered from any number of design flaws, the Kan assumed that some sort of plumbing problem was responsible for the unfortunate incident and entered the cell to check.

Effectively blinded by the section of natal tissue that still covered its head, but conscious of the intruder nonetheless, a nymph extended its neck. Jaws snapped just short of the Kan's right leg, which forced him to back along the wall. Then, well clear of the twins, Tze-Gas bent to examine the hole.

Qwas was only units from the top when the warrior looked down into the pipe. Both beings froze—but the marine reacted first. It was impossible to miss as he tilted the submachine gun upward and squeezed the trigger. A steady stream of slugs ripped the warrior's head apart. The Ra 'Na felt something warm splatter against his facial fur, watched the Kan fall back out of sight, and reached for the rim. His arms pulled, his legs pushed him up, and he was up and out. Terrified that even more Saurons would suddenly appear, Qwas took a moment to check his surroundings.

The birth chamber was crowded. The carcass of a dead

Fon lay to his left, its abdomen split nearly in two, hoses leading this way and that. The Kan's headless corpse lay next to him, gore leaking out of its neck, while the nymphs continued to peck at it.

Qwas gulped. "I made it . . . but ran into a spot of trouble . . . so please hurry."

Twan needed no urging—nor did Pol. He had caught up, thanks to the momentary delay, and felt reenergized. As before, hands reached down to pull him up. The scene that waited to greet him was gruesome beyond belief. "By all the blue devils," Twan said in wonderment, "would you look at that!"

"It's hard not to," Pol said dryly. "Please note the Kan's condition. I see no signs of swelling. There could be more like that, so keep an eye out. Remember, it's the hatch we're after, so focus on that."

Then, having switched to a second frequency, Pol sent a message. "Ra 'Na One to Bone One . . . Objective one is ours . . . Repeat, objective one is ours."

The return message came quickly, so quickly that it seemed as if Smith had been waiting for it, which he definitely had. "Good work, One. We'll see you at objective two."

Pol clicked twice, just as Farley had taught him to do, and gestured toward the entry. "Qwas, you take the point. Twan, you walk drag."

Both marines nodded. The file leader edged his way around the still-agitated nymphs and stuck his head out into the hallway. The screams were less frequent now, but the stench was incredible, and a layer of slime covered the floor. Qwas looked both ways, stepped outside, and looked up. Gallery after gallery of birth chambers climbed until the highest levels were hidden by darkness. Good, that meant he was on the ground floor, which put him on the same level as the all-important door. Then, with his back to the wet, lichen-covered walls and his weapon at the ready, the marine edged sideways down the corridor. The others followed.

Meanwhile, not far away, and still making his rounds, Centum Commander Nis-Sta rounded a curve and looked for Tze-Gas. Seeing no sign of the warrior, Nis-Sta stuck his head into a series of birth chambers and repeatedly called the Kan's name. "Tze-Gas? Tze-Gas? Come on out."

There was no reply. Finally, having entered an especially noisome cubicle, the Centum nearly tripped over the body. It took the officer less than a unit to compute the most likely scenario and trigger his com set. "A slave murdered Tze-Gas! Find the interloper and kill him!"

Ninety-eight Kan heard the orders via their radios, pulled their t-guns, and joined the hunt. Many, bored by guard duty and unnerved by the din, were glad of something to do.

Qwas had just rounded a curve and spotted the gigantic door, when a Kan spotted him from above. A t-gun barked, limestone chips hit the side of the marine's face, and he yelled to the others. "Run! Run for the door! I'll cover you."

Then, tilting the submachine gun upward, Qwas fired. The first Kan stepped off his perch, fell through a virtual hail of .22-caliber bullets, and was dead by the time he hit the floor. But others had heard and jumped from above. The marine counted three, four, five, more than he could keep up with, and tried to back toward the door. The gun clicked empty, and the file leader had just reached for a new magazine, when something brushed his shoulder. That's when the pincer closed around the Ra 'Na's throat, his spine snapped, and his mind floated free.

Twan was halfway to the door by then, with Pol screaming through his earplugs. "Concentrate on the door! I'll keep them off you."

The marine wanted to turn, wanted to defend himself, but resisted the urge to do so. The grenades made a cracking sound as Pol underhanded them down the corridor. A Kan squealed loudly but fell silent when the cleric opened fire. Though not a true prayer, the toth was heartfelt nonetheless. "May my grenades rip you apart! May my bullets pierce your flesh! May the Great One curse you and your entire race!"

Meanwhile, Twan, hands shaking, opened the access panel. The lock was controlled by a key pad identical to its shipboard counterparts. The firing was closer now, so close he could hear empty casings tinkle as they hit the deck, soon followed by Pol's yelling. "Open the damned thing! I can't hold them any longer!"

A dart exploded against hull metal. The marine knew he lacked the time required to connect the computer leads and run the thousands of combinations required to do the job right. So, heart in his mouth, Twan decided to take a guess. The Zin were comfortable with numbers, but other castes were less so and had a tendency to forget things. So, that being the case, which digits would a Fon choose?

Twan took a deep breath, stabbed the numbers 1, 2, 3, and 4, and was rewarded with a groan as the door started to open. That's when the marine gave the Ra 'Na equivalent of a war whoop, and used the submachine gun's grip to smash the key pad. Then, turning toward his right, the tech prepared to fire.

The Kan's automatic weapon made a sound similar to ripping cloth as it sent a stream of darts into Twan's chest. He staggered, fell onto his back, and felt sunlight hit his face. The clouds! They had disappeared! Then he was gone.

Pol, still firing three-round bursts, heard some sort of yell, realized it was human, and knew help was on the way. That was when the sledgehammer hit, the impact threw him up into the air, and he fell into the water-filled moat. There was a splash, and he disappeared.

"Follow me!" Smith yelled, and ran onto the bridge. Franklin was there, with the .9mm clutched in his hand and

Manning at his side. So were the rest of the bodyguards, all trying to protect him, but caught in the mad charge.

The first rank of humans fired, as did the Saurons, and members of both sides went down. Then, as the two came together, the *real* fighting began. Manning heard rather than saw Franklin fire his weapon and struggled to maintain his position. "Keep it tight!" he urged the team. "Don't let the bastards in!"

Kell, who was stationed on the chief executive's left side, knew what Manning meant. "In" referred to the protective bubble in which the president floated. He saw a Kan fire his t-gun, put two .9mm bullets through the alien's skull, and kept on going.

Forward of the president, right behind Smith and the lead elements of the assault force, Garly Mol and Jill Ji-Hoon struggled to make a hole and keep the Saurons from coming straight back. Both agents had emptied their weapons by then, and with no time to reload, were using their backups.

For Mol that meant knives, one in each hand, both of which were used like ice picks. Her arms moved like pistons as each blow punched a hole through enemy chitin.

Ji-Hoon, who preferred an old-fashioned nightstick, hit anything that morphed. Those around her could hear the solid whack as the baton made contact with chitin, often followed by a loud craack as it shattered, and a subsequent squeal of pain.

But the contest was hardly one-sided. Unlike the humans, who could do little more than press forward, the Kan could jump and used that ability to considerable advantage. Manning first became aware of the threat when the sky seemed to shimmer and warriors fell on the mob *behind* him.

The crowd seemed to expand as people backed away, shuddered when the Saurons fired, and closed as the Kan ran out of ammo.

Now, thorax to torso with the humans, and unable to

reload their t-guns, the Kan employed their graspers like clubs. Humans fell as the rock-hard extremities crushed their skulls and broke limbs.

Not to be outdone, some of the ex-slaves swung their assault weapons like battle-axes, while others produced big ball peen hammers, and gave as good as they got.

Meanwhile, still protected by his bodyguards, Franklin had the opportunity to reload his weapon. That's why he had a fresh magazine in place when one of the warriors fell short and landed right in front of him. The president could *hear* the grunt of expelled air, *smell* the alien's breath, and *see* the hatred in his eyes.

The t-gun fired first but the dart missed by an inch. Gozen Asad never felt a thing. One moment he was there, guarding, the Big Dog's six, the next moment he was gone.

Franklin struggled to drag the handgun up and into position. It seemed to weigh a ton. Then, having squeezed the trigger, he followed the Kan down. It was only when he heard Manning yell, "He's dead, Mr. President," that the politician realized that his weapon was empty and took his finger off the trigger.

The Kan had been forced to give ground by then, so, rather than give the aliens an opportunity to regroup, Smith led a second charge. "All right, people! We have the bastards on the run! Let's finish this thing!" So saying, the deacon and his demons thundered across the bridge and poured through the door. But Nis-Sta was waiting, and no sooner had the humans entered, than thirty Kan fell from above.

Manning felt something heavy land on his shoulders, was thrown facedown onto the limestone floor, and knew he was about to die. But that's when he heard a roar of outrage, felt the weight disappear, and rolled onto his back.

The Kan struggled as Jonathan Wimba lifted the warrior up—only to throw him down. There was a thud as the body hit limestone, and the Sauron lay dead. The battle had moved on by that time which meant there was a momentary respite as Manning got to his feet. "Thanks, Jonathan. Not bad for a sociologist. Where's the Big Dog?"

"I saw him go thataway," Mol responded, as she pointed toward a ramp, "with Kell in hot pursuit."

Manning said, "Shit!" slammed a new magazine into the butt of his weapon, and ran for the ramp. The sounds of battle grew more distant as the others followed. Now, as they climbed, the humans could hear intermittent screams, waves of the staticlike clicks and pops, and the sound of their own footsteps.

Many of the nymphs were active by then, already peeking from their birth chambers or venturing out to explore a bit. One of the juveniles, a Kan by the look of him, leaped at the humans as they passed by. Ji-Hoon fired without breaking stride. The .9mm slug caught the nymphling in the side of the head and threw him into a wall. Both of his brothers pulled back.

Manning paused as he arrived on yet another level and took a look around. "Damn Franklin anyway . . . Does anyone have a clue as to where he was headed?"

"I heard him say something about Hak-Bin," Wimba volunteered.

Hak-Bin! Of course! The bastard was *here*! Ra 'Na intelligence had verified that . . . but where? Then it came to him. Knowing the Sauron social structure as he did, Franklin would naturally head for the top gallery. "Come on!" Manning shouted. "He's on the top level!" Boots pounded as the security team continued to climb.

Meanwhile, a few levels higher, Franklin ran out of ramp. This was it, the highest gallery there was, and the place where Hak-Bin was certain to be. But in which chamber? Now, all alone, the politician regretted the haste with which he had sped to the top. Still, that's where he was, and it was best to keep moving. That's what he told himself anyway as he turned to the left. Slowly, the .9mm held straight out in front of him, the president eased his way down the corridor. There was less noise on the top level—as if the Zin nymphs had less to say. But they were aware of him, as he checked their cubicles, and he could feel their animosity.

Then, as if alerted by some sixth sense, Franklin knew he was close. He could *feel* it, or thought he could, and tried to extend his senses. That's when Kat-Duu slipped out of a shadow, took one step forward, and wrapped a chitinous arm around the politician's throat. The other grasper sought the gun, locked onto it, and jerked the weapon free. The .9mm went off, a bullet bounced off the opposite wall, and the gun fell. Kell heard the gunshot and ran toward the sound.

Franklin felt the arm tighten, rammed the Kan with his elbow, and hit the alien's rock-hard exoskeleton. Desperate by then, the politician stomped on one of the Sauron's pod-like feet, felt the grip loosen, and stomped again. Then, sensing some give, the human threw himself forward as Kat-Duu attempted to pull the foot back. The hold broke, Franklin fell forward, and dived for the gun. There were two reports . . . quickly followed by a third.

The politician waited for the darts to strike, wondered how the Kan had missed, and flipped himself over. "Got the bastard," Kell said happily. "That's one less to worry about."

Franklin was about to agree, about to thank Kell for saving his life, when the automatic weapon started to chatter. It belonged to Kat-Duu, and the jet-black nymph could barely control it. Struck from behind, the agent jerked like a puppet on a string as darts tore at his legs.

The politician did a desperate backstroke as he felt for the pistol, found it, and brought the weapon forward. He fired two shots. One missed entirely and the other blew one of the Sauron's arms off. The nymph screeched pitifully, tried to jump, but fell as the last bullet took it in the head.

Franklin fumbled for a fresh magazine, realized he was out, and let the wall support his shoulders.

Manning heard the rattle of automatic fire followed by the steady bang, bang, bang of a .9mm as he topped the ramp and made the turn. Mol knelt next to Kell as the security chief extended a hand to Franklin. "Not bad for a politician, sir, but the security team would appreciate it if you'd let us do some of the shooting."

"Sorry," Franklin said contritely, "I got carried away. This is where Hak-Bin should be—and I want to nail the bastard."

"Sounds like a plan," Manning said understandingly. "But it might help if we were a little more systematic. All we need to do is find the largest chamber—that's where the bastard will be."

What the security chief said made sense. Franklin nodded, bummed a fresh magazine from Ji-Hoon, and gestured to the larger body. "See the big one? I saw him with Hak-Bin. He's here . . . I can feel it."

"All right," Manning said. "Wimba, Alaweed, get Kell to the aid station and give Dr. Sool my best. The rest of you check the cells. One person on point—the other two on backup. Understood?"

The security agents nodded, and Manning remained with Franklin as Mol, Ji-Hoon, and Orvin began to check the birth chambers. Less than a minute had passed when they met with success. "Over here!" Ji-Hoon shouted. "*This* cell is larger!"

Manning motioned for the team to close in, ordered the rest of the agents to take up positions facing outward, and approached the entrance.

Though not yet mature, the new Hak-Bin was aware of the overall situation and realized he had little choice but to deal with it. He heard noise, knew the slaves were going to enter, and called out, "President Franklin? Is that you?"

Manning heard the voice and peeked around the corner. The cell *was* larger than the rest. The coal-black nymph sat before an already rotting body. Flies, drawn from the outside, buzzed as they circled the corpse. "Ah," the nymph said, "when the slave appears—the master will follow."

"There are no slaves," Franklin said, his shoulder brushing past Manning's. "Not anymore."

"And here he is," Hak-Bin said sarcastically, "the collaborator turned conqueror! I enjoyed the way my progenitor toyed with you. Still, your race proved much more resilient than he thought it would. Please accept my congratulations . . . Victory is yours."

"No," Franklin said, "not yet." Somewhere, on the levels below, weapons were being fired. The president jerked his thumb back over his shoulder. "Hear that, Hak-Bin? Notice how regular those shots are? That's because the battle is over . . . That's because ex-slaves are going chamber to chamber killing every nymph they find. *Thousands* of them. Later, when all of them are dead, *that's* the moment when the allies will be victorious."

The nymph hung his head. His voice was low, and Franklin was forced to move closer in order to hear. "The previous Hak-Bin named your planet Haven. Did you know that? A somewhat ironic choice, wouldn't you agree? Even now his ancestors berate him. The entire race . . . brought to its knees by slaves! They can hardly believe it. But, just before I die, I have a message for you. . . ."

Franklin took an unconscious step forward, Manning shouted a warning, and the nymph's elongated head shot up and out. The politician felt hundreds of tiny needle-sharp teeth sink into his throat, staggered under the unexpected impact, and struggled to breathe.

Then, determined to fight back, Franklin wrapped his hands around the long, sinuous neck. The Sauron tightened his jaws, the human started to squeeze, and a bullet broke the impasse. Manning shot the nymphling in the thorax, waited for its jaws to open, and shot it again.

That's when Franklin rubbed his throat, realized that it was still in one piece, and wiped the blood off on his shirt. "I don't know about you," he said, looking around the room, "but I'm thirsty. Who'd like a drink?"

"Sounds good," Manning said, "but the nearest drink is back in Bellingham."

"And that's where you're wrong," Franklin proclaimed. "The nearest drink is on Lifter Two! We have something to celebrate, and the president is buying!"

Epilog

The Ra 'Na remained in the vicinity of Earth long enough to remove the debris from orbit, repair their ships, and provide medical treatment to thousands upon thousands of humans. Among those so served were First Lieutenant Darby . . . and a group known as The Crips. Then, eager to return to Balwur, the Ra 'Na left for the long journey home. Among them, still recovering from his wounds, was an initiate named Pas Pol, who, with Shu at his side, would found a new navy.

Some of the Saurons who had hidden themselves away in caves, subways, and basements managed to give birth. Most of their nymphs were located and killed. Some, no more than a thousand, were able to survive. Surprisingly enough, it was a group of ex-slaves who sought to protect the aliens from genocide and eventually succeeded in doing so. A reservation was established in the American Southwest, where the Saurons were imprisoned.

Elections were held, Alexander Franklin was confirmed as president, married an anthropologist named Maria Sanchez-Jones, and served two full terms. He, along with successor Boyer Blue, worked long and hard to help other countries recover from the invasion. Full reconstruction would take a long time, but there was plenty of time to work with.

Jack Manning resigned his position as security chief to teach geology, married Dr. Seeko Sool, and for reasons neither could fully explain, settled near Bellingham, Washington.

Others, extraordinary people like Deac Smith, the man named Patience, and the nurse known as Dixie, went back to where they came from: the streets of America.

And it was there, safe within the embrace of a small town, that Ella Howther Ivory secured a small frame house, married a man named Joseph Mack, and raised her daughter Rose.